Praise for *Haven Point*

"From losing relations to dealing with infidelity, hurricanes, war conflicts, and confidences held, we get an inside view of how these women survived through more than seven decades yet remained strong and steadfast in their devotion to each other."

—*New York Journal of Books*

"*Haven Point* has all the proper ingredients for anyone looking for a great summer read. The characters are realistic and potent, and Hume brings them to life in a very rich setting with compelling dialogue, intertwining romance, mystery, and history into the story of several generations of American women."

—*Washington Examiner*

"You will love curling up with this one under your beach umbrella!"   —Martha MacCallum, host of *The Story*

"*Haven Point* is a novel that had me making excuses to go to bed early so that I could return to the story that had me daydreaming all day. I loved the characters, setting, historical references, dialogue, romance, and mystery. Virginia Hume has written a book that I can't wait to recommend to all of my friends."

—Dana Perino, former White House press secretary

ing their character and family bond. A powerful novel of families trying to understand the forces that shape them just as the ocean shapes the elegant coastline they're summering on."

—Brooke Lea Foster, author of *On Gin Lane*

"A shimmering debut novel about four generations, a summer community in coastal Maine, and the secrets, grief, and prejudices that are unwittingly passed down through the years. Rewarding and atmospheric, with deeply drawn characters and a setting you won't soon forget. Delicious!"

—Jennie Fields, author of *Atomic Love*

"Taking readers from the wartime corridors of Walter Reed hospital to the contemporary summer sing-alongs in the rec hall, this wistful debut is perfect for those who want to follow characters through their lifetimes, examine complex family relationships, or enjoy a good redemption story. For fans of Elin Hilderbrand's *Summer of '69* and J. Courtney Sullivan's *Maine*."

—Modern Mrs Darcy

HAVEN POINT

VIRGINIA HUME

St. Martin's Paperbacks

This is a work of fiction. All of the characters, organizations, and events portrayed in this novel are either products of the author's imagination or are used fictitiously.

Published in the United States by St. Martin's Paperbacks, an imprint of St. Martin's Publishing Group.

HAVEN POINT

For information, address St. Martin's Publishing Group, 120 Broadway, New York, NY 10271.

www.stmartins.com

Library of Congress Catalog Card Number: 2020057518

ISBN: 978-1-250-88992-8

Our books may be purchased in bulk for promotional, educational, or business use. Please contact your local bookseller or the Macmillan Corporate and Premium Sales Department at 1-800-221-7945, ext. 5442, or by email at MacmillanSpecialMarkets@macmillan.com.

Printed in the United States of America

St. Martin's Press hardcover edition published 2021
St. Martin's Griffin edition published 2022
St. Martin's Paperbacks edition / July 2023

10 9 8 7 6 5 4 3 2 1

For my husband, Drew Onufer

PROLOGUE

August 2008
Haven Point, Maine

MAREN

Maren took her mug of coffee outside and sank into the wicker love seat. Skye would finally arrive the following day. Maren had so much she needed to tell her granddaughter. The conversation was long overdue, but Maren was still uncertain how to go about it, or even where to begin.

From the water came the sound of a horn, and Maren looked up to see a race underway. For the next half hour, she watched sailboats fly across the bay, white sails trimmed to harness the brisk breeze. The boats rounded their mark and went behind Gunnison Island, but from her perch high on the cliff, Maren could still catch glimpses of the mastheads when they emerged from behind clumps of spruce, like stealthy hunters gliding between coverts.

The cannon shot signaling the end of the race startled Maren from her reverie. She had been like this since her daughter died six months earlier, wavering between agonizing grief and a strange fugue state. Most days she had found herself sitting in this very spot for hours, just staring out at the water.

If Georgie was right (and she usually was), the hurricane barreling toward the coast could cause problems on Haven Point. It was hard to imagine, given the crisp air and sapphire sky today, but Maren had spent enough summers here to know how quickly the skies could change. With no more effort than it took to wipe a cloth across a dusty shelf, a storm could mock their efforts to tame this wild peninsula. *Go ahead. Build your roads. Carve your paths. Plant your gardens. Never forget who's really in charge, though.*

She and Skye would be fine in Fourwinds, of course. The old house had faced down plenty of weather in its day.

Maren sat listening to the ocean engaged in its violent, noisy, age-old battle with the rocks below. That strangely pacifying sound was the heartbeat of this house. She'd always thought of Fourwinds as a living thing—pulsing, thrumming, speaking to her. She had loved it from the first, even when she so mistrusted the community outside its doors.

Skye did not know it yet, but Fourwinds would be hers someday. Maren had planned to leave it to both her children, but a few years earlier, Billy had made his wishes clear:

"I love it there, but I've lived abroad my whole adult life. Let Annie have the house," he'd said.

"She wouldn't want it."

"You never know," Billy replied with a gentle smile. "She just might decide to come back to Haven Point someday."

Billy had been right. In the end, the very end, Annie had wanted to come back.

Her granddaughter did not know this yet either. After the memorial service, Skye had asked what they would do with the ashes. "We can figure it out later," Maren had said. Skye had been satisfied. She had no reason to imagine her mother—flaky on her best day, downright reckless on her worst—had left detailed instructions on that (or any) subject. There was so much Skye didn't understand about her mother.

Maren rose and went inside to the living room. Her eyes took in the books, trophies, and pictures that crowded the shelves. They were all there, the Demarest women, layered over one another like a fossil record. Even Annie. Her daughter might have abandoned this house, but Fourwinds had not returned the favor. She was everywhere: her name next to Charlie's on the Stinneford Cup trophy, her face in photographs, her soul in paintings and drawings.

And she lived on in Skye, too. Maren smiled at the memory of Oliver's reaction all those years before, when Annie told them she had decided to have a baby.

"Ah, artificial insemination." Oliver had nodded in his doctorly way, as if she had told him she planned to try a new heartburn medication. "What an interesting idea. Do clinics provide this service to single women?"

"I think so. I'm still looking into it," Annie had said breezily. "If not, Flora said she would pretend she's my lover."

How Oliver had not fallen out of his chair at that moment, Maren would never know. But of course, he was careful with Annie, after everything that happened. They promised to love Skye, to do all they could to help raise her. They hadn't realized what they were signing up for, but it never mattered. From the first moment, they were so beguiled by the little redhead, they would have cheerfully laid down their lives for her.

Still, Skye saw Haven Point as her mother had: beautiful on the surface, petty and snobbish underneath. Maren understood; she had once felt just the same way. It was only in the worst moment of her life that she realized what she'd missed. Just as the big storms wiped out Haven

Point Road, exposing the bedrock beneath, it had taken grief and pain washing everything away for Maren to finally see the community's sturdy foundation, its titanic heart.

Maren recalled a maxim Annie used to share with her art students at the start of each semester: *Everything depends on the quality and direction of light.* It was only in the last year that Annie had finally applied this lesson to her own life, that she relinquished the story she had clung to for so long, about what had happened here and who was responsible. By then, it had been too late.

But it was not too late for Skye.

CHAPTER ONE

August 1994
Washington, D.C.

SKYE

Skye Demarest had ten minutes to decide whether to lie to her best friend.

Skye didn't like to lie, but if the choice was between honest and normal, she was obviously going to pick normal every time. As far as she was concerned, that was just survival.

The trick was knowing what qualified as normal. In Skye's experience, the definition was pretty slippery.

When she was little it was so much easier. Back then, Skye didn't have to lie, because she thought she was just like every other kid. That lasted until the summer after first grade, when Gretchen Hathaway clued her in.

Skye and Gretchen were both attending the little day camp at the community center. One day, Gran showed up at the edge of the playground and called Skye over.

"Hi, love. Your mom needs to go away for a bit, so I'm taking you up to Haven Point with me this afternoon. I've let the camp director know."

Skye had looked away and tried not to cry.

"You need to get your things," Gran said kindly. "I've packed your suitcase already."

Gretchen had followed Skye into the building. (She told the counselor she was going to help her friend, but she just stood there and watched as Skye shoved things into her backpack.)

"Where are you going?" Gretchen asked.

"Up to Maine with my grandmother," Skye said.

"Why do you have to go all of a sudden?"

She felt a nervous bubble in her stomach. This was not the first time Gran had showed up out of the blue and taken Skye somewhere. She just hadn't thought to question it before. When she saw the *this is weird* look on Gretchen's face, though, it hit her: It *was* weird. *Normal people know about vacations ahead of time! They talk about them and make plans!*

The honest answer to Gretchen's question was "I don't know," but some voice inside told her that the reason, whatever it was, needed to stay a secret.

It was amazing, how easily the lie slid out of her mouth. Unfortunately, it wasn't a very good one.

"My mom is sick. Gran is taking me so she can get better."

"What's she sick with?"

Skye scrambled to come up with something bad, but not *too* bad.

"She has to get her tonsils out."

Gretchen was an absolute pro at using her face to make people feel inferior. All she had to do was tuck her chin and scrunch her eyebrows, and *I think you're weird* turned into *I think you're lying.*

It got worse when Skye came home from Maine and ran into Gretchen and Emily Walker at the park. (Emily was like a little trained poodle who followed Gretchen everywhere and obeyed all her orders).

"While you were gone, my mom brought a casserole to your house," Gretchen said accusingly. "She said your mother wasn't even home."

Skye felt her face get red. It wouldn't have been as bad coming from anyone else, but Skye worshiped Gretchen's mom. Mrs. Hathaway was the room mother and the Brownie troop leader. She had pretty brown hair, perfect clothes, and bubbly excitement about whatever her kids were doing.

Skye fantasized about her all the time. She'd imagine herself on a chilly night, curled up on the Hathaways' front stoop. Mrs. Hathaway would open the door and find her there.

"Oh no. Oh, my dear Skye!" she would say, her eyes filled with worry, as she scooped Skye up and brought her inside. (Skye always pictured herself really quiet and stoic throughout the ordeal, so while Mrs. Hathaway was obviously deeply concerned, she also admired Skye for being so calm and brave.)

Skye never mentally sketched out why she was on the Hathaways' doorstep. She didn't want to imagine her mother dead (or to even make her the bad guy), so she just left her out entirely. She wrote the rest of the Hathaway family out, too, while she was at it. She barely knew Mr. Hathaway, and it totally broke the spell to imagine Gretchen or her little brother there.

Despite the unsatisfying holes in the story, it had been Skye's favorite fantasy. When things were bad at home and she couldn't sleep, she'd replay it over and over in her mind until she felt calmer.

Skye was so humiliated by the idea that Mrs. Hathaway knew she lied about her mom's tonsils (or, worse, that things at Skye's house were "not normal"), she could barely speak. She mumbled something about her mom staying with a friend then walked away, cheeks still burning, while Gretchen and Emily whispered about her.

Of course, Skye's lesson from the experience was not

that she should tell the truth. She just needed to get better at lying. That was one good thing about constantly changing schools. Just when she felt like a lie was about to catch up with her, her mom would get a new teaching job at another nearby private school. Since Skye's tuition was always part of the bargain, she had to go with her. New school, new and improved lies!

She still had close calls, like two years earlier in sixth grade when Max Zilkoski asked who her dad was. Skye gave him her usual answer.

"He died in the war," she said, then looked down sadly. (Until third grade, she'd just said "He died," but kids started asking "How?" so she'd added the war part.) The sad look was key, because it made people uncomfortable, and they stopped asking questions. Unfortunately, Max was book smart but people dumb, so he missed his cue.

"Which war?"

Skye froze. Her many schools with different history curriculums had given her an encyclopedic knowledge of the Revolutionary War and Civil War (and, weirdly, the Peloponnesian War). However, in a panicky search through her brain for some war that had happened since she was born, she found a gaping hole where twentieth-century military history should be.

"The Cold War," Skye replied, finally. She tried to sound certain, though she had a sneaking suspicion the answer wasn't quite right, and Max's confused expression was not comforting. But then he suddenly got excited.

"Wait, was he a *spy*?"

Once again, Skye was dumbstruck. Fortunately, at this point Max's social cluelessness came in handy. He assumed the answer was classified.

"I get it. You can't talk about it." He nodded knowingly.

The next month, Skye's mom announced she'd accepted a job teaching art at some hippy-dippy school in Maryland. Skye was a little bummed, since she had just started making friends, but at least she could quit worrying about whether Max Zilkoski could keep a state secret.

Now, once again, she was being whisked off to Haven Point. The situation wasn't exactly the same as that time with Gretchen, though. First, Skye didn't know what was going on back then. Now she did. In fact, she knew it so well, she'd been able to hide it.

Skye's grandfather had died in May, just six weeks after being diagnosed with pancreatic cancer. Gran had kept a close eye on her mom after that, looking for any hint a relapse was coming. Instead of leaving for Maine over Memorial Day weekend, like she usually did, she stayed in her apartment, just a mile from Skye and her mom. If Skye's mom had gone off the rails then, Gran would have figured it out first, like she always had.

Skye also knew the signs that Anne was about to start drinking again, but it wasn't until Gran left for Haven Point in early July that she began to spot them. At first it was just exaggerated versions of her normal behavior: staying up later at night, hanging out with sketchier friends, acting more irritable than usual.

The sure sign was when she stopped feeding the birds.

Keeping seed in the bird feeder was the one household task her mom normally stayed on top of (at least partly because it didn't have to be done at an exact time—"lunch at noon" was way too specific, but "birdseed low" she could handle).

Resisting the temptation to fill it herself, Skye watched the bird feeder as if it were a countdown clock. The seed level got lower and lower, and sure enough, soon after it was empty, bottles started appearing in the trash outside.

Skye knew she should tell Gran her mom was drinking, but she also knew if she did, Gran would take her up to Haven Point, which would blow up all of her plans with Adriene for the rest of the summer. So, she kept it a secret. If the phone rang when her mom was drinking, Skye would race to get it. If it was Gran, she'd say her mom was out with one of her non-sketchy friends, or doing some other Sober Mom–sounding thing.

Skye was used to doing everything herself anyway, so it worked out fine. Well, until Gran called the night before, while Skye was out. First thing in the morning, Gran had showed up at the house and gone straight to her mom's room. She came out a half hour later and found Skye in the living room.

"Skye, your mom needs help, as I suspect you know. I'm taking you to Maine tomorrow morning. I need a few hours here, though. Can you go somewhere for a bit?"

Skye felt a little guilty, seeing how tired Gran looked, but she steeled herself with the reminder that this was just what she'd been trying to avoid. She rose from the love seat and marched to the front door.

"I'm going to Adriene's," she'd said, slamming the door shut behind her.

Now, as Skye headed through the swampy heat to her friend's house, she considered the other big difference between this situation and the one years before: Adriene was nothing like Gretchen. Skye had known that since they first met, the summer before.

Skye had been at the pool when a girl about her age walked up and asked if the lounge chair next to her was taken.

"I don't think so," Skye said.

Skye, who had to sit under an umbrella, because her skin would fry in about five minutes otherwise, watched with envy as the olive-complexioned girl angled her chair to face the sun. Once she was situated, she turned to Skye.

"I'm Adriene, by the way. My family just moved into the neighborhood."

"Nice to meet you. I'm Skye."

Before they could say anything else, a little girl appeared. She wore a shiny purple bathing suit and huge mirrored sunglasses. She looked like a mini-Adriene—with the same complexion, and thick, almost blue-black hair.

"What do you want, Sophia?" Adriene asked.

"Natalie says she gets to name the baby turtle."

"So, let her," Adriene replied.

"But I want to name it!"

"Oh my God, Sophia," Adriene said wearily. "Go back to the baby pool. Seriously."

"Okay, but I'm telling Natalie you said I could pick the name!"

"Fine." Adriene sighed. Sophia turned on her heels and marched back to the baby pool.

"Sorry. My sister's a lunatic," Adriene said.

"Who's Natalie?" Skye asked.

"Sophia's imaginary enemy."

"She has an imaginary *enemy*?" Skye laughed.

"Yeah. Natalie's supposedly really mean, but I hear how Sophia talks to her. I can't blame her."

"And the baby turtle?"

"Also imaginary."

Over the next half hour or so, Skye picked up some key facts. Adriene Maduros was one of six kids. Her family had moved into D.C. from Rockville, Maryland. She went to a school way out in Virginia ("super-strict Catholic, the closest my parents could find to Greek Orthodox") that sounded like the complete opposite of Skye's.

It left them in the same position, though: open to friends outside of school.

When Skye spotted Gretchen Hathaway at the sign-in desk, her heart had sunk.

That'll be the end of that, she thought.

As usual, Gretchen looked like she'd jumped off the set of *Beverly Hills, 90210,* with her wispy blond bangs and her white denim overall shorts (one side of the bib unbuckled, obviously).

Skye had left public school in second grade, when her mom got her first teaching job. Eventually, most of the neighborhood girls also scattered to various private schools, but the posse got together over holidays and in the summer, and Gretchen was still totally in charge.

Adriene didn't strike Skye as Gretchen's type. For one thing, Adriene seemed like she could actually have a conversation, without constantly scanning her surroundings for people she might need to impress (or gossip about).

Skye had years of experience watching what happened when Gretchen was around, though. Even the most normal-seeming girls would start auditioning for an ensemble role in The Gretchen Show.

Skye avoided making eye contact, but Gretchen walked right over anyway. To her surprise, the two girls already knew each other.

"Hey, Skye. Hey, Adriene," Gretchen said.

Adriene didn't seem interested in Gretchen, which was good, except that it activated Gretchen's radar for threats to her place in the pecking order.

"So, Skye. Are you still at that world peace school, where you call teachers by their first name?"

"Mmm," Skye replied, though Gretchen had actually mashed up two different schools.

"Wait, really?" Adriene turned to Skye, eyes wide. "That sounds awesome."

"Yeah. Skye's mom teaches art," Gretchen added, trying to up the ante.

"That's so cool. Like painting? Pottery?"

Once Gretchen realized she could not enlighten Adriene about Skye's inferior social status, she left to find someone less hopeless across the pool.

"How'd you guys meet?" Skye asked, nodding toward Gretchen's receding form.

"Our new house is down the block from theirs. They invited our family for dinner to welcome us to the neighborhood." Adriene rolled her eyes.

"You didn't like her?"

"I don't know." Adriene shrugged. "I just didn't have that much to say to her."

"What did you think of her mom?"

"She's pretty. Their house is pretty, too, I guess," Adriene said. "I just wasn't that comfortable there."

Skye felt something shift inside. She had never really felt comfortable at the Hathaways' either. She'd just been too busy idolizing Mrs. Hathaway and trying to get in Gretchen's good graces to realize it might not be her fault she felt that way.

"I wonder where Gretchen learns it," Adriene said.

"Learns what?"

"That look." Adriene twisted her face into an exaggerated version of Gretchen's sneer.

"Maybe there's a school."

"Can you imagine?" Adriene laughed.

Could she imagine? There was nothing Skye liked more than attaching "can you imagine" to some weird scenario. It was just hard to find other people who liked it as much as she did. Not everyone obsessively watched *Kids in the Hall* and *Saturday Night Live,* after all.

"They probably have a class on facial expressions," Skye said. She wagged her finger like a schoolteacher. "No, no, no. How many times have I told you? Both eyebrows up, but just one side of your lip!"

"And one on brainwashing techniques, so they can attract followers," Adriene added.

They spent the rest of the afternoon laughing as they made up more classes and lesson plans. The next day, Skye invited Adriene over to her house. If anything about her life was going to push Adriene away, she wanted it to happen sooner rather than later. Plus, her mom was in relatively good shape at the time, and who knew how long that would last?

Adriene thought everything about Skye's house was cool: the drop cloths and easel in the dining room, the coffee table with ceramic high-heeled shoes as legs, the wavy stripes on the staircase risers. As they walked upstairs, Adriene looked over the paintings of baby wrens and chickadees along on the staircase wall.

"These are amazing," Adriene said.

"Yeah, my mom's kind of known for those. She sells a lot."

The way her mom painted them, with a few bold strokes of brightly colored impasto oil, the little birds that looked tiny and vulnerable in the backyard now appeared stout and hardy.

Adriene looked around Skye's room, taking in the neatly made bed, orderly bookshelf, and little containers for school supplies on her desk.

"So, you're the organized one," Adriene said. From anyone else, it would sound like a jab at the rest of the house, but from Adriene it just sounded like an observation. She peered at a photograph on Skye's dresser.

"You play ice hockey?"

"My grandfather got me into it. He used to be one of the team doctors for the Capitals."

"I didn't know girls played," Adriene said. "That's neat."

"Gretchen thinks it's weird."

"Of course," Adriene said, without looking up from the picture. "But if she found out she was good at it, suddenly it wouldn't be weird anymore."

The last stop was the back patio. As they reached the sliding glass door, they could see Anne outside, waving around a handheld butane torch as she talked to Flora.

Skye's mom was pretty, though she hid it well. Her blond hair was chopped short, tucked behind a bandana, and her baggy cotton pants and oversized men's T-shirt hid her slender figure. She was one of those lucky blondes who could actually get a tan. (Skye had her mom's height and long legs, but she was pale with red hair and freckles. Under the circumstances, she thought this was a pretty raw deal.)

Flora had on a giant caftan and big plastic hoop earrings, and her prematurely gray hair reached all the way down her back. Though she looked every bit the daffy artist, Flora was actually her mom's steadiest friend. It was always a good sign when she was around.

Skye slid the door open and brought Adriene outside. After she made the introductions, Adriene asked her mom what she was doing with the torch.

"It's called flame painting. I use it to put a design on this copper sheet. When I'm done, I'll bend it into a dome like this." She picked up the sheet and folded one side under the other. "It's for the bird feeder. Keeps the squirrels from getting the seed."

"I am here to make sure she does not do a mistake and burn the house," Flora said in her thick Portuguese accent.

"I am not going to do a mistake and burn the house!" Anne laughed. Skye liked when her mom laughed. It made her eyes shine.

"Only because I make you be outside!" Flora said, throwing her hands up.

Skye and Adriene hung out with them for a while. Skye's mom was in funny art teacher mode, and Adriene obviously got a kick out of her. This was better than thinking she was strange, but in Skye's experience, people who were dazzled by her mom at first often wound up disappointed. Artist Anne Demarest could be irreverent and freewheeling, but at some point, they expected a more mom-like version to come out. Adriene learned pretty quickly that Anne had no other gear, but she liked her anyway, just how she was.

Over the year, Skye had told Adriene things she had never shared with anyone. She even let her know the truth about her dad, that her mom had picked him out of a catalog at a sperm bank. (And not a very detailed catalog. Skye knew three words about her father: "healthy graduate student.")

"Is your mom a lesbian?" Adriene asked, her eyes wide, apparently thrilled by the idea.

"No. She wanted a baby, but she doesn't believe in marriage." Adriene looked disappointed, so Skye added, "She does have some lesbian friends, though."

"Does she have a boyfriend?"

"Not now. She's gone out with a few guys, but she never gets really serious with anyone."

Adriene nodded to signal her understanding, then looked thoughtful for a minute.

"We should call him Don," she said finally.

"Who?"

"Your dad. Short for 'donor.'"

So "Don" he became (or sometimes "Don the Mon," or "Don Juan"—Adriene was still trying to come up with a last name). They joked about him all the time.

By the end of summer, Skye and Adriene were inseparable. When school started, they got together every weekend, and since they lived so close to each other, they sometimes did homework together during the week.

But one thing kept nagging at her, like a kid tugging on her mom's skirt: Adriene liked the sitcom, but what would she think of the drama? Skye had hoped she would never find out. There was always the chance her mom's last rehab visit would be her final rehab visit, right? No such luck, unfortunately.

Skye had not lied to Adriene once in the year since they'd been best friends. As she reached Adriene's house, she decided that the only thing worse than revealing the truth would be to lie and have Adriene find out later.

"Get this. My grandmother came over this morning. She's taking me to Maine tomorrow." Skye tried to look annoyed, instead of nervous.

"What? No way! Why?" Adriene sounded disappointed.

"So, I haven't told you this, but my mom is an alcoholic," Skye said, fiddling with a Japanese eraser on Adriene's desk. "She's going into rehab. Gran's at my house figuring it out right now."

"Oh my God, really?"

Skye nodded.

"That sucks. My uncle Kostas is an alcoholic, too."

To Skye's relief, Adriene looked sympathetic, not scandalized.

"I didn't think Anne even drank. She never has wine at our house."

"She's a binge alcoholic. It's like an on-off switch," Skye said, reverting to Gran's terminology. "She quit cold turkey when she was in her twenties but started drinking again when I was three. Flora's been sober for thirty years, and she took my mom to Alcoholics Anonymous. That worked for a while, but she's been relapsing every couple of years. This will be her third time in rehab."

"At least she quits for a while," Adriene said with a sigh. "My uncle has never tried to stop. How does your mom act when she's drinking? Does she get, like, angry?"

Skye hesitated. A month ago, the answer would have been a decisive "no," but Skye had seen a different side of her mom recently. At first it was directed mostly at impersonal targets, like traffic and politicians. (For some reason, she was especially mad at Newt Gingrich.) In the past week, it had circled closer and closer to home, like a burglar looking for an open window. The night before, the unthinkable happened and her mom had turned on her.

Skye didn't want to get into that now, though. As a rule, her mom was still mellow to a fault.

"Not really," she said finally. "You know how she is normally? Sort of out there?"

Adriene nodded.

"She's like that, but times a hundred. Less bouncy, though. More lazy."

"I see. I couldn't imagine her being like my uncle," Adriene said. "He's a horrible drunk, screams and throws mugs and plates and stuff."

"Wait . . . he throws plates?" To Skye's surprise, the

nervous knot in her stomach was gone, and in its place a giggle was forming.

"Or whatever's nearby, I guess."

Skye burst out laughing.

"What?" Adriene demanded, wanting to be in on the joke.

Skye managed to stop laughing just long enough to get a question out.

"Sorry, but isn't throwing plates a Greek thing?"

"Oh! Yeah. I guess they do it at weddings and stuff in Greece," Adriene said, still confused.

Then it clicked, and Adriene started laughing, too. Soon she was on her feet, pretending to clean a house. "Don't mind him, it's a Greek thing," she said, waving her hand as she ducked imaginary plates.

Once they squeezed all the humor they could from the scenario, Skye's mind returned to the original subject.

"Anyway, while my mom's in rehab, I have to stay with my grandmother in Maine."

"That probably makes sense," Adriene said. "What's it like up there?"

"The house is cool. Really old, up on a cliff. It's in this place called Haven Point, where everyone knows each other. It's almost like summer camp. They even have teams, green and blue. Every family is one or the other, and they compete all summer in golf and tennis and stuff. It's supposedly for the kids, but grown-ups get really into it, too."

"It sounds fun, at least?" Adriene said.

"I don't know. I liked it when I was young." Skye shrugged. For some reason she couldn't name, her visits in recent years had left a bad taste in her mouth.

"Why doesn't your mom take you there?"

"She hasn't been to Haven Point since before I was

born. She hates it, says it's full of 'elitist hypocrites.'"
Skye lifted her fingers in air quotes.

"Does it bug her that you go with your grandmother?"

"Probably." She shrugged.

Definitely, she thought, as she felt something unpleasant curl inside her.

The night before, Skye had come home from babysitting to find her mom sitting at the dining room table, drinking from a mug. (As if Skye wouldn't notice the half-empty bottle of wine on the table.)

"Hi, Mom," Skye said as she headed toward the staircase.

"So, Skye, Gran's coming in the morning to take you to Haven Point," her mom slurred. Her voice had a nasty edge.

Skye's stomach pitched, as shame and disappointment warred inside her.

Gran knows.

Skye had a million questions, but she continued toward the staircase without asking them. She knew better than to try to talk to her mom when she was drunk, never mind drunk and angry.

But Anne was not finished.

"Poor Skye. Couldn't take care of herself. Had to call your grandma, didn't you?" The last words ran together—*hadtocallyourgrammadinyou*—but the mockery was unmistakable.

"What?" Skye spun around to see her mother openly sneering at her.

"And now you get to go to Haven Point to be with all the pretty people," she jeered.

Skye felt a terrible tightness in her chest, like something had grabbed hold of her heart. She clenched her jaw and continued up the stairs, determined not to let her mother know she'd gotten to her. She closed her bedroom door, dragged a wastebasket to her bed, and sat down, head between her knees, thinking she might throw up.

When the wave of nausea finally passed, her mother's words echoed in her mind. It was all so bizarre, so twisted. Skye had spent weeks trying to avoid going to Maine, and now this was supposedly what she secretly wanted? Skye only went to Haven Point when her mom was in rehab. She'd never once asked to go.

And I need Gran to take care of me? What a joke. Skye's mom was hopeless on the best of days. Schedules, forms, three balanced meals a day—all the stuff other moms worried about, Skye always had to handle on her own. Gran might help with ways to work around her mom's shortcomings, but ultimately Skye had to take care of herself.

It was so ludicrous she might have laughed, but it was too sickening to be funny. Skye thought she had built sturdy walls around herself to protect her from what was going on at home. Now she realized her fortress had been nothing but a bubble. And with just a few snarling, slurring words from her mother, it had burst.

CHAPTER TWO

October 1944
Walter Reed Army Medical Center,
Washington, D.C.

MAREN

As usual, there were three hours of work left and two hours in which to do it. Maren smiled as she watched Dorothy imperiously demand compliance from a soldier who refused to turn away from the wall so she could change his bandages.

"Listen, Corporal Hines. I know you've had it rough, but we must get to this at some point."

The soldier had come by his nasty mood rather honestly. He had left an arm behind in France, and under the bandages, the right side of his face was badly disfigured. He had no right ear to speak of.

His attitude was not uncommon on the amputee ward. After a time, the soldiers moved on to convalescence, a more hopeful place where they were fitted for prosthetics and learned to adapt. But here, still recovering from surgery and new to their loss of limb, their spirits suffered.

Dorothy didn't give everyone the "dowager duchess treatment," as Maren called this particular tactic. But Dorothy, who could read a soldier's emotions like they were running across his forehead on a ticker tape, adapted her approach accordingly.

Corporal Hines scowled, but compelled by her tone, he finally turned over.

"Thank you, Corporal. Much better," Dorothy said in a cheerier voice as she shot Maren a look of amused relief.

Though Maren's patient was also badly wounded, he gave her less trouble than Dorothy's, as he was in a drug-induced slumber. She worked furiously anyway, conscious of the endless row of soldiers awaiting attention. As she was about to finish, she heard footsteps approaching their corner of the ward.

"Hello, Dorothy." Maren turned to see a doctor addressing her friend. He was young, probably no older than thirty, tall, and thin, with well-defined cheekbones and large dark eyes framed by thick lashes.

"Oliver! Oh dear, I mean, Dr. Demarest," Dorothy said with a little laugh. "How *are* you?"

"Very well, thank you. I suspected I'd run into you before long." He gestured toward Corporal Hines. "Will you introduce me to your friend?"

"Corporal Hines, this is Dr. Demarest. See? I promised you would get the very best care here at Walter Reed, and here's my proof. I've known Dr. Demarest almost all my life. He is the best doctor there is." Dorothy's tone carried its usual note of conviction.

Maren returned to the bandages, but after a moment snuck another glance. She had never seen the doctor before, but that was not unusual. Walter Reed was enormous, with multiple wards. Even after several months, she was still meeting new doctors and nurses daily.

Dorothy ceded her spot at the soldier's bedside to Dr. Demarest and moved to her next patient.

"Doc, I feel so much pain there." The soldier pointed to where his amputated arm had been.

"It is unfair, isn't it? To lose your arm, then experience pain where it was? Phantom pain is unfortunately quite common. It is also generally temporary." His tone was formal but sympathetic.

When Dr. Demarest finished his examination, Maren concentrated on her work, not daring to look up even as she heard him approach.

"Hello, Nurse . . ."

Maren raised her eyes to see him looking at her fixedly. She quickly finished bandaging and stood up.

"Larsen. My name is Nurse Larsen." Her heart raced in a manner foreign to her—not a pleasant sensation, a cousin to anxiety.

"Hello, Nurse Larsen," he said. He held her gaze a second longer than necessary, then picked up the chart at the end of the bed. "Can you tell me about Private Gregory?"

"He was injured at Ardennes, Doctor. His leg was amputated below the knee. His wound is clear of infection."

Dr. Demarest peeked under the bandages and appeared satisfied. He caught Maren's eye again, gave her a slight smile, then moved on. He left the ward soon thereafter.

They were so busy cleaning wounds, changing bandages, and dispensing medications for the rest of the afternoon, Maren had little time to consider the queer effect Dr. Demarest had on her. But when her shift ended and she left the ward, she saw him talking to Dorothy at the end of the hall. He walked away before Maren approached, headed down one of the corridors, somewhere into the building's byzantine depths. Fortunately, she did not have to wait long before Dorothy satisfied her burning curiosity.

"Oliver Demarest went to boarding school with my brother. That's why I called him 'Oliver.' I wasn't thinking. *Such* a faux pas," Dorothy said, though she didn't sound particularly troubled. "He invited us to go to the pictures tonight at the Greenhouse Theater. I told him I thought we could. Please do come with!"

"I'd love to, Dorothy, but perhaps you'd like to catch up, just the two of you?"

"Oh no you don't, silly. I'm pretty sure he cooked up the whole outing as a way of seeing you again. He specifically asked if you might be available." She raised one eyebrow and gave Maren a gentle nudge. "I knew someone was going to catch on to you!"

"Oh really, Doro! He just met me for a moment," Maren said. But as they headed down the hall and out the door toward the nurses' residence, she felt a twinge of excitement. She thought he had noticed her, but she hadn't been sure. She had no experience reading the signals of an East Coast man who appeared to be at least ten years her senior.

The truth was, she had thought little about men of any age during her first months at Walter Reed. The work was overwhelming, the stream of boys arriving every day with their grievous, life-changing injuries. She had tried to see some of the city beyond the campus, but there had been little time even for that.

She and Dorothy had come to Walter Reed through the Cadet Nurse Corps, a program cooked up in Washington to address the shortage of home-front nurses. High school graduates were fast-tracked through nursing school, with the government picking up the tab for tuition, books, and uniforms.

Like many senior cadets, Maren and Dorothy were spending their final months training in a military hospital. Though some of her classmates grumbled about staying on American soil, Maren had no such misgivings. The detritus of the war that passed before her eyes told her all she needed to know about the mayhem and misery that lay beyond American shores. This was no time to see the world.

"Oh, will you feel that air." Dorothy sighed, throwing her arms out wide.

Leaving the ward after a long shift always felt like a rebirth, but particularly so today. They had emerged into an exquisite autumn afternoon, the air cool and dry. Tree branches moved in the light breeze and tossed their leaves along the path like offerings.

Though signs of illness and injury were everywhere—doctors and nurses in uniform and patients wheeled between buildings—in many ways, Walter Reed resembled a university more than a hospital, with its brick buildings and landscaped grounds. The nurses' dorm, Delano Hall, was a rambling structure with grand white pillars, high ceilings, sun porches, music rooms, and large parlors. It even had a ballroom where the nurses hosted dances.

It would be nice lodgings at any time, but it was positively luxurious for 1944 Washington, D.C. The city was stretched to the seams even before thousands of "government girls" moved to town to fill wartime administrative jobs. In some apartments, girls lived three to a room, sleeping in shifts. Maren and Dorothy's suite in Delano was quite comfortable—a bedroom with twin beds and a nightstand, and a small sitting room.

"So, what shall we wear?" Dorothy asked as she threw open the closet door and gestured at the contents. Dorothy used her long arms to great effect, with grand, balletic gestures.

"I don't know, Dorothy. What do you think?"

"Ugh, I loathe all these rules," Dorothy said as she flipped through the items in her closet. "I miss all my gewgaws." Wartime garment restrictions meant dresses with fewer pleats and trimmings. Buttons were for utility, never ornamentation. Limitations on dyes meant muted tones. Even so, Dorothy's wardrobe still generated a wealth of options.

"How about this for you?" Dorothy held up a bottle green jacket with padded square shoulders.

If they had selected roommates based on ability to share clothing, they could not have done better than putting tall and slender Maren and Dorothy together, though Maren hadn't much to offer in the bargain. Dorothy was adamant that Maren wear anything in her wardrobe. "We're in uniform so much, my things are barely used," she insisted, as if her clothes required airing and exercise.

"I love that jacket, Doro. Are you sure?" The matching skirt was knee-length, flared with a single pleat.

"Of course." Dorothy reached to the top of the closet and grabbed a small green hat. She perched it on Maren's head and held it there, squinting critically.

"Perfect," she said with a decisive nod. "Oliver won't know what hit him."

After Maren put on the outfit and a pair of pumps, she looked in the mirror and smiled. Back home, she'd been considered pretty. Anyone would have called her that. But a healthy blonde with blue eyes and high coloring was hardly an exceptional sight in Ada, Minnesota, and she had never been particularly conscious of her looks. Since arriving at Walter Reed, Maren had discovered her appearance was not as commonplace outside the upper Midwest. She could not help but notice the appreciative stares she seemed to attract around the campus.

Dorothy had not only been generous with her wardrobe. Maren had also turned a keen ear toward her speech. Though not ashamed of her accent, she had a "When in Rome" view of matters. Though she missed her family, she did not expect to return to Minnesota. If she was to stay in the east, she might as well sound the part. Maren and Dorothy had spent many late nights in their suite, amid riotous laughter, with Dorothy acting as Henry Higgins to Maren's Eliza Doolittle, helping smooth out her long *O*s and sing-songy tones.

"You all look like you have big plans." At the sound of the shrill voice, Maren looked up to see Caroline Sturgeon in the doorway. Dorothy, who came from a prominent New York family, was a minor celebrity in Delano Hall. Caroline fancied herself a Philadelphia version of similar breeding and was forever trying to find out what Dorothy was up to.

Maren focused on selecting a pair of earrings from the ceramic dish on the dresser. Maren's birth was too low to be of interest to Caroline, who paid little attention to her. Maren generally returned the favor.

"Hello, Caroline. What are *your* plans tonight?" Dorothy asked evenly. Maren smiled inwardly at Dorothy's tactic. Caroline would not dare confess she was without anything to do.

"Some of the girls are talking about going to the Trans-Lux Theater down Fourteenth Street." She tossed her hair, which hung in a neat pageboy.

"That sounds *wonderful*," Dorothy said encouragingly, reaching into the closet and pulling out a brown dress with a rounded collar. "They have *Above Suspicion* playing, that film with Joan Crawford."

Caroline took the bait.

"You're welcome to come along!" she said. "You, too, Maren," she added after a beat, flattening her tone to ensure Maren knew she was an afterthought.

"Oh, we've already seen that film, but thank you. Have a wonderful time!" Dorothy said, faking regret.

Now on the record with specific plans, Caroline would not wish to sound nosy or pathetic by continuing the interrogation. She soon slithered away in defeat.

"Ugh. Caroline Sturgeon's voice could cut metal," Dorothy said. "She's the last thing we need hanging around. Not that she's any competition, but you can bet if she got her claws into Oliver Demarest, she wouldn't let go."

"Why do you say that?" Maren asked.

"Oliver's from a positively ancient family. He's related to all those old Bostonians who came over on the *Mayflower*—the Coffins, the Peabodys. That's the sort of thing Caroline cares about."

In many ways, the war had acted like an ice cutter, driving through people's prejudices. Caroline, however, still considered her family name a trump card and clung to it tenaciously.

Maren had never questioned her status growing up. Her father ran a successful farm. He was educated and well respected in their town. Other farmers and town leaders sought his opinions. She had been raised in comfort, taught to consider herself privileged.

For the first time, Maren wondered how someone like Oliver Demarest would see her. She was encouraged by Dorothy, who cared little about pedigree and thought nothing of their divergent backgrounds. She appreciated Maren for her energy and sense of fun, and her desire to learn and be useful, qualities Dorothy also held in abundance.

Dorothy's mother, who thought the cadet program was unseemly, had urged her to volunteer for the USO or the Red Cross like other respectable young women in New York. Dorothy, however, whose brother was an Army Air

Corps pilot somewhere in the Pacific, wanted to do her part and to do it soon. She needed no subsidy for her education, but the expedited nursing school program appealed to her. Her father, a Manhattan financier, was proud of his daughter's commitment and overruled her mother. After studying nursing at St. Luke's in Manhattan, she arrived at Walter Reed, just weeks before Maren.

Dorothy's face was narrow and her smile a little toothy, but she had fetching eyes and a cap of chestnut hair, cut in fashionable curls. Something in her carriage suggested dance lessons, perhaps finishing school. She also had an air, a breezy confidence Maren suspected came from one thing: money. Unlike Caroline, however, Dorothy was in no hurry to settle down.

"My mother has quite exalted ambitions for my marriage," Dorothy had laughed the first night they met. "I'll take my time, if only to annoy her."

A half hour later, Maren and Dorothy were downstairs in the reception room, waiting for Dr. Demarest. They stood by the open door to the screened porch, while Dorothy blew cigarette smoke into the cool air outside.

When he walked in, accompanied by a friend, Maren once again experienced a lurching sensation. He looked even more striking in his elegant dark suit than in the white coat he'd worn earlier. She propelled herself forward with Dorothy to meet the gentlemen in the middle of the room.

"Hello, Dorothy. Nurse Larsen. May I introduce Dr. Arnold?" They shook hands all around and walked outside into the crisp autumn air, rich with a homey smell of fallen leaves and chimney smoke.

Dorothy quickly struck up a conversation with Dr. Arnold, who insisted they call him Michael. Maren managed to learn only that Michael was from New Jersey and also studying orthopedics before Dorothy maneuvered him ahead.

"Dr. Demarest, thank you for taking us to the picture this evening. This is my first time to the Greenhouse Theater," Maren managed.

"I'm pleased you could come. I wish you would call me Oliver," he replied.

"Thank you. I will, if you'll call me Maren."

"All right, then." Oliver smiled. A pleasant smile, but one that fell short of engaging his entire face.

The subdued smile of a wartime surgeon, Maren thought.

"Have you liked your time at Walter Reed, Maren?" Oliver asked.

"Very much. It is hard, of course, all these boys and their terrible injuries. Dorothy and I are on the amputee ward most of the time. But I'm learning so much. How did you come to be here?"

"I was in medical school, and enlisted when we entered the war. Most of the other doctors ended up overseas. It was a great relief to my parents that I went on active duty as a surgeon here. My older brother is fighting in Europe."

"Oh dear. What do you hear from him?" Maren asked.

"Very little. We believe he is in France somewhere." Oliver spoke with a reserve that didn't invite further discussion, so Maren changed the subject, asking him about Walter Reed's eminent head of orthopedics.

"It is a rather spectacular education. In fact, on his recommendation, I plan to continue with orthopedics after the war. I'm ashamed to admit I'm benefiting from this dreadful mess, but I indisputably am," he said as they arrived at the theater.

The Greenhouse Theater was a wonderful example of

wartime ingenuity. The post engineer had disassembled an old greenhouse, salvaging enough wood and glass to build a theater, then pressed the Army Motion Picture Service for a screen and equipment. The result was not fancy, but it provided a nice diversion for the sixty doctors and nurses it accommodated.

They found four seats, and Dorothy contrived to ensure Oliver and Maren were next to each other. They were showing *Stage Door Canteen,* which was fortunately a thinly plotted film, since Maren was too distracted by Oliver's presence to follow along closely. When the movie ended and they left the theater, Maren thrilled at the feeling of Oliver's hand on her back, gently steering her through the crowd.

On the way back to Delano Hall, the foursome took a detour to the formal garden in the southeast corner of the campus, where Dorothy quickly guided Michael in another direction.

"How did you learn of the Cadet Corps, Maren?" Oliver asked as they walked along a garden path.

"I would have had to try hard *not* to know about it," Maren said, trying her best to relax in his presence. She had always conversed comfortably, but she found herself choosing words with unusual care, conscious of what she was saying, how she must sound. "The posters were all over my hometown, Ada, Minnesota. And they were so enticing! My best friend took the first one they put up in our town hall, hid it under her sweater, and brought it to straight to my house."

She smiled at the memory of Helene's act of treachery, how she had burst into Maren's room, eyes gleaming, and unrolled the poster. It featured a beautiful blonde, walking with great purpose. She wore the smart gray cadet uniform, with scarlet trim, epaulets, and a Maltese cross on the sleeve. Her shoulder-length hair glistened under the dashing gray Montgomery-style beret.

Be a Cadet Nurse! The Girls with a Future!

The instant she saw it, Maren's eyes were as alive as Helene's. It was so obviously *The Answer*. Not for Helene, who would marry Nels and live on the land her father had promised them, but for Maren.

"It sounds as if she thought this was a matter of great urgency," Oliver said with a smile.

"I should confess. My friends and family were despairing a bit about my future," Maren replied.

"Oh?"

"My father is a farmer. He and my mother always hoped I would eventually take an interest in the farm. They finally realized my problem was not just lack of interest in agriculture, but lack of instinct for it."

"What finally convinced them?"

"A lot of things. There was my brother Anders, who is terribly earnest about farming. And my cousin Margit. She's my age and was practically queen of the local 4-H Club."

Something in Oliver's manner had begun to encourage her. He was reserved but not cold, and gave off an air of calm acceptance. Maren had the impression there was little she could say that would surprise or disappoint him.

"Though I suspect it was the Junior Goat Show that finally did it," she added in a breezy tone.

"It's always the Junior Goat Show, isn't it?" Oliver played along, shaking his head. "What happened?"

"It's a very painful memory, but if you must hear it . . ."

"I must."

Maren sighed. "Well, all right, then. How much do you know about goat showmanship?" She looked up at him innocently, pretending they didn't both know the answer.

"I'm afraid goat showmanship is a lamentable hole in my education," Oliver said with mock gravity.

"Oh, that's all right," Maren replied. "It's very involved, you see. The goat must be healthy and well groomed, of course, but he also has to behave, which means working with him at least an hour a day so he grows accustomed to being handled. And really, who has time for that?"

"Your cousin Margit?"

"Whose side are you on?" Maren asked indignantly. "Anyway, I trimmed his coat nicely, and he was clean as a whistle. I actually felt pretty confident when I arrived at the fair and led him into the show ring. The judges examine the animal from different angles, though, so you have to move the goat, pick up his hooves. Not being used to this, my goat resisted. I dropped his lead somehow, and he was off like a shot. Next thing I knew, he was by the fence, chewing on some girl's ponytail."

"Oh my."

"You wouldn't believe the fuss. I really thought they overreacted. It wasn't as if he chewed her ponytail *off*."

Oliver laughed out loud, and Maren wondered if she had ever heard such a beautiful sound.

He led her to a bench under the pergola, between two Doric columns. At his prodding, she told him about her mother's determination that Maren continue her education, and how the Cadet Corps program had helped overcome her father's initial resistance.

"College is an unusual choice for women in my community, but in the Cadet Corps, I'd not only be helping our country, but my parents' Norwegian homeland in the process. I studied at University of Minnesota before I came here. I hope to continue with nursing after this war finally ends, God willing. So, you see, you're not the only one benefiting from this terrible mess."

Maren tried to draw Oliver out on his family and life before Walter Reed. She wasn't sure if he was reticent or private, but he provided scant details. She learned he was raised in Boston, that his family had a summer home in Maine, but little else before he steered the conversation in another direction.

He wasn't animated, precisely, but he seemed as interested in her thoughts as she was in his, and listened in his intent way to her observations. It was a nice turn of events. The few men she'd met in Washington cared little for the opinions of a twenty-year-old woman.

Eventually Dorothy and Michael found them, and they headed to Delano Hall. To Maren's dismay, just as they reached the dormitory, Caroline Sturgeon approached along another path. She had Juliet Gibson in her wake, a plain, dull-witted girl from Maryland who thought Caroline was the pinnacle of taste at Walter Reed, a one-sided adoration that was the only possible explanation for their friendship. Caroline's eyes narrowed as she saw them.

"Hello, girls. Hello, Dr. Demarest," Caroline said in her grating voice.

"Hello, Nurse Sturgeon, Nurse Gibson," Oliver said politely, and introduced Michael.

"Have you heard about the ball at Delano Hall next weekend?" Caroline asked. She cocked her head and smiled up at Oliver.

"We have, thank you," Oliver replied. "We will be there."

"I hope you'll save me a dance," Caroline said. Dorothy nudged her foot against Maren's, a gesture of solidarity.

When Juliet went inside, Maren hoped Caroline would follow, but she lingered, forcing Dorothy and Maren to say their good-byes in her presence.

"Thank you for taking us to the pictures," Maren said. She looked Oliver in the eye and extended her hand.

"Thank you for joining me." Oliver took her hand in his. Maren noted with pleasure his use of "me," rather than "us," implying the previous three hours had been more date than group excursion.

"I'll see you again soon, I hope. At the ball, certainly," he added. Maren felt Caroline's eyes on her and could do nothing more than nod and smile in a way she hoped was encouraging.

When she and Dorothy reached their room, Maren went to the window to lower the shade, and paused to watch Oliver's tall form disappear into the darkness.

"I think he liked you," Dorothy said.

"Do you?" Maren turned to face Dorothy. She felt uncertain.

"I do. Oliver has lovely manners, but if he wasn't interested, he would have come up with some excuse to end the evening after the picture, so he could go home and stick his nose in a book. He's terribly hardworking and serious. His brother Daniel is just the opposite. They're different as chalk and cheese."

Dorothy's words squared with Maren's observations. He did seem kind, but serious, too. And so much older.

"Could you believe Caroline?" Dorothy asked as she unrolled her stockings. "She told Mary Grady she joined the Cadet Corps hoping to marry a doctor. Imagine her disappointment when she discovered most of them are old civilian grandfathers. Except Oliver, of course. I'm sure she's after him. She gives us all a bad name with her scheming."

Sleep did not come easily for Maren that night. While she found Caroline's behavior distasteful, she was a bit in awe of her single-mindedness. Maren was artless, in her way, but she'd had her fantasies through the years, fueled by Clark Gable films and her beloved nineteenth-century literature. At their center was always some handsome, cultivated man.

She knew real life wasn't like films or novels. Romance sometimes needed to be helped along, but she had never had to throw out lures. How did one capture the attention of a man ten years one's senior, one from a completely different world?

She had no idea, but for the first time in her life, she wanted to find out.

CHAPTER THREE

Maren stood at the bedside of Private Brian O'Neill, nearly overcome by the pungent odor of decaying skin. No matter what the burn unit nurses said, she would never grow accustomed to this smell. They had suggested menthol under the nose, but it barely helped.

Private O'Neill had had the good fortune to live through his tank being hit by a shell, but he was otherwise the unluckiest of soldiers: both amputee and burn victim. His leg was blown to pieces below the knee, and his left arm was burned from the shoulder to the tips of his fingers.

But for all this, he was still a flirt. Everyone adored him.

"Hello, Nurse Larsen," he said, looking her up and down. His smoke-damaged voice was still thin and raspy, even weeks after his injury. In his Boston accent, her name sounded like "Lah-sen."

"Hello, Private O'Neill. How are you today?" Maren smiled indulgently and forced herself to master her stomach.

"I'm fine, now you're here. Care to give a poor burned, legless soldier a kiss?"

"You're not legless, Private O'Neill. You still have that

one over there, on the other side." Maren pointed over his stump to his remaining leg.

He faked a look of confusion then pretended an idea had come to him. "Okay, then. Care to give a poor burned *one-legged* solider a kiss?"

Maren laughed and blew him a kiss.

"When are the other nurses coming?" Brian asked. His light tone, Maren knew, masked great apprehension at the excruciating pain he endured when the burn unit nurses removed unhealthy tissue from his arm.

"They won't be here for a bit, Private. You can rest easy."

The field surgeons had done their best with Brian in primitive battlefield conditions. They'd amputated below the knee, casted his leg, and sent him home. When he continued to suffer infections and pressure sores, the surgeons at Walter Reed had to amputate again, this time above the knee.

The scarring on his arm was so thorough, his fingers appeared webbed. If he lived, which remained an open question, the doctors would spend months just trying to separate his fingers enough to bend.

As Brian was a burn patient first, he was kept in the hot rooms of the burn unit. Maren had been dispatched from the amputee unit to care for his leg wound. It was meant to be a two-day rotation, but it was obvious to everyone that Brian's mood lifted when Maren was around. The ordinarily austere and rule-bound Nurse Blair, who oversaw the cadets, had altered the schedule to let Maren attend to Brian as much as possible.

Maren had always feared the burn unit—its smell and damp heat, and the disfigurement and suffering of the patients. The doctors and nurses there were serious and sober, almost clannish. They ate together in the cafeteria and spoke in hushed tones, on and off the unit. They had an almost spiritual devotion to their patients and to one another.

She was still in awe of them, but helping Brian had buoyed her. Until now, she had not done anything at Walter Reed that any cadet could not have handled. The fact that her particular efforts seemed to raise the spirits of one precious patient suited her innate desire to find meaning in her work.

"Will you write a letter for me?" Brian asked. Maren fetched a paper and pen and sat in a chair next to his bed.

"Dear Mother," he began. "I am sitting here with my wife-to-be. . . ."

Maren put down the pen and looked at him, amused and exasperated.

"I'm just trying to cheer her up!" Brian said. His mother, a widow, was home in Fall River with a passel of younger children. She could not visit, but Maren knew from reading her letters to Brian that she was worried. Maren smiled and waited.

"Okay, sorry," Brian said with a smile. "Just say I'm better, and you're all taking good care of me here."

The burn unit nurses arrived just as Maren finished. Brian stiffened when he saw them.

"Will you stay, Nurse Larsen?" one of the nurses asked. Maren agreed, and held Brian's good hand until they finished their ministrations.

He finally fell asleep, as he always did after the ordeal. As Maren was leaving the unit, she caught sight of the clock and groaned. She had left herself little time to get ready for the ball that evening.

I'll bet Caroline Sturgeon's been at it for hours, she thought as she raced out the door.

She was out of breath when she reached her room, certain she could never be ready in time. Dorothy, typically efficient, was already in her burgundy sheath dress.

"Don't worry. I'll help," Dorothy said, reading her mind. She handed her a towel, and Maren quickly showered.

She had put her hair in pin curls the night before, but most of the waves had been defeated by the humid air of the burn unit. Dorothy helped her clip back one side with an elegant rhinestone barrette.

She quickly stepped into the pale blue dress Dorothy had insisted she wear. It was lovely, with an organza A-line skirt and off-shoulder portrait collar. She put on her lipstick, smacked her lips, took a quick look in the mirror, and they headed downstairs.

The ballroom's parquet floors gleamed, and the sounds of the musicians warming up their instruments bounced off the high ceilings. Entertainment for most dances consisted of one of the more musical nurses playing on the baby grand piano in the corner of the ballroom, but tonight they were to enjoy a real dance band. Nurses stood in clusters, chattering excitedly and admiring one another's dresses.

With the rush behind her, Maren felt some restraint of spirit. Even as the guests began to arrive and the band finally struck up a number, Maren felt as if some part of her was still back in the burn unit with Brian.

The room filled with the lush voice of the singer, a voluptuous redhead with a lovely contralto, and a young soldier approached Maren and asked her to dance.

"I'll just say I'm sorry now," he said as he led her onto the floor. "I'm a terrible dancer."

He was not being humble, Maren discovered, but what

he lacked in skill he made up for with energetic enthusiasm. By the time the song ended and he escorted her from the floor, Maren had begun to enjoy herself.

She stood talking to Dorothy, casting the occasional furtive glance toward the door, looking for Oliver. Just as she had begun to worry that he would not come, he appeared at the entrance, dazzling in his dress uniform. She had not laid eyes on him all week, except one brief sighting in the hallway. He had been in earnest conversation with several other doctors but caught Maren's eye and smiled.

His glance swept the room and stopped when it reached Maren. Her heart fluttered as he headed in her direction. Out of her peripheral vision, she saw another soldier taking steps toward her, but she kept her eyes determinedly on Oliver, and the young man turned to another nurse instead. By the time Oliver reached her, Maren's heart was pounding.

"Will you dance, Maren?" he asked in his mild way, smiling down at her.

As they walked onto the floor, Maren bade a silent thanks to her mother for insisting she take dance classes. It took her little time to realize, however, she need not have known how to dance at all. Oliver guided her through the foxtrot with ease, the slightest pressure of his fingers on her back signaling their next move.

"How is Private O'Neill?" he asked as they glided across the floor. As a surgeon, Oliver would be familiar with the case, but his question suggested he was aware of Maren's unofficial role as Brian's private nurse.

"As well as he can be. He's dear and brave and everyone adores him."

They talked about Brian and other hospital news, but Maren was so consumed with the sensation of his arm about her waist, she could barely keep up her end of the conversation. She had never felt her movements so anticipated and synchronized. Even with the rigidly determined steps of the dance, even in this crowded room, Maren felt an abandon, a sensual pleasure entirely new to her. When that song ended, the band struck up Glenn Miller's tune "A String of Pearls." Oliver kept her on the dance floor.

His nearness, the rhythmic song, the contrast of the men's formal uniforms to the swirling skirts and gaily arranged hair of the nurses, all acted as enchantments. Maren felt transported, completely relieved of her earlier mixed feelings. As the song came to an end, Oliver leaned toward her, his mouth near her ear.

"They are circling," he whispered. She looked around and saw several men, apparently eager to cut in. With his thumb and index finger, Oliver lifted her chin and locked her in eye contact.

"I don't think I'm ready to release you yet, if you don't mind." He smiled. She nodded. Seeing the pair was unlikely to present an opportunity, the competitors gave up, and Maren and Oliver danced until the band took a break after a few more songs.

In the absence of music, Maren's mood began a descent to earth, but remnants of euphoria lingered as they headed for the refreshment table. Oliver filled glasses of punch for them, and two more when Michael and Dorothy approached. They had a few pleasant moments before Caroline appeared. Juliet was by her side, wearing a poufy pink dress and her usual daft expression.

"That woman is like a homing pigeon," Dorothy whispered. Maren felt the spell begin to break. The conversation began congenially enough, but Caroline could not leave feathers unruffled for long.

"This music is wonderful. They remind me of a terrific

dance band we have in Philadelphia." Caroline turned to Maren. "I imagine this is a far cry from entertainment in Minnesota."

"We do have dances in Minnesota, Caroline," Maren said. She did her best to hide her impatience.

"Really? I am trying to envision a big band out in farm country," Caroline replied, tilting her head as if Maren were a fascinating anthropological specimen.

"Well, it might be hard to imagine, but so it is." Though her resolve to remain in charity with Caroline was fast dwindling, Maren managed a little shrug and smile, then turned to Dorothy and began to speak. Caroline would not be put off. She interrupted before Maren could finish a syllable.

"Really, Maren. I'm dying to hear. Where does one even *hold* a dance in Ada, Minnesota?"

Maren's temper flared. "Why, we just throw open the doors to Daddy's barn. It is *so* dreamy." Maren elongated her *O*s in an exaggerated Minnesota accent and widened her eyes in her best country-girl-in-the-big-city impersonation.

Caroline raised her eyebrows, obviously gratified to have provoked her, and Maren immediately regretted the outburst. Oliver looked amused, but Maren felt certain such childishness would only highlight their difference in age. She resolved to be more careful. Caroline, however, had no such compunction. When the music started up again, she parried with another tactic.

"Dr. Demarest. It's a Ladies' Choice dance. Shall we?" Caroline held her hand out to him.

He assented politely and led her to the floor. What little was left of Maren's exhilaration was gone. Dancing in Oliver's arms, it was easy to believe his attention toward her was special, but watching him move across the dance floor with the abominable Caroline Sturgeon reminded her how sought-after he was. She felt as if she were swimming far out of her depth.

The moment that song came to an end, a sweet-faced young soldier asked Maren to dance. After that, another took his place, and then another. She caught glimpses of Oliver, first at the refreshment table, then talking with some other doctors, and then dancing with Dorothy, who attempted to angle him in her direction, but was thwarted by the crowd.

After nearly an hour of this, Maren extricated herself from the dance floor. A few nurses stood near a potted tree by one of the ballroom's tall windows. Maren tucked behind them and sat on the low windowsill, hidden from view by the plant and the shimmering skirts, safe from requests to dance. The window, slightly ajar, admitted the cool night air. She leaned back, closed her eyes, and breathed in, trying to conquer what felt like irrational disappointment. After a moment she sensed a presence, a shadow blocking the light.

"I hope you aren't hiding from me." Maren opened her eyes to find Oliver standing over her, hand outstretched. She took it and let him pull her from her perch.

"Are you too tired for another dance?" he asked.

"Not at all. I was just getting a little air," Maren answered, forcing her voice to rally. She was pleased he'd come to fetch her, but the previous hour's insecurities were still fresh.

He led her onto the floor as the singer approached the microphone. When the band played the first notes of "When the Lights Go On Again," the dance floor quickly filled. The song had become an instant anthem when it was released the previous year. Its lyrics spoke to the great yearning for an end to war, painting a tantalizing picture of a day when the boys would finally be home again, when there would be time for love and a return to simple pleasures. The singer performed without affectation, allowing the words and melody to deliver the sentiment.

As Maren and Oliver moved wordlessly around the dance floor, she felt a tension in his arms she'd not noticed earlier. He pulled her tighter, and she felt his breath on her ear.

She tried to imagine how he felt—his brother fighting God only knew where, and the war's most appalling consequences paraded before his eyes, day after day.

How he must worry, Maren thought.

She allowed him to hold her closer than she was accustomed to, closer than she would ordinarily allow.

The following day, Maren raced through her duties on the amputee ward so she would have time to visit Brian. One of the burn unit nurses had told her in passing that he had spiked a fever and passed a difficult night. When she finally reached his side, he smiled weakly.

"Hello, beautiful," he said, his voice even thinner than usual.

"Hello, Private O'Neill," she replied. "How are you feeling?"

"Not real well," he said.

Maren sat and took his good hand in her own. What was it about hands that made them so personal? Brian's was thin and freckled, his youth evident in its smoothness. He was just eighteen, after all.

Feeling sad for him, and more worried than she thought she should be, she released his hand and attended to his bandages. When she finished, he indicated a book by his bedside.

"Will you read to me?"

She hesitated. The ward nurses had encouraged her attention toward Brian, but she had begun to think the situation called for some professional distance, which she had no idea how to achieve. She picked up the book and examined its spine. It was one of the Armed Services Edition paperbacks sized to fit in cargo pants. They were ubiquitous at the hospital.

"Not your kind of book?" Brian asked.

"Oh, no, I adore a good Western." Maren smiled. She found the earmarked page and read aloud until Brian fell asleep.

An hour later, Maren entered her room and flopped on her bed without removing her cap. She had walked out of the hospital into a cold, drizzling rain, a full fourteen hours after she'd walked in.

"Gads, you look tired," Dorothy said.

"And wet, I know. I stayed after with Brian again. He's not doing well."

"I don't suppose you want to go to the diner?"

"I don't think so, Doro. I grabbed something in the cafeteria before I went to the burn unit. I'm so tired."

"I'm afraid caring for poor Private O'Neill is wearing you to the bone."

"I was thinking something similar today," Maren said, eyes still closed. "But they depend on me. They're all such heroes on the burn unit, and so busy. I don't feel like I can cut back right now."

Maren dragged her cap from her head, used her left foot to nudge the shoe off her right, then repeated the move on the other side. That little bit of effort sapped her of what energy remained, and soon after Dorothy left, she fell asleep in her uniform.

As it happened, she couldn't see Brian the next day.

She was detailed to the post-surgical room and the amputee ward, and by the time she arrived at the burn unit to check on him, he was asleep.

As she was leaving, she saw Nurse Latham, the burn unit's head nurse, who informed her Brian had been a bit better that day. His fever persisted, but he was stable. They were still watching him closely.

"He asked after you, of course," Nurse Latham added.

As she left the building, Maren felt a little more herself. She was only a short way down the path toward Delano when she heard a voice calling her name from behind. She turned to see Oliver in his white coat, walking briskly in her direction. She felt a smile pop onto her face as she waited for him to catch up.

"Hello, Maren. I noticed we both have Thursday off, and I wondered if you might like to spend some time away from the hospital."

"I would love to, thank you," she said, pleased he had taken the time to check her schedule.

"If the weather holds, I was thinking a picnic in Rock Creek Park?"

"Wonderful."

"I'll fetch you at Delano at eleven thirty." Oliver smiled briefly and patted her on the arm, then turned to hurry back to the hospital.

On Thursday, Maren wore a navy woolen skirt, white blouse, and cardigan sweater, all from her own closet. If Oliver was going to be disappointed by seeing Maren in her own clothes, rather than in one of Dorothy's fashionable dresses, she wanted to get it over with now. (Though Dorothy did insist on wrapping a silk scarf around her neck before she left the room.)

She found Oliver waiting outside. He kissed her cheek

and smiled at her in his understated way. He didn't blink at her humble attire. In fact, he opened with an apology for his meager picnic.

"Not much of a meal." He held up a brown paper bag. "No basket or anything. But it's lunch."

They walked across Sixteenth Street toward one of the paths that led into Rock Creek Park. The two-thousand-acre forest and its byzantine network of trails had once been on the edge of the city that had long since grown around it. Through its center, the aptly named Rock Creek ran noisily over its stony bed.

"Teddy Roosevelt loved this park," Oliver said. "He used to bring unsuspecting ambassadors here for long hikes."

"I bet he was hard to keep up with," Maren replied.

"His motto was 'Over, under, or through—never around.'"

Though a corner of her mind was occupied with Brian, Maren filled her lungs with the autumn air and took in the splendor.

"I hear Private O'Neill's had a rough go of it lately," Oliver said, seeming to read her thoughts.

"Yes, running a fever, and his spirits are low."

"I'm sorry to hear that. He's like a cat with nine lives, that fellow. Amazing story. I know everyone is pulling for him, and you've been very devoted."

Maren thought she detected a note of concern in his voice. He was so hard to read, though; she couldn't be sure.

They ambled along a wooded path, quiet, though not awkwardly so. The trees, at the peak of autumn beauty, formed a colorful canopy far above their heads. Dappled sunshine made its way through the patchwork of scorching red maples and vibrant yellow elms. Browned leaves, defeated and fallen, crackled under their feet. The noise sent squirrels and birds under the growth and up to the branches.

"It's funny, isn't it," Oliver said, almost absently, as he looked around. "How nature seems to celebrate decay each year in all this beauty."

Maren nodded. She knew what he had left unsaid, the contrast to the human decay they left behind at the hospital. There was no beauty in that, nothing to celebrate. She pulled her sweater a little closer.

They arrived at a picnic table in a clearing, shaded by soaring trees. Oliver laid out sandwiches and sodas. He was his typical well-mannered self, leading her in conversation about nothing in particular, interested in anything she had to say, though there wasn't much of it. Maren simply couldn't summon her usual liveliness. If Oliver noticed, he didn't show it. He was kind, not overly solicitous. He seemed to expect nothing more than her presence.

When they returned to Delano Hall, Oliver left her with a kiss on the cheek and a promise to "see each other again soon."

She went to her room wondering if she was the only woman he was seeing, and whether she was doing the right things. He seemed to enjoy her company, but he was reserved, inscrutable.

I should have been more animated. She sighed.

Caroline Sturgeon would never have let such an opportunity go to waste.

In the following weeks, it became hard for Maren to imagine when Oliver could possibly be seeing someone else. Despite his grueling schedule, he made time to take her to the Glen Echo Amusement Park and the National Gallery of Art. Many of the museum's greatest works had been spirited away to some unknown location for the duration of the war, but Maren was so enthralled with what remained he'd practically had to drag her out when it closed.

In between, the days seemed endless. She frequently stayed at the burn unit for hours after her scheduled shifts. The extra work began to take a toll. Even Nurse Latham, who treasured help from any corner, suggested Maren take time off. Brian's condition remained perilous, though, and he brightened so much when she came around, she couldn't stay away.

One afternoon when Maren arrived at the burn unit, she was pleased to find him cheerier. His condition was still so unstable that a long-scheduled surgery for his hand had been postponed indefinitely. Still, Maren discerned a definite change for the better.

"You know, Nurse Larsen, I can't wait to get out of here. I think I'm going to go soon," he said.

Maren thought that was unlikely, but she smiled at his optimism. They talked about inconsequential things. He showed her a letter from his mother, at the bottom of which one of his sisters had colored a picture. It was obviously meant to be Brian, though the figure was unnaturally long, with freckles that looked more like large spots.

"Maybe she's forgotten me and thinks I'm a giraffe," Brian said, laughing as much as his tired lungs would allow.

"Either that, or she thinks you're in the hospital with measles," Maren said.

"I'd like you to meet my mom someday," Brian added.

"I'd like that, too," Maren said.

She read to him until he fell asleep, then left the ward, feeling as tired as ever, but hopeful that Brian's body might soon catch up with his mood.

CHAPTER FOUR

The following day, Maren was not due at the hospital until afternoon. She was catching up on the papers in the reading room when one of the other cadets brought a message from the burn unit, asking her to come straight-away.

Maren went to her room, threw on her uniform, and raced to the unit, wondering what had happened. *Was Brian asking for me?* Nurse Latham met her outside, a distressed look on her face.

"Nurse Larsen, please sit," she said, indicating a pair of chairs along the wall. Maren sat, her heart beating in growing alarm. Nurse Latham took the other seat.

"What is it?"

"Private O'Neill took a turn last night. It was a cascade of events. You know how unstable he was. To put it simply, his system simply couldn't take any more. He died early this morning. I wanted you to hear it from me. I know he had become dear to you, as you had to him."

Maren went slack, first her face, then her shoulders and arms. Her head fell to Nurse Latham's shoulder, an entirely involuntary movement. Tearless, silent, Maren willed her mind to emerge from its fog. Some kind soul came out of the unit and handed her a glass of water.

How can this be?

After a few minutes, the realization that she was keeping Nurse Latham from her work began to prick at her conscience. She managed to sit up and drink the water. She asked no questions, said nothing except "Thank you."

"Are you all right, Maren?" Nurse Latham touched her forearm. She'd never used Maren's first name before. The gesture struck Maren as unbearably tender, and tears threatened. Desperate to keep herself from becoming a spectacle, Maren forced herself to stand. Though she was shaky, her legs seemed willing to support her, so she thanked Nurse Latham again and said good-bye.

It was chilly outside, and she wore only a thin jacket over her uniform, but she took the path to the rose garden. She craved the dry, brisk air, a contrast to the stultifying atmosphere of the burn unit where she'd spent so much time recently.

No blooms graced the stalks, but even the ghosts of flowers appealed to her. She sat on a cold stone bench and looked around blankly. As her head cleared, she remembered Brian's words the day before.

"I am going to go soon," he had said. She smiled weakly, realizing what he'd left out. He hadn't said "go home" or "move to convalescence." He had known, in the way some people do, that he would die. He made a particular point of wanting Maren to meet his mother. She would have to find a way, though she couldn't begin to imagine how.

Twining around her grief was a thread of shame. How capable she had thought she was, how *helpful*. For weeks she had operated under the unconscious belief that if she tried hard enough, she could keep Private Brian O'Neill alive. Preposterous, of course, but looking back, she realized it had underscored all her actions.

The realization gave rise to an unpleasant thought. What did it mean that she hadn't been successful? What did Maren have to offer that was special? Just as she was adding disappointment to the growing list of horrible emotions warring inside her, a crunching sound announced a visitor. She turned to see Oliver ambling down the gentle hill that led to the rose garden. He sat on the bench and put his arm around her.

"I heard about Private O'Neill, Maren. I'm sorry." His expression, normally so difficult for Maren to read, contained a distinct note of compassion. Unable to speak, she merely nodded. As his hand lightly stroked her back, she felt a lump form in her throat.

She tried mightily to keep the tears at bay. She had been able to keep from crying in the face of almost all of it, the cumulative effect of days of overwork, the anguish and sense of futility. But this was too much. Unable to resist yet another act of unexpected kindness, she put her face in her hands and wept. Oliver held her silently. When the tears abated, he offered a handkerchief. She used it and gave him a gentle smile.

"I'm dreadfully sorry. I know I scarcely knew him, but I was so hopeful. And I'm so tired."

"Please. Don't be sorry." Oliver looked at her intently, his eyes searching hers. He leaned a little closer, giving her a chance to object. When she did not, he closed his eyes and kissed her. He was tentative at first. But when she put her hand behind his neck and pulled him closer, his ardor increased. He held her face with his free hand and she felt, if only for this instant, completely within his protection.

Maren pulled back after a spell, a little embarrassed, but Oliver continued to look at her, stroking her cheek with his thumb. His demeanor suggested nothing here surprised him. It was all perfectly natural, expected. He saw nothing odd about her caring so much for Brian O'Neill or in her tears at his death. And nothing was unusual about their rather passionate midday kiss in the rose garden.

His acceptance comforted her in a way nothing else could have at that moment, and as she felt herself emerging from the wild emotional swings of the previous hour, she realized how attached to Oliver she had become.

And even as she gloried in this moment, even as she was certain he appreciated her, she still had little idea of his feelings beyond that.

"Better?" he asked, his hands moving to hold hers.

Just as Maren was about to respond, she caught a glimpse of the watch on his left wrist. She gasped, pulled away, and leapt to her feet.

"Oh dear! I am better, thank you so much, but I'm also late. I am supposed to be starting a shift now."

She looked at him, uncertain what to do next, how to bring an end to this scene, one that certainly called for some kind of close. How young she felt around him.

"I'll walk you back," he said helpfully. He stood, offered her an arm, and they headed toward the hospital.

"Maren, I'm invited to a party Friday night. Would you join me? It's for the Dutch ambassador. I don't know him from Adam, but the party is at the home of a family friend."

It was hard to imagine putting on a dress and smiling at strangers, but Maren knew the distraction would probably be helpful. And she was pleased he had asked.

"Thank you. That would be lovely."

They reached the door to the amputee ward. A number of people were in the hallway, but he looked down at her and smiled gently.

"Friday, then," he said quietly. Before he walked away, he brushed the back of his hand against hers—a discreet touch and feather-light, but it was several minutes before her heartbeat returned to normal.

Over the following days, Maren began coming to terms with Brian O'Neill's death. One lingering concern was how to honor his wish that Maren meet his mother, but that problem was solved for her. Through Herculean contortions, Mrs. O'Neill arranged for neighbors to care for her other children, so she could come to Walter Reed to thank the staff who'd cared for Brian, and to accompany his body on its last journey home to Massachusetts.

Nurse Blair arranged an audience, and Maren met Mrs. O'Neill in a small reception room in the main building. Maren was apprehensive, uncertain of her ability to handle tears or histrionics, but her fears were unfounded. Patricia O'Neill was tiny, probably not five feet, but she had an unmistakable dignity. She sat straight in the worn antique love seat, dressed neatly in a sensible plain black suit. The only sign of stress was the grip with which she held the black patent handbag in her lap.

Even through the sorrow in Mrs. O'Neill's countenance, Maren detected the life and humor that had been so evident in her son. She had his freckles, his bright green eyes.

"I am so sorry for your loss," Maren said as she took Mrs. O'Neill's hand in her own. "I spent a good deal of time with Brian. I came to know and like him better than any patient since I've been here."

"I am glad he had so many who looked after him in his final days." Her voice caught slightly, but she lifted her chin and mastered herself. "I thank you."

Maren told Mrs. O'Neill about her last conversation

with Brian, and her hindsight realization that he likely knew he was facing the end, that he seemed at peace.

"Well, he had his faith," Mrs. O'Neill said. "He might not have shown it, but he was a good Catholic boy. He knew where he was going."

They spoke comfortably until a hospital representative came in to discuss details with Mrs. O'Neill. Maren returned to the dorm, feeling she had received as much, if not more, comfort than she had given.

"I bet I know why you've been asked to come in uniform," Dorothy said, filing her nails as Maren dressed for the party on Friday. "It's because of Roosevelt and his parasite comment."

"What comment?" Maren asked. Oliver had sent a note on Thursday, saying he'd fetch her at six o'clock and that they were "both to be in dress uniform." Maren had wondered about that, but she'd been too busy to give it much thought.

"It was in the society column. Didn't you see it?"

Maren shook her head. She read the papers in the Delano Hall reading room when she could, but the society columns were meaningless to her. She knew no one who was mentioned.

"Well, you know Roosevelt and the cave dwellers never have gotten on," Dorothy began.

"Dorothy, back up." Maren laughed. "Parasites? Cave dwellers?"

"The cave dwellers are the old Washington families. They've never much liked Roosevelt, who filled up the city with all his New Dealers even before the war. He doesn't like them either, says they just travel and have parties and don't do their part for the war. 'Parasites,' he called them. It got in the papers."

"Oh my!" Maren said with a smile. "I'm going to a parasite party?"

"They thought it was funny at first, but then he started threatening to annex their houses. That got them nervous."

Maren could well imagine, given how many buildings around the city had been annexed. Girls from a nearby school were about to return from a break when they discovered the army had taken their school building to use for a convalescent wing. That was understandable, since Walter Reed was so short on bed space, but other annexations seemed more capricious. When the Statler family's new hotel near the White House was still under construction, they were so afraid the navy would try to nab the lovely new building, they kept things quiet until it opened, at which point they immediately invited a host of luminaries, including Mrs. Roosevelt, to a tea. As they hoped, the clientele became so attached to the venue, the navy wouldn't dare snatch it out from under them.

"Anyway, the *Post*'s society editor wrote a column defending the cave dwellers," Dorothy continued. "She said their parties were serving the war. She called them 'parties for a purpose.'"

"Well, there's an expression with wiggle room!" Maren said. "Don't all parties have a purpose, even if it's just to drink champagne and dance?"

"I suppose, but hostesses have taken it to heart. Everyone wants to claim they brought important people together to relax and discuss the war effort. They're all competing to attract the right guests."

"And Oliver Demarest makes a fine prop in his uniform," Maren said.

"Rather! A Demarest of the Boston Demarests *and* a doctor at Walter Reed? A star guest, in or out of uniform. And they'll get a lovely cadet nurse, to boot."

"Any points of cave dweller etiquette I should know?" Maren asked.

"Maybe say 'how do you do' instead of 'pleased to meet you,'" Dorothy replied, though she sounded agnostic even on this small point. "Truly, Maren, you have better manners than many people you will meet in Washington society. Or New York's or Philadelphia's, for that matter."

Oliver arrived promptly in his fine dress uniform. Maren had replaced the standard-issue pumps with a nicer pair, but otherwise looked like a model for the sort of re- cruitment poster that had originally lured her into the Cadet Corps.

They headed into the chilly November night. Soon after they arrived at the stop at the corner, a streetcar pulled up, one of the World War I models, resurrected to accommodate wartime demand. Oliver guided her up the rickety stairs, and she felt a rush of pleasure at the pres- sure of his hand on the small of her back. They switched to a more crowded car at U Street, and Maren enjoyed the second leg of the journey even more, pressed into Oliver's side as he smiled down at her in his distracted way.

They walked the last few blocks through the neighbor- hood dubbed Millionaires' Row. Even in the darkness she could make out the federal-style town houses, their commanding façades softened by urns, stone swags, and fluting over the doors.

The hostess, he explained, was Mrs. Edward Bell, a widow. She and Mr. Bell had lived in Boston until he'd been called to work in the Wilson administration. Mrs. Bell, a native South Carolinian who had never acclimated to Boston winters, had stayed on after her husband's death.

"This must be her fifth invitation, and I've not been to see her once. My father mentioned my negligence in a letter. I would never hear the end of it if I didn't show my face."

Even before they turned onto the flagstone walk that ran along the circular driveway, Maren could hear the music, voices, and tinkling glasses that swelled and ebbed with the opening and closing of the door. Oliver took Maren's hand and led her to the entrance, where a uniformed maid gestured them into the large marble hallway.

After the maid took their coats, they entered a ballroom off the hall, quite large for what from the outside had appeared to be a compact property. Queen Anne chairs lined creamy yellow walls. In the far corner, a piano player's talents were barely audible over the voices, which echoed in the cavernous, uncarpeted, almost completely unfurnished room.

The women were mostly middle-aged, with helmets of white coiffed hair, red lipstick, and elegant but shapeless dresses. Oliver led Maren across the room, where a bartender was pouring drinks. They attracted some notice as they moved through the crowd. *The uniforms,* she thought.

When they reached the bar, a portly woman with silver hair and a great green dress waddled up, her voice high and trilling.

"Oliver, dear, you've finally come!" she exclaimed, her arms outstretched. Maren detected a vestigial Southern accent.

"Hello, Mrs. Bell." Oliver accepted her embrace and gave her a kiss on the cheek. He introduced Maren, whom she greeted pleasantly.

"Oliver, there are so many people here who'd love to meet you. But you must tell me first, how is your family? How is your *mother*?"

Maren detected an emphasis on the word *mother,*

a subtle note of concern. Was Oliver's mother ill? He hadn't mentioned it, but he was so reticent about his family.

"Much the same, thank you," Oliver responded, offering no clue to the question's provenance.

"We have wanted to get to Haven Point to see them, but these rations! Whenever we try to fly, we are bumped off by soldiers, though God bless them, we do understand. I hope this war will be over soon so we can all go back to normal."

Maren smiled to herself. Washington's upper echelons were notorious for their resistance to privations of war. Gas rations were allocated based on one's relative importance, and the poor schoolteachers charged with doling them out were terribly harassed. A waitress became a minor celebrity when a customer demanded more sugar after already receiving his share. "Stir what you've got!" she'd snapped in reply. Washingtonians were not good at "stirring what they'd got."

After Mrs. Bell excused herself, Oliver got Maren a soda water, and a scotch for himself. He soon attracted the attention of a group of older gentlemen, and Maren listened as he answered their questions about research and advancements at the hospital. After a few moments, one of the gentlemen pointed toward the door.

"Oh, there's the ambassador," he said. They briefly turned for a look then resumed their conversation. Maren wondered at such a figure being so commonplace that his arrival heralded little more than a murmur.

Oliver eventually extricated himself from the conversation and guided her toward the buffet, or what remained of it. A few small dishes of salted peanuts sat near a larger silver bowl, which contained only melting ice cubes and a lonely shrimp tail that hinted at a long-gone appetizer. Maren was surprised at the paucity of refresh-ments. Even in wartime, she would have been far better fed at a Minnesota hot-dish supper. Maren did not say anything, but once again Oliver seemed to know what she was thinking.

"This is why cocktail parties are so popular," Oliver explained. "It's cheaper and easier than trying to figure out an elaborate meal on war rations. The British think it's passing strange, people gathering for drinks with noth-ing to eat. I suppose if you attend enough events in one night, you can cobble together a reasonable meal."

"Enough events and the right timing. Twenty minutes earlier, we might have had a piece of shrimp!"

"Yes, that's how it's done. A shrimp at one house, a peanut at another, and eventually you've had the equiva-lent of dinner. But if you don't mind, I'd rather have it the old-fashioned way. I made us a dinner reservation. Shall we greet the guest of honor and get on our way?"

Maren nodded, and they wriggled through the crowd toward the ambassador. Oliver introduced them, and they had a brief exchange. Maren made some mental notes to share with her parents, who would actually be interested. After they said their good-byes, they got a cab on Con-necticut Avenue.

Washington, not a gourmet town to begin with, was even worse for rationing. Even after setting aside certain days as meatless, the number of points available to most restaurants limited how many filet mignon and other choice cuts they could serve.

Oliver, however, had finagled a reservation at the Oc-cidental, which had been exempted from ration rules un-der the theory that a few restaurants should be available for high-ranking diplomats and military officials.

Maren glanced about the room as the maître d' led

them to their table. A long, deep, dark wood bar with comfortable stools and a brass rail ran along one side. The dining tables were small, but chairs had substantial leather seats and deep arms. Photographs of notable patrons lined the walls, mostly politicians and generals, with a few actors and artists sprinkled in.

"Robert Frost!" Maren said.

"How like you to note the poet amid the politicians." Oliver smiled. Maren felt a bubble of pleasure at his having formed this assessment of her. When they sat and opened their menus, Maren gasped aloud.

"Red meat!" Oliver said.

"I don't know when I've ever been so thrilled."

It was not the best meal of her life, coming as she did from a working farm, but recent deprivations made it seem as if it was. The filet was tender and juicy. The crispy skins of the roasted potatoes were flavored with salt and rosemary. The asparagus was served plain and delicious. For dessert they shared a root beer float, a quirky Occidental tradition.

As they rode back to Walter Reed, Oliver sat close to her in the cab, holding her hand loosely in his as they watched the blur of nighttime sights out the window. On several corners they saw older uniformed auxiliary policemen, recruited to take the place of the younger men who had been called to war. Oliver pointed out the outlines of 40 mm antiaircraft guns, visible in the moonlight on some rooftops.

The cab left them at the hospital's Sixteenth Street entrance. It was dark now, and it had grown colder. As they followed the path toward Delano Hall, Maren stopped to pull her coat a little tighter.

"Let me do that," Oliver said. He turned her toward him, buttoned the top buttons, and retied the sash, pulling

Maren slightly closer to him as he did so. He popped up her collar and then chafed her hands in his.

"Warm enough?"

She nodded slowly. He leaned in and kissed her, one hand behind her neck. She put her arms around his back and returned the kiss. He pressed her more closely to him and they enjoyed a repeat of the interlude in the rose garden.

When she finally pulled back, he took her arm and led her back to her dorm. A few steps from the circle of light cast by the fixture at the entrance, he kissed her once more.

After they finally said good night, she walked to her room, a smile on her face. As keenly as she had felt her youth during the previous challenging weeks, there was something attractive in how *in charge* Oliver seemed all the time.

CHAPTER FIVE

Maren sprang out of bed the next morning, grabbed a book, and headed downstairs, hoping to find a comfortable place to read and relax. Brian O'Neill's death had pulled her down to a level unusual for her, but it was the natural inclination of her mood to rebound. The evening with Oliver had given her a new charge. He was working today, but he'd promised to get in touch soon. She had finally begun to feel more certain.

As she approached the reading room, she heard Caroline Sturgeon's piercing voice.

"Oh, good Lord, will you listen to this?" Caroline said. Maren heard the crinkling of a newspaper.

"'Mrs. Edward Bell hosted the Dutch ambassador, Dr. Alexander Loudon, at her S Street mansion last night. Dr. Oliver Demarest of the Boston Demarests was one of many guests in attendance. An orthopedist at Walter Reed Army Medical Center, Dr. Demarest had a ready audience for his news about advancements in prosthetics to help our wounded soldiers.'"

Mission accomplished, Maren thought. *Party with a purpose!*

"'Dr. Demarest was accompanied by Maren Larsen. Miss Larsen, a representative of the successful Cadet

Nurse Corps program, was quite striking in her trim gray corps uniform.'

"Can you believe that girl?" Caroline added. "What pretensions!"

Maren felt a chill. She knew what Caroline Sturgeon thought of her, but it was unpleasant to have it laid before her so starkly.

Maren heard someone murmur in response to Caroline. Juliet, she presumed.

"Does she imagine she has a chance with Oliver Demarest? She hasn't any idea of his family or their expectations for him," Caroline said in her all-knowing tone. Maren looked around then took a silent step closer to the entrance of the reading room.

"His mother won't allow him to end up with some farm girl, I can tell you. She can enjoy her little dalliance, but it won't last. I saw him at the diner with some brunette last week. She looked much more the thing."

Maren quietly returned to her room. At first, she discounted Caroline's assessment. It didn't square with the Oliver Demarest who had sat in the cab with her, holding her hand with such calm familiarity. Throughout the day, however, doubts crept in. She had proved her naïveté again and again since her arrival. What instincts did she have worth trusting? Maybe the reason Oliver never wanted to talk about his family was because Maren was too unsuitable to ever meet them.

In Ada, Minnesota, Oliver's behavior would have signaled serious interest, but she knew nothing of his world. For all she knew, he could also be dating some "brunette who looked much more the thing." He certainly liked her. He clearly found her attractive. Beyond that, of what could she be sure?

As one day passed, and then another, her confidence ebbed. She was consumed with thoughts of the mysterious brunette, desperate to know who it had been. She could not be someone who worked at the hospital, or else Caroline would have referred to her by name.

She said nothing to Dorothy, so her muddle of emotions built, unvented. One moment she felt rejected and foolish, the next moment annoyed with herself for allowing a man to threaten her normal confidence.

From time to time, she would revisit the idea that Caroline was wrong. Was it not folly to give credence to the words of someone so spiteful? The belief that perhaps she was not so terribly mistaken, that there *was* something special between her and Oliver, would pierce her gloom. Invariably, the doubts returned.

A few days later, Oliver sent a note to Delano asking if he might see her. By this time, Maren was thoroughly exhausted and terrified by the prospect of seeing him again. She had only just begun to master herself, forcing anger to prevail over other, more vulnerable feelings.

He is a snob. He has loads of women in his life. I'm just another plaything.

That would not do for Maren Larsen. She deserved better. Not only did she refuse to respond to his note, but she also asked for shifts on the convalescent wing at the Forest Glen annex, a few miles away. She would never see Oliver there.

"Maren, *what* is going on with Oliver? Why are you avoiding him?" Dorothy asked one night, a week after the Bells' party. Maren had visited the library and was now ensconced in a Victorian novel, as anesthetic to her as vodka to a drinker.

"I don't know. It just didn't work out," Maren replied,

barely looking up. Dorothy looked sad, and a little skeptical, but she let it be.

The days went by. Oliver left another message.

Dear Maren,
I wonder if you hadn't received my earlier note? And if you had, whether there was something wrong. Either way, I would be grateful to hear from you.
All my best,
Oliver

Again, Maren did not reply. She knew it was impolite. She owed Oliver an explanation, but she had no idea what to say. Honesty would mean even more vulnerability, and she already felt as if her skin had been turned inside out. When no further messages came, she considered it confirmation of her suspicions. If he was so taken with her, would he not try harder?

She almost began to enjoy her self-imposed solitude. Maren was a social creature, but she had the ability to lose herself in books and work. She added a fresh-air element to her exile. Raised with the Norwegian attitude that there was no bad weather, just bad clothing, she bundled up whenever possible and took long walks in Rock Creek Park. Occasionally, when she remembered the picnic she had enjoyed there with Oliver, she forced her mind in other directions. The painful moments grew fewer and farther between.

On the Friday evening before Thanksgiving, Maren was reading in their room when Dorothy entered the suite, eyes red-rimmed, her face the picture of despair. Maren sat up in alarm.

"Dorothy, what is wrong?"

"It's terrible." She sank into the love seat next to Maren and buried her face in her hands. "It's Oliver's brother, Daniel. He was killed in France. The family just learned the news."

"Where is he?" Maren leapt up. "Where is Oliver?"

"He's at the Moores', friends of the family. They live in Georgetown. Oliver stays there sometimes. Maren, could you go to him? He would want you to."

Dorothy's expression was eager, almost pleading, but Maren needed no convincing. Whatever Oliver thought of her, even if he had the brunette with him, Maren knew she must offer her consolation in person. Dorothy gave her the address, and she grabbed her coat.

"I'm sorry for your loss, too, Doro." She hugged Dorothy tightly before racing out the door.

She ignored the bitter wind as she ran to the streetcar stop. After she sat down in the rattling car and took a breath, she felt an instant of hesitation, but immediately brushed it aside. Her mother's words echoed in her mind. *You can't go wrong if you do the right thing.* When someone died, you went to the family. It didn't matter who was there with Oliver. Even if she turned around and left right after, she needed to address him in person.

She got off at P Street, briskly walked two blocks to the narrow house, compelled herself up the staircase, and rang the bell.

To her surprise, Oliver answered. She breathed in sharply at the sight of him. He wore dark trousers and a white button-down shirt, half tucked. He held a drink. His face was pale, the soulful eyes and beautiful angles shadowed with misery.

"Maren," he said. His wooden expression changed

slightly, and she detected a hint of relief in his voice, as if instead of saying "Maren" he might as easily have said "finally."

"Oh, Oliver. Dorothy just told me the news, and I am so sorry." To her own surprise (and, she imagined, Oliver's) Maren burst into tears, right there on the front stoop of the elegant little townhome. She kept her arms by her sides, uncertain whether she should enter, or what precisely she should do besides say what she'd come to say.

Oliver stepped from the doorway, reached for her arm, and led her into the house.

"Maren," he repeated, his voice rough. He shut the door behind her, then wrapped her in a crushing embrace. He released her and she glanced around the foyer. It was dark, and she could hear nothing inside. A flickering light from a room off the hall hinted at a fire.

"I don't want to interrupt, Oliver. I just wanted to come, to tell you . . ." She faltered.

"There is nothing to interrupt," he said, looking at her with his intense gaze. "I'm alone."

Though she did her best not to show it, Maren was dumbstruck. This would be unthinkable at home. How could people allow him to be by himself at such a time?

"This house belongs to family friends, but they're in Florida," Oliver said, reading her thoughts, as always. "I stay here from time to time. Mrs. Bell came by earlier with her daughter, but I told them I had to leave early in the morning."

"Oh, well . . . I just wanted to tell you . . ." Maren stepped back and eyed the door, thinking perhaps she too should take her leave.

"No, Maren. Please." He reached for her again. "You must stay. Will you?"

She nodded. It was clear Oliver was not on his first

drink, though he seemed to be in reasonable possession of his faculties. He gestured toward the living room off the hall. She headed, a little uncertainly now, in that direction, Oliver with his hand, as ever, on the small of her back. He took her coat and hung it in the hall closet.

The fire blazed in a generous fireplace, framed by an elegant white mantel. Large windows looked down on the street. Despite its grand proportions and accents, the room was cozy. They sank into the toile sofa.

"When did you hear?" Maren asked.

"This morning. We don't have details, except that it happened in the Battle of Metz in Lorraine." Oliver leaned his head back on the sofa and looked up at the ceiling. Maren looked up, too, taking in the decorative plasterwork, angels and curlicues. Despite what they saw day in and day out, they were still so far from the war. "The hideous thing is, the Allies are taking Metz. He'll probably be one of the last men we lose there."

Maren squeezed his hand.

"Do you know what, Maren?" Oliver closed his eyes.

"What?"

"Somehow, I don't know how, I always knew he wouldn't survive."

"Oliver . . ." she said, unable to mask the heartbreak in her voice.

"Would you stay here with me a while?"

She nodded. He pulled her closer and kissed the top of her head. Even amid her sorrow for him, she felt a hint of pleasure at his need for her. They sat quietly, staring at the fire.

"I'm going to get another drink," he said after an interval. "Can I make you one? Perhaps some wine?"

"Wine would be nice." Maren virtually never drank, but the occasion seemed to call for it. She wanted to make

Oliver comfortable, and she couldn't imagine it was comfortable to drink alone.

He returned with a glass of white wine and another drink for himself, something strong-smelling in a highball glass. He resumed his place next to her, his arm around her back. Maren sipped at the wine, enjoying how it warmed her. She'd not eaten, but her vague concern that she probably should not drink seemed a small matter next to what Oliver was going through.

Under tacit agreement that he deserved pleasant conversation, they talked of inconsequential things. He managed a laugh as he told her about the family that owned the house. Despite an overly indulgent mother who turned a blind eye to their unruliness, the Moore children had grown into respectable adults. Maren detected admiration, perhaps even envy, as he spoke of them.

The conversation wandered into a good-natured debate about poetry, with Maren making the case for the romantic Victorians and Oliver for the spare imagery of Wallace Stevens and the modernists.

"I'll show you," he said, getting up. A little unsteady on his feet, he entered a darkened adjacent room, a library evidently, and turned on a light. Maren heard him shuffling before the light went out again, and he emerged with a volume of poems.

"See here, Maren," he said in a mock professorial tone. He sat, opened the book, found his line, and began to read. *I placed a jar in Tennessee. And round it was, upon a hill . . .*

"See how economical he is with words?" Oliver said, when he'd finished. "How much he tells with how little?"

"Now why would you ever do that, when you can crush so many great words into a poem?" Maren teased. Oliver smiled and pulled her closer.

He was not precisely himself. More than once he withdrew into long silence, but despite the unspeakable circumstances, the evening wore on in its easy way. Maren continued to enjoy her wine. *Perhaps it is a* good *wine,* she thought, though she had little basis for judging. She finished two glasses.

At some point, Oliver found crackers and nuts, which they treated as a small meal.

"Would you tell me more about Daniel?" she asked finally. He did, though with his usual brevity and spare biographical details. He had gone to Harvard (all Demarests went to Harvard). He was a good athlete, had played rugby. Maren had learned more about Daniel from Dorothy.

As the fire died down, Oliver turned to look at her.

"I don't know where you have been these past weeks, Maren," he said. She cast her eyes down. She could not possibly explain her petty concerns at this moment. "It's all right. I don't think I want you to tell me."

She looked up at him again. He wanted to kiss her and was seeking her permission. He must have found it in her expression, because he leaned over and pressed his lips to hers.

It was partly the wine, but only partly. Maren felt like she was cracking through a shell she'd erected around herself in the previous weeks, and his attentions, even on this miserable occasion, reacquainted her with some lost joy. She still was not sure of him, but she wanted him. He paused after a moment, took their drinks and placed them on a side table, then gently pulled her down so she was lying alongside him on the sofa.

"Maren," he said as he kissed her neck, her chin, her mouth, with increasing passion. She returned the kiss eagerly.

After a few moments, he pulled back, took a deep breath, and put his hand over his eyes.

"I'm sorry. This is wrong of me, and at such a time." He opened his eyes again and looked at her. "You are hard to resist, and I've missed you," he said simply.

Maren looked into his great brown eyes, which had always hinted to her of the brilliance and roiling thoughts behind them. She felt disappointed.

"But now I am afraid we have a challenge," he said, looking at his watch. "It is awfully late to get you back to Delano. I hope you don't mind my asking, but there are plenty of rooms upstairs. Would you consider staying here? We can get a message to Dorothy."

"I'll stay, Oliver," she replied quietly. "Dorothy knows I've come, so we needn't worry there."

Dorothy did know where she was, of course, and she wasn't on the schedule for the following day. It felt daring, a little bit wrong, but when he extended his hand, she took it and let him lead her up the staircase off the front hall. When they reached the landing, Oliver led her to a bedroom that looked out on the small yard at the back of the house. The four-poster bed had a canary yellow canopy and matching area rug. A row of Madame Alexander dolls lined a shelf on the wall.

"You can sleep in here. Let me grab you something to wear." He disappeared for a few moments and returned with a nightshirt, obviously his.

"Highly improper nightwear," he said. "But surely more comfortable than your clothes. I'll come back in a bit and tuck you in."

So, he really is going to sleep in another room, she thought with some relief, not sure what she might have done had he thrown temptation in her path. She changed and climbed into the bed. Between the girlish room, the oversized nightshirt, and the fact that Oliver planned to "tuck her in," she felt very young again, a little foolish. But the feeling dissolved when he came back to the room in his pajamas and a navy flannel robe, looking vulnerable and sad.

He sat down on the edge of the bed, and she moved over to make room for him. He took her hand in his, pondering it for a moment, looking first at its back then turning it over and tracing a finger along her palm. His mind seemed elsewhere, but the distracted gesture nearly took her breath away.

He looked her in the eyes for a long moment, then leaned over and kissed her lightly on the lips.

"I am not going to start this business again, I promise," he said, pulling back, as if she had been the one to put a stop to it before. "But can I lie here with you for a bit?"

She nodded and made more room. It was a chaste arrangement—Oliver, still in his robe, on top of the covers, and Maren beneath them. He put his arm around her, and gently pulled her toward him so her head rested on his chest. She could hear his heartbeat through the flannel and detected the faint smell of alcohol on his breath.

"Thank you, Maren. For coming here tonight," he said, his voice lazy. In moments he was asleep. Maren listened to his even breathing. She still felt uncertain, no idea of anything beyond this evening, but she was glad she had been with him on this terrible night, glad he had needed her. For now, that was enough.

In the middle of the night, Oliver woke with a start and Maren woke with him. He sat up and looked around the room. She watched his expression change from confusion to sadness, seeming to freshly recall why he was there, what had happened.

When he turned to her, his face softened, as if he had just become aware of her presence. He lay down again and pulled her toward him.

"Maren. Maren, you're here." His voice was sleepy. He pulled her closer still. Before dropping off, he murmured, quietly but unmistakably, "I love you."

She was stunned, not certain whether he was even truly awake. Within seconds, he was snoring gently.

It took her much longer to fall asleep.

The gray dawn light peered through the blinds and cast striped shadows on the bed. Oliver was not there, but his words rang in her ears. She rubbed her eyes.

In a few moments he entered the room, fully dressed, and sat down on the bed next to her. Something in his appearance and demeanor sent a cold chill up her spine.

"Hi," she said tentatively.

"Hi, Maren." He looked drawn and tired. "I'm afraid I didn't behave well last night."

"What do you mean?"

"I think I was a little bosky, as my father might say."

Maren's uneasiness increased. Was he referring to his words in the middle of the night? Perhaps he didn't remember. There was something formal, almost nervous in his tone. He was so hard to read on the best of days, and this was certainly not one of those.

"I wish I didn't have to leave," he said. "God knows, how I wish that." He looked away.

"I understand. I'll get up now, Oliver."

"They have someone who cleans, Maren, so don't bother with the room," he said as he left her. Maren dressed, then hurriedly stripped the bed and pulled the coverlet neatly into place, too much her mother's daughter to leave it otherwise. She found Oliver in the hallway downstairs, holding her coat. She took it and gave him his pajamas in exchange. He tossed them on top of his suitcase at the foot of the stairs.

"I will be thinking of you, Oliver. I am so sorry," she said, taking his hands and looking up at him.

"Thank you for everything, Maren," he said in a formal tone. He leaned down to give her a kiss on the cheek. "I feel terrible I haven't a car to take you back to the hospital."

Maren brushed aside his concern and moved toward the door. Oliver opened it for her, and she walked out into a gloomy morning, the air damp and cool, the sky the color of slate, almost indistinguishable from the pavement. There was no one about.

She started down the street, miserable for Oliver and his loss, for all the horrid losses that just kept coming and coming, and miserable on her own behalf, though she felt selfish for it. That moment in the middle of the night had raised her hopes of him back to their formerly stratospheric level, and the chilly good-bye had sent them plummeting back to earth. She wanted only to get back to her warm room, to put her nose in a book and forget.

She was several blocks away before she heard a voice and turned to find Oliver jogging toward her with his graceful gait. She assumed she had forgotten something back at the house and looked instinctively at her arm to see that her handbag was, indeed, hanging from it.

"Maren . . ." he said as he caught up with her. "Maren, I can't say good-bye to you like this."

She looked at him curiously.

"There is something I have to say."

Maren dreaded the words that might be coming. Perhaps he wanted to explain his coldness, or the brunette. She cast her eyes down, not sure she could bear it.

"I have no right to do this. This might be the most self-ish thing I've ever done, and I am sure I am putting you in the worst possible position. You deserve so much better, but I can't wait another moment."

Maren looked up again. Whatever was coming did not sound like what she had feared.

"Maren, will you marry me?"

She looked at him, stunned, her mind turning over all the possible explanations, other than the one she hoped for but refused to believe. Did he think she had been *compromised* in some way by spending the night? She wouldn't have thought his sensibilities were so old-fashioned, but once again, what did she know?

"Won't you please tell me you will think about it, at least?" He sounded earnest, but Caroline's words came back to her.

"But Oliver, you can't. Your family . . ." She closed her eyes against the pain of the conversation she thought they must have. When he didn't respond, she opened them again and peered up at him.

He looked confused, but then an awareness appeared to dawn in his eyes. He took a step closer, so he was right before her. He lifted her chin with his finger, forcing her to look him in the eye.

"What about my family?" Oliver enunciated each word, a new firmness in his tone. She hesitated a moment. How could she put this?

"I just . . . I heard Caroline Sturgeon say something. It sounded like they had, that your mother has, well, other *expectations* for you. And Caroline had seen you with someone else. . . ." Her voice trailed off.

He paused, his expression incredulous. "Let me see if I have this right. You've been avoiding me all these weeks because Caroline Sturgeon, of all people, said *you* weren't good enough for my family? For my *mother*?"

"I suppose." Her voice was tentative. She didn't understand the wry, almost angry look on his face.

"Maren," Oliver said, his voice filled with conviction. "Let me assure you in the strongest possible terms that Caroline Sturgeon, in addition to evidently being a wretched person, is completely wrong."

He put his hands over his face and sighed. Finally, with what seemed like supreme effort, he looked up. His eyes still looked tired, but his expression was tender.

"Maren, I am blundering terribly, I'm sure. I am dreadful at this. I wish I had the right words, but you must hear me. You must know. I have loved you from the first moment I saw you."

She shook her head, still unwilling to believe.

"Yes, Maren, that moment is imprinted on my mind like no other in my life. You were treating that soldier, the one injured at Ardennes."

Oliver must have seen her soften, because his words came more forcefully.

"I had no reason to look over that soldier's chart. I approached his bed just to speak to you. When we sat together in the arbor that night after the pictures, I wondered how it was possible that someone so beautiful could also be so kind and clever and funny. You were like a miracle, and I've thought it more every time I have seen you. The last weeks have been an agony. Please, you must believe me." He looked almost anxious now. "You are the *only* beautiful thing now, the *only* beautiful thing."

A tear fell down her cheek.

"Please, Maren? Please, will you at least consider it?"

In that moment, Maren realized her heart had been whispering to her for some time, though in her doubt and uncertainty, she had not dared listen. She heard it now, though, clear as a bell. *This is what you hoped for,* her heart told her. *This is what you want.*

She smiled and stepped forward to close the gap between them, pressing her now damp face against his chest.

"Yes, Oliver. I will marry you."

CHAPTER SIX

August 1994
Haven Point

SKYE

Skye spent the flight to Portland alternating between moodily staring out the plane window and complaining to Gran about all she was missing out on.

She secretly hoped Gran would lecture her about keeping her mom's drinking a secret, because she had planned some really great comebacks. (Her favorite was "Every time my mom messes up, I'm the one who gets punished!" She'd felt a rush of furious satisfaction when she came up with that one.)

Gran didn't scold her, though. In fact, she agreed with all Skye's complaints, and sometimes even kicked them up a notch. If Skye said something was unfair, Gran would say it was *so* unfair.

It was late when they finally reached Haven Point, so Skye went straight to bed. Early the next morning, she was awakened by the sound of an engine. She opened one eye and looked out the window to see a lobster boat idling just offshore. For a few minutes, she watched the lobstermen in their orange oilskin jumpsuits as they pulled in their traps, and felt a tickle of pleasure at the cool air. When the lobster boat motored off, Skye tucked herself further under the covers and fell back asleep.

When she woke up later, it was raining, which reminded her she was supposed to be crabby. Skye grumbled about the weather at breakfast, but once again, Gran just sympathized. Skye finally gave up. Trying to get a rise out of Gran was not worth the effort.

The truth was, she was glad it was raining, because it gave her a chance to get reacquainted with the old house.

Skye's neighborhood in D.C. was filled with little colonial-style houses—nice, but predictable. If you looked at the front, you pretty much knew what the rest of the house would look like. Fourwinds looked like some giant kid had made it with building blocks. The roof was different-size triangles facing every direction, and the windows were all different shapes—squares, rectangles, and even a big half circle over the front door.

The house sat on a piece of land that jutted out from the peninsula, so three sides looked out on the water. (Fourwinds was a good name for it, since the breezes blew from every direction.) It stood right up on the cliff, as if on a dare. Upstairs, unless you pressed yourself against the window, you could see nothing but water beyond. It was like being on a cruise ship.

Skye wandered around the long living room, with its wall of windows and stone fireplaces at the ends. The middle of the room was the dining area, with a big table in front of a bay window. Shelves along the beadboard walls were crowded with books and mementos, but it didn't feel cluttered like her house in D.C.

The bedrooms on the second floor were loosely decorated by color. Skye's was the "blue room," with a blue gingham curtain, old blue dresser, and blue coverlets on the twin beds. At the south end of the hall were the master bedroom, which was mostly yellow, and the smaller "green room," which had a little shallow porch off of it, with screens on the casement windows, and a twin-sized daybed with a quilt and throw pillows. The memory of hours spent reading here when she was younger sent Skye up to the third floor in search of a book.

She poked around the attic rooms. Servants had once slept up there, when they'd needed lots of them to keep up the house. Now it was mostly for stuff that was not good enough to be downstairs, but not bad enough to be thrown out: old children's books, suitcases, games and toys.

Skye found a shelf with a bunch of teenage novels from the 1940s and 1950s. The girls on the covers had high ponytails, or shoulder-length hair curled up at the ends. She grabbed a few and headed down to the green room's porch.

When Gran called her for lunch a couple of hours later, Skye reluctantly put the book aside. As she headed for the kitchen, it occurred to her that this was the first time that summer she had allowed herself to get lost in a story.

Skye would never have admitted it to Gran, but she realized now how exhausting it had been—first worrying that her mother would relapse, then keeping it a secret when she did. She was always on edge, always trying to pretend nothing was wrong. Now it felt like something inside her had uncoiled. She was not altogether hopeful that rehab would be a permanent fix, but at least her mom was someone else's problem for the moment.

It rained for three days. Other than a trip into Phippsburg with Gran, Skye spent most of the time cocooned on the little porch of the green room, reading about girls with names like Tippy and Tobey, all of whom had two parents, siblings, and uncomplicated, easy-to-solve problems.

Ironically, it was when the sun came out that things

took a turn. On Sunday, they were invited to go sailing with Gran's friends Georgie and Cappy and a couple of their grandkids.

When Skye stepped onto the yacht club lawn, she was hit by a sudden, unexpected wave of grief for her grandfather. Skye had loved her grandfather, and she'd been sad when he died, but Pop had not been that involved in her day-to-day life. Gran was the one who knew when Skye got out of track and hockey practice, what size shoes she wore, and that when the Good Humor man came, she'd want a toasted almond and not a Sno-Cone.

Skye thought she was done being sad about Pop dying, but when she looked out at the water, she was flooded with memories of sailing on his beautiful boat. They used to go out, just the two of them, and have a picnic on Gunnison Island. He'd ask her lots of questions and was always interested in her answers. He'd called her Skye Bird, which always made her feel good, because she knew how much he loved birds.

When they climbed onto Cappy's sailboat, Skye sat in the bow, hoping if anyone saw the tears in her eyes they would think it was from the spray. It wasn't until they were past Gunnison Island that Skye had pulled herself together enough to look around.

As they made their way to the east side of the point, Skye noticed a smaller cove, nestled on the other side of the rocks at the end of Haven Point Beach. A bunch of kids were playing on the sand and in the water. She could hear their voices, and strains of music. A lawn led from the beach up a hill to a huge white house, with a few smaller buildings around it. It almost looked like a resort.

"What's that?" Skye asked Gran.

"That's the Donnellys' house. You met Mr. Donnelly at the hardware store in Phippsburg."

Skye remembered him: a big man, loud and charming.

"Maren Demarest, I can't believe you're old enough to have a grandchild of this age!" he had said when Gran introduced her. Skye got the feeling he was flirting with Gran. (Gran was polite but definitely didn't flirt back.)

Georgie's granddaughter Nora, who was a few years older than Skye, spoke up from her seat in the stern.

"Guess what! I heard Posy Harwood is dating Kevin Donnelly. They're, like, super serious. Posy's cousin told me she thinks they'll get married!"

"Oh Lordy, that'll get the tongues wagging," Georgie said, shaking her head.

"Why?" Skye asked.

"The Donnelly kids hang out with Haven Point kids, but a marriage? That would break new ground." Georgie smiled, as if she didn't care one way or another, but when they returned to the yacht club a half hour later, Skye was still turning those three words over in her head: *Haven Point kids.*

While Cappy was tying his boat to the mooring, Skye heard shouts of laughter and turned to see a group of kids on the dock that held the prams, the single-person dinghies they used to teach beginner sailors.

Those are Haven Point kids, Skye thought. The Donnellys were not Haven Point kids. And, Skye remembered, neither was she.

When Skye was little and visited Haven Point, Gran and Pop had filled her days with blueberry picking, exploring the tidal pools, and trips to Freeport to buy clothes for school. Sometimes Gran's friends brought their grandkids to play, and once, her uncle Billy came with his wife and two daughters. Uncle Billy was in the foreign service. They had just left a posting in Japan and were about to move to Egypt.

Her cousins, Maren (named after Gran) and Victoria, were older, but they doted on Skye, and she was so blissed out being with them, she didn't have eyes for anyone else on Haven Point.

As Skye got older, kids still came over, but at some point they'd have to leave because they "had sailing" or "had golf." They weren't "going sailing" or "going to play golf." These were things they did with other kids, at a specific time.

And while Skye would come for a week or two, the Haven Point kids were there all summer long, just like their parents had been. They talked about the same people and shared the same inside jokes. Skye felt a little like a foreign exchange student. The kids were nice enough, but they didn't really expect her to speak their language.

This was why Skye had felt so ambivalent after her recent visits to Maine. She had realized there was a whole other world on Haven Point, one to which she didn't belong.

She got another taste of it that night when Gran took her to the weekly sing-along at the yacht club. They picked up songbooks and found seats, and at first everything was fine. Gran loved the sing-along, and Skye had always liked going with her. She got a kick out of how seriously everyone took it, like when the song leader pulled the rope of a ship's bell on the wall and everyone immediately turned toward him and quieted down.

"That's Julian Stevens," Gran whispered to her. "His

grandfather was the one who started the sing-along during the blackouts back in World War Two."

"Good evening, ladies and gentlemen. Welcome to the Haven Point Sing-Along. Before we get started, some announcements. Children, this one is for you." He looked over his glasses like a schoolteacher. "I have been asked to comment on a new fashion on Haven Point: bicycle helmets with chin straps hanging down."

Some parents in the audience clapped.

"If you fall off your bike with helmet unbuckled, what will happen?" He looked around. Some younger kids raised their hands.

"Annabelle?" He pointed to a little girl in the front row.

"It's gonna fall off your head," Annabelle replied.

The girl had a really loud voice for a tiny person, which Skye thought was funny. She reminded her of Adriene's little sister, Sophia.

"That, Annabelle, is exactly right. Seventeen and under, you ride with a helmet . . . buckled! Remember, freedom with safety!"

Skye looked around as the audience clapped, and that's when it hit her. Other than Skye, only little kids sat in the folding chairs with the adults. All the kids her age sat together on the benches along the walls, or out on the south porch behind the piano player.

Skye tried to push it from her mind as they sang "Loch Lomond," "On Top of Old Smokey," and a few others.

Then Julian pulled out an envelope. Before he could speak, everyone started whooping.

"All right, all right, quiet down now," he said, smiling. "It's time to announce the winning team this week."

He opened the envelope like he was announcing an Academy Award.

"And, it's . . . the Blue Team!" All the Blue Team kids cheered, then got up to sing their team song.

> *Blue Team has got the spirit*
> *We'll raise the roof on this old joint*
> *The world is gonna sing our praises*
> *The best team on Haven Point*

It wasn't just the kids. Even the grown-ups on the Blue Team sang along. A few parents held babies in the air, like Rafiki with Simba in *The Lion King*.

When Skye was younger, she was glad when the Green Team won the week. She had never done anything to help them win, but Gran had told her that Demarests were on the Green Team, and that had been good enough for her. This time she was glad Blue won. She would have felt like an imposter joining in.

After the sing-along, Skye went back to being angry. Most of the time, she stayed inside and read. When she did leave Fourwinds, all she saw was packs of kids together, riding their bikes to tennis or sailing, or gathered on the beach (where Skye sat under an umbrella, wearing sunglasses and a baseball cap, protecting herself from both the sun and from people noticing she was alone).

One night, while she and Gran were eating dinner, the phone rang. Gran went to the hall to answer it.

"Hang on, Bill. She's here. I'll ask her," she heard Gran say. A second later, Gran's face appeared in the doorway.

"Skye, I have Bill Jackson on the phone. He has a daughter your age who was supposed to run a leg of the baton relay on Saturday, but she sprained her ankle. Georgie told him you were a runner. He's wondering if you could take his daughter's place."

"Um, sure, I guess so," Skye said. She tried to sound

casual, but her spirits rose a little. The baton relay was a big deal, the final Blue-Green event of the season.

She knew she wouldn't have been asked if Gran's best friend hadn't mentioned her, and it would hardly make her a Haven Point kid. Still, if she did something for this team, even once, she might feel like a little of this place belonged to her.

On Saturday, Skye and Gran headed to the beach club, where her leg of the relay would begin. Skye, curious who she would be running against, scanned the crowd for a blue pinny. She finally spotted it among a cluster of girls about her age. The girl wearing it had a lean, athletic build and obedient brown hair, pulled back in a glossy ponytail. She looked familiar, but it was not until she laughed and rolled her eyes at something one of the other girls said that Skye realized who it was.

Oh my God, Skye thought. *I'm running against Charlotte Spencer!*

Skye *hated* Charlotte Spencer.

Once, when Skye was younger, she made the fatal error of going to the kids' tennis clinic. She only went because she loved the tennis skirt Gran had bought her. It was white with pleats and had a band of navy grosgrain ribbon around the hem.

Skye felt like an outcast before the clinic even started. Gran had brought her to the courts early to introduce her to the tennis pro, so she saw the other girls arrive together on bikes (all carrying their racquets Haven Point–style, threaded head-up on their handlebars).

While they were standing around waiting for instructions from the pro, Charlotte had turned and looked Skye up and down.

"Your skirt looks so *new,*" she said.

The moment Charlotte said it, Skye realized her skirt

was all wrong. Everyone else wore faded tennis clothes and old sneakers. Next to them, she felt like the bit of titanium white her mom used to make some detail stand out in a painting.

When she got back to Fourwinds, she had shoved the skirt in the back of a drawer. She never went back to the clinic.

"Your skirt looks so new" were the only five words Skye could remember Charlotte ever saying to her, and she added no new ones to the count now. Even when they were given instructions about where to stand to wait for the batons, Charlotte acted like Skye was invisible. Skye ignored her right back.

Gran had explained that the race was sort of a figure eight: up the beach, out one of the gravel lanes to the main road, back south over the causeway, then in a loose circle around the point.

The youngest pair of girls ran the first leg and then handed off the baton to the youngest boys. The relay alternated between pairs of girls and boys, with each leg getting longer as the runners got older.

People gathered at spots all along the route. Some kids rode bikes alongside the runners, and others acted as messengers, racing ahead to report on who was in the lead.

From their spot outside the beach club entrance, Skye could see the start of the race down on the beach. Even when runners were out of sight, cheers echoed around the cove.

The guys handing off the batons to Skye and Charlotte would be coming from the causeway. When Skye heard the cheering from that direction, she felt a surge of anxiety as she waited to see whether the blue or green runner was ahead.

The blue pinny appeared first. The Green Team supporters gathered at the beach club groaned, but Skye felt relieved. She didn't want to be the one to lose the lead for the team.

The blue runner handed the baton to Charlotte, and she took off. It was at least ten seconds before the green runner reached Skye.

The first part of their leg was uphill, along the east side of Haven Point Road. Halfway up the hill, they were to turn into the Haven Point Sanctuary, a nature preserve in the middle of the point. They would run through the sanctuary and emerge on the other side, just north of the yacht club.

As they ran up the hill, Skye did not feel like she was gaining on Charlotte, but she wasn't falling behind, at least.

The path through the sanctuary was too narrow for spectators, but a group had gathered outside the entrance. Skye could hear "Go Blue!" and "Go Charlotte!" when Charlotte entered. (She noticed they just said "Go Green!" for her.)

Skye and Charlotte's route took them along the little boardwalk path that cut the twenty-acre preserve in half at the longest point. Once Skye entered the sanctuary, she felt like she was in another world. The towering trees blocked out the white noise of the waves crashing into the cliff and voices echoing around the cove.

The path was not perfectly straight, so from time to time, Charlotte disappeared from view. At one point when she reappeared, Skye thought she looked larger. After the next bend in the path, she was sure of it.

I'm gaining on her!

When she was within twenty feet or so, Charlotte sped up, but Skye kept pace. As she got closer, Skye trained her eyes on Charlotte's twitching ponytail. Charlotte Spencer might be Haven Point perfection, but Skye was faster. She knew she was.

She pulled up the mental image of Charlotte acting so snotty at the tennis clinic all those years before, and used it to fuel a burst of speed. Charlotte was not about to give way on the narrow boardwalk, so Skye waited. When they reached a part of the path with enough clearing on the side, she jumped off, sped ahead, and jumped back on.

See ya! The sound of Charlotte's feet behind her grew fainter as Skye increased her lead. Just as she was really beginning to enjoy herself, she heard an "Oh!" followed by the sound of stumbling. She looked back and saw Charlotte on all fours.

It felt like one of those "angel on one shoulder, devil on the other" situations. In the end, Skye turned and ran back to Charlotte, though not because she listened to the angel. She was just worried what people would think if Charlotte broke her ankle or something, and she hadn't stopped to help her.

"Here," Skye said, sticking out her hand.

"I can get up," Charlotte snarled.

"Okay!"

Well, that's nine words she's said to me now, Skye thought as she turned on her heels and took off again. The sound of Charlotte up and running again came soon after, but by this point Skye heard voices and knew she was near the other side of the sanctuary. It seemed they could hear her, too.

Someone's almost out! Who is it?

She heard other voices yelling at the next runners.

Get ready! get ready!

When she emerged around the last turn on the path, she saw light through the trees that formed an arch at the entrance, and faces lining either side. Soon she could see the next two runners, about ten yards past where she would come out.

It's green! . . . She's ours!

Skye had been told to pass the baton to a guy named Ben Barrows. As she got closer, she realized she recognized him, too. She'd seen him on the beach, playing football with some friends. He was on that border between cute and goofy—tall and kind of skinny, with a mess of wavy brown hair and a little acne.

"Here, here! Give it here!" he said encouragingly, a big grin on his face.

After she passed Ben the baton and he took off, Skye was surrounded by people patting her on the back and congratulating her. Even Charlotte's buddies, Cricket Belmont and Darby Palmer, were excited. *We heard Green was behind! You must have been so fast! That was awesome!*

Charlotte took longer to come out than Skye expected. When she did, she was half jogging, half limping.

Faker, Skye thought.

Up until the last bend in the path, she had been able to hear Charlotte running behind her. Skye figured she was using her skinned knee as an excuse for falling behind.

As it turned out she had bigger plans.

The Green Team won the relay. There was a party at the country club that night, a kind of end-of-season thing. When Skye arrived, she got more congratulations from friends of Gran's, and when she was at the table getting cheese and crackers, Ben Barrows walked up and gave her a high five.

"Good run! You clinched it!" he said.

Skye was having a decent time until Charlotte showed up with a massive bandage on her knee.

A little Band-Aid would have done the trick, Skye thought.

When a group of girls surrounded Charlotte, it dawned on Skye that she was probably going to pay a price for her victory. It seemed she had beaten the Gretchen Hathaway of Haven Point. A few minutes later, Nora Ormsby confirmed her suspicion.

"Way to go today," Nora said.

"Thanks," Skye said.

"Get this," Nora said, laughing. "Charlotte's telling people you tripped her."

Skye looked at Nora, appalled. "I didn't trip her. I tried to help her up. And I heard her running just fine after that!"

"Duh, of course you didn't trip her. No one believes her. She's just mad because we won!" Nora said, high-fiving her.

When Skye glanced toward the corner of the room and saw Charlotte sitting at a table, "injured" leg resting on a chair, she knew Nora was wrong. Skye couldn't hear what was being said, but Charlotte gave her more than one dirty look, so she could guess. Even Cricket and Darby glanced at Skye a couple of times with *oh my God how awful* expressions on their faces.

Skye knew running the relay would not make her instantly popular on Haven Point, but she thought she'd at least found the portal to the parallel universe there. Now the portal door had slammed shut, and she wondered if it had been better when she was invisible.

She suddenly felt desperate to leave the party, so she hunted down Gran and Georgie. Fortunately, they were also ready to go.

They reached the door just as another woman was entering. She was about Gran and Georgie's age, but skinny and stiff, with pursed lips and short curled hair that looked normal until you realized the curls didn't move at all.

"Maren, Georgie." The woman nodded.

"Hello, Harriet," Gran said coolly, while Georgie just nodded.

The woman stopped and looked down at Skye. "Harriet, you remember my granddaughter, Skye Demarest. She passed the baton to your grandson today. Skye, this is Harriet Barrows."

Skye was about to extend her hand, but Harriet kept her arms stiffly by her sides.

"Yes. I remember," Harriet said. Her eyebrows came together in a question. "That red hair. You didn't get that from your mother."

Skye felt a prickle at the back of her neck. She didn't know what this woman was up to, but she was sure it wasn't anything good.

"I assume that came from your father's side?" she continued.

The prickle at her neck turned into a shiver down her spine. Skye could not have replied if she tried, but Georgie saved the day.

"Harriet, you never met Maren's brother. Anders has red hair, just like Skye's."

Harriet's mouth opened halfway then closed, like she wanted to keep interrogating her but couldn't figure out how. She mumbled something like *Mmm . . . I see . . .* then walked off without another word.

"I'm sorry about that, Skye," Gran said as they headed for the causeway.

"Don't people here know how my mom got pregnant?" Skye asked.

"Some, but not her. Not that there's anything to be

ashamed of, because there's not. She's just a bitter old woman, and ridiculously old-fashioned."

"Don't let that old dragon get under your skin, Skye," Georgie added.

"I won't," Skye lied. It was too late. The old dragon had indeed gotten under her skin. Just about everyone on Haven Point had gotten under her skin.

A couple of days later, Gran told Skye her mom was out of rehab. Gran had talked to both Anne and Flora, and she felt comfortable taking Skye back to Washington.

Skye had been dying to leave Haven Point. As soon as Gran told her the news, though, her heart sank as she realized she dreaded going home just as much.

Skye mostly divided her mom into two categories: Drinking Mom or Sober Mom. She had forgotten about the third version: Post-rehab Mom—fragile and so eager to please, it made Skye feel horribly uncomfortable.

The first night Skye was home, her mom tried to make a casserole. An actual dinner at something like an actual dinnertime was weird enough. When it came out of the oven a liquidy mess and Skye saw tears in her mom's eyes, she couldn't bear it.

When they sat down at the table to eat the terrible casserole, it was painful how hard she was trying to be cheerful. Skye didn't care if her mother never tried to make another meal as long as she lived. All she wanted was for her to stop acting so weak.

But then her mom asked the perfect question.

"How was Maine?"

Skye felt a wave of relief. Now she could make things right again. Skye skipped over every part of the trip that had been good and went straight to the story about Charlotte and the baton relay.

As she told it, she watched her mom's face transform. First came a smile at Skye's account of passing Charlotte in the sanctuary, then an eye roll and an *Oh, come on . . . seriously?* when she described Charlotte limping out at the end of the race and her drama-queen act at the party.

When she got to the part about the rumor Charlotte had spread, Skye was surprised to feel tears in her own eyes.

"Even Darby and Cricket were looking at me and whispering. And they're on my team," she said as one of the tears rolled down her cheek.

Skye had not expected to feel so bad when she told the story, but it was worth it. Her mom put her fork down and looked directly at Skye, one hundred percent sure of herself again.

"Skye, that place only has one team that matters. If you're not one of them, you're not on it."

CHAPTER SEVEN

August 1945
Haven Point

MAREN

I t's amazing," Maren said. Everything on the cliff seemed to be standing guard. The gables on the houses looked like shaded eyes, the porches like mouths stretched in grim determination. The spruce and fir trees were the grenadiers. Even the seabirds perched on the granite cliff had a martial appearance, as if unwilling to believe that Nazi U-boats had surrendered at Portsmouth Harbor.

It was Maren's first glimpse of the Atlantic Ocean, of *any* ocean. She felt she could look at it all day.

"I thought you would like it," Oliver said, smiling as he gently urged her toward the house.

Gideon Douglas, the Demarest caretaker who had driven them from the train station in Bath, stood by the car, eager for her reaction.

"So? What do you think?" He was a great Siberian husky of a man, down to the snowy head of hair and crystal blue eyes.

"I've never seen anything like it before."

"Nor will you, except right along this coast. There is nothing like it," Gideon said knowingly, as if he had traveled the world to compare, though he admitted earlier he'd never left the state.

"People must have been nervous here during the fighting. It seems so exposed."

On the map Oliver had showed her, Haven Point looked like a clenched fist, brandished southward into Casco Bay. From where they stood, she could see the islands to the south and west, but nothing to the east except the vast ocean.

"We were. The North Atlantic Fleet was headquartered at Portland Harbor," Gideon said, pointing toward the city to the southwest of them. "Closest big port to Europe. Ships refueled over there at Long Island before heading out. We never knew what might be under that water. Folks still got bored here during the blackouts. They covered the windows of the yacht club and started a singalong on Sundays and bingo on Wednesdays. Anything to keep them from turning the lights on."

Gideon turned to Oliver. "I put your bags inside, Dr. Demarest. I'll be off now. Mrs. Douglas left you some dinner."

After Gideon drove off, Maren followed Oliver through the front door, her nerves jangling. Oliver's father would not arrive until the next day, but she was about to meet his mother for the first time.

Wartime had provided a neat excuse to do what Oliver wanted to do anyway: get married quickly. Travel challenges made it impossible for their parents to be there, so with a handful of friends in attendance they had married just before Christmas in the little stone chapel on the grounds of Walter Reed.

Maren's parents had been kind and understanding when Oliver called to ask their blessing. Though Oliver's father said all the right things to Maren, she had detected little warmth. His mother sounded vague and a little unwell. Oliver assured her they were fine with it. It was too soon after Daniel's death to expect ebullience, and quick weddings and understatement were the way of things now. She was still worried.

Maren followed Oliver through the front door and to the kitchen. As they passed the seemingly endless main room, she took in the great wall of windows overlooking the sea.

"Mother?" he called. "Mother, we're here!"

Silence.

A white handbag sat on the kitchen table, and Oliver touched a yellow cardigan that hung over the back of a chair. He seemed to be reading these as *Mother is home* signals. He called out again as they walked back to the big room, then opened a door that faced the ocean, and she followed him as they traded the quiet inside for the gusty outdoors. They walked around the porch, which spanned three-quarters of the house.

Finding no one, they reentered through the front door. Oliver sat on a sofa in the living room. He looked confused. Maren sat quietly. She knew better than to prod Oliver when he was puzzling something.

After a moment, she thought she heard a sound upstairs. Oliver looked up. He had noticed it, too. It was muffled, hard to make out. Then it came again, this time louder, a thump. Maren watched as Oliver's look of mild confusion was overtaken by a more forbidding expression.

Slowly, but with purpose, Oliver got up and headed for the staircase. He neither told Maren to come with him nor to stay put, so she followed in his wake up the stairs, through a large hallway space at the top, then into a corner bedroom.

Half-opened windows faced east and south. The breeze seemed to blow in every direction. Thin white curtains billowed out, almost perpendicular to the walls. The large bed had a brass frame, ruffled pillow shams, and a heavy quilt folded at the foot. Medicine bottles cluttered the nightstand. A yellow dress draped over a faded upholstered chair in the corner looked small enough for a child.

Oliver seemed unaware of Maren's presence. She had never seen him so tightly coiled, and it gave her a bewildered, disoriented feeling.

His eyes scanned the room and stopped at the closet in the far corner, from which a dim light emanated. He moved in that direction with Maren close behind. The closet was large and deep, almost a room in itself. Inside, a rickety fold-down staircase led to an attic.

They peered up into the opening. Maren could see nothing but an empty rectangle of space lit by one bare bulb. Oliver was fixed to his spot. By the look of his jaw, his teeth were tightly clenched. His tension was contagious. Her heart was beating like a trip hammer.

"Mother?" Oliver said again, more slowly.

A few long seconds of silence followed.

"Mother!" Oliver said more loudly.

There was silence again, then a flash of motion. Maren jumped backward as a thin arm flopped across the opening of the attic. A small hand dangled flaccidly.

Horrified, Maren was ready to run for help, but then she heard Oliver let out a long, slow breath. It suggested resignation, perhaps irritation, but definitely not alarm.

"Please wait here, Maren," Oliver said. He closed his eyes for a moment, as if to summon forbearance, then opened them and climbed the stairs.

"Hello, Mother," Maren heard Oliver say, his tone sardonic. Though Oliver was out of view, she saw the limp arm rise from the opening as he lifted Mrs. Demarest.

He turned as he began his descent, careful to keep the small figure draped over his arms from hitting either side of the opening, then continued down the remaining stairs in an awkward sideways movement. Given his light burden, Maren suspected the flush she saw in his face was from annoyance rather than exertion.

Maren stepped from the closet entrance to let him pass. As he did, his mother looked hazily in her direction and lifted her hand in vague greeting. Maren caught a sticky-sweet whiff of alcohol.

Oliver laid his mother on her bed, carefully, though without tenderness. She was tiny, the skin on her arms and face almost translucent, as if there was nothing between it and the bones beneath. Though her short brown hair was tousled, Maren could see the suggestion of leftover styling. Even in her diminished face, Maren saw Oliver's lashes and cheekbones. She was frail and insubstantial, but pretty.

She mumbled something, perhaps his name. He took the blanket from the end of the bed and unfolded it with a shake more vigorous than necessary, the only outward sign of emotion in an otherwise frighteningly controlled demeanor. He spread the blanket over her, and she fell asleep.

Oliver went back up the attic stairs, returned with two empty liquor bottles, and moved to the staircase without a word. Maren followed him down in much the same way she had followed him up, with him scarcely aware she was there. He moved to the kitchen and threw the bottles in the trash can.

"I'm going to bring the suitcases to our room and go for a sail. Would you like to settle in?" His jaw was still set, his coloring high. He looked around the kitchen, avoiding eye contact.

Maren was stung. She would not have wanted him to feign a smile or extend a half-hearted invitation to join him if she wasn't welcome. She just wished more than anything she was.

"Yes, I'll settle in." She thought for a second before adding, "Will your mother need anything?"

"What she needs is to sleep it off," he said, his tone laced with contempt.

After Maren unpacked, she sat on the window seat in their room. Oliver had said little about his mother, but while Maren had sensed something was amiss, she had never pressed. Daniel had just died, and she assumed Mrs. Demarest was grief-stricken.

Now, however, she recalled the party for the Dutch ambassador, and the strange emphasis she had heard in Mrs. Bell's voice when she had asked about Oliver's mother—that had been before Daniel's death.

As she looked out at the water, she saw a sailboat with what appeared to be one man aboard. It might have been Oliver, but Maren wasn't sure. She couldn't tell from this distance.

She wondered, not for the first time, how well she knew him, even up close.

On the hunt for clues and insights, she decided to give herself a tour of the house.

When they had pulled into the driveway earlier, Maren had been rather daunted by the house, so large that even from fifty feet away, it spilled over the frame of the windshield. The fieldstone foundation and faded gray shingles made it look like it had sprouted organically from the cliff, held fast by a half century of root growth.

Her first impression of the interior, however, was that it was not particularly imposing. It seemed reasonably well maintained, if a little shabby, with bare floorboards and an eccentric mix of furniture and accessories.

After a while, in bits and pieces, Fourwinds began to speak to her. The living room stretched almost the entire length of the first floor, and its windows offered a breathtaking view of the ocean. But she spotted little touches that lent an unlikely coziness to the cavernous space—comfortable furniture arranged in front of the large stone fireplaces at either end, needlepoint pillows, baskets of blankets, and a collection of quirky wood bird feeders. The room had been designed for loafing.

She peered at the spines of books and looked over the trophies, photos, and children's art projects that lined the built-in bookcases. As she waited for Oliver to return, she wished whoever had filled these shelves with memories was there to fill in the gaps.

He walked in a few hours later. She had hoped his mood would be easier, but he was still tense. She kept up an easy banter as they ate Mrs. Douglas's casserole by lamplight in the dining room, but as she cleaned up, she wondered if they should prepare a tray for her mother-in-law.

"Do you expect your mother to wake up this evening?"

"I don't." Oliver sat at the kitchen table with his long fingers tightly interlaced between his knees. He hesitated a moment, looking down.

"My mother has had episodes like this before," he said finally. "I'd hoped we had seen the last of them, but perhaps Daniel's death was a setback. I apologize."

"You have nothing to apologize for, Oliver." Maren used her best matter-of-fact nurse's tone. "I only want to know how and if I can help her."

"I expect we will see her in the morning, and if past is prologue, she will behave as if nothing happened."

"And we . . . ?"

"We do the same."

Alone in the kitchen the following morning, Maren felt a jolt of nerves when she heard soft footsteps on the staircase. While Oliver's mother was obviously not the alarming aristocrat of her imaginings, she wondered if this might be worse. How would she react to Maren having witnessed her in such a horrible condition? Would it make her angry somehow?

Mrs. Demarest entered the room with an expression so vague and innocuous, Maren's fears dissipated. Maren detected a hint of unsteadiness, and the ankles and wrists that peeked out from her pink shirtwaist dress looked like they could snap like twigs. Still, she moved with a certain grace, like a young ballerina.

And she seemed perfectly delighted to meet her daughter-in-law.

"Hello, dear Maren!" she said in a thin, silvery tone. She embraced Maren feebly then held her at arms' length, which was not very far away. "I know we have spoken on the phone, but to see you in person! Oliver said you were pretty, and so you are. Welcome to Haven Point. I am so glad to finally meet you. Will your parents come to Maine someday? I wish you will please call me Pauline. . . ."

She went on in this way. Though her individual utterances would be cogent standing alone, they were thrown together in such a disjointed fashion, Maren felt like she had conversational whiplash. She did her best to answer politely where she could.

"I am so sorry I wasn't able to see you last night," Pauline finally said, her face the picture of innocence. "You must have come in late!"

Maren was dumbfounded. How did Pauline think she had gotten to bed?

"Well, it is a pleasure to finally meet you," Maren managed, just as Oliver entered.

"Hello, Mother," he said as he bent to kiss her formally on the cheek. True to his word, he pretended nothing had happened. His mother, who seemed beyond the ability to pick up small cues, did not seem to notice the distance in his manner.

"Hello, dear. Look at you. You're so thin! Are they working you to the bone? I've been having a nice chat with your beautiful wife." She turned and smiled at Maren.

At least she's nice. Pauline was miles from the formidable character of Caroline Sturgeon's description, the one who supposedly had such high marital aspirations for her son. She was sweet, if a little fuzzy around the edges, and seemed inclined to like anyone Oliver brought around.

Oliver bolted down toast and coffee while they talked, then took Maren's hand and led her to the kitchen door.

"Mother, I'm going to show Maren around the point," Oliver said. "We'll be back later."

"All right, dear," Pauline responded, busying herself straightening items on the counter.

Oliver led Maren outside. She disliked leaving so soon after meeting her mother-in-law, no matter how bad off she'd been the previous afternoon, but she knew better than to protest. Fortunately, Pauline had not seemed offended.

They took a dirt path that ran along the cliff. Short stretches of fence had been erected in front of spots where the cliff was steepest, though they hardly looked strong enough to prevent calamity. Scraggy bayberry and sea rose bushes grew in abundance, their ambition to obtrude onto the path, Oliver explained, blunted by the dogged efforts of the Ladies Auxiliary.

The view from the very edge of the cliff was even more magnificent than the one on the lawn where they had stood the previous day. Maren marveled that this spectacular prospect was for the pleasure of fewer than a hundred families. It seemed such an extraordinary privilege, yet they didn't pass a soul as they walked.

"Where is everyone?"

"Most of the men aren't up for the weekend yet. I expect many of the women are squeezing in their tennis games today. The tournament tomorrow will keep the courts busy."

"But when they are here, do people often walk this path?"

"Honestly, they don't," Oliver answered. He had the decency to look sheepish. "I suppose we get inured to the view."

I will not let that happen to me, Maren promised herself.

They followed the path to the beach, signed in at a desk at the beach club entrance, then walked past rows of faded yellow cabanas to the wooden staircase that led down to the sand. They slipped off their shoes at the top, placing them among the dozens of other pairs scattered around, and descended the stairs.

After so much time in the antiseptic environment of the hospital, the fresh air was a rare pleasure. They had meant to walk the length of Haven Point Beach, but when Oliver was swarmed by friends, Maren realized they would have to abandon that plan.

Oliver fetched chairs from the Demarest cabana, and they spent the next hour and a half in conversation with an unending line of people. She understood their interest in Oliver and eagerness to welcome him home. Maren had not expected a red carpet. However, as the afternoon wore on, she could not help noticing that Oliver's friends treated her civilly, but without warmth. Several looked her up and down conspicuously.

The few questions directed to her were repetitions of what people already knew. "You work as a nurse at Walter Reed?" "You were married in December?" "You're from Minnesota?" This last statement-masked-as-question was usually accompanied by raised eyebrows, as if her home state was an outlandish place, difficult to locate on a map.

The question she heard most often was "What do you think of Haven Point?" Maren thought they might as well have asked, "What do you think of *us*?" Beyond this, there was a complete lack of curiosity.

Maren tended to like everyone, and with the odd exception of a Caroline Sturgeon or two, the feeling was usually mutual. But she sensed she had found herself among people who were not inclined to like her, or to even try. She suspected there wasn't a woman outside of Haven Point whom this little world would think fine enough for its favorite son.

Oliver had spent all his boyhood summers here. As they trudged back up the hill, she wondered if he assumed his children would, too.

"I hope that wasn't too boring for you," Oliver said.

"Not at all," Maren replied, forcing a smile. "I gather I've married the prince of Haven Point."

"Oh no." Oliver sounded as if he truly believed this wasn't true. "I just haven't seen them in ages. Some were at Daniel's memorial, but I was there such a short time."

Oliver had indeed raced back to Washington after the service. He used work as the excuse, but the instant he returned, he had found Maren at Delano Hall. Maren recalled how he took her face in his hands and looked at her hungrily, as if he'd been gone a year.

When they returned to Fourwinds, they went out to the porch, where Pauline had settled in with some needlework. The house protected them from a stiff west wind. Except for the occasional gust attempting a skirmish from the east, the air was still.

Maren's disquiet at the reception she'd been given by Oliver's friends began to ease. The sound of the ocean crashing against the rocks pacified her. Oliver sat beside her on a wicker love seat, reading a medical journal, while she chatted with Pauline, whose vague responses suited her own lethargy.

Pauline had said Oliver was the Audubon of the family, so she interrupted him occasionally to inquire about birds that swooped and perched before them.

"What's that one, stretched out on the rocks, Oliver?"

He looked up briefly.

"A cormorant," he said, his eyes already back on his reading material. It was evidently commonplace. "Double crested. That's how they dry their wings."

A while later, a delicate white bird with a slim black bill and long black legs alit on the rocks. The wispy plumes on its head, breast, and back looked more like tufts of fine curled hair, its yellow feet like gloves. It was pretty and slight, so unlike all the oversize creatures Maren had seen, incongruous with the rugged coast.

The Pauline of birds, Maren thought.

"What about that one, Oliver?"

Oliver looked up, lazily at first, but then he sat up straighter and put his reading aside. "Well, will you look at that? That's a snowy egret! Mother, do you see it?"

Pauline looked up, too, more attentive than Maren had yet seen her. "Oh, it is." She clasped her hands together.

"Are they very rare?" Maren asked.

"They shouldn't be, but they were nearly hunted out of existence for their feathers. You ladies and your hats!" Oliver said. "An ounce of their plumes was once worth more than an ounce of gold. Fashions changed and they passed some laws to protect them, just in time to prevent complete extinction. Right, Mother?"

"That's right."

"Mother took an interest in the snowy egrets," Oliver explained.

"I'll get the binoculars," Maren said, and went inside to fetch them from a table by the door.

When she returned, however, the egret was gone, and two women were approaching down the long porch. One appeared close to Oliver's age. The other, bounded by black Labs on three sides, was obviously the first woman's mother. There was a masculine quality to the way they moved, certain and strong.

"Georgie! Maude!" Oliver said, getting up. He petted the dogs and gave both women a hug and kiss. Pauline smiled and murmured some unheard welcome from her seat.

"I want you to meet my wife, Maren. Maren, this is Georgina Franklin, and her mother, Mrs. Franklin." Maren returned their firm handshakes. Oliver had mentioned the Franklins. They had a house on Haven Point and lived in Portland the rest of the year. Oliver and Georgie had grown up together, and he'd told Maren Georgie's mother was like an aunt to him.

"Georgina will have your head if you call her anything but Georgie. And call me Maude. That's what Oliver and his brother always called me," she said in a tone of gruff, good-natured resignation.

"Dogs, down," Maude said. The dogs looked at the

tip of their master's pointed finger and moved to the appointed spot, as if trying to follow her instructions with maximum precision.

Georgie's straight, thick brown hair was parted in the middle and pulled back with barrettes. Other than small pearl earrings, she wore no adornments. Her brown eyes turned downward at the edges, giving her a slightly blasé appearance. She wore a brown cardigan, khaki-colored trousers, and a pair of saddle shoes that hinted at a golf game in the offing.

Her mother looked like a preview of Georgina in a quarter century, with the same face, just more lived-in; the same hair, only gray. They exuded health and vitality. "Good stock," Maren's father would call them.

"How are you, Pauline?" Maude said as she sat on a wicker ottoman next to Pauline's chair. She took Pauline's hand in hers, in a gentle and familiar manner Maren found affecting.

"Hello, Maude," Pauline said comfortably. Maren, Oliver, and Georgie pulled chairs to form a circle.

"So, welcome to Haven Point, Maren," Maude said, sitting up a little straighter, like a reporter about to commence an interview. "I understand you are a nurse at Walter Reed?"

"I am. I came to Walter Reed as a cadet nurse."

"And you're from Minnesota?" she asked. Maren sighed inwardly. The conversation was taking a familiar turn.

"Yes. A small town called Ada near the North Dakota border," Maren replied. "My father is a farmer."

Maren never hesitated to share this information. She was proud of her family, and if anyone was inclined to judge her, she figured they could go ahead and begin doing so immediately.

"The Grahams, my family, have farmed in Maine for hundreds of years," Maude replied.

Maude was not precisely warm, but Maren, who was ready for table scraps at this point, began to relax. At least she had tried to make some connection, rather than treating her like a zoo animal.

"We all have the Grahams to thank for Haven Point," Oliver said. "Maude's father once owned this entire peninsula."

"Sentimental old fool could have sold it off to a speculator to build a hotel, and we'd have been sitting pretty," Maude said. She shook her head and sighed, but a hint of a smile again suggested good-humored resignation. "As it is, here we are."

"So, tell us about the wedding," Maude asked after they finished exchanging the basics. Maren saw something in Maude's expression, an intensity that hadn't been there before. Georgie stopped petting one of the dogs and looked up, as if to listen more carefully.

She felt a resurgence of the concern she had harbored, that their whirlwind courtship and marriage had been a bone of contention here. While the rest of the world might accept speedy wartime weddings, perhaps Haven Point was more hidebound. Did they feel Maren and Oliver had snubbed his parents, or maybe everyone there?

"Bettina was at the wedding!" Pauline piped up, smiling.

Maude and Georgie both looked at Pauline, eyes filled with solicitous interest.

"Was she, Pauline?" Maude said, with a sweetness Maren suspected she reserved for a select few. "Well, of course, that makes sense. She lives not far from Washington."

"Yes, Bettina was there," Oliver said. He also had a smile on his face, but it was for Maren alone. Oliver's second cousin Bettina turned out to be the mysterious brunette Caroline had seen with him at the diner, the one over whom Maren had spent so many restless nights. Caroline had evidently not been at her strategic best, because she had failed to notice Bettina's wedding ring.

At this point, Maude and Georgie seemed to soften toward Maren. It seemed confirmation of Maren's suspicion: They had indeed been troubled by the fact that Oliver and Maren had married without his parents in attendance. However, if Pauline was comfortable with it, they would be, too. They stayed another twenty minutes, peppering her with questions, friendlier ones now, and occasionally directing some comment or kindness toward Pauline.

"See you tomorrow night for your big debut," Georgie said as they rose to leave. She glanced at Oliver, and Maren saw something in her eyes: a flash of pity, or perhaps commiseration.

There had been talk of a party in honor of Oliver and Maren, but the packed Haven Point social schedule made it impossible. Oliver's father was playing in the forty-and-over doubles championship the following day, which would be followed by a cocktail party.

Maren did not know what was behind the look Georgie gave Oliver, but she had enough anxiety without borrowing more. She took comfort in Maude's and Georgie's kindness and appreciated that they seemed protective of Pauline.

Maren knew her mother-in-law was helpless, perhaps even feckless, but she had quickly developed tender feelings toward her. Pauline seemed in need of friends and defenders from any quarter. She had obviously been a trial for Oliver, but it was jarring to witness the disdain with which he had treated her. She hoped his father had a little more forbearance.

A few hours later, she discovered he had far less.

CHAPTER EIGHT

From the moment Gideon brought William Demarest from the train, the balance of the household tilted unpleasantly in his direction.

When Oliver introduced Maren, his response was a chilly "How do you do." He looked her over, brusquely answered her polite inquiry about his journey, told her to call him William, then moved on to other subjects. But William's rudeness to Maren was nothing compared to his behavior toward Pauline, whom he treated more like an irritating child than a spouse.

Maren had helped with dinner and was pleased to note Pauline's competence in the kitchen. Though she knew it was probably force of habit and rote memory, it was heartening to see her do anything well. When they sat down at the long dining room table, she hoped Pauline might earn some praise or gratitude. Perhaps the family would rally for mealtime, as some did.

Not the Demarests. They picked up their forks, the eating interrupted only occasionally by wooden conversation. Maren ventured a few questions, but William's answers were abrupt and Oliver said almost nothing, so she stopped asking.

When Pauline asked her husband who his partner

would be in the tennis tournament the following day, he looked at her as if she was a perfect idiot.

"Bull Trumbull, for Chrissakes. The same doubles partner I've had for two years!"

"Oh, yes, of course," Pauline replied mildly, seeming oblivious to William's tone.

Or maybe she doesn't care, Maren hoped. More than once that day she had wondered whether her mother-in-law was cleverer than she seemed.

Maren was stabbed by a rare pang of homesickness. Her father was taciturn, but he had none of William's anger. At the Larsen table, meals began with a prayer then quickly devolved into noise and chatter and movement. Her mother was in and out of the kitchen, buzzing and bustling and asking whether everyone had what they needed.

Even when Maren's high spirits landed her in trouble, as they sometimes had, the dinner table was a sanctuary. Maren couldn't be sure what sins were being punished here at the Demarest table, but there was clearly no granting of mealtime asylum.

She came away from dinner with two distinct impressions about her father-in-law. First, disagreeing with him on any subject would be a ridiculous waste of time. Second, while he was willing to like her well enough, he wasn't accepting applications for new loved ones, thank you very much. She had been eager to make a good impression. Now she found she hardly cared.

When she and Oliver retired that night, she did not expect him to speak of the shadow of ill feeling cast by his father's arrival. In fact, he had been so remote all evening, she was surprised when he took her into his arms. But she welcomed him, eager to find some warmth in a house that had grown much colder.

*   *   *

The next morning, Maren followed Oliver out the kitchen door to their ramshackle garage. The heavy barn doors squeaked noisily. Great patches of light shone through holes in the roof, revealing a riot of cobwebs, life preservers, and cans of gasoline. (Rations be damned!) Tools and garden implements were piled in a corner, though Maren knew from Gideon Douglas that gardening and repairs were outsourced. Demarest men, in her short experience, were fit and healthy, but not at all handy.

Leaning against one side of the garage was an impressive quantity of dilapidated bicycles. Oliver extracted his own from the jumble before eyeing the rest and picking one for Maren. Its only qualification seemed to be that it was the proper height. It was rusty, the seat rent from front to back, and an odd lack of symmetry in the handlebars hinted at some long-ago catastrophe. But once the tires were pumped, it seemed willing to carry her, so she hopped on and followed Oliver down the hill and across the causeway to the country club.

Maren was puzzled by the Demarests' derelict collection of bikes. This was the primary mode of transportation on Haven Point, after all. Surely they could afford some decent, updated models. When they reached the bike rack near the tennis courts, she discovered it was endemic. It looked like a chaotic bicycle museum, with one ancient model knocking carelessly into the next.

The country club itself was surprisingly lovely, though—a lodge-like structure of green wood with a stone foundation and wraparound porch. A broad staircase faced the grass tennis courts, and the back side of the porch looked onto the golf course and across the bay.

After she and Oliver found seats on the porch, Maren surveyed the crowd, which spanned all ages. Toddlers squirmed in their mothers' arms. Four ancient, sour-faced women in shirtwaist dresses and flats, evidently the dowager uniform of Haven Point, sat in a row farther down the porch. In addition to heads of hair so thoroughly styled and sprayed no comb could possibly penetrate, they all wore expressions of intense discontentment.

"I see you noticed the Founding Fathers," Oliver whispered.

Maren looked at him, eyes wide. "*What* did you say?"

"It's a parlor game on Haven Point, deciding which of the Founding Fathers each of those four widows most resembles."

"That's terrible!" Maren scolded. A moment later she chanced another glimpse at the women then leaned back toward Oliver.

"But the one with the reddish hair?" Maren whispered.

"Yes?"

"That's Jefferson, right?"

"Naturally." Oliver smiled and threaded his fingers through hers in a way that still made her heart jump.

A respectable crowd had assembled to watch the women's match, but soon after Maren and Oliver arrived, the rest of the porch chairs filled up, then the stairs and the backless benches around the courts. When the seats were filled, latecomers leaned against nearby pine trees.

Every person on Haven Point seemed to be in attendance (with the exception, Maren noticed, of Pauline). Most women appeared to be dressed in anticipation of some athletic endeavor. Some wore white belted tennis dresses with pleated skirts and Peter Pan collars. Others were in pants, striped shirts, and jackets, as if they might hop on a sailboat the instant the tournament ended. The rest had on longer skirts, button-down blouses, and golf shoes. In her simple sundress, Maren was one of the few who didn't look like she'd jumped from the pages of *Sporting Woman* magazine.

Maren had watched a tennis exhibition match in Minneapolis once and thought the game looked like great fun, one of a few sports she thought she might try if ever she had time or opportunity. But ten minutes of watching these men put her off that idea.

She was not intimidated by the talent on display. She was athletic and didn't mind being a novice. And she was impressed by the way the men ran down every ball, even flailing themselves into the fences if need demanded.

They just did not seem to be enjoying themselves. Other than the occasional victorious smirk, she saw no smiles. It was not the genteel game played by accomplished amateurs she'd expected.

Oliver's father and Bull Trumbull won the first set, but it did little to improve William's temper. He snapped at Bull more than once for being out of position. Their opponents seemed to hit their stride in the second set. William appeared particularly annoyed when he lost two points serving.

"Watch my father here. He can't bear to lose serve," Oliver said. Maren heard a hint of weary resignation in his tone.

After his next serve went in, hard and to the outside, William rushed the net. The return came back high. William picked it out of the air, and slammed his volley directly into his opponent's stomach.

There was an audible gasp. While most eyes were on the injured party, Maren watched William return to the baseline. She was certain she detected a smile.

"Does the losing team get fed to lions?" Maren whispered to Oliver.

"It's much worse."

"What happens?"

"The losing team loses," Oliver said.

William and Bull went on to win that game, and then the set and match. Moments after the four men shook hands, the courts were filled with players eager to get in their own games, and the rest of the crowd dispersed to their various activities.

William, who also had a bike, joined Maren and Oliver on the return trip to Fourwinds.

"Congratulations, Father. That was quite a game," Oliver said as they rode up the hill. Maren picked up some irony in Oliver's tone, though William did not.

"I thought we were done after that first set. Bull was a disaster," William replied. His mind seemed back on the court. He had derived no joy from the outcome.

"I think it made a real impression on Maren," Oliver said. "Didn't it, Maren?"

"I don't think I've ever seen anything like it," Maren said brightly, wondering why Oliver had put her on the spot. "They should call you the Fearsome Foursome!"

"Ha! The Fearsome Foursome," William repeated, wrinkling his brow as if considering the label. "I rather like that." He looked over from his bike and gave her a genuine smile, the first she'd earned from him.

So, this is the way to his heart, Maren thought, though she was annoyed rather than pleased with the discovery. Her father-in-law had more than enough people to remind him of his magnificence.

That evening they headed to the country club for the cocktail party. Pauline, in a full-skirted pink dress, looked like a little girl next to her husband. No one mentioned the fact that she had not attended the tennis match, and Maren didn't ask. It was just another of the many pieces of the Demarest family puzzle scattered about. She wasn't sure she'd ever complete the picture, or if she wanted to.

When they entered the country club, Maren thought she understood Georgie's look of commiseration the previous day. All eyes were on them. This was indeed their debut. Or hers, really.

She was glad she had consulted Dorothy about her wardrobe.

"It's not fancy, Maren. No evening wear required." Maren's simple blue cap-sleeved dress with a matching belt and square neckline seemed in keeping with what other women wore.

They made their way to the makeshift bar, a long table with a tablecloth, staffed by one of the tennis pros. On the way, Oliver introduced her to several friends she had not yet met, all of whom gave the same impression the others had: Everyone wanted to meet her. Few wanted to know her.

While they waited for their drinks, a woman near Oliver's age approached. She was slim, and her tan brought out her blue eyes, but a haughty expression added harshness to an angular face. Her russet hair was curled to a perfection Maren knew could only have been achieved with great violence.

"Hello, Harriet. You look well. I'd like you to meet my wife, Maren. Maren, this is Harriet Hyde."

"How do you do?" she said to Maren, smiling just enough to avoid appearing uncivil before returning her attention to Oliver.

"Oliver, you've finally come. How long will you be on the Point?"

On the point. Maren chafed at the phrase, which she'd heard some of Oliver's friends use earlier (along with its reverse, "off the point"). It seemed to imply that life beyond the Haven Point causeway was somehow devoid of meaning.

Oliver responded politely to that and a few similar inquiries until he was pulled into conversation with a few friends nearby. Harriet abandoned the smile.

"So, you're a nurse?" Harriet said.

"Yes." Maren, sensing hostility, was not inclined to help the conversation along.

"Is that how you met Oliver?"

"We met through a mutual friend." Dorothy's introduction, Maren had realized, provided a veneer of legitimacy—an antidote to suspicion that Maren had been a nurse in the Caroline Sturgeon mold, on the hunt for a doctor husband.

"You got married so quickly."

"Yes." Maren let the silence hang.

"We wondered about that," Harriet said. She held her chin up and tilted her head at an odd angle, as if she was somehow trying to look down on Maren, who was actually taller.

"What, exactly, did you wonder?" Maren understood the implication but had a perverse desire to hear her say it out loud.

"We just wondered why you had to get married so fast." Harriet changed her tone to one of friendly conspirator, as if Maren might be fooled into sharing some confidence. Her eyes moved slowly but unmistakably toward Maren's midsection.

Maren suppressed a flash of fury. Harriet had surely done the math. If she had been pregnant at their wedding, Maren would have a baby by now. Either she was feigning obtuseness, or, worse, implying Maren had tricked Oliver. Just as Maren was about to respond, Georgie approached.

"You wondered why we would *have* to marry so quickly?" Maren asked. This seemed like a good way to bring Georgie up to speed.

"We just didn't know . . ." Harriet faltered. It seemed Georgie's presence had thrown her off.

"We?"

"Some of us. I mean, again, it was rather sudden," Harriet said quickly.

"Harriet," Georgie cut in, her voice clipped. "I think your mother might need you. Why don't you go check on her?"

Though vanquished, Harriet still gave Maren a final once-over, as if Maren were an item at a flea market that she had considered, but found wanting.

"Well done. You have a knack," Georgie said after Harriet walked away. She nodded in grudging respect.

"For what?"

"For handling Harriet. She probably thought she had the mouse under her paw the second she met you."

Just as Maren was about to ask Georgie to elaborate, a man with a cheerful, ruddy face approached and slung his arm over Georgie's shoulder. Maren's initial thought was that he must be Georgie's brother.

"Maren, this is my fiancé, David Ormsby. Everyone calls him Cappy. Cappy, meet Maren."

He smiled and gave her a hearty handshake. In response to Maren's inquiry, they explained they'd known each other since middle school.

"When did you all actually start dating?" Maren asked.

They answered in such a disjointed fashion, with so much talking over and contradicting each other, Maren was laughing heartily by the end of it.

"Where did you get your nickname?" Maren asked Cappy.

"He was barking orders at everyone from the first time he set foot on a boat," Georgie said. "Hasn't quit."

Cappy smiled and shrugged.

Maren had noticed a tendency on Haven Point toward making perfectly good names ridiculous. She had already met a "Twink" (Mary), a "Tug" (Robert), and an "Orry" (Orwit).

Cappy's nickname was more forgivable once he explained that his first boating experience had not been on a sailboat, but on his grandfather's lobster boat, which he spoke of with nostalgia.

A bark of laughter from the side of the room attracted their attention, and they looked over to see William Demarest and his tennis partner, Bull Trumbull, both bent at the waist, laughing noisily.

Probably at someone's expense, Maren thought. Bull's eyelids were heavy, and his fleshy face as red as if he'd just come off the court. A woman with ashy blond hair and a feline expression stood near them, smoking a cigarette. She did not look amused.

"Who is that with them?" Maren asked.

"Bull's wife, Adelaide Trumbull," Georgie said, rolling her eyes. "They're a pair. She wants to be known as 'Lady,' but we all call her Adelaide. They live in New York. She doesn't come up here much. Too rustic for her."

The couple gave off a whiff of something unpleasant, and Maren kept one eye on them until Oliver approached and slipped his hand into hers.

"We'll leave you newlyweds," Georgie said, as she led Cappy away. Oliver pulled her close and looked down at her with the gentle smile that made her heart turn.

"Let's get out of here, shall we?"

Maren nodded, delighted to escape. As they slipped out, the last thing Maren saw was Adelaide Trumbull watching Bull through narrowed eyes as he lurched toward the bar with a look of drunken determination.

When William left Sunday, the house seemed to exhale. For the next few days, she and Oliver were mercifully free of social obligations and spent much of the time reading on the porch. Just as Maren began to relax, the world intruded.

They awoke Tuesday to news that a bomb, bigger and more destructive than any before, had been dropped on the city of Hiroshima in Japan. Amid the horror of the destruction, there was hope.

"Maybe this is it," Oliver said, looking up from his newspaper. "Maybe he'll finally give up."

When another bomb fell on Nagasaki, it was certain. It would only be a matter of days before Emperor Hirohito would surrender. The war's end did not mean the end to their work, however. It was time to return to Walter Reed, to do what they could for the men who would suffer the war's consequences for months—many for years or even lifetimes.

On the eve of their departure, Maren went downstairs to get her book from the porch. As she returned to their room, she took her time looking over the dozens of pictures along the staircase wall. She stopped at one of William and Daniel, standing on the cliff, shotgun barrels against their shoulders. She had noticed it but had not taken the time to look at it closely until now.

Daniel, smiling broadly, held a small bird by its feet. With his thumb and forefinger, William held one of the bird's feathers in the band of his hat, a jokey gesture. The bird was delicate, white with wispy plumes.

A snowy egret. It was the bird they had seen on the rocks that first day. Maren felt sick. Every day, Pauline had to pass this photograph of her husband and son, fresh from killing the bird she so admired.

She heard a sound and looked up to see Pauline on the landing, peering down at her. Pauline, who had evidently seen the stricken look on Maren's face, lifted her fragile shoulders in a slight shrug.

Maren read the question in her eyes: *What could I do?*

CHAPTER NINE

August 1997
Haven Point

SKYE

How's this?" Adriene asked as she came to the living room, where Skye sat waiting with Gran. Adriene was wearing one of Skye's plaid button-down shirts tucked into a pair of jeans.

"That's fine," Skye said.

"Good. I want to blend in."

"Adriene's like the guy on *Wild Kingdom*," Skye said to Gran. She made a motion with her hands like she was parting grasses and lowered her voice. "I'm here at the yacht club, observing the creatures in their native habitat."

"I just want to see these people in action," Adriene said, unapologetic. Skye looked at Gran and raised an eyebrow. Once Adriene decided she was interested in something, things tended to get unpredictable.

"Oh, it will be fun," Gran said.

"You don't get it, Gran," Skye said. "She asks the most outrageous questions."

"Yes, but they let her, don't they?" Gran said.

"True," Skye acknowledged with a sigh. Adriene got away with being nosy because she didn't seem like she was digging for dirt. Everyone was fair game, even herself. Once, when Skye was thumbing through Adriene's

CDs, she made the mistake of asking Adriene where she got her terrible taste in music.

"I know. It's so sad," Adriene had replied, as if her appreciation for Neil Diamond was a chronic affliction, like having one leg shorter than the other. Skye thought that was the end of the discussion when she heard the dreaded "But wait . . ."

The next hour was spent analyzing where *exactly* Adriene got her terrible taste in music. Was it genetic? Was she subconsciously rebelling against what was cool? Could it be a reaction to some traumatic moment in childhood when good music had been playing in the background?

Skye had since learned to be careful with rhetorical questions.

"All right, we're off, Gran. Wish me luck," Skye said. They put on jackets and headed out into the cool evening.

After the baton relay summer, Skye and Gran had struck a bargain: Skye would never try to hide her mom's drinking again, and if her mom had a relapse during the summer, she could stay with Adriene.

Skye hadn't been to Haven Point since. She liked being at the Maduroses' house. With all the kids and countless relatives in and out, there was plenty of chaos to hide behind. At the same time, Adriene's family stuck to the basic rules of domestic grammar: days punctuated by regular meals and routine. It was a nice change of pace from Skye's own home, which was more like a garbled run-on sentence.

It also helped that Mrs. Maduros was not shocked by her mom's issues. They fit nicely, in fact, with her fatalistic view of humanity. When Skye would arrive for one of her stays, Mrs. Maduros would wrap her in a great hug.

"Oh, my poor Skye. Your poor mother. It's a fallen

world, so much suffering," she'd say in her thick Greek accent (while Adriene did a pitch-perfect imitation behind her mother's back, complete with eyes to the heavens and the sign of the cross).

Skye's mom had been clean for a while, but spring of junior year, Skye began to spot signs of trouble on the horizon. Her mom stayed up so late, Skye had to plead with her to get her out of bed in the morning. Then that bitter edge came out. *Those jackasses don't pay me enough anyway.* Sometimes Skye's efforts failed, and her mom simply wouldn't go to work, leaving it to Skye to make excuses for her.

Her mom's students still adored her, but supervisors were another story. Whenever she got a new job, she'd get the star treatment for a while, but eventually the disappointment phase set in, and Skye had a front-row seat. She would cringe at the increasingly fake concern. *Your mom has been ill a lot lately. Is everything okay?*

She had begun to realize her mom's constant job changes were less about chasing the shiniest new object in arts education and more a strategy to leave before she completely drained the reservoir of goodwill.

Somehow her mom managed to stay sober through the school year and even wrangled another contract, so at least Skye wouldn't have to change schools for senior year. From the start of summer, though, Skye had been on red alert. The fear of a relapse nagged at her constantly. The third week in July, Skye came home from babysitting and found her mom passed out on the couch, an empty bottle of wine on the floor. Skye called Gran, who made the usual arrangements. Her mom was off to rehab, and Skye was off to Adriene's.

Like always, Skye felt relieved. The bad thing happening was never as bad as waiting for the bad thing to happen, and it was always nice when her mom was in someone else's hands.

What she didn't feel anymore was hope. It was like the Escher print her mom had on her art room wall, of ants on a Möbius strip. You think the ants will eventually reach the other side, but there is no other side. They always end up back in the same place.

The hiccup came three days after she arrived, when Adriene's parents were called to Greece for a family emergency. After a bunch of phone calls between Gran and Mrs. Maduros, it was arranged that both Adriene and Skye would go to Haven Point.

Skye knew it would be different with Adriene there, but she had pictured it like summers when she was little, when she enjoyed Haven Point without thinking about the fact that she didn't belong. As they headed to the party, she realized she had not taken into account how much Adriene could be like an anthropologist.

When they arrived at the lawn above the yacht club, Adriene looked down, surprised.

"That's a yacht club?" Adriene asked, pointing. Except the porch around two sides, the yacht club looked like a big square wooden shed.

"Yeah. Fancy name, not a fancy place," Skye replied.

The party, which was for the high schoolers, was a typical low-key event. Other than a table with sodas and a few bowls of chips and popcorn, the only thing that said "party" was the stereo in the corner blasting Bruce Springsteen. Adriene looked around and laughed.

"Your mom wasn't kidding. This place is so white," Adriene said.

Skye had grown up surrounded by all kinds of people: black, white, brown, gay, straight, old, and young. But other than occasionally saying they should move to a less "vanilla" neighborhood (a statement she was way too disorganized to act on), her mom didn't make a big point about it. She just seemed to like people who were interesting, who had distinct points of view, and she'd chosen a career and workplaces where she'd find them.

She never hesitated to point out how homogenous Haven Point was, though.

"That place doesn't even have canine diversity," she said once, rolling her eyes. "Labs and goldens, goldens and Labs."

Skye didn't disagree. Neither did Gran, for that matter. Skye once commented to Gran that all the kids on Haven Point looked the same—so different from what she was used to. (In comparison, Skye's schools were like little United Nations meetings.)

"Change does come to places like this." Gran sighed. "Just very, very slowly."

Adriene, of course, managed to find the potential benefit.

"You know, I'm actually kind of exotic here," she said.

They grabbed bottles of water from the cooler on the table. As Adriene opened hers, she looked around. The inside of the yacht club was prettier than the outside. Nautical pendant lights hung from exposed beams, and the glossy wood-paneled walls were crowded with sailing paraphernalia.

"Wait, is that your mom?" Adriene pointed her bottle at a large placard hanging between a signal flag and an old ship's wheel. It listed the winning crews of the annual Stinneford Cup Junior Sailing race. Near the top of the second row, it read *1966: Charles Demarest, Anne Demarest.*

"Yeah. I forgot about that," Skye said. "That's her and my uncle Charlie, the one who died before I was born."

Her mom had never mentioned it, but Skye had once noticed the silver cup from the race on a shelf at Fourwinds, and Gran told her the whole story.

"I can't really imagine your mom sailing," Adriene said, squinting as if she was trying to do so. "It seems so, I don't know . . ."

"Preppy?"

"That's it." Adriene laughed.

"My uncle was the real sailor. He was the skipper in that race, even though my mom was older than him. I don't think she was that into it."

As soon as the words came out of her mouth, though, a memory from years before flashed through her mind. Gran and Pop had stopped by one evening when Skye and her mom were in the dining room, Skye doing homework at one end of the table, while her mom stood in front of a tabletop easel at the other end, putting the finishing touches on an oil painting.

Gran was always interested in her mom's art, which Skye found annoying. She thought Gran should spend less time encouraging her mom to be an artist, and more time encouraging her to be a mom.

Gran had stood for a moment looking at the painting: two bold converging lines, slashes of red in the space between.

"It looks like a sailboat," Gran had said finally.

"Well, it's not," Anne had snapped, eyes flashing.

Pop had changed the subject, but Skye remembered how the tension had lingered. To this day, she had no idea what was behind it. But she never saw the painting again.

"So, do you know any of these people?" Adriene asked, taking in the crowd.

"Not really, though I've met most of them," she said. She looked around and spotted Charlotte.

"Over by the door to the porch. Dark hair, green Choate sweatshirt. That's the girl who told everyone I tripped her during that relay."

Adriene looked over and squinted. "Got it." She nodded. "Hate her."

A few minutes later, Ben Barrows walked over, a friend in his wake.

Ben had gotten cuter. His shoulders were broader, which made him look less gangly, and his skin had cleared up. And he still had that wavy brown hair and big smile she remembered.

"Hey. Skye, right? I'm Ben. I don't know if you remember me."

"Of course. Green baton relay team, 1994," Skye said. She would have been more flattered by his approaching were it not so obvious that his friend was angling for an introduction to Adriene.

"This is Flip Devereaux," Ben said. Flip had freckles, a sunburned nose, and spiky blond baby-fine hair.

Skye greeted him and introduced Adriene.

Flip seemed a little dazed, but Skye was used to that. Adriene and Skye had both enjoyed metamorphoses in the preceding years. Skye had grown taller (not that she needed to be any taller) but she was no longer flat-chested, at least. Her red hair had darkened to more of an auburn, and she'd tamed it with a better cut and a little effort. She knew she wasn't like Charlotte, the type who people immediately looked at and said "She's pretty." Skye was more the "She's pretty, actually" type, like people had to think about it for a second.

Adriene was absolutely gorgeous. She had never been skinny, but her weight had redistributed itself strategically, and she embraced her curves. She wore her thick, dark hair loose around her shoulders. Adriene always drew the eye, but she had been right about standing out in the all-American, pastel blur that was this crowd. Next to her, Flip almost looked like a different species.

"Flip? Is that short for something?" Adriene asked.

"Philip," he replied.

"Oh? Do you spell Flip with a *Ph*?"

"No, with an *F*," Flip replied earnestly. A second later, he laughed, embarrassed. "Oh, you're joking."

As Skye was marveling at Adriene's power to tease guys and make them like her even more, she noticed Charlotte and Cricket heading their way. Her spidey sense told her she and Adriene were poaching on their territory.

Charlotte approached the table, grabbed a Diet Coke, then looked over at Ben and Flip.

"You guys have your talent ready?" Charlotte asked, her tone challenging.

Adriene shot Skye a look. Skye knew she'd have a heyday later with Charlotte's ruse of getting a soda, which allowed her to toss something into their conversation without having to acknowledge Skye's existence.

"Yeah, we're working on it," Flip replied.

"Mmm-hmm," Charlotte said, as if she didn't believe him.

"What's this about a talent?" Adriene demanded, after Charlotte and Cricket walked away.

"We're Junior Sailing counselors, and they have a talent show on Wednesday night. It's mostly for the campers, but the girl counselors usually do one act and guy counselors do another," Flip explained. "Ben and I are the only two guys this summer, though, so we're going to blow it off."

"Blow it off?" Adriene said, in a tone that suggested this was the most poor-spirited thing she'd ever heard. "Come on. You must have some talents."

"Ummm . . ." Flip started, flummoxed.

"Flip sings in the chorus at St. Paul's," Ben said. Skye saw a twitch at the corner of his mouth.

"That's great!" Adriene said encouragingly. Flip looked pleased for an instant, but then he seemed to realize what Ben was up to.

"Yeah, well, Ben plays guitar," he said, glaring at Ben.

"Oh?" Adriene looked at Ben hopefully.

"Well, I can play 'Wild Thing' by the Troggs," Ben admitted.

"What, you only know two chords?" Adriene rolled her eyes. When she returned her attention to Flip, Ben looked at Skye and held up three fingers.

Three chords, he mouthed, pretending to be serious. Skye acknowledged his correction of the record with a solemn nod. After a brief sidebar with Flip, Adriene told them the plans.

"Okay, Ben, you'll play 'Wild Thing.' Flip will sing and do a dance. I'll choreograph." She made a "spit spot" motion with her hands. "Where can we practice?"

Skye stifled a laugh. Adriene might have taken a few dance classes in school, but as far as Skye knew, she had no experience in choreography. Flip, however, had the *whatever it takes to please you* expression that was familiar to Skye. He'd probably put on a tutu and sing opera if that's what Adriene wanted.

Ben, for his part, had the look guys get when they're torn between stopping a friend from doing something really stupid, and kind of wanting to see what happens. He turned to Skye, his brown eyes dancing.

"Well?"

Skye put her hands up and shrugged, as if to say, *How can we resist?* Without another word, they had entered into conspiracy.

"Okay, then. To my garage," Ben said with great decisiveness, as if it were the most normal thing in the world to submit to the demands of a little spitfire he'd never seen before that night. As they headed for the door, Skye leaned over and whispered to Adriene.

"So, I guess we're not going to use binoculars and watch through the grasses."

"No way. We're going full *Gorillas in the Mist*."

Twenty minutes later, they were sitting in four inner tubes on the floor of Ben's detached garage, drinking beers. Ben's older brother had transformed the garage into a party space. It was decorated with discarded lamps on discarded tables, a refrigerator, an old boombox with CD and cassette player, and some beer signs on the walls.

Adriene was drilling the guys about Haven Point.

"So, what do you people do here? Croquet? Polo?"

"Oh my God, Adriene." Skye laughed and looked up at the ceiling.

"We don't play croquet or polo," Ben replied, pretending to be indignant. "We're way too busy fox hunting."

He's funny! Skye thought. This was a revelation. And funny at Haven Point's expense, to boot.

Flip, who until that point had seemed too intimidated to speak, finally got a question out.

"So, where do you all go to school?"

"I go to this super-strict and holy Catholic school out in the sticks," Adriene said. "Though I'm Greek Orthodox, which means I also have to go to Greek school in the summer to unlearn all the wrong stuff they're teaching me."

"Why'd your parents send you to a Catholic school?" Flip asked.

"I think they went around the D.C. metro area and

graded each school, one to ten, based on how repressive it is. They didn't stop until they found an eleven," Adriene said. "Skye's mom does the same, except on the one-to-ten repression scale, she's always looking for the one."

Ben and Flip turned to Skye and insisted she elaborate.

Skye used to hate the school question. She knew it was supposed to set up the name game, which she could never play. *Oh, you go to Deerfield? Do you know . . . ?*

But things Skye had once been ashamed of were just fodder for analysis to Adriene. Nothing seemed quite as scary once it was taken out of hiding and put under her microscope. And when they had thoroughly dissected that formerly shameful thing, and all the parts were laid out on the table, Skye was able to make her real contribution to the partnership: spotting the absurdities, finding the comic potential.

At first, it was just the two of them, laughing as they idly deconstructed anyone and anything. But one night, Skye had a revelation while watching a stand-up comic on late-night television. The comedian had mined her crazy family for material—found the through lines and matched them up with stories. Yes, the audience laughed, but the comedian got there first.

That's what Adriene and I do! Skye was no pro, obviously, but she wasn't trying to get on Johnny Carson. She just wanted to get through high school.

Over time, she and Adriene had taken the show on the road. And since they'd spent hours analyzing Skye's schools, which Adriene found endlessly fascinating, Skye was more than prepared to respond to Ben and Flip.

"Hmm, let me see. . . ." Skye paused and looked up, as if summoning something from memory, then began ticking them off on her fingers. "There was the grade school with faceless dolls and pine cones for toys, the 'invent your own knowledge' school, the one where we sang hymns to Gaia and buried coffee cans filled with cow manure to please the earth spirits, the one that believed there were no wrong answers, even in math. . . ."

Ben and Flip laughed.

"I was so jealous," Adriene said. "Total anarchy."

"Yeah, until she worked with me at a frozen yogurt shop and realized I couldn't calculate change without the cash register," Skye said. "As you probably figured out at your schools, there actually *are* wrong answers in math."

"I'm still jealous," Adriene insisted.

"Are you artistic, too?" Ben asked, after Skye described her art teacher mom's never-ending quest for the perfect school.

"Not one little bit." Skye sighed. "My poor mom."

"Oh please," Adriene said. "She's creative, and her mom knows it. Skye's a writer. She even won a humor writing contest."

"Adriene, stop," Skye said, embarrassed. Why was Adriene talking her up? They were only there because Flip had given Adriene an opening to do her Jane Goodall thing.

"Oh, all right. She's being humble. Anyway, it's time we got working on your talent," Adriene said.

Flip looked a little disappointed, as if he hoped Adriene had forgotten, but Ben hopped right up.

"I'll go grab my guitar."

They spent the rest of that evening and the next in Ben's garage. Ben played his three chords, and Adriene choreographed a ridiculous dance for Flip, which involved a lot of stomping and hand gestures. Skye was in charge of costumes.

On Wednesday night, Skye and Adriene arrived at the

country club moments before the talent show began. The room was filled with parents and siblings of campers sitting in folding chairs in front of the portable pipe and drape they used as a stage.

Skye hadn't had much to work with in the costume department, but when the curtain opened on Flip and Ben, the crowd went crazy. Flip really did look like a "wild thing" in his dark shirt and dark pants and the floor-length wig Skye had made by stringing together pieces of dried seaweed.

Ben and Flip were awarded an honorable mention for their effort—a triumph, especially since the judges overlooked Charlotte and her friends' Spice Girls act.

After the talent show, the four of them went to the beach. Adriene, prepared to finally reward her adoring protégé, promptly disappeared into the darkness with Flip.

"Mission accomplished." Skye laughed. When she turned to Ben, Bud Light bottle raised, she saw he was peering at her closely.

"Not quite," he replied.

She looked at him questioningly, not sure she understood his meaning. Or, rather, afraid of the disappointment if she misunderstood it. They had laughed so much, and Skye had felt a powerful tug of attraction, but it was hard for her to believe he felt the same.

"While his friend's mission was accomplished," Ben said, in a deep narrator's voice, "he had a mission of his own."

He took her hand, led her out of the light of the beach club, and kissed her. It was soft and sweet, and she felt it from the top of her head to the tips of her toes. They didn't separate until they heard Flip and Adriene's voices.

"You should have done that for the talent show," Skye

whispered, before Flip and Adriene were close enough to hear them.

"I don't know," Ben said, pretending to consider it. "Flip's not really my type."

The four of them had another five days together before Adriene's parents returned from Greece and she had to leave.

Skye, who was staying on Haven Point for another week, worried things with Ben might die out once Adriene was gone, but she and Ben continued to see each other whenever he wasn't working.

It was easy and familiar, lots of laughter; like one of those years-long friendships that turns romantic, only compressed. In the afternoons, they would hang out on the cliff and talk. If it rained, they would go to Fourwinds, where Gran would leave them alone. At night, they'd go to the beach or Ben's garage, if neither of his brothers was around.

Skye told him more about herself and life with her hippyish, paint-under-the-fingernails, disorganized art teacher mom—the messy house, the under-planned vacations and inconsistent meal preparation. She stuck to the practiced funny bits and used her *doesn't bother me* tone, but he still heard more than she normally shared.

She even told him about her father. A couple of years earlier, Adriene had finally come up with a last name for "Don."

It was right after Skye's mom broke up with Elliott, a handsome black accountant, whom Adriene had seen as an excellent prospective stepfather for Skye. Skye had known better than to hope. Her mom always broke up with guys when they got too attached. Adriene was disappointed, though.

They were in the kitchen with Skye's mom, Adriene

grilling her about why she'd ended things, and Anne giving her usual non-answers.

"Adriene, you know my philosophy," she said finally, pointing at the "woman needs a man like a fish needs a bicycle" refrigerator magnet.

Adriene sighed and was quiet for a minute, but then her eyebrows went together. "But you know, Anne, you did need Skye's dad for something."

"Oh God, Adriene." Skye put her face in her hands. Skye and her mom almost never talked about this.

"What? She did!" Adriene insisted.

"Nothing but his original contribution," Skye's mom said drily.

"That's what I meant." Adriene nodded, satisfied.

Later, after Anne had left to meet Flora, Adriene said, "Well, now we finally know your dad's last name."

"What?"

"Fishbike!"

Skye had not forgotten Ben's grandmother trying to get this information out of her years before, but she didn't tell him about that conversation. Somehow, she knew he wouldn't tell Harriet about theirs.

The only real shyness she felt was when Ben urged her to tell him about the writing contest she had won. *The New Yorker* "Shouts and Murmurs" column had run it for high school humor writing.

Skye described her submission, a mock treatment of a teen film. She had parodied all the tropes: the klutzy new girl in school who ends up on a road trip with a brooding hero, during which they outsmart evil adults (and vampires), and also discover the heroine's parents aren't her real parents, because she's actually royalty.

"So, it was autobiographical," Ben said, when she finished.

"Well, obviously. Except the road trip, the brooding hero, outsmarting adults and vampires, and finding out I'm royalty. Other than that, story of my life," she said. Ben laughed.

Skye told him she hoped the prize would help her get into Northwestern, which had a great creative writing program.

Ben told her about his plans, too. He wanted to play lacrosse in college, hopefully at Williams. He would study history, go to law school, and eventually become a judge like his grandfather.

"Probably sounds boring," he said.

Skye thought it sounded normal (which worried her a little, since she felt like she wasn't). But she was never bored with him. She loved his smile, and the way he kissed, and the feel of her fingers in his wavy hair.

Throughout the week, Ben occasionally made comments like "We'll have to go to a hockey game together," implying they'd see each other during the school year. On her last night, he was more direct. They were lying on a blanket on the beach, looking up at the stars.

"We can talk on the phone. And write, too," he said, threading his fingers through hers.

"Definitely," Skye replied.

"I have an October break. Maybe you could come to Hartford, or I could go down to D.C."

"That would be awesome," Skye said.

Part of her even believed it. She felt like a girl in one of those 1950s teen romance novels she had inhaled on her previous visit to Haven Point. It was all so sweet, so simple. *Of course we'll see each other!*

Then she got home.

Nothing was particularly unusual. The house was a mess, but that was par for the course. Her mom was irritable and scattered. (Anne had long since given up the post-rehab eager-to-please routine—by this point, they were both too used to Skye being the competent one.) But Skye had seen this version of her mom before. She had seen them all.

Still, in returning to the grim, unfunny reality of her life, she realized what a carefully edited story she had told Ben. She hadn't lied, but she'd scrubbed out all the pain.

Ben called a few times and suggested getting together, but she put him off and eventually let it fizzle out. She was doing exactly what he would have done if she'd ever let him see the whole story. She knew it wouldn't really matter to him. Ben was a Haven Point kid, and Haven Point kids were like rubber bands. He had stretched a bit in his fling with Skye, but he would snap right back.

And sure enough, the following summer, Ben started dating Charlotte Spencer, commencing their long reign as the "It Couple" of their generation on Haven Point.

CHAPTER TEN

August 1949
Haven Point

MAREN

Maren did not know what had awakened her, just that it must have been loud. She was so tired these days, she practically gulped down sleep.

There it is again. It was clearer now. It sounded like someone coming up the staircase, accompanied by banging and mumbling. She looked at the clock. 1:00 A.M.

There was no crime on Haven Point, and she knew she had little reason to be frightened. Her heart did not seem to agree, however. It was beating at an alarming rate. She reached over to the bedside table to get the flashlight, wincing as she opened the noisy drawer, which was swollen with salt air like everything else in this house. She got out of bed and opened the door a crack, her anxiety now compounded by the terrible nausea that was her constant companion.

She could just make out the silhouettes of two figures as they reached the landing and headed toward Pauline's room. Maren cursed Oliver for leaving her here alone. The idea that she could somehow protect Pauline in her sick and ungainly state seemed ludicrous, but she screwed up her courage, turned on the flashlight, and flung her door open.

"Who is that?" She tried to sound firm as she pointed the flashlight at the intruders.

In the center of the circle of light was Georgie, one arm around a semiconscious Pauline. The scene contained echoes of another one four years earlier, when Oliver had found Pauline in the attic.

"Aw, damn. I didn't want to wake you." Georgie grimaced.

"*What* is going on?"

"Pauline's drunk."

"I gather that, Georgie. But I don't understand. She went to bed three hours ago."

"Give me a minute, Maren." Georgie continued toward Pauline's room. "I'll be right back."

When Georgie returned, she looked weary.

"I know we need to talk, but can it wait until tomorrow? I have to get back to bed before Cappy wakes up."

"All right," Maren reluctantly agreed.

Maren crawled back in bed, but she struggled to sleep. She could not remember ever feeling as lonely as she did at that moment.

She had been violently ill from the very start of her pregnancy. When the expected relief did not come at three months, her doctor explained some women were sick all the way through. Maren had nearly wept.

After the Washington, D.C., summer had set in with its usual vengeance, Oliver suggested she go to Haven Point.

"It'll be cooler there. Safer," he'd insisted. The memories from her one visit four years earlier were fresh enough that Maren did not relish the idea, but she had no energy to fight. She had arrived a week earlier. It was definitely cooler. She wasn't sure about safer.

* * *

Until now, Maren had only seen Georgie's house from the outside. It was a large shingle-style home like Fourwinds, though even more rambling and asymmetrical, as additions had been made throughout the years to accommodate family proliferation.

Georgie's family clearly adhered to the coastal Maine tradition of farming out of one side of the house and fishing out of the other. Off the north side of the porch, she could see down into the kitchen garden, which appeared to thrive, despite the inhospitable soil and weather. The porch was lined with fishing poles, nets, and colorful buoys. These were interspersed with plants and flowers potted in any kind of container, from old lobster pots to a chair with a hole carved in the seat. Maren felt a pang, thinking of her own family in Minnesota, of a simpler life.

Georgie had invited her to come over while her two-year-old daughter Susan took a nap. She appeared at the screen door, and held it open for Maren.

"Come in. I just got Susan down. I'll go get us some iced tea."

While she waited, Maren looked over the pictures along the board and batten walls of the entryway. When Georgie returned, two glasses in hand, she nodded toward a large picture, apparently from Haven Point's earliest days.

"That's Elizabeth Demarest and Nora Graham, Oliver's grandmother and mine," Georgie said.

Maren looked at the photograph: two women in long white dresses, sitting on a blanket on the beach. She did not need to ask which was Georgie's grandmother. Nora Graham had Georgie's straight hair, turned-down eyes, and candid, no-nonsense expression.

Elizabeth Demarest was beautiful. Her dark hair was

falling out of its loose knot, and she leaned back on her hands and smiled directly at the photographer, in defiance of the nineteenth-century rule that one must look stiff and miserable in photographs.

Georgie led Maren outside and nodded down the porch to two chairs.

"I know Haven Point was built on your land. How did it actually get started?" Maren asked.

"My grandfather, George Graham, wound up at Harvard and somehow fell in with Ambrose Lawrence, Jerome Demarest, Fritz Hyde, and some of the others whose names you've heard."

Maren had indeed heard those names. She had wondered why people on Haven Point referred to Maude and Georgie as "Grahams," and Harriet Hyde (now Harriet Barrows) as "a Hyde." Evidently it was a way to acknowledge the early Haven Point families—an informal version of those lineage societies like Colonial Dames and Sons of the American Revolution that Caroline Sturgeon had been so obsessed with.

"My grandfather was no aristocrat, never pretended to be. He was funny as all get-out, though."

A few years after graduation, Georgie explained, he invited his Harvard friends to hunt and fish on Haven Point.

"It was basically an island back then," Georgie said. "The connection to the mainland is underwater, except during high tide, and this was before the causeway was built. The steamships were carrying people to all the islands, though, and you could get here by rowboat, too."

Her great-grandparents were considering selling the land to a speculator, but Ambrose Lawrence had another idea, and a pile of money to go with it.

"Ambrose had seen some of the other summer spots

along the coast, which all started with a hotel. Cottage lots and communities came after. Ambrose wanted to skip the hotel and go straight to the community."

Ambrose bought the land and found a lawyer to work out the legal niceties. Fifteen families, including Oliver's grandfather, bought parcels and built their houses immediately. The yacht club and beach club were constructed right before the turn of the century, and the causeway and country club soon after.

"It all could have turned out differently. We were lucky, in some ways," Georgie said.

"How so?"

"Ambrose and Serena Lawrence were fashionable, but fortunately for us, these shingle houses were in fashion. Ambrose was also a terrible snob. The reason he didn't want a hotel was because he thought they attracted the wrong sort. Needless to say, my grandfather knew you didn't have to be rich to be the right sort. He managed to convince Ambrose to carve out some smaller, more affordable lots."

Maren nodded. She'd noticed a wide range in size among the houses and lots on Haven Point. The community had its share of families like the Grahams—comfortable, but without the kind of money that begets more money. On the other hand, while Haven Point frowned on ostentation, Maren knew it also had its share of extraordinary fortunes. The Lawrences, for one, were "smashingly wealthy" according to Dorothy, who knew them from New York.

The Demarests were not in that category, but they had the blithe lack of interest in the subject of money that Maren associated with the very well-off. She rarely heard Oliver talk about finances. Other than the occasional half-hearted grumble about the cost of maintaining

Fourwinds, which was an asset on paper, but a liability in practice, William was the same. (Of course, William and Pauline were also proof of the weak correlation between money and happiness.)

"What was that all about with Pauline last night, Georgie?"

"Let me ask first: What do you know about your mother-in-law?"

"I know she had problems with alcohol in the past. I was under the impression it was not a regular occurrence."

"That's good," Georgie said, as if she approved. Seeing Maren's confusion, she continued. "Oliver gets his information from his father. Sounds like William Demarest is in the dark, which is where we want him."

"What are you talking about? Who is *we*?" Maren asked. She was confused and, for some reason, vaguely irritated. "Are you suggesting Pauline is often drunk?"

"Pauline Demarest is as sweet a woman as ever lived. But yes, she is often drunk."

Maren felt a twinge of shame at her ignorance. She had not seen Pauline drunk since her first visit to Haven Point, but they hardly saw her, period, and Oliver had made it abundantly clear he had no desire to discuss Pauline's drinking.

"What happened last night?"

"She wandered into a party at the Ballantines'. Before people caught on, Nellie Fitzsimmons steered her into the kitchen and called me. Pauline does this sometimes, but we have a bit of a system worked out."

"A *system*?" Maren sat up, her irritation more focused. Who were these people, and why where they making decisions about *her* mother-in-law?

"Why has no one told Oliver?" *Or me?* she wondered silently.

"It's a long story," Georgie said wearily. She proceeded with the tale of a young Pauline Powell, a petite brunette with a way of unconsciously making men feel like kings. Pauline's once-fine Virginia family was impoverished after the Civil War. Pauline knew her duty: She was to marry well.

William met Pauline while visiting a college friend and courted her with his usual single-mindedness.

"According to my mother, she didn't so much fall in love as relent to it," Georgie said. "At first, she drank for Dutch courage, trying to keep up with his family. It went downhill from there. It was terrible when Daniel and Oliver were little."

"I can only imagine," Maren replied. Twelve hours earlier she could not have conceived of anything more miserable than her unrelenting nausea, but it was getting a run for its money now. Half of her ached with pity for all Oliver had endured, and the other half was appalled at her trifling knowledge of his family.

"She was delicate as an orchid," Georgie went on. "Kind, and bright, too, for all her wide-eyed ways. She used to make up darling poems, right off the top of her head. And she'd stay sober for spells. When Oliver and I were toddlers, Daniel pulled a hot iron onto himself while she was passed out on the couch. She went several years without drinking after that."

"Did she ever go for treatment?"

"To several institutions, but she always fell off the wagon at some point."

"Did William send her? It sounds like he wanted to help."

"He did, but never believed it would work. Eventually he refused to spend another dime on 'those quacks,' as he called them. Drinks like a fish himself, but he can't fathom getting sloppy. Oliver's grandfather, Jerome, was the same. To them, it's weakness. She should just *will* herself to drink less. William even keeps alcohol in the house." Georgie shook her head. "That's Demarest men for you."

Maren considered pretending she understood Georgie's last comment, but more information seemed worth the cost of betraying her ignorance.

"What do you mean by 'Demarest men'?"

"They're bulls in china shops. Daniel was pure Demarest, may he rest in peace. My mother says the Demarest bloodline needs tempering from the right women. She believes some qualities can't be trained out." In response to Maren's look of incomprehension, she added, "She sees it in her dogs."

A few days earlier, Maren had summoned the energy to walk to the beach, where she saw Maude putting two black Labs through their paces. Maude would throw a ball into the ocean, and the dogs would sit stock-still, sleek bodies buzzing with anticipation. When she finally gave the command, they were off like a shot into the water.

"Do you believe that?" Maren asked.

"Demarest women need to be strong. Elizabeth Demarest was wonderful. We all adored her, and she stood up to Jerome."

Maren nodded, remembering the photograph of Elizabeth Demarest, her level gaze and the casual confidence in her posture.

"Pauline is many things, but she's not strong," Georgie continued, her expression hardening. "William's response to weakness is cruelty."

"Has anyone talked to Pauline? If treatment was her idea, couldn't William be convinced?"

"We've talked to her until we're blue in the face. Fruitless. Try it sometime. You'll see."

"What about speaking to Oliver?" Maren said.

Georgie didn't respond for a moment. When she did, she sounded hesitant.

"My mother brought it up with Oliver a few years back."

"Since we were married?" When Georgie nodded, Maren's heart sank. She had put a mental grandfather clause in place. She could accept Oliver not sharing something that occurred before their marriage. It was a terrible sting to discover he had withheld things since.

"Oliver went straight to William, who just kept humiliating Pauline," Georgie continued.

Maren thought for a moment. Oliver had nothing like his father's cruelty, but at a minimum he had been heedless about how William might use the information about his mother. Maren saw a casual negligence in this, which was not entirely unfamiliar.

She had noted it recently, in the effort to replace Maren in Oliver's orthopedic practice. Maren had found a nurse from rural Maryland whose niece had been a fellow cadet at Walter Reed. She was knowledgeable, practical, and dependable. Without even consulting Maren on the matter, Oliver instead chose to hire Khaki Trumbull, one of Bull Trumbull's daughters.

In addition to the nonchalance with which Oliver rejected her candidate, Maren also couldn't help noticing his preference for a nurse from his own milieu over a better-qualified one with a background more like Maren's.

Initially, Maren felt sorry for Khaki. Her parents, Bull and Adelaide Trumbull, had managed to blow through an entire fortune in one generation. Khaki was skinny and flat-chested, with frizzy hair and an unprepossessing manner. She could not easily go the route of Pauline Powell and find a wealthy husband. She had pursued her nursing degree out of sheer necessity.

The time spent training Khaki had drained Maren's sympathy, however. Khaki learned the job well enough, but she hadn't an ingratiating bone in her body.

Maren knew it was not entirely fair, but the episode had contributed to a sense that she had been exiled—first from the practice, and now from D.C. Before she was pregnant, Maren had worked alongside Oliver, so his long hours had not bothered her. She had been unable to relate to the other young wives at the Kennedy Warren, their apartment complex, who one-upped one another with tales of woe about inattentive husbands.

She still struggled to understand why anyone would battle for the title of Most Aggrieved, but she had developed some compassion for the feelings that underscored the competition.

"Tell me about this 'system' of yours," Maren said.

It was nothing formal, Georgie explained. Maude and Georgie had identified a dozen or so women on Haven Point who they knew had Pauline's best interests at heart, and who would make sure gossips did not catch on.

"We don't want someone like Harriet knowing what's up with Pauline," Georgie said.

That's for sure, Maren thought. She had not forgotten her previous interaction with Harriet. The following year, Harriet's older brother had invited some friends from college to a house party on Haven Point, James Barrows among them. James was so bewitched by the place, he proposed to Harriet before the week was out. From all accounts, it was a miserable union and had done nothing to improve Harriet's disposition.

"Originally we tried to make it harder for Pauline to

find alcohol," Georgie said. "One night, Pauline had run through the stash she had hidden and tried to drive William's car to the liquor store in Phippsburg. She ended up in a ditch."

"I'm not surprised," Maren said. Pauline disliked driving, and didn't even have a license.

"It took a big conspiracy to keep that quiet," Georgie said. "Sad to say, Pauline might drink herself to death. I'm not sure we can stop that. But if we can help it, she won't die in an accident, and we can try to minimize her humiliation. That's all we can do—keep her safe, get her home. That, and keep it all among the women. The men are too loyal to William."

"Cappy wouldn't tell, would he?"

"No. He doesn't like William Demarest. But if I tell Cappy, the others will tell their husbands, and it will all unravel. Plus, it would eat at Cappy. He'd want to fix it."

Maren was surprised. Georgie and Cappy seemed the sort of good-friends-turned-married-couple who share everything. The enterprise around Pauline seemed to create a strange gender schism on Haven Point, or perhaps exacerbated one already there. She was hardly one to judge, though, given how much her own husband had obviously kept from her, and what she was all but agreeing to keep from him.

"Well." Maren lifted her chin. "She's my mother-in-law, and I'm here now. I would appreciate people calling me from now on. I should be the one to see her home."

"In your condition?" Georgie looked at her skeptically.

"I'm not an invalid," Maren sniffed.

"All right, fine," Georgie said. She looked at Maren appraisingly. "My mother likes you, you know."

"That's nice to know. I like her, too," Maren replied, wondering what Georgie was getting at.

"She worried at first you were too pretty."

"What?" Maren was unable to mask her annoyance.

"Oh, don't get angry, Maren," Georgie said with sigh. "Remember, she's spent decades watching the wreckage from the last time a Demarest man married a beautiful woman. She knows now you're not Pauline. We all do."

"Nor is Oliver his father," Maren added, still riled. "He doesn't exactly fit your description of the Demarest man."

"No, Daniel was much more his father's son. Oliver is not pure Demarest," Georgie said.

Maren noticed Georgie's emphasis on the word "pure," and the strange ambiguity it left hanging in the air.

Georgie made good on her promise. Five nights later, the phone rang after midnight. Maren swam from a deep sleep and struggled to the landing to pick up the phone.

"Maren?" It was a woman, whispering.

"Yes, this is Maren."

"It's Lillian Belmont. I just came downstairs and found Pauline passed out on our front porch. She must have been on her way home from somewhere. She's dead weight. I called Georgie, but she wasn't sure she could get out without waking Cappy. She said to try you."

"I'll come," Maren said, gratified. "Just leave her there."

"Okay. I have to get back to bed or Bill will wake up." She hung up the phone with care.

Maren was impressed. She'd met Lillian Belmont and thought she seemed meek, the type to defer to her husband. It was testament to Maude's influence that Lillian had joined this band of conspirators.

Maren stumbled into a dress, slipped on her tennis shoes, and walked out into the chilly night. With the help of light from the nearly full moon, she made her way to the Belmonts' house on one of the interior roads, near an entrance to the sanctuary.

Pauline lay on her side on a wicker love seat, hands pressed together under her cheek. She looked like a child tuckered out from a long day of play. Maren approached quietly. When she got closer, the smell of liquor dissolved any innocence that the scene evoked.

Maren tried to rouse her, but Pauline wouldn't budge. When she attempted to lift her, Maren understood what Lillian meant by "dead weight." Dismayed, she realized she had not thought this through properly. This was not a job for one very pregnant woman.

She looked around for inspiration and spotted a wheelbarrow next to the detached garage. In the absence of a car, which would be too noisy anyway, it seemed the only answer. Maren tiptoed over, dumped the soil from the wheelbarrow into a flower bed, brushed it out, and wheeled it to the porch.

Her next task was to move Pauline onto the floor, then down the stairs. She grabbed cushions from a matching love seat on the other side of the porch and placed them beneath Pauline, then half dragged, half lifted her off the love seat. From there, it was a small task to drag the makeshift raft to the edge of the porch.

But how to get her down the stairs? Maren groaned. Why on earth had she said she could do this alone? She had finally been entrusted by the group of women responsible for Pauline, and she had set herself up to fail her first test.

Just as tears began to sting, she heard a sound behind her and spun around to find her salvation: Georgie, in a nightgown, gray cardigan sweater, and green rubber boots—bleary-eyed, but approaching with her usual clunking purpose.

"Sorry," Georgie whispered. "I had to wait until Cappy fell back asleep." Georgie's eyes moved from Pauline to the wheelbarrow. "I think I see the plan." She smiled.

"Can you help me lift her in? Even you can't carry her all the way home. Trust me."

Georgie eyed the scene one more time. "Wait a second," she said. She quietly climbed the porch stairs, took a smaller cushion from a porch chair, and put it in the wheelbarrow. Then she grabbed Pauline under her shoulders, while Maren took her feet. Together they carried her down the stairs and placed her in the wheelbarrow, back against the cushion near the handles, legs hanging over the front. Pauline's skirt had ridden up, so Maren pulled it down, sparing her this one indignity.

"I'll come back later and put the cushions away," Georgie said. "Let's get her out of here."

Maren picked up the handles, lifted the wheelbarrow, and began to push as quietly as she could manage. They froze when they heard a noise from the house, and only breathed when it was silent again.

"Probably just Buster," Georgie whispered. "Don't worry. He's the dumbest dog in Maine."

They rolled Pauline to the road and started toward Fourwinds. Maren felt a little thrill at their achievement, but her sense of triumph was short-lived. They were not a hundred yards down the road when she felt a surge of the nausea that accosted her with the slightest exertion. She pushed the wheelbarrow a little faster, hoping to get home before the inevitable.

"Are you okay?" Georgie asked, squinting at her in the moonlight.

Maren felt her mouth begin to sweat, the sure sign she'd reached the point of no return. She put the wheelbarrow down, held up her index finger, covered her mouth with her hand, and scurried behind a hedgerow in front of the Ballantines' house.

She got sick behind a juniper bush and said a silent prayer that rain would wash it away before Dee Ballantine, the most attentive gardener on Haven Point, caught sight of the mess. She returned to the road, wiped her mouth, then lifted her chin and picked up the handles of the wheelbarrow again.

"Fine now. Let's carry on." Maren began pushing Pauline forward, doing her best to stand up straight and regain what remained of her own dignity. After a few steps, she realized Georgie was no longer beside her.

She looked back and saw Georgie crouched in the middle of the road, hand over her mouth. Unable to make out more than her silhouette, Maren wondered if Georgie was sick now, too, or maybe in pain. She lowered the wheelbarrow and went to Georgie's side.

"Are you okay?" Maren asked. Georgie's shoulders were shaking.

Maren soon realized that Georgie, far from suffering, was laughing so hard that tears streamed down her face. Georgie looked up at Maren, a hint of apology in her eyes, but she was not sufficiently chastened to stop laughing.

Soon Maren also began to laugh. Georgie tried to stand, but was too convulsed to achieve a completely upright position. Before long, neither could Maren. They held on to each other, doubled over in the middle of the road. Occasionally they would catch their breath, but one glimpse of Pauline's motionless limbs sprawled in every direction would set them off again.

Eventually they pulled themselves together enough to push the wheelbarrow the final distance to Fourwinds, occasional bursts of laughter emerging as unladylike snorts that made them laugh harder still.

They managed to get Pauline to her room and Maren walked Georgie back to the front porch. Georgie promised to return the wheelbarrow and cushion to the Belmonts' house. She took off without bothering to say good-bye, but Maren didn't mind. Effusion was not Georgie's way.

Somehow, she knew everything had changed now—for the better.

CHAPTER ELEVEN

January 2008
Washington, D.C.

SKYE

Hurry up, will you?" Colette said into the intercom. "It's colder than a cast-iron commode out here."

"Be right down," Skye said. She pulled on her suede boots, locked the door to the apartment, and headed down the elevator. Colette was outside, rubbing her hands together and doing a little dance to try to keep warm.

They race-walked through the snow to Soulas, where they left the frigid air for the cozy warmth. Adriene and a few of her colleagues from the U.S. attorney's office were at the bar, seated at one of the high-top tables.

Skye and Colette reached them just as Adriene's uncle Nico was coming out of the kitchen. Nico plopped a plate on the table then greeted Skye with a kiss on each cheek.

"You're too thin. You eat some of that." Nico nodded at the plate of pan-fried feta before bustling back to the kitchen. Skye laughed. Nico had greeted her the same way since she was fourteen years old.

"Eat! Eat!" Adriene threw up her hands in imitation. "Such a cliché."

"I see you got him to paint over the mural, though," Skye said, nodding toward the warm neutral walls of the restaurant area.

"It was the worst," Adriene explained to Colette. "Pillars, blue domes. Looked like a gift shop in Santorini."

Skye greeted Adriene's colleagues, introduced Colette, then slipped onto the bar stool next to Adriene.

"So, who's this mystery guest?"

"You'll see." Adriene looked Skye up and down, taking in her jeans and green cashmere sweater. She nodded in approval. "Looking good."

Adriene had called that afternoon to tell Skye she had invited someone to join them for drinks.

"Smarten yourself up. I don't want to see you in your uniform," she said.

"It's called a capsule wardrobe. This isn't another setup, is it?"

"It's someone you know," Adriene replied.

Adriene, of course, had come straight from work but still managed to make her conservative suit look like a "sexy prosecutor" Halloween costume.

"So, how's work, girls?" Adriene asked as her cousin Petra delivered glasses of wine to the table.

"Same as always. Mac's crazier than a shot-at rat," Colette said, in her southwest Virginia accent. "We've got this new fund-raising consultant, Jennifer Heubert. She's been prancing around the office in skirts so short you can see her religion."

Adriene shot Skye a look that said *huh?* Skye loathed almost everything about her job, but at least she had Colette. Not only was she the only other sane person in the office of Virginia congressman Randall Vernon, trying to decipher her Southernisms gave Skye and Adriene something to do.

"Now Jennifer's got the congressman's attention, which I'm sure is what she was after," Colette continued. "That Vernon's a hard dog to keep on the porch as it is, and you can bet Shelley Vernon's watching Jennifer close."

"I can't imagine a more vigilant species than the third wife of a billionaire," Adriene said drily.

They had been chatting for a while when Skye noticed Adriene sit up a little straighter.

"And there he is." Adriene smiled and waved in the direction of the door.

Skye had not laid eyes on Ben Barrows since the summer she and Adriene were on Haven Point together, but she would have known him anywhere. Evidently some muscle in her heart also stored the memory, because it fluttered involuntarily.

"Ben? What brought him to town?" Skye asked.

"He *lives* here." Adriene raised her eyebrows.

Ben caught Skye's eye, smiled, and headed in their direction.

"He's clerking for a federal judge. I ran into him at a legal event," Adriene quickly added, before he was in earshot.

Skye rose, and he greeted her with a kiss on the cheek.

"Good to see you, Skye," he said. "I didn't realize you'd moved back from Chicago until Adriene told me today."

"Good to see you, too," Skye said, surprised he even knew she had lived in Chicago.

Petra reappeared and helped Adriene move coats and drag stools from another table, while Skye managed the introductions. Adriene, with customary command, ordered everyone around until Skye found herself at the end of the table next to Ben.

Ben had gotten ridiculously handsome. He had tamed

his wavy brown hair with a shorter cut. His face was more defined than she remembered, but had none of the harsh angularity of his grandmother's. He did not seem particularly aware of the transformation, however. He still had the same easy, unaffected smile she remembered.

They filled each other in on the intervening years. After playing lacrosse at Williams, Ben worked for the mayor of Hartford. He ended up at UVA Law School and had started his clerkship the previous September.

Until the year before, Skye had been on a reasonably steady path, too. After she graduated from Northwestern, she got a job in corporate communications for a Fortune 100 company and eventually became one of the CEO's top speechwriters.

When Ben asked what brought her back to D.C., however, she found herself slipping into her old habit of selective editing.

"Oh, it just felt like time. And political communications is a pretty natural transition from what I'd been doing," Skye said. It was all true, just wildly misleading.

"Is your mom still teaching?"

"She's just selling her own work now," Skye replied, omitting the fact that her mom would not even be doing that had Flora not found galleries and online retailers to market giclée prints of her mom's old bird paintings. Anne hadn't worked on anything original in more than a year. When Skye moved home, she discovered she wasn't even depositing checks from what she did sell.

Fortunately, before Ben could ask more questions in that vein, Colette interrupted from the other end of the table.

"Skye, these guys don't believe me about Mac and the height discrimination. Tell them."

"So blatant. Every time our chief of staff fires someone, which is about once a week, he brings in one of his henchmen as a replacement. They're all shorter than him."

"Mind you, Mac McCarthy's about five foot six," Colette added.

"Line them all up, they look like little henchmen nesting dolls," Skye said. Ben laughed, and she felt a familiar thrill at the sound.

"Wait, though. How have you survived?" Ben asked. "You must have at least four inches on the guy."

"She'd be out, too, if she didn't look like such a Girl Scout. I mean, seriously." Colette gestured in Skye's direction with an upturned hand. Ben leaned back and squinted, pretending to examine her critically.

"I see what you mean. Green eyes, freckles, cute nose. Not very intimidating."

Cute nose? Skye decided she'd take it.

"Ha! Little does he know, Skye's mom wouldn't let her join Girl Scouts," Adriene said.

Ben looked at her with a question in his eye.

"Oh, you know, because of the fascism," Skye said with a casual wave of her hand, as if the despotic nature of the Girl Scouts was common knowledge.

"Oh, yes, of course," Ben said. Another laugh, another thrill.

Petra delivered more drinks, and Adriene and her colleagues entertained them with stories from the U.S. attorney's office. Adriene, who had decided she was not nearly nice enough to be a psychologist, had found that prosecuting drug crimes was a good outlet for her fascination with human behavior.

To Skye's relief, she and Ben steered clear of the subject of Haven Point. She didn't want him to ask the "Have you seen anyone from . . . ?" question. Skye had visited Gran on Haven Point a few times over the years—when work brought her to New England, and once after attending a wedding in Camden, but that was about it.

The only person remotely connected to that world with whom she'd had any contact was Ryan Donnelly, whose family owned the property just beyond Haven Point Beach.

Skye had met Ryan at a hearing on Capitol Hill. He worked for a congressman from Long Island, where she knew the Donnellys lived, and he had the Donnelly look—the jet-black hair and blue eyes. And while he didn't have his grandfather's build (amid the lean patrician men of Haven Point, Finn Donnelly stood out like a buffalo in a herd of deer), he definitely had the swagger.

"Are you related to the Donnellys who have a house on Haven Point in Maine?" Skye found herself asking.

"Well, not *on* Haven Point." Ryan had laughed in response. "That place never quite knew what to do with my grandfather, so we never got past the gates."

"My grandmother has a house there, but I never got more than a baby toe in either," Skye commiserated. They often joked about it when they ran into each other. Ryan was a social gadfly and a bit over the top, but he was amusing.

It was a work night, so the evening wrapped up early, but before they said good-bye, Ben asked for her cell number and said he'd love to get together.

"He's still into you!" Adriene said, excited, as they trudged home through the snow to Adriene's apartment.

"I'm not sure about that."

"You're crazy as a Betsy bug," Adriene said, using one of her favorite Colette-isms.

To Skye's surprise, Ben called her at work the very next day.

"I remember you were a hockey player. Still have your skates?" he asked.

"I've only worn them a few times since high school, but yeah, I still have them."

"The canal is frozen for the first time in years. What do you think?"

"Sounds great," Skye said. Her heart signaled agreement, fluttering as it had when she saw him the night before.

After she and Ben made arrangements, Skye called Adriene.

"Told you he's into you!"

"We're going skating, Adriene. That's like a friend thing. He's probably lonely. He doesn't know that many people in D.C."

"Skye, you kill me." Adriene laughed. "Yeah, he's *soooo* lonely. Well, I'm glad you're doing the poor lonely boy a favor and going out with him."

Though Adriene had been right about Ben calling (and quickly, Skye noticed) she was less certain he was "into" her. She also found the whole idea of resurrecting some old summer fling vaguely ridiculous, like the plot of a cute Hallmark movie. Skye's life was many things, but "cute" wasn't one of them.

Still, as the weekend got closer, she found herself eagerly anticipating seeing him again.

Her skates were at her mom's, so Friday after work, she picked up groceries and headed over there. She found Anne in the living room, wearing leggings and a tattered Fleetwood Mac T-shirt. The television was on, but Skye could tell she wasn't paying attention. Her mom had never really watched TV.

"Hi, Mom."

"Hi, hon." Anne looked up at her, managed a closed-mouth smile, and waited.

This was their routine. Her mom would answer any question Skye posed. *Have you seen your sponsor? Your therapist? Have you been eating?* If Skye criticized, she did not defend herself.

She just didn't do much of anything. *This is it,* her attitude suggested. *This is all I have now.* Skye could not have imagined missing her mother's bursts of stubbornness or impulsivity, but she would have given her right arm to see a little fight in her.

Skye put the groceries away and straightened up the kitchen. The house had never been neat, but the mess had a more depressing quality now.

When Skye was young, Anne occasionally tried to clean, but something invariably distracted her before she made any progress. She'd work on a painting, or notice a bird at the feeder and grab her camera, or go outside to talk to their sweet but senile neighbor Mrs. Bradley, who roamed around in a quilted housecoat, picking dandelions.

What Skye had not appreciated back then was that the mess in their home was a living thing, with its own energy. All Skye saw now was lifeless neglect—no works in progress, no signs her mom took an interest in anything.

Skye did a quick check of some old hiding places but didn't find any alcohol. She got her hockey skates from the basement and returned to the living room.

"I'm off, Mom. Do you need anything?"

Her mom gave another half smile and shook her head, a hint of apology in her eyes.

Skye left, almost wishing she had found some bottles. It would force them past the inertia, at least.

* * *

The previous March, Gran had called Skye in Chicago to say that her mom had been found at one o'clock in the morning, passed out on a bench in Meridian Hill Park.

"How did she end up there in the middle of the night?" Skye had asked. Her mom loved Meridian Hill Park, which had been a gathering place for civil rights activists in the 1960s. When Skye was little, Anne sometimes took her there on Sundays to watch the weekly drum circle and wander among the people juggling, meditating, playing soccer, or picnicking.

"I gather she had been at a cocktail bar on U Street," Gran said.

"A bar?" Everything about this was bizarre. Skye's mom was not a barfly. "Who was she with?"

"We're not sure. Flora thinks some new artist friends."

Anne, who never checked the weather, had been duped by one of D.C.'s teaser March days, when spring-like daytime temperatures plummet to freezing at night. She evidently wandered out of the bar and ended up in the park. Fortunately, a good Samaritan found her and called 911. She was admitted to the hospital and treated for exposure.

Gran, who was still listed as her emergency contact, had gotten her out of the hospital and into another rehab facility. She was there for six weeks.

She was supposedly sober when she got out, but otherwise seemed no better for the ordeal. Skye grew increasingly alarmed by the persistent gray listlessness she heard in her mother's voice, but when she started talking about moving home, Gran tried to discourage her.

"You have your life, Skye. I think you should live it."

It was when her mom did not return to work after her leave of absence expired that Skye's already amped-up anxiety went into the stratosphere. She gave notice at work, packed up her apartment, and arranged to move into Adriene's apartment in D.C.'s Penn Quarter. (Adriene was delighted to have a roommate her own age, after having a series of younger cousins foisted upon her.)

Skye abandoned her normally meticulous career planning and took the first job she could find, on the communications staff in Congressman Vernon's office.

After she moved home, she quickly saw why Gran had tried to dissuade her. Nothing could penetrate her mother's gloom. It was maddening to watch her do nothing to arrest her decline.

So, Skye did the only thing she could: She slipped into her old role as Imposer of Order on Chaos—she put food in the pantry, paid the bills, called the lawn guy to mow the grass.

And through it all, she tried not to let her resentment show.

Skye often ran on the towpath, originally built to accommodate the mules that pulled barges up and down the Chesapeake and Ohio Canal, but she couldn't remember the last time she had skated there. The afternoon was chilly and cloudy, but after she and Ben put on their skates and headed down the canal, she felt invigorated.

Around the first bend, they came across a group of boys who had cleared out a big rectangle to play hockey.

"You look like you could use a couple of players," Ben said to one of them.

Skye raised an eyebrow. The boys could not have been more than fourteen.

"You got sticks?" the kid asked.

"I do. They're in my car."

Skye shot him a questioning look.

"Just happen to have them there," he said.

"I guess you never know when a hockey emergency will arise."

"Well, yeah!" Ben gestured at the game in progress. "Hockey emergency, right here."

Ten minutes later, Skye found herself in a rousing pickup game. She had played right wing in high school, but this was definitely more of a free-for-all. Within ten minutes, they had their coats off; within twenty, their sweaters, too.

Ben was pretty good, though Skye noticed he was setting up his teammates to score. As the only girl, however, Skye felt no need to lower her level of play. She even managed to score a goal on a breakaway.

When it started getting dark, they headed back to Ben's car. She directed him to a casual burger place near Skye and Adriene's apartment where their disheveled appearance would not matter. They chatted about Ben's brothers and about his clerkship, and she told him more about her infamous boss.

"He has that H. L. Mencken quote on his wall, 'Every normal man must be tempted at times to spit upon his hands, hoist the black flag, and begin slitting throats.'"

"And not because he likes pirates?" Ben asked.

"No. It's pretty much his motto. Bit of a bunker mentality in that place. Most days I feel like I've infiltrated a doomsday cult," Skye said in a light tone that belied how much anxiety the job caused her. "A day is a light-year in politics, though, so I'm learning a lot."

After dinner, Ben drove her home. When he pulled up in front of her apartment building, he put the car in Park.

"So, um, Skye . . ." He paused, ran his fingers through his hair, then looked at her. "Are you dating anyone?"

"I am not," she said.

"Good to hear." He smiled.

"And you?"

"I am not." He quirked an eyebrow.

More than once, through all the laughter and easy banter that afternoon, Skye's mind had flashed back to her time with Ben on Haven Point. It was not the specific memories (though some of those had come back, too), but more an echo of how she had felt—that wonderful sense of reprieve, of taking a break from her real life. It had made her aware of a powerful longing she had to push the Pause button again.

She and Ben still felt like make-believe, but there was no denying the reality of the attraction, and this seemed like too good a moment to waste. She looked him directly in the eye, smiled slightly, and let the silence hang between them.

He reached over, took the side of her face in his hand and gently pulled her toward him, matching her gaze, then closed his eyes and kissed her, gentle and undemanding.

She melted into the sensation. It had been so long since anyone had kissed her like that.

Has anyone else ever *kissed me like that?*

She resisted the temptation to invite him upstairs, and he was too much the gentleman to presume, so she said good night.

As she rode the elevator up to her apartment, she shook her head a little, as if to bring herself back to reality. By the time she reached the apartment, where Adriene was waiting up for her, she felt like she had her feet back on the ground.

"So? How was it?" Adriene asked.

"Fun," Skye said, hoping the residual heat she felt in her cheeks did not give her away.

Adriene threw up her hands in exasperation. "Come on. You have to give me more than that."

"Okay, it was really fun," Skye said, unable to repress a smile. "I know it's not going anywhere, but we had a great time."

"Why are you talking yourself out of him already?"

"I'm not talking myself out of him. He's just not my type."

Adriene snorted. "Well, thank God for that. Your type is weird. I swear, it's been a parade of severe personality disorders since college."

"You just want to be able to say you were there when it all began," Skye teased, hoping to steer the conversation away from Adriene's assessment of her love life, which was indisputably accurate.

"No, no, no," she corrected, wagging her index finger. "I want to be able to say, *I orchestrated the entire thing.* Don't forget my sacrifice, making out with that friend of his, Phillip Buckley Brooks Brothers the Fourth, or whatever his name was."

"You were a conniving little somebody back then," Skye acknowledged, laughing.

"What do you mean I *was* a conniving little somebody?" Adriene said indignantly. "I'm still a conniving little somebody."

The following morning, Ben called to see if she'd like to get breakfast at Eastern Market on Capitol Hill. They met in the market building, picked up croissants and coffee, then went outside. It was chilly but sunny, so they sat on a bench, people-watched, and chatted about nothing in particular.

When they got into a good-natured dispute about overtime shootouts in hockey (Skye, ever the lover of certainty, liked that shootouts eliminated tie games, while Ben thought they were just skills competitions), Ben held out a clenched fist.

"I know how we can settle this," he said. "Rock, paper, scissors."

"I thought you didn't like shootouts," Skye teased.

"Only in certain circumstances."

"Things will be interesting in your courtroom someday."

"I will keep the wheels of justice moving," Ben said with a grin.

Afterward, they wandered toward the Capitol Building and sat on the steps of the Supreme Court.

"So, Skye, I don't want to seem weird or stalkerish," Ben said with an awkward little laugh she found endearing, "but I read something you wrote a while back. I thought it was really funny. It was about the McMansion neighborhood."

"Oh, thanks. Yeah, that was a few years ago." She'd written the piece for *The Weather Vain,* an online humor magazine. It was a satirical account of a homeowners' association arguing over applicants for the "neighborhood oddball" they planned to hire to add authenticity to the glossy new development. *I realize the woman with the parrot has a mysterious past, but the old man is grizzled* and *he limps!*

"Where'd you get the idea?" Ben asked.

"A running joke with Adriene. She always ragged on her old neighborhood. She said it was a bunch of huge, no-soul houses, and they had no town characters like we have in the city. I said they should have hired one, and, well . . . you know Adriene. It devolved from there."

Ben laughed. "Well, it was great. Have you written anything recently?"

"Floor speeches and press releases." Skye smiled. "I'll get back to it, though."

Ben didn't seem to be judging her, but the conversation still reminded Skye how much she had lost sight of what she had once wanted.

In college, Skye took every comedy-writing course available to undergrads and wrote for the sketch troupe. For a while after she graduated, she managed to continue creative writing as a sideline. She took the Second City comedy-writing class at night and wrote some pieces like the one Ben mentioned. At work, her diligence, competence (and, she had to admit, instinct to please) were always well rewarded. The flip side, though, was an ever-increasing workload, which eventually left little time for anything else.

She knew she didn't want to be a freelance writer. As the daughter of an artist, she was far too familiar with the chaos of that kind of life. She thought she had found a happy medium as a working writer. But now she wasn't really writing, and she definitely wasn't happy.

Skye remembered that summer on Haven Point, when she and Ben had sat on the cliff, spilling their dreams into the night air as the moon rose over the water. It was hard not to notice that while her life had gone completely sideways, Ben's was right on track.

CHAPTER TWELVE

August 1955
Haven Point

MAREN

Pauline was missing. Again. Maren would gladly have left her to her fate, indeed would have *relished* leaving her to her fate, but the Ladies Auxiliary meeting would start soon. It would not do for every woman on Haven Point to be across the causeway and out of reach if Pauline turned up drunk somewhere.

Maren arrived at the beach club, the last stop on her tour of spots where Pauline (or evidence of her drinking, at least) had been found through the years. The beach cabanas had neither windows nor ceilings, but surfboards stored over the top of the Demarest cabana provided some shelter, and there was space enough to unfold a beach chair. It was as good a place as any for one of Pauline's benders, as evidenced by the empty gin bottles Maren had found there on more than one occasion.

Today, however, the cabana was closed and locked from the outside, the key in its usual spot above the door.

Where is she? Maren thought as she slumped against the wall. What had been a drizzle when she left the house was now a downpour. She was soaking wet, out of ideas, and almost out of time. Georgie and Maude were due to arrive at the house soon to take her and Pauline to the meeting. Maren was certain to face the wrath if she didn't show up.

Harriet had been elected head of the Ladies Auxiliary two years before. It might as well have been a lifetime appointment, like the Supreme Court, since no one dared run against her. She had been insufferably power-drunk since.

At this point, however, blowback from Harriet was the lesser of two evils. If Maren could not find Pauline, she would not go.

The rain lashed at her face as she trudged up the hill from the beach club. When a bolt of lightning lit up the sky just north of Haven Point, she picked up her pace, bending into the wind and dodging the muddy streams where gravel had washed away during this rainy month. When she heard a clicking sound, she realized it was now hailing, too.

What next? she thought miserably. *Locusts?*

Her question was answered by another bolt of lightning that forked treacherously in every direction, followed almost immediately by a deafening thunderclap. Then, closer to earth, came a great cracking sound, as a limb from an enormous red oak crashed to the ground not twenty feet from where she stood.

Maren stopped in her tracks. Her heart pounded unnaturally. What had been cold, wet, and supremely annoying now felt foolish and dangerous. Her mind raced as she looked around at nearby houses, deciding which to approach and how to explain why she was out in this weather in her condition.

She heard the sound of an engine and turned as a sleek black Cadillac Eldorado pulled up beside her. The driver rolled down his window.

"Get in!" he shouted, the only way to be heard over the storm and surf. His tone was peremptory, but Maren appreciated it under the circumstances. She went to the passenger side but hesitated when she opened the door and saw the beautiful leather interior.

"I'm soaked!" she said, dismayed.

"Jesus Christ, of course you're soaked. Get in!"

Maren slid in and slammed the door shut.

"You have to turn around," Maren said. "A huge branch fell up ahead. You can't get by."

He turned around in a clearing next to a detached garage. As they headed down the hill, another bolt of lightning lit up the sky. When they were out from under the tree canopy, he pulled over.

"We'd better stop here until the worst of this passes," he said as he turned off the engine.

"Agreed."

"Finn Donnelly." He extended his right hand to Maren and lifted his brows in inquiry.

"Maren Demarest." She accepted his grip, her hand immediately lost in his much larger one.

She knew who he was, of course. She would have known even if all the chin-wagging about him had not included elaborate descriptions of his flashy car. Virtually every conversation on Haven Point looped back to this infamous man who had rented Bull Trumbull's house for the month of August.

Most of the breathless speculation surrounded where he had made his money, of which, reportedly, he had obscene quantities. Between known entities were shadowy corners, illuminated by people's worst imaginings.

There is some real estate. Lots of it, but terribly downscale, and other businesses, too. Who knows what, exactly?

He's in everything. I think he even has a carpet business!

Carpet!?

That last rumor had given Maren a chuckle. If an alleged *rug merchant* was allowed into the Haven Point Country Club, it would certainly go down as the moment all standards had been abandoned. She had been itching to meet him.

"Thank you for picking me up," she said.

"Couldn't leave a damsel in distress," he replied with a subtle tilt of his head and lift of an eyebrow.

Is he flirting? she wondered. The notion seemed absurd, especially given how cold, wet, and pregnant she was. When she glanced down, however, she realized her midsection was obscured by the folds of her voluminous poncho.

"So, Maren Demarest, what were you out looking for in this weather?"

"How do you know I was looking for something? Maybe I was coming home from a friend's house when the sky opened up." She was surprised at the arch tone she heard in her own voice. *And now I'm flirting back?*

"I know you weren't at a friend's house. I was leaving the point an hour ago and saw you coming out of the yacht club. You were clearly looking around." He smiled, raised an admonitory finger, and added, "Too late to tell me it was a dog, because you would have said so right away."

She looked at him as she considered her answer. Finn was near Oliver's age and almost as tall, but she noted little similarity otherwise. He had broad shoulders, a ruddy complexion, and black hair, graying at the temples—the kind of rough good looks that hinted at hard living. He might be a flirt, but he amused her, and something told her she could trust him with the truth. Or part of it, at least.

"I was looking for my mother-in-law. She tends to, um . . . wander."

His expression immediately changed from idle inquiry to a mix of urgency and bafflement.

"Why didn't you say so?" He faced forward, turned on the car, and put it in gear.

"No, no," Maren said quickly, waving her hands as if to erase the misunderstanding. "We don't need to look for her. She's not senile or anything. That's not the problem."

He turned the engine off again then looked at her, awaiting further explanation.

"Would it be possible, Mr. Donnelly, for me to leave it at that?" Maren sighed. She suddenly felt very tired.

"Fine," he said, after a beat. "If you'll call me Finn."

"All right, Finn. Please call me Maren." Disconcerted by the intensity of his eye contact, she felt herself blush and peered out the windshield.

"We can probably get going, though," she said. "I think it's letting up."

It was still pouring, but the wind had died down enough to see in front of them. He turned the car on and pulled back onto the road.

"So, how do you like the Trumbull house?" she asked as he followed her directions around the point toward Fourwinds.

"Hmmm. How shall I answer that?" He furrowed his brow in a charade of deep thought. "I'll just say it reminds me a bit of my uncle's house in Ireland."

"Oh? Did you like your uncle's house?"

"My uncle's house was so decrepit, when he died, the fire department burned it down for practice."

She laughed. Haven Point had an uneasy relationship with renters. Not all families could readily afford the taxes and upkeep on an old coastal house. Some chose to sell, and rent something smaller. Others held on by renting out their house for part of the summer. The supply of the former was not sufficient to satisfy the demand of the latter, though, so it was necessary to look beyond the community for prospective renters.

Technically, owners could rent to whomever they chose. This caused some angst (*anyone* can come?!), but since access to the amenities—beach, boat launch, and golf and tennis—was limited to club members, there was little reason to be on Haven Point without at least being proposed for membership to the clubs.

Renters, by definition, were aspirants to the community, and Haven Point brooked no fussing. They were expected to be submissive, like dogs showing their bellies. Finbar Donnelly seemed prepared to bare his teeth, if need be.

I can't blame him, she thought as they passed the yacht club. He had paid a pretty penny to rent the Trumbull home, the Trumbulls being in need of as many pretty pennies as they could find. Bull's daughter Khaki still worked as a nurse in Oliver's practice. She was as sour and supercilious to Maren as ever, but Maren felt sorry for her. She had even hired her to watch their kids from time to time, and to housesit when they were away.

Bull had sweetened the pot by putting Finn's name up for membership in the trifecta: the beach club, yacht club, and Haven Point Country Club. Maren wondered if Finn and his wife knew how empty the gesture had been. They had limited access until they were admitted, and they would never be admitted. Harriet, among others, had already declared she would not tolerate this vulgar Catholic family joining the community.

That reality did nothing to stop the anxiety the Donnellys' arrival had occasioned. It was as if their mere presence could remove the proverbial finger from the dyke. Haven Point was suddenly in danger of being flooded with the wrong sort of people. Soon they'd be transformed into Newport or one of those nouveau riche spots in the Catskills—with lavish parties, gambling, and other unwholesome pursuits.

And the men will all drive flashy cars like this one, Maren thought, smiling inwardly, as Finn pulled up in front of Fourwinds.

"So, the mysterious wanderer is your mother-in-law?"

"Yes."

"This house belongs to your husband's family, then?" He leaned forward to look up at Fourwinds, squinting as if mentally assessing its worth.

"Yes, it does," Maren said.

"You didn't come here as a girl?"

"I did not," Maren said, almost laughing.

"Not your kind of summer spot?" He smiled conspiratorially.

Maren wondered at Finn having pegged her as an outsider. Was her ambivalence about Haven Point etched on her forehead?

She loved Fourwinds and the rugged Maine coast, but other than Georgie and Maude (for whom she daily thanked the friendship gods) she had not warmed to the community. She found an enervating sameness to the society. The obsession with the Donnellys highlighted what bored her most—the constant fretting on Haven Point about Haven Point.

Georgie and Maude treated it as an article of faith that there was a legacy worth cherishing there, but at least they didn't feel the need to talk about it all the time.

That said, while she had enjoyed what had been a rather subversive interval with Finn Donnelly, she realized she had probably said too much.

"Oh, it's lovely here, and wonderful for the children," she said, as brightly as she could manage. She opened her car door. "I'd best get inside. Thank you for your help."

"It was a pleasure to meet you, Maren Demarest." He smiled meaningfully. "I hope to see you again soon."

"You, too," she said as she climbed out of the car. She was only a few steps away when she heard his voice again.

"Let me know if I can ever help with your problem," he said. In response to her confused expression he added, "With your mother-in-law, I mean. I'm Irish, after all. An expert."

He smiled a little roguishly. As he drove off, window still open, she heard him sing. "'Well, baby, I'm resigned . . . to having you for life, but no peace of mind . . .'"

What he lacked in talent he made up for in volume. Though his voice was soon swallowed up by the sound of the rain and surf, she knew the rest of the words.

Because gentlemen prefer blondes, but the only blonde that I prefer is you.

Clara Douglas, the wife of the Demarests' caretaker, Gideon, was rinsing blueberries at the sink. Annie galloped around the table while Billy sat quietly, looking at pictures of birds in an old Audubon book. Maren greeted the kids, then joined Clara at the sink.

"That was some fierce weather, Mrs. Demarest. Someone's cat must have been swishing its tail. I was glad to see you get a ride home."

Maren was relieved Clara hadn't noticed who her knight-errant had been.

"Any sign of her?" Clara added under her breath.

Maren shook her head.

"I'm afraid we're not done with the storms. It's getting dark again." Clara nodded her head toward the window. Maren looked out. The sky was a softer gray now, the rain almost invisible, but darker clouds in the distance were heading in their direction.

Their attention was brought back to the room by the sound of a broom hitting the floor, knocked over by Annie in her high-speed perambulation.

"Annie, stop your pranking and capering and sit back down," Clara said, her voice kind but firm. Annie stopped abruptly and climbed onto her chair next to Billy.

Maren smiled in wonder. Georgie's kids, whom Clara also watched, had shown the same mysterious willingness to do her bidding. Maren and Georgie were convinced Clara was some kind of sorceress, given her odd superstitions and magical way with children, but they were not about to complain, since she was using her powers for good.

Annie stood on her chair and began to sing as she leaned over to spin the lazy Susan in the middle of the table.

"Row, row, row your boat, gently down the stream. Merrily, merrily, merrily, merrily, life's a butter dream."

"Life is *but a* dream," Billy corrected without looking up from his book.

"*Butter* dream," she insisted. She stopped playing with the lazy Susan and stared at him, her expression serious. He looked up, but just as he was about to correct her again, she grinned impishly. Annie was as impulsive as her brother was thoughtful, but there was no denying her precocious comic timing. Even Billy had to laugh.

It was a toss-up, whether Annie had been more challenging before or after she was born. With Billy, Maren had traded up from nine months of morning sickness to an easy baby. Nearly six years old now, he was still steady and placid. With Annie, she'd again been sick from the beginning of the pregnancy to the end, but swapped that for monstrous sleep deprivation. Annie, now "two and free quarters," as she put it, had five times Billy's energy and slept about half as much.

"Demarest brains like her dad, Demarest pluck like her uncle" was the consensus on Haven Point. By this thinking, Maren observed, she herself was merely a vessel to deliver Demarest intelligence and high spirits to a new generation. It might have annoyed her had she not recognized what a good insurance policy it would provide. People would be more forgiving of Annie's mischief, of which she was certain there would be plenty, if it was deemed a Demarest trait.

Maren left the children in Clara's capable hands and called Georgie to let her know Pauline was missing again and she would not go to the meeting. Georgie promised to check in on their way back.

Maren had never questioned the wisdom of joining Pauline's band of protectors. The "system" wasn't perfect. People certainly saw Pauline in her cups from time to time, but they managed to keep such instances to a minimum. As Georgie had said, the occasional drunken incident didn't cause much chatter.

William helped by assiduously avoiding his wife. He traveled, attended parties, sailed, and played cards, golf, and tennis, all without Pauline. On the few occasions Pauline slipped the leash and William saw her drunk, the contempt with which he treated her strengthened Maren's resolve to keep it hidden from him.

She had begun to think, however, that she should at least try to talk to Pauline about her drinking. Everyone claimed it was useless, but Pauline had been finding new ways to get in trouble. In July, fellow caretakers told Gideon someone had been breaking into unoccupied houses. The intruders didn't leave much of a trace, other than the odd gin bottle. Figuring it was teenagers sowing oats, they hadn't told the owners. But Gideon told Clara, and Clara told Maren.

"Showing up drunk at a party's one thing, Ms. Demarest. Breaking and entering's a whole 'nother."

It's time to give it a try. Maren resolved to finally confront her.

Of course, she'd have to find her first.

The next round of thunderstorms rolled in soon after Clara and Maren got the children to bed. Gideon called to let them know he would not be able to pick up Clara, because a tree had fallen in the road just past the country club. Even in the unlikely event they cleared it, the causeway would likely be flooded by high tide.

"You're welcome to stay here, Clara," Maren said, "but I know you keep things in the Grahams' guest cottage."

"I don't mind stayin', Ms. Demarest. I know how it is when Pauline's out getting a snoot-full, and you oughtn't wait up in your condition."

"I promise I won't wait up. Pauline is on her own tonight."

By the time Maude and Georgie pulled up in their old LaSalle, it was raining biblically.

"Still missing," Maren told them.

"I bet she's holed up somewhere," Maude said, her

raspy voice strangely soothing. "She doesn't much like the outdoors, even on the best of days."

"I'm sure you're right." Maren had also comforted herself with the thought that Pauline had found shelter. And after a very wet afternoon hunting for her, Maren didn't much care who found her. "How was the meeting?"

"If that tree had fallen a little farther south, we'd have had a slumber party," Maude said. Maren cringed at the thought.

"Harriet asked where you were," Georgie said, shooting her a rueful look.

Maren sighed. Harriet was as miserable as ever. The shambles of her marriage hadn't helped. She and her husband lived almost entirely apart.

"Marry the woman, and not the house," James Barrows warned anyone who would listen. "And if you must marry the house, marry the permanent residence. Three months of a summer home will not get you through the rest of the wretched year."

She was particularly nasty to Maren. Harriet already resented her (probably for withholding the reverence to which she felt entitled) but it had been compounded by the fact that Annie often upstaged Harriet's daughter Polly.

Life to Harriet was a zero-sum game. Someone else's child was permitted talents or good qualities, as long as she was certain her own children had them in greater abundance. But when it came to pure charisma, there was no competition. No one had more charisma than Annie.

"We're going to head back. You coming, Clara?" Georgie asked.

"Do go, Clara. I'll be fine," Maren said. She urged Clara out the door, reiterating her promise not to wait up for Pauline.

As she got ready for bed, Maren began to worry again, but she knew Maude was probably right. Pauline was not much for the outdoors. In all likelihood, she had made herself at home in an unoccupied house. She finally fell into a restless slumber.

At two o'clock in the morning, Maren tried to convince herself that the loud, slurring voice belting out "Singing in the Rain" was a dream, rather than Pauline coming up the porch stairs, literally singing in the rain. She was about to turn and put a pillow over her head to block out the noise when she was roused by a recollection.

Oh Lord. She's at the front door. Maren had closed it tightly before she went to bed. Warped and swollen like everything in the house, it was tricky to open, no job for a drunken Pauline.

If she wakes Annie, I will murder her, Maren thought as she raced downstairs. Maren took the knob in both hands and simultaneously lifted, turned, and pulled, the only sure way to get it to budge. As fate would have it, she wrenched the door open at the exact moment a very wet and surprised Pauline was trying to turn the knob on the other side.

Pauline stumbled, and her hands flailed as she sought something to grasp onto. All she could find was Maren's nightgown. Pauline seized a fistful of it before dropping to her knees. Maren stumbled, too, but she tightened her grip on the doorknob and kept herself from falling.

She would have remained upright, but Pauline listed and her shoulder hit the door, causing it to swing farther open. Maren's feet slid out from under her, and she landed hard on the floor. A pain shot through her hip, so sharp it took her breath away.

She lay motionless for a moment, waiting for a wave of nausea to pass, then pushed herself up—first on her elbow, then gingerly to a sitting position. She carefully moved her legs. The pain was intense, and she knew she'd have a great bruise. To her relief, however, her limbs seemed to be working as they should.

I am definitely talking to her tomorrow, Maren thought.

Despite her annoyance, she almost laughed when she looked up and saw Pauline still on her knees in the doorway, hands pressed against the doorjamb, trying to pull herself up. She looked confused, unable to compute why she could not rise. Evidently she did not realize the screen door had shut on her bottom, immobilizing her lower legs beneath it.

Maren stood carefully, took two painful steps toward Pauline, and held the screen door open with her foot as she helped the dripping woman to her feet.

"What am I going to do with you, Pauline?" Maren said. Pauline mumbled something in response. Maren put her arm around the tiny shoulders.

At least Annie didn't wake up, Maren thought, relieved, as she guided Pauline up the stairs. She was so eager to get back to bed, she could practically taste the sleep.

They were halfway up when Maren felt the dampness between her legs.

She stopped and looked down. A spasm of fear clutched at her heart as she saw a slow, steady trickle of fluid down her leg. She stood up straighter, and the trickle came faster.

Oh no. Oh God, no. Her water had broken.

CHAPTER THIRTEEN

Maren let go of Pauline, who teetered a little on the staircase. Maren cursed under her breath, helped Pauline back down the stairs, and pointed to the wooden chair by the hall table.

"Sit!" she commanded. Pauline stumbled toward the chair and sat down.

Maren tried to stay calm. Did she have time to wait for an ambulance? Billy and Annie had come quickly once her water broke, but in both cases, she had already been in labor. If it was the fall that caused her water to break, maybe labor would be slower. She was not due for five more weeks.

There were no doctors on Haven Point at the moment, so an ambulance seemed the only hope. She hobbled to the hall table, picked up the handset of the old candlestick phone, and put it to her ear.

Nothing.

She pressed and released the brass switch hook. Still nothing. She tried a few more times, growing more frantic with each attempt, but she could not hear even a hint of static. She grabbed hold of the edge of the hall table and closed her eyes. It was the storm. The phones went out constantly. They were lucky to still have electricity.

She tried to think of the best way to get to Phippsburg.

Georgie. She could take her in the LaSalle. That was even better than an ambulance, because they wouldn't have to wait for it to arrive.

But then, with a groan, she remembered the fallen tree. And even if it had been cleared, the causeway was almost certainly flooded. An ambulance could not have gotten in, and the LaSalle could not get her out.

A powerful contraction took hold. It started deep inside, and grew stronger until it felt as if someone had grabbed hold of a vital organ and twisted it mercilessly.

Damn.

Maren looked at Pauline, who was mumbling something, her eyes closed.

Why? Why can I not have a competent mother-in-law, someone resourceful and helpful?

And then it hit her.

Clara. Competent, resourceful, helpful Clara was from Androscoggin County in rural Maine, where women had babies at home, not under twilight sleep in tidy hospitals. Clara was not a midwife, but she had assisted in many births, including several of her grandchildren's. And she was just a little way down the road, at Georgie's.

All that was left was to fetch her. Maren knew she couldn't, shouldn't go. Pauline seemed scarcely more capable, but it was her or Billy, and she did not want to wake Billy.

"Pauline!" she barked. Pauline's head lolled, and she half opened one eye.

"My water broke," Maren said sharply. "I am going to have this baby. You have to go to Maude's and get Clara."

"Oh, I can't," Pauline slurred, waving her hand, as if Maren had asked her to do something trivial, something optional. "I have to go to bed."

Maren's pain and fear and helplessness all faded into the background, overtaken by white-hot fury. This woman, this feckless drunk, the author of this catastrophe, had to *go to bed*? If Pauline Demarest could form a sentence, if she could cheerfully sing a show tune while walking home from wherever she had been drinking, she could damn well get to Maude's house.

Maren leaned forward until her face was just a few inches from Pauline's.

"Get out of that chair and get over to Maude's house. NOW!" Maren snarled. She barely resisted the temptation to smack Pauline across the face, like Scarlett O'Hara slapped Prissy the maid.

Pauline looked fearful, but she rose unsteadily. Allowing no time for a change of heart, Maren helped her up and into a rain slicker, grabbed a flashlight from the hall closet, then took Pauline's face between her hands.

"Listen to me. Go to Maude's. Bang on the door. Tell her the baby is coming. I need Clara."

Pauline nodded, but Maren worried she was merely placating her.

"What did I say, Pauline?" Maren heard the edge in her own voice.

"Maude, the baby, Clara," Pauline slurred.

Maren practically pushed her out the door and watched her stumble across the yard. Once she determined Pauline was lurching in roughly the right direction, Maren hobbled upstairs to her room. Just as she got on top of her covers, she felt another contraction.

Please make it. Please make it. Maren didn't care if a tree branch fell on Pauline's head and killed her, just as long as it fell *after* she'd fetched Clara.

She tried to breathe and think reassuring thoughts.

My body will know what to do. . . . The baby is not so

*very premature. . . . Billy and Annie were big babies, so
this one won't be so small. . . .*

A memory of Oliver at her bedside at Billy's and Annie's births floated into her mind. She could almost feel his hand as it brushed the hair from her face, the love and tender concern in his eyes. Her need for him was almost a physical being, his absence a presence, like the phantom limbs of the amputees at Walter Reed. Tears spilled down her cheeks.

It took little time for her to realize her hope for a longer labor had been a vain one. The contractions grew closer together and the pain more intense, until she began to lose track of time and place. It felt as if the world collapsed in on itself until there was her, this bed, and this baby. A baby, who, by hook or by crook, would soon come into the world. Had it been ten minutes since Pauline left? An hour? Two?

She wasn't sure, but soon the contractions were right on top of each other, almost no respite between. Then came the pressure low in her pelvis and an entirely new pain, as if her hips were being torn apart. And then the urge, the overwhelming urge, to push.

Some instinct told her to resist. *They will come. They must come.* She breathed, but it came out as a whimper. The urge grew stronger until she felt she had no choice but to relent. She bore down.

Pauline didn't get there. They don't know.

Through the fog, Maren realized it had been folly to send her. She should have gotten Billy up and had him get Clara. Now it was too late. She was going to have this baby alone. She was so tired she could not imagine how, but she had no choice. She took a breath, trying to summon strength from somewhere deep within.

Just as she prepared to push again, she thought she

heard something. She froze and listened. It was unmistakable now. Voices, women's voices. Her head fell back against the pillow as she reveled in the miraculous sound of Clara, Maude, and Georgie coming up the stairs. The bedroom door opened. Maren looked up and smiled weakly, then let her mind go blank as she relinquished the need to think.

The next twenty minutes were a blur. She could hear Clara's voice, her comforting tone of authority. *Warm water, towels, clean scissors, syringe . . . Don't push yet, dear. . . .*

Then pain, pressure.

All right, now push . . . wait . . . all right, dear, push again. . . .

A swirl of pain, more pressure and burning . . . *One more push . . .*

And then, *It's a boy, Mrs. Demarest. It's a boy.*

Maren let her head sink into the pillow and breathed deeply. She was still in pain, but nothing like before.

A boy. Charles, after Maren's own father. She and Oliver had agreed.

She luxuriated in the silence, until the foggy peace was pierced by a terrible realization. It should not be so quiet. *My baby hasn't cried. Why hasn't my baby cried?*

"What's wrong?" No one answered, so she screamed louder. "Where's my baby?"

She forced her eyes open and saw four silhouettes: Clara in the armchair by the window, Maren's silent son facedown across her legs, Maude and Georgie bent over her. Clara's entire arm was moving back and forth, as if she were scrubbing a pan.

Maren heard a sound, one plaintive word. *"Nooooo!"* She knew somehow it had come from her own throat.

Three heads turned in her direction, but just as Maren

prepared herself to see sorrow and horror on their faces, she heard a loud and lusty wail, and then a great cheer from Georgie and Maude. Weeping, Maren held out her arms to welcome her son.

The next day, Georgie filled in the blank spots from the night before. Pauline had managed to rouse her and Maude and explain the circumstances, albeit somewhat incoherently. They put Pauline to bed in a spare room, fetched Clara, and came straight to Fourwinds. At some point in the morning Pauline had stumbled home and gone directly to her own bed.

That afternoon the phones were still down, but the roads were clear, so Gideon would fetch the doctor in Phippsburg. Maren was awaiting their arrival when Pauline entered her room. She smiled at Maren, not a hint of self-consciousness on her face, and leaned over the bassinet.

"Oh, aren't you a pretty boy!" She reached in and tickled the baby's chin.

"Pauline, can I talk to you?" Maren asked.

"Of course," Pauline said, still gazing adoringly at her new grandchild.

"You need help, Pauline." Maren's voice had a hard edge.

"With what?" Pauline looked up now, uncomprehending.

"Pauline, can we *please* stop pretending? You came in drunk last night. You pulled me down as I was opening the door. I fell and my water broke. That's why Charlie was born early. *You're* why Charlie was born early."

"I don't remember that," she said, skeptical.

"You had been drinking, Pauline. Do you remember that much?"

"Well, everyone drinks on Haven Point," she said innocently.

"That wasn't my question," Maren said, beginning to feel insane. "My point is, you drink too much."

"Well, it's just the way it is. I take the first drink and the next ones take themselves." She spoke nonchalantly.

Maren tried to come at it from a few more angles, until she finally realized she was on a verbal merry-go-round, and the only way off was a change of subject. She finally understood what Georgie and the others meant when they said talking to Pauline went nowhere. There was no helping her.

As she watched Pauline coo at the baby, however, a strange thing happened. To her astonishment, rather than anger, Maren felt a surge of tenderness.

For all her flaws, all her terrible glaring weaknesses, Pauline had one redeeming quality, one Maren realized she honored above all: pure and unadulterated love for her grandchildren.

William picked and found fault. Billy was too bookish, Annie too wild. But Pauline was thrilled whenever the children entered the room, even if it had only been fifteen minutes since she'd last seen them. The kids felt it. They adored "Nonnie," as they called her.

In that moment, Maren decided anyone who loved her children as much as Pauline loved Billy, Annie, and now Charlie, deserved a measure of her devotion.

And, for what it was worth, at least Pauline was standing here in this room. Oliver didn't yet know he had another son.

CHAPTER FOURTEEN

February 2008
Washington, D.C.

SKYE

You have got to get a new job, Skye." Adriene was perched on the vanity stool in the bathroom, painting her nails, while Skye got ready. Skye had just returned from a two-day trip into the congressional district. The entire time, she had felt the chief of staff's eyes on her, scanning for signs of disloyalty.

"You shouldn't have to put up with this," Adriene continued.

"I know." Skye sighed. She wished she could be more like Adriene, who was impervious to the moods and judgments of people around her. Skye was too porous, too vulnerable to toxicity. In other jobs, she had placated angry bosses or colleagues by meeting, or exceeding, even the most unreasonable expectations, but Mac McCarthy cared little about performance. The most worthless true believer was valued far more than Skye, who was highly capable, but unable to fake worshipful devotion to a congressman she did not respect, or a siege mentality she found baffling and ridiculous.

"You look great," Adriene said, looking up from her nails to check on Skye's progress.

"Good thing I've pared down the routine," Skye replied. "He'll be here in like three minutes."

Years earlier, at Adriene's urging, Skye had given up on foundation and powder.

"I'm telling you, the Celtic ginger look is in," Adriene had insisted, pointing to a Benetton ad, featuring a Scottish model with Skye's auburn hair, pale skin, and light freckles. Skye was down to blush, eye makeup, and tinted gloss on her full lips. In the cold, dry air it took only a few minutes to coax her hair into subtle waves past her shoulders. She finished just as Ben buzzed from downstairs.

They had dinner at a restaurant in upper Georgetown, then wandered around the historic neighborhood. Like many Washingtonians, Skye tended to avoid Georgetown, especially on weekends. She had forgotten how pretty it was at night. As they walked along M Street, the sound of people singing along to a piano emanated from one of the bars. Ben looked at Skye and smiled.

"Shall we?"

"I can't sing, but sure," Skye replied.

"Me neither, but sounds like it won't matter much," Ben replied as he led her inside. They got beers at the bar and joined the crowd of drunken patrons, singing along (badly) to "Sweet Caroline," "Piano Man," and "Brown-Eyed Girl."

When they left an hour later, Skye was not exactly drunk, but she felt pleasantly buzzed, having exceeded her normal two-drink limit.

As Ben lifted his arm to hail a cab, he looked over his shoulder at Skye.

"Any chance I could talk you into coming over?" he asked casually.

"Sure," Skye replied, before she could stop herself.

"Thirteenth and Q, please," Ben said as they climbed in. Ben and Skye shared an affection for the quirky, often overeducated cabdrivers in D.C. On their way to dinner, they'd gotten a passionate lecture about bottleneck dolphins from a student pursuing a Ph.D. in biology at Georgetown University.

The driver that picked them up now was older and taciturn. In response to Ben's friendly questioning, they learned he was from Baltimore ("Bawler, Merlin," as he pronounced it), but not much more. Ben smiled at Skye and shrugged, as if to say, *Can't win them all.*

When they arrived, the driver leaned over his steering wheel and looked up at the little town house Ben shared with a fellow clerk. "This where you live?" he asked.

"Yep," Ben said as he pulled bills from his wallet.

"Bit close to the pentagram for my taste," he said, shaking his head.

"Pardon me?" Ben asked.

"The pentagram," the driver said, as if this should be obvious. "You know the Illuminati designed Washington, don't you?"

"I did not know that," Ben said, now smiling triumphantly at Skye. "Tell me more."

The driver outlined the elaborate conspiracy theory about the Freemasons who had incorporated occult symbols into the original plan for the capital.

"Just look at a map. You'll see it. Pentagram, right there in the middle, pointing at the White House," the driver said. He nodded his head southward. "Logan Circle over there? That's one of the tips."

"Good to know," Ben said. He handed over the bills. "Thanks."

As soon as the cab left, Ben and Skye burst out laughing, and kept laughing as he led her up the walk and into the house. When they got inside, Ben leaned against the inside of the front door and turned Skye to face him. The laughter was gone, replaced by a look of searching intensity. Skye felt a quiver of excitement.

He pulled her closer and kissed her. Skye loved how she felt in his arms, how his strength was tempered by his youthful air, his well-bred charm. She loved that he never preened.

He pulled back and smiled gently.

"Will you come to my room?" he asked; no expectation, no pressure. She nodded.

What followed was sweet and gentle and passionate, a combination Skye had never experienced or even known to hope for. Ben's face had a way of lighting up, of looking as if he was constantly discovering something fresh and appealing about her. She always felt like she was escaping when she was with him, but especially so that night.

The following morning, when Skye woke up, she turned to look at Ben. He was still asleep, his wavy hair tousled, his expression peaceful and untroubled.

Ben's eyes opened slowly, as if he'd sensed her looking at him. He turned to her, smiled lazily, then pulled her toward him.

"Come here. I'm worried you're too close to the pentagram," he said. Skye laughed, then obliged him by nestling into the crook of his arm. As his eyes closed again, he said, "You're really something, Skye."

Skye appreciated the sentiment, even as she worried that she might not be the "something" he thought.

The following week, Skye and Mac were to accompany the congressman to the district, where he was making a speech to local business leaders. When the driver pulled up, Skye was dismayed to see Jennifer Heubert already seated in the Escalade.

Skye climbed into the cramped third row, as befitted her lowly station. Mac sat in the passenger seat next to the driver, while the congressman sat next to Jennifer in the middle row.

The affair was common knowledge among the Vernon staff, but Skye assumed the congressman and Jennifer were at least trying to be discreet. As they made their way to the district, she discovered that was not at all the case. They flirted and touched each other ostentatiously, not a hint of concern that Skye was sitting directly behind them.

When they arrived at the event, the congressman and Jennifer walked ahead, arm in arm.

"We've got to do something about this," Mac said, steaming.

"Agreed," Skye said. She had long thought Randall Vernon was an arrogant spoiled billionaire, but she was pleasantly surprised that Mac also thought the congressman had crossed a line. She quickly learned she had misread his comment.

"We have to find a way to throw her under the bus," he continued. "She's going to ruin his reelection chances. And if Shelley finds out, God knows what she'll do. That woman can be a real battleax."

Skye felt a surge of fury. *Of course. It's their fault— Jennifer the temptress, Shelley the fishwife.*

"Mmm-hmm," she replied, trying to keep her voice from betraying her.

Mac turned and looked at Skye closely. "Any ideas?" he asked sharply.

"I don't know. Tough one." Skye shrugged, her anger shape-shifting to anxiety. Once again, her attempt to sound earnest had not fooled Mac.

Skye knew she'd been hasty in taking this job, but she had consoled herself with the fact that Congressman Vernon was a businessman. His tentacles reached into so many sectors of the economy, which could help when she finally returned to the private sector. What she hadn't considered until now, when Mac had her in his sights, was that those tentacles could just as easily choke off opportunities as open them.

Meanwhile, Skye's mom showed no sign of emerging from her terrible torpor. Skye still felt resentful. She knew Anne had not forced her to move back home, or to take this disastrous job. It was hard not to notice, though, how much her professional life had unraveled once she got back in her mom's debris field.

And for what?

"I'm just working through some things, Skye" was as much as she would say, with that sad half smile. Skye knew Gran had spent a lot of time with her mom, but Gran was strangely reticent when Skye asked what they could do, how they might help.

The situation with her mother was dark. Work was crazy. She felt like a pinball bouncing between the two. *Dark, crazy, dark, crazy, dark, crazy.*

Ben was light and sane, but Skye still felt like she was presenting him with the highlight reel, leaving so much on the cutting room floor.

They never talked about that summer they dated—if you could even call it that—but from time to time he'd mention Haven Point or talk about visiting a Haven Point friend in Greenwich or Bronxville or Newburyport. When he did, Skye would be forcefully reminded of this key fact about Ben: He was a Haven Pointer in the truest sense—the perfect educational pedigree, traditional family, and childhood of summers that had cemented a sense of belonging and certainty of his place in the world.

Ben seemed to think Haven Point was something they had in common. Skye, however, was beginning to see it as an irreconcilable difference.

One evening, Skye and Ben planned to meet for a quick dinner on Capitol Hill. Congress was debating an economic package to stimulate the economy, and Congressman Vernon was trying to insert some pet project into the legislation. The effort was doomed to fail (and not making him any friends) but Mac insisted the staff work around the clock anyway.

Skye had been doing her best to feign enthusiasm and determination, but that evening, when Mac spotted her leaving for dinner, he raised an eyebrow.

"I hope you won't be gone long, Skye," he said, looking at his watch.

"Back soon!" she replied.

She arrived at the restaurant late. Ben had already grabbed a table. He had changed out of his suit and into khakis and a button-down shirt.

"Sorry. Things are crazy," Skye said as she slid into her seat. She gave him a quick rundown, ending with Mac's comment as she was leaving. Ben rolled his eyes.

"People gotta eat," he said, handing her the bread basket.

"Eat? While the rest of the staff slaves away on this vitally important, totally futile exercise?"

Ben laughed, and they moved on to other subjects, but Skye was unable to shake the tension from work. Ben's relaxed humor and general cheerfulness were usually contagious, but tonight they just highlighted how messed up her life was.

Easy laugh, easy life, she thought, when he chuckled at something she said.

"Listen, some friends of mine are having a party at Thompson's Boathouse next Saturday," Ben said, after they got their entrees. "Can you come? Band, kegs. You're welcome to bring friends."

"Sounds great, thanks," Skye said. She felt a little kick of pleasure at the invitation. She hadn't met many of Ben's friends, so it seemed like a step forward.

"I think a few guys from Haven Point might come down from New York," Ben added.

The pleasure receded, eclipsed again by her doubts.

He assumes I'll be thrilled by this? For some reason this annoyed her, which probably accounted for what she asked him next.

"That reminds me, you know Ryan Donnelly works on the Hill, right? Will he be there?"

She was not sure what Ben thought of Ryan, but it was no secret that his grandmother despised the Donnelly family. Anne had told her as much through the years. Harriet's family owned the last house on Haven Point Beach. When the Donnellys had built their mansion on the other side of the rocks, they had effectively become her next-door neighbors, and she'd never forgiven them.

Ben paused.

"You're friends with Ryan?" he asked finally, his tone colorless.

"Sure. I mean, not great friends, but everyone knows him," Skye said, pretending not to notice his shift in mood.

Here we go, she thought as her irritation was joined by something almost like satisfaction.

"I hadn't asked him, but you're welcome to," Ben replied stiffly.

Skye lifted her chin. "I will, thanks."

After a few moments of silence, Ben's good breeding overrode his petulance and the conversation got back on track, but his response stuck with her throughout dinner and continued to pop into her mind in the days that followed. She knew she might have misread him, but she could not help feeling that he had failed a test she had unconsciously administered.

She had not actually planned to mention the party to Ryan, but when she ran into him a few days later in the cafeteria of one of the House office buildings, she found she couldn't help herself.

"Listen, you might know Ben Barrows is living here," she said, after they had caught up for a few minutes. "His friends are having a party at Thompson's on Saturday night. Do you want to come?"

Ryan looked at her closely. "This is Ben's party?"

"No, some friends of his, but I told him I would invite you."

"What did Ben say?" The usual jocularity was gone from Ryan's tone.

"He said fine."

"Oh. Okay. Well, unfortunately, I'm heading up to New York that night, but thanks for thinking of me."

The coolness in his tone surprised Skye. "Do you have an issue with him, Ryan?"

"Honestly, Skye, I don't have an issue with Ben. But he has one with me," Ryan said with a sigh. "It's the old Hyde-Donnelly thing, I guess. He's just kind of a jackass to me."

Skye walked away, wishing she hadn't said anything. Ryan clearly sensed Ben didn't like him, and she'd only succeeded in reminding him of it. Skye would not have guessed Ryan Donnelly's seemingly boundless confidence could be vulnerable to such petty judgment, but evidently it was.

Skye was too busy to give the issue much thought. Adriene had agreed to go to the party with her, and she figured she could give Ben a chance to explain himself (assuming he *could* explain himself).

In the end, it was all moot, because the night before the party, Skye's world fell apart.

Two unreturned phone calls to Anne hadn't worried her. Even the third could be written off as typical flakiness. But the fourth had set off alarm bells. Skye had left work at the earliest possible moment.

She turned the key to her mother's house, her heart thudding in her chest. She stepped into the hallway and looked around at the usual disarray.

"Mom?" she called.

Nothing.

After checking the basement and around the first floor, she climbed the stairs to her mother's room. She breathed a sigh of relief when she saw the bed unmade, but empty.

She's gone away. She forgot to tell me.

Then she noticed her mother's batik print purse lying open by the closet door, and her heart resumed its hammering. Her mom was not one to change accessories with outfits, but Skye still had some faint hope as she moved toward the purse. When she spotted the keys and wallet inside, she felt a terrible clutching sensation in her chest.

"Mom?" she called, her voice trembling.

Nothing.

She made her way to the far side of the room, where a hall led to the small master bathroom. She felt as if her legs were moving through wet concrete. When she saw the sliver of light coming from under the bathroom door, her knees buckled. She had to extend an arm to brace herself against the wall.

Part of her wanted to run, for someone else to be responsible for whatever was on the other side of the door. Only the tiny chance her mother might be alive and in need of help propelled her to push it open.

For the briefest instant, Skye tried to convince herself that the figure in the tub was not her mother, but a work of her mother's art. The face was too waxen, and the pose—knees up, covering the chest—too modest.

It lasted only until she took in the bluish tint to the skin, the hand draped over the side, as if reaching for the pills that had spilled from their bottle onto the tiles.

"Oh God, Mom. Oh God." Skye stumbled toward the tub and fell hard on her knees. She already knew when she lifted the cold, heavy hand, but she felt for a pulse anyway. Her stomach churned as she half crawled back to the bedroom and picked up the phone.

Swim to the surface, swim to the surface.

She dialed 911 and somehow made the words come out. She returned the phone to its cradle and squeezed her eyes closed as whimpers escaped between shallow breaths. When she picked up the phone again to call Gran, her fingers were so numb, she had to dial three times before she got the number right.

"Gran. I'm at Mom's. Something's . . ."

"Skye? Are you all right?"

"She's . . . the bathtub. I'd called four times. I left work. I came to check . . ."

Skye, who made a living arranging words, could not seem to find any to arrange. It was as if her mind had deconstructed the previous few hours into a series of discrete images but expelled the knowledge of what they added up to.

"The bathtub . . ." she repeated numbly.

"What is it, Skye?" Gran asked quietly.

"She's dead. My mom . . ."

"I'll be right there."

CHAPTER FIFTEEN

August 1960
Haven Point, Maine

MAREN

The screen door slammed violently, Irina's signature manner of announcing her presence. She soon stood before Maren and Dorothy, hands on hips, face flushed.

"This monkey, I cannot stand," she said. In her thick Russian accent, it sounded like "Zees minkey." Dorothy stifled a giggle. The summer's two new additions to the household, Pauline's nurse, Irina, and the pet monkey, Sassafras, hated each other with a passion.

"Yes, I know, Irina. But Sassafras has a room to herself now. Can't you just stay out of there?"

"But Pauline . . . she brings her out!"

"All right, Irina. I'll talk to Pauline." Maren sighed. Irina looked dubious, and slammed the door again as she went back in the house.

"Maren, this is absurd," Dorothy said, pointing at the spot where Irina had just stood. "Why do you put up with Oliver being gone all summer like this? Three kids underfoot, and now all this nonsense?"

Maren and Dorothy, still in knee-length skirts and polo shirts from golf, lounged with iced teas in hand. In what had become an annual tradition, Dorothy had come up from the Hamptons to play in a women's golf tournament. The weather, which would have felt like a miracle in D.C. in August, was tropical by Maine standards. For weeks it had felt like the Maine coast was stuck under a damp, warm blanket.

"Oliver's working a lot this summer."

Dorothy sniffed and waved her hand impatiently, and Maren prepared for one of her trademark diatribes.

"I'm sorry, but he's presently at a medical conference in Manhattan. That's not 'working.' He could get up here easily from there."

"But he's a speaker. It's on arthroscopy, and you know what a pioneer he has been. Also, I refuse to be one of those whiny wives. What do I have to complain about anyway? Look at this place." Maren made a sweeping gesture toward the view.

"If it's not your dread of sounding like a complainer, it's your guilt. So, because this place is beautiful, you have no right to want your husband around more?"

"Maybe a little. But mainly it's that I knew what I was getting into when I married him."

"Ah, so that's it! You knew he was a hard worker when you got married, so you must reap what you've sown. Boy, he's off the hook no matter how you come at it."

"Sort of," Maren said, a little sheepishly.

"Allow me to point out a few facts," Dorothy said. She began ticking off items on her fingers, like a lawyer addressing a jury. "One: When you got married, you didn't know you would have to spend three months a year with his mother. Two: You did not know said mother would be so *thoroughly* pickled. Three: You did not realize you were signing up for a good bit of time with his highly unpleasant father. . . ."

Maren opened her mouth to object, but Dorothy put up her right hand.

"I'm not done! Or, four, that upon William's death,

God rest his miserable soul, he would be replaced with one of the nastiest Russians ever born. And, five—*la pièce de résistance*—that Pauline would then bring that wretched monkey into the little tableau."

Dorothy's long arm was raised now, index finger wagging in the direction of the upstairs room, from which came the nervous, high-pitched shrieks of Sassafras, who was, indeed, a wretched monkey.

"Yes," Maren said with a wry laugh. "Sassy does add a certain flair to the summer, doesn't she?"

"Where on earth did she get that thing?" Dorothy slumped in her seat, as if fatigued by the climax of her closing argument. "Couldn't she have bought some little dog?"

"She saw an ad in the back of one of Billy's comic books. *Squirrel Monkey! America's Most Amusing Pet!*" Maren said, using her best pitchman's voice.

In May of the previous year, William had died of a heart attack. To Maren's thinking, Pauline outliving her husband had to be one of the greatest ironies in Demarest history.

Not a month later, a neighbor found Pauline in a heap at the bottom of the outside stairs of her Boston home. Pauline was not drunk at the time, but alcohol was still the culprit. A doctor at Massachusetts General Hospital informed Maren and Oliver that Pauline had alcoholic neuropathy, a form of nerve damage that weakened her muscles and numbed her extremities.

Maren found the meeting with the doctor both uncomfortable and terribly sad. When the doctor suggested inpatient treatment, Oliver flatly refused.

She and Oliver rarely spoke of his mother's drinking, but she had held out hope he might see things differently after William died. At that moment she realized he had simply taken over as the enforcer of the long-standing Demarest position on Pauline: Her drinking was a weakness, not a disease. Oliver did, at least, agree to the compromise solution: a full-time nurse.

Pauline's choice of Irina over many other qualified candidates might have seemed odd, but Maren thought she understood. After years of submitting to William's subtle (and sometimes not so subtle) abuse, she suspected Pauline actually liked doing battle. A tough-as-nails White Russian, Irina was impervious to Pauline's feistiness. She was certain her time in America would be brief, lasting only until her people finally rose up and reclaimed the homeland. They fought "like Kilkenny cats," as Clara put it, which didn't wear well on the rest of the household.

And then, that spring, Pauline purchased Sassafras. It was hard to believe a creature just a foot tall could bring such chaos to a home, but chaos was Sassafras's particular talent. She was tiny and slender like Pauline, with small hands that looked eerily human. She was a disgraceful slob, and tended to bite when she was nervous, which was almost always. Irina could no longer wear sandals, as Sassy bit her toes at every opportunity.

Initially the children were thrilled—*a monkey*! They soon discovered, in addition to biting, Sassy liked to throw her own droppings. Annie still held Sassy in grudging admiration (any creature who got away with such misbehavior deserved some respect), but overall, the kids had cooled toward her.

"I think you are taking too much on, Maren," Dorothy said.

"Maybe . . ." Maren trailed off. Part of her longed to tell Dorothy that Oliver's usual summer neglect was the least of their problems, but she did not know how to explain what she barely understood herself.

She was spared the need to do so by the appearance of the children, who had been out hunting for sea glass.

"Look! Four reds! And one of them is big!" Annie said, after they clambered onto the porch. She dumped her box of treasure on the wicker coffee table.

"I got some, too!" Charlie put his hand in his pocket, grimacing as he worked to reach the bottom with his chubby fist.

"Here!" He opened his hand to reveal some small pieces, all green, the easiest to find.

Billy opened his mouth, and Maren flinched, certain he was about to school Charlie about how little his sea glass was worth. Billy was not unkind, but he was terribly literal. Charlie had a hair-trigger temper, and he hated being bossed or corrected. Maren was about to step in, but Annie beat her to it.

"That's good, Charlie!" Annie shot Billy a look.

From the time he had made his dramatic entry into the world, Annie had adored Charlie. He was difficult and prickly, but Annie had a miraculous ability to keep him happy. She had his unswerving loyalty in return.

After a few minutes, Billy and Charlie followed the smell of Clara's cookies inside. Annie swept her sea glass back into the cardboard box and then looked up, as if an idea had struck.

"I'm going to the Donnellys," she said. She jumped up and darted down the porch, blond ponytail swinging behind her. Annie never planned. She just *did*.

"The Donnellys?" Dorothy asked, eyebrows raised, as she and Maren rose to get ready for the ladies' golf cocktail party at the country club. "Of gaudy mansion fame?"

"Annie's friendly with their son, Patrick. He's nine, just a year older than her."

"How does Oliver feel about a Donnelly breaching the Demarest ramparts?"

"He hardly knows him." Maren shrugged. "Patrick isn't intimidated by Annie. She needs that."

However great Finn Donnelly's influence, it had not been sufficient to throw the world off its axis. The Donnellys had not been admitted to the Haven Point Country Club. A few people were willing to relent, but Harriet Hyde Barrows was not going to let that happen.

Finn had his revenge, however. A family from Phippsburg owned land on the other side of the rocks at the end of Haven Point Beach. Finn had bought it and built his palace: a sprawling marble house with pillars, cupolas, and an enormous turret on the southeast corner.

"Besides," Maren continued as they walked upstairs, "all the kids go over there now. It's like an amusement park. Trampoline, croquet, a chip and putt course. You name it, they've got it."

"I bet the country club wishes they'd bought that land when they had the chance," Dorothy said.

"It was a terrible lot, rocky and uneven. They never imagined anyone building there. They didn't reckon on a buyer with an entire construction company at his bidding."

"And the desire to stick it to this place for saying he wasn't good enough," Dorothy added.

"Precisely."

From the start, something about the party felt off.

At first Maren thought it was the atmosphere. When they entered, Percy Faith's "A Summer Place" was floating feebly from the old RCA record player. Maren loathed the tune, ubiquitous that summer. The doors facing the bay were open, but the breeze was listless and did little to cool the room. Japanese lanterns cast an odd, mournful light, exacerbating the gloom.

The only thing Dorothy noticed initially was that Bert, the bartender from the Red Lion Inn in Phippsburg, was pouring drinks.

"Oh, thank God. You've got that big fellow serving. Come on, he makes the best Tom Collins."

Maren smiled. Some years earlier, Dorothy had obliged her mother by finally marrying well and becoming a card-carrying member of New York society. Dorothy enjoyed visiting Haven Point. It gave her a respite from unrelenting social demands and extravagant entertaining of East Hampton. She missed the Hamptons' cocktails, however. Bert, she claimed, was the only person within fifty miles of Haven Point who could mix a decent drink.

As they made their way to the makeshift bar, Maren felt eyes on them. At first, she thought Dorothy's gorgeous yellow sheath dress was attracting the attention. It was when they turned to speak to Margeaux Peabody and Dee Ballantine, who had been in their foursome that morning, that Maren realized something was wrong. Both were civil, but Dee's smile seemed unnaturally bright and Margeaux struggled to maintain eye contact.

A short while later, Maren noticed Harriet in the corner. She was talking to Frances Morrell, who had a hand cupped to her ear to better hear whatever gossip Harriet was pouring in it. When Frances realized Maren was looking at her, she quickly pulled her hand down.

This didn't necessarily mean anything, since irritating Maren was one of Harriet's chief and constant ambitions. But as the evening wore on, the strangeness intensified. For every normal interaction, there was a conversation that stopped abruptly when Maren and Dorothy approached. For every friendly face there was an uncomfortable or sheepish one. Taken in isolation, no one incident or inter- action would have registered, but together they added up to something amiss. Maren grew increasingly uneasy. She wished her normal social anchors, Maude and Geor- gie, were there, rather than at a family event in Portland.

The awards ceremony was the final straw. The golf pro approached the podium, and the women gathered. Maren felt as if an invisible buffer had formed around her and Dorothy. Everyone stood just a little bit apart, as if she'd contracted a terrible social disease, and they feared it was contagious.

Maren knew she was not particularly popular on Haven Point, but it had never bothered her. Her friend- ship with Georgie had been enough to satisfy her, and, to some extent, everyone else. While she would never be at the top of anyone's guest list, Georgie's and Maude's esteem acted as a Good Housekeeping Seal of Approval. Tonight, however, she felt a sense of alienation she hadn't experienced since her first visit after she and Oliver were married.

"Let's go," Maren whispered to Dorothy when the golf pro had finished his remarks. Dorothy nodded and they slipped out.

"That was odd," Maren said as they walked along the causeway toward the point, following the bobbing beams of their flashlights. It was dark under the cloudy sky, and the air was still thick.

"Agreed," Dorothy replied. She had been to enough Haven Point events through the years to know there had been something singular about this one.

"What do you think was going on?" Maren asked.

"I don't know." Dorothy was in shadow, but Maren

saw her nose wrinkle, as if she had picked up the scent of something and was trying to place it.

That night, Maren struggled to sleep in her warm room. She woke up in the middle of the night, her mind traveling to the darkest and grimmest places, as it always did during her rare bouts of insomnia. By morning she had only managed to cobble together three or four hours of sleep. When she arose, the air still hung heavy over the point. She wished it would go ahead and storm, so they could get past the terrible stillness. She made coffee and stumbled through the morning, getting the kids fed and out the door to a sailing event.

She and Dorothy were sitting at the kitchen table, drinking coffee and idly talking, when a knock came at the door. On Haven Point, a knock was not a request for permission to enter, but rather a warning one was about to do so. Maude limped into the kitchen, huffing a bit.

Maren greeted her, surprised. She visited Maude often, but not so much the reverse.

"Maren, can I speak with you for a moment?" she asked after the niceties were behind them. She appeared to have a purpose, and not one she was happy about.

"Of course. Please sit down." Maude lowered herself into a kitchen chair.

"I need to get upstairs to pack," Dorothy said. She took her coffee and headed up to her room.

Maren poured coffee for Maude, and watched as she stared into the mug, hands clenched around it as if she was warming them, though she surely wasn't cold.

"Maren, I have something to tell you. It's hard to know how," she said finally.

"What is it?" Maren asked. Somehow, she knew she needn't panic. A death or illness wouldn't elicit such awkwardness.

"Harriet has been spreading a rumor about Oliver."

"About *Oliver*?" She briefly wondered if it was something that denigrated him professionally, but she discarded the idea almost as soon as it struck her. Maren was the enemy, not Oliver. "What sort of rumor, Maude?"

"You've met Harriet's friend Betsy Chase, haven't you? She's up here all the time." Maren nodded. Betsy was one of Harriet's hangers-on from Hartford.

"Betsy called Harriet from New York yesterday. She said she saw Oliver at the Waldorf Hotel. He was getting into an elevator with some woman, and they looked rather, um . . ."

Maren felt a horrible jolt, as if something or someone had yanked her underwater. Maude continued to speak, but Maren couldn't hear her over the swirling rush, the great white noise that filled her ears.

It took an enormous effort, but Maren forced herself to the surface. Maude had been so uncomfortable, coming to deliver this terrible message, and she did not wish to make it harder for her. She grabbed on to that scruple as if it were a life ring and tried to keep her head above water.

"They looked . . . *intimate*?" Maren managed. As her mind emerged from the turmoil, something else was beginning to take hold—humiliation and the seeds of rage.

"Yes," Maude replied, still clutching her mug. She looked as woebegone as Maren had ever seen her. "Of course, I don't know if it is true, or if it means anything, but I thought you should know she was saying it."

Maren took Maude's hand. "I know you don't like being the messenger. Thank you," she said, as warmly as she could manage.

Maude looked up from her mug. Though her expression was still filled with regret, Maren saw some of her customary self-possession reemerge.

"Maren, you know you don't have to tell me anything, and I'm not fishing. But if you don't mind my saying, you don't look surprised."

Maren thought for a moment. The greatest surprise, in fact, was how *possible* it seemed. She should be thinking *Never! It's not true!* But with the initial shock behind her, Maren found she was able to believe the story, even given the source.

"I don't know if I am surprised," she said finally.

Her mind flashed to a street artist in Washington. A performer of sorts, he attracted a crowd when he worked. His paintings appeared abstract until the final brush strokes revealed them to be something recognizable, a famous person or landmark. Maren felt as if an artist were putting the final touches on a painting of her marriage. She'd seen all the brush strokes, but only now was the full picture emerging.

"We don't know that it's true. Harriet would make the worst out of whatever she heard. And Maren"—she looked at her directly—"I know your husband loves you."

It was such an uncharacteristically tender thing for Maude to say. Maren felt a catch at her throat.

"Thank you, Maude," she said.

"I don't want to be thanked for this," she replied. She got up and headed toward the door, shaking her head sadly.

A half hour later when Dorothy entered the kitchen, Maren was still at the table, staring into the middle distance.

"What on earth is going on?" Dorothy asked, sitting in the chair next to her. "You look as if you've seen a ghost."

"Maybe I have, in a way. And now I know why last

night seemed so strange." Maren relayed what Maude had told her.

"I don't believe it," Dorothy said firmly. Though Dorothy had railed against Oliver's neglect the previous day, it was clear this had never entered her mind.

"You know what? I do believe it, Dorothy," Maren replied. "Or maybe I should say I *can* believe it."

"What?" Dorothy's eyes were wide.

"Doro, he's changed so much lately. I don't know how to explain it. I might not have come up with the possibility on my own, but when Maude told me, I just had this sense . . . it rang true."

"Maren, are you sure? It seems so out of the blue. Just yesterday you wouldn't even fault him for spending so little time up here, but now you're willing to believe he's seeing another woman?"

"I know it sounds crazy, but I have been sitting here thinking about it, and it's like puzzle pieces are coming together. I hadn't wanted to face it."

"An *affair*? You can't think he is capable!"

"He's been so distant, especially since William died. I wrote it off as grief, but that never made sense. You know Oliver wasn't close to his father—to either of his parents, for that matter. I kept waiting for him to climb out of this . . . this *thing* . . . but he didn't."

"Climb out of what, exactly?"

"It's hard to describe. I know you think he's never here, but it's not just his absence. He's never been here much. But before, even when he was incredibly busy and overwhelmed with work, when he did finally see me, it was like he was relieved."

Dorothy pulled her chair closer, took Maren's hand, and looked at her questioningly. Sweet and shrewd in equal measures, Dorothy was a gift at this moment. Maren took a breath and tried to summon the words for what had been percolating in her mind.

"I used to feel like I was *home* to Oliver, and he was so glad when he finally *got* home. He was never much for words, but I could always see it, especially in his eyes. The way he would look at me, Doro . . . it was like I was the most important thing in the world, that he couldn't believe his great luck." She blushed at her immodesty. But it was true. Oliver had treated her like his miracle.

"That look made me feel safe. Even through all of the absences. But he hasn't looked at me like that for a long time. I meant what I said earlier. It's not that I need him here all the time. But Septembers were awful. It took longer and longer to get back to normal after summer, until it never did get back to normal. When his father died last year, it felt as if we went off a cliff. Never mind looking at me like I'm so vital to him. It's as if he doesn't see me at all."

"I know other marriages where couples grew apart. That happens all the time. It doesn't have to mean *this*. I just don't think it fits. Oliver cheating? He *worships* you." Now poor Dorothy looked distraught.

"I don't know what to say. Except again, the second Maude told me, it was like a light bulb went on. It would explain a lot, actually."

They were quiet for a moment.

"Well, there's only one thing to do then," Dorothy said finally, a touch of her businesslike demeanor returning. "You need to call Georgie."

"Georgie?"

"Yes. Get her to watch the kids. We should go to New York. He's still there, right?"

"Yes. He's supposed to be there until Tuesday."

"I don't really have to be back in the Hamptons for a couple of days. Let's just go, Maren."

"What's the point?"

"Because if Oliver is there with someone . . ." Dorothy hesitated, not wanting to say it out loud.

"I have a chance of catching him with her?" Maren's stomach turned.

"I believe Oliver loves you more than anything in the world. But in spite of that, or maybe because of it, you know he would lie like a rug if you confronted him."

Dorothy's plan seemed like a reach. Oliver usually stayed at the Waldorf when he was in New York, so that part fit. Still, how likely was it they could catch him with this woman, or some artifact of hers? What if it was a one-night stand? Even if it wasn't, she might not be staying with him at the Waldorf.

Long shot or not, however, Maren felt like the only thing worse than going would be to stay on Haven Point, sitting on her hands. It seemed like a sign that Dorothy was with her when she'd received this news. She couldn't imagine anyone better to have at her side.

Three hours later she had made arrangements with Georgie, and they were in Dorothy's red Cadillac convertible, speeding down the Maine Turnpike. Sleek and straight, the "Mile-a-Minute Highway" was a boon to summer travelers. Given where they were racing, Maren almost wished they were still bumbling along the rough, two-lane roads closer to Haven Point.

"What will we do when we arrive?" Maren asked.

"Leave it to me," Dorothy said. "I'll do the thinking. You know how I like to be useful."

Though Dorothy gave her a gentle and encouraging smile, Maren saw no glint in her eye, none of the adrenaline-fueled chatter Maren would have expected

had they undertaken this adventure on behalf of someone else. Still, she knew Dorothy's mind was clicking
away on all cylinders. She had always thought Dorothy
would make a marvelous detective. She was as clever as
they came.

In the rush to get out the door, Maren had little time
to think, but now, as she left Dorothy to her plotting,
her mind wandered. She had no idea what the woman
looked like. She conjured a vision of her own physical opposite—someone dark and tiny, but voluptuous,
maybe foreign. When her imagination painted in huge
smoky eyes, she felt nauseous.

She tried conceiving of a positive outcome. She would
knock on Oliver's door and find him alone, no woman
in sight. The entire episode would turn out to be an ex-
plainable misunderstanding. She could not come up with
the details to flesh out the scenario, but it ended with a
wonderful, productive talk. He would be chastened that
his remoteness could have led Maren to believe such a
horrible thing was even possible. All would be well. As
the city grew closer, she clung to the fantasy with all her
might.

By the time they pulled into a garage near the Waldorf, it was dark. They entered the hotel through a lesser-
used entrance, and Dorothy outlined the plan.

"You wait in the lobby while I check the bars and restaurants. If Oliver saw you down here, he could explain
away anyone we found him with. If we catch him, it has
to be in his room."

Maren did as she was told. As she stood, obscured in
a darkish corner, hopes for her fantasy outcome ebbed.
The art deco lobby reminded her ominously of the lobby
of the Kennedy Warren, where she and Oliver had lived

as newlyweds. She jumped when the enormous carved bronze lobby clock chimed.

Dorothy returned, shaking her head.

"He's not in the bar or any of the restaurants. Come with me."

"Where are we going?" Maren asked, following dumbly behind.

"To a house phone. I found one hidden away." She dragged Maren to a bank of phones down a hallway. Dorothy picked one up and dialed for the operator.

"Hello, Operator, could you connect me to Oliver Demarest's room?" She paused. "Thank you."

She looked at Maren and smiled slightly. Maren's stomach fell. She had held out hope that Oliver was not even staying at the Waldorf this trip, but that was now dashed.

"Oh, hello—eet ees room service. Is zis zee Thompson room?" Dorothy used a peculiar accent, with shades of Irina, just odd enough to be credible. Maren's sleepless night and emotional day were catching up with her, and she was beginning to feel a little punch-drunk. She giggled in spite of herself.

"No? Oh, pardon me, I am zo confused. Eez zees room 520? No? So sorry, what room eez zees? Room 617? Oh, so sorry!" She hung up.

Dorothy grabbed her hand and led her across the plush carpet to the elevator. Maren's heart was in her throat when they reached the sixth floor and headed toward the room.

It almost felt as if they were in a Renaissance painting with linear perspective, the long hallway growing narrower toward a vanishing point far in the distance. An older woman opened one of the doors, stepped into the hallway, and eyed them suspiciously. She wore all black, except a rope of pearls that hung long from her neck, like a flapper's, as if she'd forgotten to double them up. She seemed to Maren like another bad omen, a raven.

As they passed by room after room, 603, 605, 607, Maren's heart thumped uncomfortably. Their footsteps were not audible on the thick carpet, but Maren still felt she should tiptoe, as if she were doing something wrong, rather than trying to discover whether her husband had.

They finally reached 617. The door, like all the others, was of a heavy dark wood with four panels and no peephole. Dorothy put her ear to it and shook her head, unable to hear anything. She knocked. After a second came a sound, then a voice—Oliver's.

"Who is it?"

Maren's stomach plummeted further. She was overwhelmed by the idea that this was a fool's errand that would end not in reconciliation, but with Oliver angry at her for not trusting him, or for being rash and crazy. Part of her wanted to run back down the hallway, away from all this. She looked around, wondering where she might hide.

"Ees room service," Dorothy answered in the same accent she'd used on the phone. Maren took a step away, so she was not immediately visible when the door jerked open.

"I didn't order room ser—" Oliver opened his eyes wide upon seeing Dorothy. Maren stepped forward and looked at him.

Her last remaining hope was that she would see innocent confusion on his face. What she saw, however, was fear. Dorothy recognized it, too.

"Oh no, Oliver . . ." Dorothy said, dismayed.

Maren slipped under his arm, through the doorway.

He made a grab for her, but she wriggled away, down the tiny dark passage alongside the bathroom and closet, and into the bedroom beyond. And there, sitting on the bed, wearing the plaid flannel bathrobe Maren had given Oliver for his last birthday, was Khaki Trumbull.

CHAPTER SIXTEEN

August 2008
Washington, D.C.

SKYE

It's good you're getting away. No one hires in August anyway," Adriene said as she turned onto Connecticut Avenue.

"True," Skye acknowledged.

And even if they did, it's not like I could do anything about it, she thought. Since being ignominiously fired a few weeks earlier, Skye's anxiety had presented itself in a new and truly hideous form, leaving her frantic about finding a new job, while too debilitated to execute the most basic task in order to do so.

"Someday you'll see this like I do. Exposing Randall Vernon is the best thing you've ever done in your career."

"Well, it is an achievement of sorts. I know people who've screwed up their lives, but not quite so thoroughly." Skye looked out the window at the throng of tourists braving the swampy heat.

"Any chance Ben Barrows might be up there this week?"

"I don't know. If Charlotte Spencer is, then probably." Skye tried not to sound defensive.

"One picture in *Washington Life,* and you make all these assumptions."

"One picture at some black-tie thing, with her hanging on his arm like she owned him." The photograph was from an auction gala in April. Charlotte lived in New York, but according to the caption, she had donated several items from the line of handbags and jewelry she designed. Though it suggested she had invited Ben to the event, not the reverse, Skye still saw it as a sign. "He's not my type, and I'm not his. These Haven Point people all end up with each other. They always revert to the mean."

"As much as 'the mean' makes a fine nickname for Charlotte Spencer, I don't think you can assume he has reverted to her. Besides, if everyone from Haven Point ended up with someone else from Haven Point, their kids would all be born with six fingers on each hand."

"Okay, maybe not with each other, exactly," Skye said, laughing in spite of herself, "but with someone just like them. It's like a benign form of eugenics, an ongoing experiment to create the perfect child."

"Oh, please. You have all the WASP cred those people could want. And the guy has liked you since you were seventeen!"

"He liked me a little when we were seventeen, and maybe enjoyed reliving an old summer fling all these years later. But I highly doubt he gave me a thought in the interim."

"I don't get you," Adriene said, shaking her head.

Skye didn't answer. Adriene could not understand that since her mother died, what she had once seen as refreshingly uncomplicated in Ben now struck her as unforgivably untouched.

When they arrived at the airport, Adriene pulled into Departures and angled her car into half a space, leaving the back sticking out in the through lane. Ignoring the cop yelling at her to move, she got out and opened the trunk. After Skye pulled out her suitcase, Adriene wrapped her in a big hug.

"Good luck with everything. Keep me updated."

"Thank you, Adriene. A million times, thank you." Skye felt a lump in her throat, but before tears could form, she saw a cop bearing down on them, blowing his whistle in an angry staccato beat. Skye managed a weak laugh.

"Oh, for Christ's sake, chill out. I'm going!" Adriene shot him a look, then took her time returning to the driver's seat.

An hour later, Skye was looking out the plane window as the Eastern Seaboard passed beneath her, thinking about how much one stupid mistake could change someone's life.

And one stupid mistake on behalf of Shelley freaking Vernon, Skye thought.

Three weeks earlier, Skye had accompanied the congressman and Mrs. Vernon to a campaign breakfast. As they headed toward the back door after the event, a reporter for the *Richmond Times-Dispatch* caught up with them.

"Hey, are you all worried about the polls tightening?" he asked.

The congressman straightened up and cocked his head, about to deliver his standard pabulum, but Shelley beat him to it.

"Nobody should worry. Randall Vernon always gets *just* what Randall Vernon wants." Shelley's smile was so fake, her tone so contemptuous, the reporter actually looked taken aback.

The congressman let out a great belly laugh and shook his head in mock good humor, as if to say, *Isn't that wife of mine a riot?* Skye had dutifully smiled, as if she, too, were in on some hilarious joke.

Skye was not entirely shocked by the outburst. She had noticed Shelley struggling to keep up her public mask in recent weeks. The only surprise was how long it had taken her to learn about her husband's affair.

Though Skye despised how Mac and the rest of the staff blamed anyone but the congressman for his behavior, she was not inclined to expend scant emotional energy on Shelley. After all, she reminded herself, Shelley had played the part of Jennifer in the breakup of Congressman Vernon's second marriage.

After the reporter walked away, Skye could tell the congressman was having trouble maintaining his composure, so she slipped out, too.

If only I hadn't parked across the street, Skye thought. If her car had been in the lot where the Vernons' driver was waiting, the congressman and Shelley would have seen Skye, checking e-mail on her phone, when they emerged from the building. They would never have knowingly enacted their little drama in front of her. She might have been spared the sight of Congressman Vernon berating his wife, and of the expression on Shelley's face as it morphed from defiance into fear.

But what she really regretted was her decision a few minutes later to pick up the phone when the reporter called.

Hey, Skye. I wasn't going to bring this up, but given Shelley's behavior this morning, I have to ask about a rumor I've been hearing. . . .

The second she got off the phone, Skye knew she had screwed up. She returned to the office and tried to look normal, while her brain was spinning like a plate on a stick, trying to conjure some way to escape responsibility.

She came up with at least a dozen ideas, each more incandescently stupid than the one before. Her last hope was that the story wouldn't run for some reason, but a few hours later, there it was on her screen.

CONCERN OVER CONGRESSMAN VERNON'S RELATIONSHIP WITH CAMPAIGN CONSULTANT . . .

The conversation had been off the record, so Skye was only identified as "a source in Vernon's office," but she knew she was toast. The timing of the story was too incriminating. Everyone knew Skye had been with the Vernons at breakfast, and that the *Times-Dispatch* had covered the event. And Skye had never been able to pull off the "Vernon Pod Person" act, especially not after her mother died.

By the time Mac summoned her fifteen minutes later, she was resigned to her fate, though she was not about to give him the satisfaction of humiliating her. As she headed to his office, she fortified herself with the memory of Randall Vernon leaning over his wife, finger jabbing at her chest, his eyes squinted in ugly rage, and of Shelley cowering, her mouth half open in fear.

Mac was at his desk. Zachary, one of his creepy deputies, stood beside him like a sentry. (Skye took some perverse satisfaction from the fact that a standing Zachary was barely taller than a sitting Mac.)

"Skye, are you the source for this article?"

"Which article would that be?" Skye asked.

"The one in the *Times-Dispatch,* obviously. And before you answer, please recall that I started my career in opposition research. I can find out anything about anyone, if I so choose."

A nice complement to your talent for character assassination, Skye thought. She looked at him thoughtfully, then raised her eyebrows as if an idea had just come to her.

"Then maybe you can find out why Congressman Vernon can't seem to keep his pants zipped?" Skye said. In a cheerful tone, she added, "It seems to me that would be a better use of your time."

"Oh my God," Zachary said, his mouth twisting in disgust, as if Skye had had just committed some grievous crime against humanity.

Skye saw Mac's jaw clench. She knew he was not as enraged by what she had done as by the fact that she was not squirming. He delighted in making people squirm.

"Skye, you're fired, effective immediately," he said, enunciating every syllable of the word "immediately." "Zachary will accompany you to your desk to make sure you only take your personal effects."

"Got it," Skye said with a nod and a smile, as if he'd just given her instructions about formatting a press release. She turned and headed for the door.

"Oh, and Skye?" Mac said. Her hand still on the knob, Skye turned back and saw the gleam in his eye. "Good luck finding a job."

"Aw, thanks, Mac!" Skye replied, as if he meant it in kindness, and not as a threat.

The Vernon staff ordinarily scurried around like a bunch of frantic water bugs, but Skye sensed a distinct pause as she strode purposefully from Mac's office with Zachary in her wake, doing a little half jog to keep up.

Ignoring the stares, she grabbed an empty box by the copy machine and headed for her desk. She opened a drawer, grabbed a handful of tampons, held them up to Zachary and raised her eyebrows, awaiting his approval. He rolled his eyes.

She went through the same exercise with a variety of personal effects, culminating with a figurine from a Washington Capitals ice hockey game.

"This is *my* Alex Ovechkin bobblehead." Skye waved it a little, so the oversized head wagged in Zachary's face.

"Fine, Skye," Zachary said, annoyed. Skye put the bobblehead in her box, then looked at Zachary with a bright smile.

"That's all, then. You may escort me out now," she said, as if they were going on a date.

I'll call you, Colette mouthed as Skye passed her desk. Skye rolled her eyes dramatically.

Zachary walked her out of the building. Skye kept up the charade of self-possession until she was in her car and out of the parking lot. She made it about a half mile down the road before, mouth sweating and heart pounding, she pulled over, then opened the door and threw up in the street.

Colette texted later that day.

This guy is slicker than otter snot. She'd included a link to a *Richmond Times-Dispatch* story. Congressman Vernon had held a brief press availability, during which he completely denied the affair, saying he was a victim of "the politics of personal destruction."

Great. Now I'm a turncoat and *a liar,* Skye thought.

The worst part was the photograph: Shelley standing by her husband's side, looking up at him from under her lashes, head ducked and tilted, the absolute picture of submission. Skye did not particularly care for Shelley Vernon, but she had thought the woman had some backbone, at least. The fact that she had willingly participated in the humiliating *devoted wife standing by her man* media ritual suggested Skye had only made things worse for her.

Skye had spent the weeks since alternating between foggy stupidity and terrible anxiety.

Gran had been oddly persistent about Skye visiting Haven Point this summer, and Skye knew she should be happy to oblige her. (Gran never asked her for anything, after all.) And if nothing else, she should be glad for a change of scenery. For some reason she could not begin to parse, the visit to Haven Point filled her with a strange dread.

Oh well, Skye thought as the plane began its descent into Portland. *As bad as things are, they can always get worse.*

CHAPTER SEVENTEEN

August 1960
New York City

MAREN

K haki. Maren froze, staring, her mouth open. Yes, she had thought it was possible that Oliver, who had been so distant and disconnected, might actually be having an affair. But in a million years, she would not have imagined this. She felt horribly, horribly stupid.

Khaki normally wore her hair in a bun, but now it was frizzed out unattractively around her shoulders. She was one of those rare women who looked better in her uniform, which elevated a homely, unruly appearance.

Oliver is with Khaki?

She wondered briefly if Oliver had seduced Khaki, if he was some sort of predator, a monster she'd never really known. But Khaki did not look like a victim. An angry expression and defiant cast to her chin told Maren she was here of her own volition, probably of her own ambition.

Maren was vaguely aware of Oliver standing off to the side, and of a sense that he was diminished, literally, by her entry—that some smaller version of him leaned against the wall, shell-shocked. She knew Dorothy was near, too, but she only had eyes for Khaki. As Khaki stared back, Maren detected something else in her expression.

Entitlement, Maren thought. *She feels entitled.*

She could not begin to peel back the infinite layers to her rage, or to sort through the multitude of questions that competed for her attention. Oliver supposedly hired Khaki to give her work she badly needed, but was that really why? How long had this been going on?

She had overlooked so much—Khaki's coldness, her ties to Haven Point. Instead, Maren had sympathized with her need to earn a living and even admired her competence in doing so.

I let her into my home, she thought. *I allowed her to care for my children.*

That last recollection caused a jolt of fury to form and radiate from somewhere deep inside. It took hold of her face. She clenched her teeth and felt herself redden. It reached her fingertips, and her hands made tight fists. Maren would have loved nothing more at that moment than to knock the smug look off Khaki's face. It was not compunction that kept her from doing so, but rather fear that it might release some of her anger, and that anger was her greatest friend.

"Get dressed and get out of here," Maren growled. "You are fired."

"You can't fire me. I don't work for you." Though Khaki's voice had a note of bold confidence, Maren saw her glance at Oliver. He was still slumped against the wall, hand over his face. If he wasn't devastated, he knew well enough to give a good impression of it. Whatever he had done, he would not help Khaki now, though Maren found little satisfaction in this.

"Oh, I can fire you, Khaki. I'll say it again: You're fired. Get. Out."

"You don't belong with him, Maren," Khaki said. "You never did."

Maren nearly smiled at the confirmation of what she had always suspected, but no one had dared say out loud. No matter how far Khaki's family had fallen, she *did* feel entitled to be with Oliver, because she was something Maren was not and never could be. She was one of *them,* one of Oliver's people.

Maren took a step closer and stared at Khaki intently. Khaki tried to keep her shoulders square and chin up, but she scooted back—the smallest movement, yet a sign of weakness Maren relished.

And then Maren felt Dorothy's hand on hers. She had just enough self-control to realize she should let Dorothy take over. She retreated, and Dorothy stepped forward.

"Listen, honey," Dorothy began, in her most condescending tone. "I don't know you from a hole in the wall—"

"She's Lady Trumbull's daughter," Maren said, emphasizing *Lady* as derisively as she could manage. Dorothy didn't even know the Trumbulls, but she took her cue. Her eyes went wide, and she laughed scornfully.

"Oh, that's absolutely *perfect.* We have *Lady* Trumbull's daughter here. Well, Miss Trumbull, I think it's time you hopped off your high horse, because there is exactly one way for this scene to end, and it's with you getting out of this room. Take your clothes, dress in the bathroom, and leave." She made a little shooing motion with her hands, as if Khaki were a bothersome pest, rather than a cancer on Maren and Oliver's marriage.

Khaki stayed put.

"What, pray tell, are you waiting for?" Dorothy asked slowly, as if Khaki was unfathomably stupid.

Khaki glanced at Oliver again. She finally seemed to realize he would not lift his eyes from behind his hand. She slid off the bed, grabbed her clothes and purse from the floor, tossed them into a little weekend bag, and headed for the bathroom, head still high.

They waited in a horrible suspended animation for Khaki to get dressed. When she emerged from the bathroom, she looked back toward the bedroom, perhaps hoping Oliver would acknowledge her. He did not. They finally heard the click of the door as she closed it behind her.

When she was safely away, Dorothy looked from Oliver to Maren.

"I'll be by the clock in the lobby," she said.

"I'm right behind you," Maren replied, her eyes narrowed and fixed on Oliver, whose face was still obscured by his hand. She did not speak until Dorothy left.

"I do not want to see you for the rest of the summer," she said, her voice low and trembling. "Don't come up to Haven Point."

"Maren, please. Please let me talk to you." Oliver's eyes finally emerged from their exile to reveal an expression of utter ruin. Maren set her jaw, determined not to melt or begin to ask the million questions, the answers to which some part of her craved.

"What, Oliver? What could you possibly say?" she asked instead, coolly.

"I have made the most terrible mistake, Maren, the most awful mistake. Can I just try to explain?" He put his palms up toward her, like a man begging on the street.

"Explain? You think you can somehow explain how you let that woman insinuate herself into our home and lives, how you allowed me to trust her? And then, while I'm up in Maine with your children, and your *mother* . . . you do this? With her, of all people?"

"This has only just happened, and it was to end here. I knew . . . It's not been all this time, please. . . ."

"Good-bye, Oliver." She walked out the door.

She spent the night at Dorothy's apartment on East Eighty-first. Dorothy was willing to accompany Maren back to Maine, but Maren needed time to think and was beyond grateful for what Dorothy had already done.

She arranged for Gideon to pick her up in Bath and boarded the train north. The mugginess that had stalled over the northeast had lifted overnight, and as she stared out the window, the nearly blinding brightness felt like an affront. She leaned back and closed her eyes.

As the train rattled and shook and hissed its way north, she relived the previous thirty-six hours—not in a linear way, but in snapshots, agonizing bursts. The image of Harriet so indiscreetly talking about her to Frances at the cocktail party felt like it was from weeks before. Her mind darted to the long walk down the hallway of the Waldorf. As anxious as she had been then, it was the last time she had a prayer this was all a mistake.

Khaki's words—*You don't belong with him, you never did*—played and replayed in her mind. Not since Caroline Sturgeon described Pauline's supposed ambitions for Oliver's marriage had Maren heard anything indicating her lack of pedigree was an issue with him. When she occasionally wondered if the women of Haven Point looked down on her for her unexalted upbringing, she would scold herself for such silly self-doubt. But what else besides the Trumbull blood, tarnished but still blue, could possibly have tempted Oliver?

She tried to banish the image of Khaki, lounging on the bed as if she belonged there, but it kept returning, and each time she felt the horror afresh.

She managed to cling to her anger, so preferable to rawness and despair. She gleaned a scrap of satisfaction in having outsmarted Oliver and Khaki, and her ability to keep it together—no yelling or wailing, no rending of garments. She savored the image of Khaki's cool mask slipping to reveal hints of humiliation in the face of Dorothy's brilliant performance. Maren knew she was indulging a regressive, adolescent pride, but that and rage were all that stood between her and a vulnerability too awful to contemplate.

Pricking through it all, like a thin line of light through nearly closed curtains, was the idea she should not have told Oliver to stay away. But when that thought obtruded, she drove it out as if exorcising a demon.

"Your husband has called twice," Irina said when Maren arrived at Fourwinds early that evening. Her tone suggested this had been a great inconvenience. "He said to call him."

Maren managed to thank her and went to fetch the children from Georgie's.

"I'll come over once mine are in bed," Georgie promised.

Two hours later, they sat in the living room, Maren sunk deep in her chair, relaying the whole horrendous tale.

"Good heavens." Georgie shook her head. Maren had been so glad for Dorothy's partnership and caressing ways, her great hug and tears when she said good-bye, but Georgie's matter-of-fact Yankee manner suited her now. "What are you going to do?"

"I have no idea. Maybe we'll be like Harriet and James Barrows. I told him I didn't want him up here the rest of the summer."

She had been unwilling or unable to consider what would come next. She could not imagine forgiving Oliver.

However, a Barrows scenario in which they essentially lived separate lives seemed no better. Divorce was unthinkable.

"You and Oliver aren't like James and Harriet," Georgie said, her tone and expression so aghast, Maren was tempted to believe her. "He didn't even love Harriet when they got married."

"Seems we're not so different from them after all. Is everyone still talking about us?"

"I haven't heard. I hate to say it, but Harriet will keep it alive."

"Naturally. No one knows it was Khaki, do they?"

"Probably not. I doubt Betsy has even met her. Khaki hasn't been here in years. Besides, if she'd recognized her, she would have told Harriet who it was. Just steer clear of people for a while. You never want to go to parties anyway. They'll find someone else to talk about soon enough."

"I wish that were true, but if I disappear, people will talk more. I need to get back in the swing of things soon. Starting with the art show party on Friday, I guess."

"You'll go?" Georgie sounded half surprised, half impressed.

"Pauline is going, so I have to anyway."

"Can't Irina take her?"

"No, she's off on Fridays." Maren smiled weakly. "I think that's when she plots against the Bolsheviks."

"Okay. I'm not sure you have to do it, but whatever you think is best."

The art show was the Ladies Auxiliary's big annual fundraiser. Professional artists from the region and amateurs from Haven Point sold their works over one weekend. It kicked off with a well-attended preview cocktail party.

Maren had been tempted to escape to her parents'. She often took the kids to Minnesota, but these visits were usually after Christmas. The idea of being on the farm during pre-harvest held a powerful nostalgic allure, but she knew leaving would only produce more chatter. Haven Point admired a kind of muscular confidence. Georgie had it, of course, but it was so much a part of who she was, she didn't even see it. Georgie could not understand that Maren needed to make a credible show of strength, so people would either believe Betsy had been wrong, or if not, that Maren was tough enough to handle whatever was happening.

Maren could not abide being pitied as Haven Point's resident Woman Scorned. She had to think like Finn Donnelly, who never cared what people thought. She had to show her teeth, not her belly.

She struggled with insomnia that week, haunted in the early-morning hours by the vision of Khaki in Oliver's hotel room, but during the day her attention was consumed by the labor of behaving as if nothing was wrong. She had never felt the women of Haven Point really knew her, and this accrued to her benefit now. They did not seem to notice the traces of unhappiness that were surely telling on her face.

Oliver called repeatedly over the next few days. Maren let the children talk to him, but when they tried to hand her the phone, she put on a smile and said to tell him she'd call back.

Billy did not sense anything amiss, but Annie, for all her high spirits and energy, had an interesting brand of sensitivity. It wasn't that she cared what people thought of her. She was almost pathologically impossible to insult, in fact. But she picked up signals and rhythms, and as Maren learned that week, was masterful at sniffing out small signs of trouble. When Oliver called for the fourth time, Annie confronted her.

"Mommy, why aren't you talking to Daddy when he calls?"

"Oh, I'm just too busy right now, love," Maren said, making a great show of cleaning one of the pantry shelves. Annie did not look satisfied, though.

On Thursday, the night before the party, Maren finally called Oliver.

"It's Maren," she said when he answered.

"Maren . . ." He sounded surprised and grateful.

"Oliver, please stop asking the children to put me on the phone. I cannot talk to you right now, and it's confusing them."

"Maren, please. I want to come up. I don't have to stay at Fourwinds, but I want to talk to you." His tone was pleading, but he spoke quickly, as if he knew his window of opportunity was small. Her stomach pitched, and she felt her resolution flicker, but she steeled herself.

"No, Oliver. No." She hung up the phone.

"Pauline, you can't bring Sassafras to the art show party," Maren said when Pauline descended the stairs with the monkey on her shoulder.

"Why not? Sassy behaves for me, don't you, Sassy?" Pauline replied, her tone playful. She nudged Sassy with her nose.

Sassafras did tend to stick close to Pauline when they were out. Besides, Maren did not have the energy to fight. Georgie looked a little surprised when she and Cappy picked them up in the LaSalle, but Maren just shrugged and rolled her eyes.

At the start of the party, Sassafras was actually a wonderful distraction. Maren expected whispering and significant looks when she entered, the kind of disturbance in the field she and Dorothy had detected the previous weekend, but all eyes were on the monkey, who was quite popular with anyone who didn't have to share a house with her. Haven Point also had a soft spot for its eccentrics, and an aging widow with a monkey certainly qualified. The perception, however wrong, that Pauline was a *grieving* eccentric widow gave her even more latitude. A cooing crowd formed around her.

Pauline stood with a languid smile and allowed the monkey to be adored. Sassafras seemed wary of the attention and intent on staying with Pauline, so Maren detached herself to walk around the show.

The room was divided by temporary pegboard walls into miniature galleries. This was one of the rare Haven Point events that was open to the general public, so it was crowded enough for Maren to browse without engaging in conversation.

She had chosen a blue floral sundress, the most cheerful in her closet, and did her best to keep up the mask she'd worn that week, a studied air of nonchalance she hoped conveyed a message: *There is nothing of particular interest in my life right now.*

She was fairly sure no one knew she'd gone to New York. As a week had passed, the rumor had had a chance to grow stale. If she could get through the evening with a convincing air of contentment, she might succeed in casting doubt on it.

Maren spotted Harriet across the room. She wore a bright pink suit, and her hair had been coerced into a gravity-defying beehive, with a little pink bow stuck preposterously right on the top.

She looks like a poodle, Maren thought.

Harriet stood near the small podium, examining a

sheet of paper, too busy preparing for her moment in the spotlight to notice Maren. Gilby Gregory, who was in charge of the art show committee that year, had attracted more artists and run the operation competently. Harriet was still head of the Ladies Auxiliary, though, and she would grab all the glory.

Maren wandered over to the east side of the room, where the sculptures were on display. She stopped to look at what Tilly Barnsworth had created. Tilly was a Haven Pointer but considered herself one of the serious artists, apart from the dabblers. She was in her sixties, a little fireplug of a woman, tiny but tough. The fact that her works never sold well at the Haven Point art show only cemented her view of herself. Haven Point taste was obviously too pedestrian for her genius.

This year's creation was a large red clay sculpture. Other artists were satisfied with tables to show their works, but Tilly had set hers atop a pedestal that looked like a Greek column. Tilly, who always gave her works cryptic names, had placed a card next to it that read *Warning*.

It took Maren a moment to puzzle out that the sculpture was meant to be a bell buoy. The fiery yellow cylinder at the top was the light. Four legs reached down to a half-spherical base. Inside, she had hung an absurd little bell that looked like it came from a Christmas decoration. She was asking fifteen dollars, extortionate by Haven Point art show standards.

The whole sculpture looked bottom-heavy and tippy, as if it might roll off the pedestal at any moment. Tilly seemed prepared for this possibility, in fact. She stood nervously by its side, glaring at anyone who got too close.

Maren felt someone materialize by her side and turned to see Finn Donnelly smiling down at her. She returned his smile, though her eyes immediately scanned the room for his wife. She had wanted to like Mary Pat Donnelly, but had found she could not. Haughty and bad-tempered, Mary Pat had quickly earned a reputation for poor treatment of anyone she considered her inferior. A few years before, Clara had witnessed Mary Pat berating a young checkout girl at the grocery store in Phippsburg.

"Mighty wrathy, that one," Clara had said, when she shared the story with Georgie and Maren. They had privately referred to Mary Pat as "The Mighty Wrathy" ever since.

She was not hard to spot this evening, overdressed in a full-skirted polka-dot taffeta dress, her smile close-mouthed and taut. For the moment, fortunately, she was occupied in conversation and not looking their way.

"Hello, Maren," Finn said. "Are you admiring this great work?" He had a glint in his eye as he gestured toward Tilly's sculpture.

"I am. May I introduce you to the artist?" Maren said, with an almost imperceptible tilt of her head in Tilly's direction. His eyes brimmed with amusement, knowing Maren had saved him from whatever he might have said next.

They might not have attracted Mary Pat's attention, but through the corner of her eye, Maren saw that Harriet had noticed them. If she wasn't careful, others would, too. Finn commanded attention wherever he went—even here, where most would have preferred him to feel invisible.

Maren did not see Finn often, but whenever she did, he invariably stood a little closer and looked at her more admiringly than he should. As a rule, she found an excuse to step away. As badly as she wished to avoid becoming the object of gossip, she was finding comfort in his presence this once. He was unlikely to know anything about her and Oliver, and there was tonic in his appreciative, sparkling eyes, his flirtatious ways.

"Are you buying or just window-shopping?" Finn asked.

"I'll come home with something. I always do, though we hardly have room for more art."

"What usually sells well?" Finn asked.

Always the businessman, Maren thought.

"Lobsters," Maren replied.

"Lobsters?"

"Yes. Anything with a lobster in it. A painting, a ceramic plate, a sculpture. Oh, red barns sell, too. It used to be lighthouses, but those are considered common now." Maren laughed.

"Oh." His face fell a little. "They are?"

"Were you hoping to find a work of lighthouse art?"

"No, well . . . It's that we've just bought a whole collection of lighthouse paintings and photographs."

"Oh dear . . . I'm sorry."

"It's okay."

"Finn, I wouldn't use sales in the Haven Point show as a way to gauge the worth of your art," she said, surprised to see him so distressed.

The look of sorrow disappeared and he grinned mischievously. "Sorry. Couldn't resist."

She laughed, but took a discreet step away when she saw that Harriet was still watching them from under her ridiculous hairdo. Fortunately, Gilby chose that moment to tap Harriet on the shoulder and whisper in her ear. It was time for the presentation.

Harriet approached the little podium. She looked toward the bar, nodded imperiously, and waited for someone to hit a glass with a spoon. The room was slow to quiet, but eventually people gathered loosely.

Maren did a quick inventory. Mary Pat was on the periphery of the crowd, monopolizing the attention of a noted local watercolor artist. Pauline had taken up a spot a few yards from Harriet, her back to the staircase that led to the country club's attic storage.

"Hello, everyone. I am Harriet Barrows," she began. Harriet used her public voice. It had a distinct modulation, a twinge of Katharine Hepburn's film accent, so "Hello" sounded more like "Hallow." "I want to welcome you to the Haven Point art show. As you have seen, we have a marvelous group of artists represented here tonight. I am sure you will all find something you simply can't live without." She looked around and beamed as the crowd responded with obligatory laughter.

Finn nudged Maren. He rolled his eyes toward Tilly's sculpture and raised his eyebrows encouragingly. Maren laughed then glanced toward Mary Pat, but she was whispering to the artist.

As Harriet droned on, Gilby stood mutely at her side. Eventually, Harriet got around to acknowledging her.

"I also want to thank Gilby, who pulled everything together this year. It's a thankless job with hundreds of little tasks, and she's been such a sport." In thanking Gilby, Maren noticed, Harriet also managed to denigrate her work by making it sound menial. Harriet looked down with a kind of maternal pride, as if Gilby were a kindergartener who had just tied her own shoes for the first time.

It was at this moment that Maren noticed with alarm that Sassafras had left Pauline's shoulder. Though she had not strayed far from Pauline, she had climbed onto the banister, her attention drawn up toward the attic storage. She was a monkey, after all, a climber.

Pauline was still blithely watching Harriet. The banister was only waist-high where she stood, but Sassafras had begun a slow ascent. If she continued, she would soon be behind Harriet, who would be furious at being upstaged.

Maren considered trying to get Pauline's attention, but she was horrible at reading nonverbal cues and would probably end up making a spectacle of them both. She could walk over and grab Sassy from the banister herself, but that would be even more conspicuous. Maren could not recruit Georgie to step in. She was working the checkout table, and was hidden from view behind one of the temporary walls. All Maren could do was cross her fingers and hope for the best.

Sassy continued to climb, but she slowed a little when she reached a spot behind Gilby, where the banister was shoulder-high. Maren looked around to see if people had noticed anything. A few guests smiled and pointed, but Haven Pointers who knew Sassy were not paying attention. Maren prayed the monkey would stay put.

"All the proceeds from the tickets and a portion of the art sales will go to the Ladies Auxiliary . . . ," Harriet continued.

To Maren's dismay, Sassy was soon on the move again. She climbed a little higher until she was over Harriet's right shoulder. Worse, her eyes were no longer trained toward the attic. From what Maren could tell, the shiny pink bow on top of Harriet's beehive had caught the monkey's attention. She cocked her little gray head left and right, which Maren recognized with utter dread as a sign of curiosity.

"And we have continued our efforts at beautification of the entrance to the beach club. . . ." Harriet's head bobbed enthusiastically as she spoke, Sassy's head now bobbing right along. This was a favorite game, one of the few the children still liked to play with her. They would shake their heads back and forth, and Sassy would mirror their movements.

Maren picked up a shift in the room as the crowd began to recognize something more entertaining, or perhaps more treacherous, in Sassy's behavior. Maren stood paralyzed, not wanting to make a move, but fearing what would happen if she didn't. She prayed Sassy would resume her climb up the staircase toward the attic, Harriet none the wiser.

It was not to be. One minute, Harriet was talking, beehive and shiny bow bobbing along, Sassy clinging to the banister and mimicking her. Then came the streak of gray, as Sassy leaped onto Harriet's shoulder and reached her long fingers into her hair, trying to get the bow.

Harriet let loose a shriek. She kept her arms glued to her sides, not wanting to touch the creature. She tucked her chin, pulled her head as far away as she could, and tried to jettison Sassy with a violent shimmying motion.

Sassy grabbed on to the beehive with her nimble fingers and held on, seeming to enjoy the ride. She looked like a water skier, little arms straight and little knees bent, moving to and fro with Harriet's movements. She finally got hold of the bow and managed to extract it from Harriet's hairdo, unraveling in the process what was left of the beehive's construction. Pins dropped to the floor and great chunks of heavily sprayed hair stuck out in every direction.

When a few people moved toward Harriet, Sassy saw it as a sign of danger and jumped from Harriet's shoulder to the podium, then to the floor. She scampered toward the refreshment table, causing a great movement in the crowd, as half tried to escape and the other half tried to reach down and grab her.

Maren remained glued to her spot, vaguely aware of

Finn Donnelly laughing heartily beside her. When Sassy turned and moved in Maren's direction, the crowd listed again, setting up the next great catastrophe of the night.

It was like watching a movie in slow motion. Billy Chambers, jumping out of Sassy's way, knocked someone into Tilly's Greek column pedestal. The sculpture teetered and began to roll off. Tilly's mouth formed a perfect *O* of terror.

With lightning reflexes Maren would not have expected from such a large man, Finn darted forward and managed to grab the sculpture with one of his giant hands. One of the four bars of the bell buoy broke, but he got his other great paw under the base and kept it from hitting the ground.

Sassy was near enough now for Maren to reach out and grab her. The monkey, evidently ready for the adventure to end, took refuge on Maren's shoulder.

A din of both laughter and alarm remained, but the crowd mostly stopped its motion. As it quieted, Maren felt dozens of eyes on her. Standing with Sassy, she realized, had the effect of making her look complicit.

She wanted to point at Pauline and scream, *"This infernal monkey belongs to her! My* husband's *mother!"* But her acting abilities were spent after their week of exercise, and she found she could only look back mutely. She had no idea how to behave.

Harriet shot Maren a murderous look as Gilby led her toward the ladies' room, presumably to try to repair the catastrophe that was her hair. Maren knew Harriet would find a hundred ways to retaliate.

What's more, Pauline was now threading her way through the crowd toward Maren, a hazy look in her eyes. Somehow, in all this, she had managed to get drunk.

"Pauline, I think we'd better be going," Maren said, her voice quavering.

"Hello, Sassy, you naughty little monkey," Pauline said, not a shred of remorse in her tone. She held out her arm. Sassy climbed on, and up to her shoulder.

"Pauline, it's time to go," Maren repeated, the effort to control her voice and expression now herculean.

"Um, excuse me." A voice came from behind her. It was Tilly, irate, holding the bell buoy in one hand, its one broken arm in the other.

"Oh . . . Tilly . . ."

It was the final insult. Overpowered by her week of indignity, anguish, and humiliation, Maren felt tears threatening. A number of people continued to stare, either blatantly or stealthily.

I must get out of this room, she thought.

"I . . . I . . . I will buy . . ." She wanted to say she would pay for the sculpture, anything to end the scene, but she couldn't form the words.

"Mrs. Demarest, you can't have this sculpture. It's mine!" Finn said in a voice filled with hearty good nature. "I've had my eye on it since I got here. I have just the place for it."

Tilly looked skeptical. She thought her art belonged in deserving homes, and clearly assumed this brute was no aficionado.

"Really," Finn said, pulling out his wallet. "I've been wanting a . . ." He looked at the thing, stumped.

"Bell buoy," Maren whispered.

"Bell boy," Finn said, covering the error with a charming smile. "All the better for the little imperfection. I love it." He looked at Tilly with great enthusiasm.

"Well, all right, then."

With Tilly somewhat assuaged, the last of the gawkers lost interest, and Maren felt she might breathe again. Finn pulled a wad of bills out of his wallet.

"Finn, you pay over there," Maren said. The episode had finally aroused her sense of the absurd. The thought of Finn's "bell boy" sculpture made her smile.

"Come show me what to do," Finn said. He caught her eye, and she saw something in his expression. Concern? Compassion? Maren led him to the table by the door where Georgie and Maude took payments, Pauline and Sassy trailing behind.

While Georgie prepared a receipt, Maren turned to Finn.

"Thank you," she said in a quiet voice.

"I should thank you," he said with a smile. "I might have bought a lighthouse if you hadn't steered me right."

When Maren finally got ready for bed, as exhausted as she ever remembered being, she heard a sound from Pauline's room. It had an odd quality, almost like coughing. She crept into the hallway and listened at Pauline's door.

The sound was muffled, as if into a pillow, but after a second Maren was able to identify it.

It was laughter.

CHAPTER EIGHTEEN

The next morning, half-awakened thoughts swam in Maren's mind. Her first reaction was to groan at the memory of Sassy clinging to Harriet's hair, but she shook it off and tried to objectively measure the night's events against what she had hoped to accomplish.

The Sassy disaster notwithstanding, she decided it had not been all bad. She hadn't planned to become the center of attention, but she did not think she had behaved in a way that would confirm any chatter about her and Oliver.

She did regret allowing Finn Donnelly to buy Tilly's ghastly sculpture. She could only imagine how Mary Pat felt about his act of chivalry. She recalled the incident years before when Finn had picked her up on the side of the road during a thunderstorm. She doubted Mary Pat was aware that this was the second time her husband had saved Maren from a difficult circumstance, but it unnerved her to again be in his debt.

I should buy it back, she thought. Even if he demurred, she could at least thank them. Doing so in person, and immediately, would surely dampen any suspicion Mary Pat might harbor.

She rose, dressed, and quickly got the kids fed and off to their various destinations before heading down the hill. It was low tide, so she walked down the nearly empty beach, past the rocks, and onto the Donnelly property. She took the flagstone path that ran alongside their great lawn, around the house to the front door.

The noise and disruption during the construction of their house had not been the end of the Donnellys' payback. The huge house was also magnificent retribution. It was hard to imagine a structure less in keeping with Haven Point architecture. Maren had not seen the inside of the house, and as she rang the doorbell, her curiosity began to conquer her flat mood.

She expected to hear barking and children, but no sound came from inside. Just as she was about to turn around, Finn opened the door.

"Maren Demarest," he said, a look of curiosity in his intense blue eyes. "Please come in."

"Hello, Finn." She stepped into the foyer. It was obvious at a glance that the interior was every bit as incongruous with Haven Point as the exterior. No unfinished panel walls or over-painted doors, this house was all gleaming surfaces and hanging lamps. The first floor was an open plan design, built out over several levels, likely a workaround to the oddly shaped lot.

The furniture was sleek and low. Built-in cabinets with glass shelves flanked a great fireplace. A spiral staircase in the corner led to the floor above. There was plenty of color, but lines were crisp and the overall effect sterile, precise. Other than a tennis racquet in the front hall and a jacket over a dining room chair, there were few hints of family life. Surprising, considering the size of the family. Mary Pat apparently ran a tight ship.

Finn gestured toward the sunken living room. She stepped into it and took a seat on a red leather love seat with a low back.

"May I get you a drink?"

"No, thank you," she said, looking around. "This is quite a home. I can see you all put a lot of work into it."

"Mary Pat told the decorator to watch the movie *Pillow Talk* and take it from there," he said as he sat opposite her, in a black one-armed chair that made him look even larger. He looked around, too, as if seeing it for the first time.

Her perch offered a glimpse out sliding glass doors to their expanse of lawn and stretch of beach below. A great portion of the view was dominated by the rocks that separated their property from Haven Point. They looked even darker and craggier from up here. Haven Point kids had agitated for a path through the thicket above the sea wall, but the Haven Point Association was not interested in easing access to or from the Donnelly compound.

"I came by to thank you, and Mary Pat, too. You saved us from an awkward moment last night, as I'm sure you know. . . ." She looked around again.

"Mary Pat took the kids to Peaks Island," Finn said, as if reading her mind. "We're alone."

Maren felt herself flush involuntarily. "Oh, well, I am sorry to miss her. I had hoped you and Mary Pat would let me buy the sculpture from you. I know you can't possibly want it."

A sly smile spread across his face. "Actually, I have plans for it."

"You do?" She glanced around. He couldn't possibly mean to keep it in this house.

"Oh, not here, of course. I plan to donate it to the Haven Point Yacht Club."

Maren smiled. "So, I assume you know Tilly Barnsworth is a member?"

"You can assume that, yes."

"And of course you know how much she would love for her great work to be displayed there."

"Yes. Indeed, I do." He seemed pleased with himself. "And I can't imagine they could find a reason to turn her down."

Maren laughed out loud, and Finn's smile broadened, as if he was happy to have amused her.

"I thought you'd appreciate it," he said.

She did admire the good cheer with which he continued to stick it in Haven Point's eye, but she had always found it odd that Finn treated her like a co-conspirator. While hardly the core of Haven Point society, until this week Maren would not have considered herself the outsider Finn seemed to think she was.

Now Khaki's words echoed in her mind. She didn't *belong* with Oliver, Khaki had said. Perhaps it was common knowledge that she was trying to live above her station, so obvious even Finn had picked up on it.

"That was quite an incident with that monkey last night," Finn continued.

"It was awful," she said.

"For you, no doubt, but I have to admit, it was rather entertaining. I seem to remember your mother-in-law putting you in a bad spot a few years back."

She felt at a disadvantage now that he'd pointed out her double indebtedness.

"Yes. Your timing was impeccable yet again," she said with a polite smile. "Thank you."

To her relief, he waved it off and changed the subject. "That girl of yours, Annie, she's a favorite of my Patrick's."

"Yes, I've seen a lot of Patrick this summer. He's very well mannered."

"Mary Pat's whipped them in shape. She won't have anyone there saying the kids aren't raised as well as the others." He gestured in the general direction of Haven Point.

Maren was sure people had indeed said that about the Donnelly kids, but she hadn't and wouldn't. She despised Haven Point's tendency to ascribe sins of fathers onto children, how the worst-behaved child of an old Haven Point family wore a halo, while the best-behaved Donnelly child was suspect.

"Annie's full of it, isn't she?" he asked, smiling.

"She's got a lot of spirit," Maren replied, then added with a small laugh, "I know I might be understating the case."

"Well, I like a girl with spirit." Finn looked at her pointedly and paused to let his comment sink in. When she didn't say anything, he continued. "So, you're here all summer."

"I am," Maren replied. "Middle of June through Labor Day."

"How do you like that?"

"Considering our alternative is summer in Washington, D.C., what's not to like?"

"Oh, I could think of a dozen things not to like," he said with a small laugh. He was on his turf now, safe and sure.

"It's lovely for the children," she said, though without much enthusiasm.

"How often does your husband come up?"

"Not often."

If possible, Finn's gaze was even more intense now. Maren felt as if she were crossing a stream on small, slippery stones.

"Because of work?"

"Yes, he works a great deal. If we lived in Boston or New York, it might be easier, but it's awfully far. He and two other doctors opened an orthopedic practice in Washington, so he's often on call."

"Well, that sounds interesting." He didn't sound at all interested. In all these years, Oliver and Finn had never met. Maren suspected Finn wouldn't like Oliver.

Finn fidgeted with a button on his jacket before looking at her again.

"If you don't mind my saying, if I were your husband, I wouldn't leave you alone here all summer long." He kept his expression determinedly benign.

"Why? Because the sea otters might get me?" Maren smiled.

"It isn't the sea otters I'd be worried about."

This was more than Finn's usual flattery, and she felt an old stirring, something she'd not experienced since those early, heady days with Oliver. The two men were so different. Oliver was attractive in his patrician way—an elegant dancer, good at golf and tennis. And brilliant, of course. But Finn was big and rugged, all muscle and power, with his strong face and sparkling eyes. Finn looked as if he could work a farm, in the unlikely event he ever had to.

Oliver couldn't work a lawnmower, she thought mutinously.

She felt as if a long-hidden switch had been flipped. And with that, she realized, she needed to get out of this house. Immediately.

"Well, thank you again, Finn, for your help last night," she said, rising. "If you change your mind, I'm more than happy to take the sculpture off your hands."

"And keep it from the yacht club? You wouldn't," he replied as he walked her to the door. Finn put his hand on the doorknob but didn't turn it immediately. He looked at her closely and moved in her direction—only an inch, but it allowed for no mistake in his intentions.

"Jesus, you're beautiful," he said, his voice low and husky. She picked up a hint of cologne, sandalwood and spice, and the smell of the man underneath.

The most infinitesimal move toward him was all it would take.

If I don't belong *with Oliver, if I don't* belong *on Haven Point, maybe . . .*

Part of her wanted to succumb. She craved his touch, to be entwined with this man, so potent, so interested. She could almost convince herself it was right, that to give in to him was to reject the false courtly manners of Haven Point in favor of the truer chivalry and kindness Finn had shown her.

Almost.

She pushed the thought aside, looked down to break the eye contact, and made a subtle move, not toward him, but toward the door. Finn opened it. He was many things, but he was no bully.

"Good-bye, Finn. Thank you again."

"Good-bye, Maren," he said, with a look of gentle disappointment.

She started toward the side of the house, planning to walk along the beach, but turned and went to the road. She was flustered, alternating between thrill and repulsion at the reawakening of her power to attract. She craved fresh air and wanted to take the longer way back.

Finn's implicit proposition did nothing to distract her from Oliver's infidelity. In fact, it put the shambles of her marriage in sharp relief. That week she had thought as little as possible about what Oliver had actually done, choosing to focus on keeping up an appearance of cheer and normalcy.

Now Maren felt as if she had stood where Oliver had—right on the edge of the same bright line with someone beckoning her across. Someone more tempting than Khaki, surely. She had opportunity. She could even argue a rationalization, where Oliver could not (at least not one she could conceive of). And she had felt the attraction, the temptation.

She had not given in, though, and it had not really been a close call. Why had Oliver crossed that line? The question pressed on her like a vise. Part of her desperately wanted to ask, to pound her fists on his chest and demand he help her understand how he could have done what she never could.

But she had held her head up so far. The fiasco at the art show was a setback, but not of her creation. She still had her dignity, and she was ferociously determined to keep it.

When she returned to Fourwinds, it was to find a letter had come. She turned the envelope over in her hands. It was his stationery, the elegant Crane envelope with their name and address embossed on the back. It briefly crossed her mind to send it back, but she rejected the idea as an adolescent gesture out of a dramatic novel.

He had written her name and address in a hand more careful than his usual doctor's scrawl. She saw the effort in that and hoped the letter might contain some answers.

Dear Maren,
I understand you do not want to speak with me.
I cannot imagine how hurt and disappointed you

must be. I had hoped you would read this and
permit me to say what I tried to say in New York.
*   I recognize I have made the most terrible*
mistake. I love you more than I can possibly ex-
press, and I vow nothing like that will ever hap-
pen again. More than anything, I would like the
chance to prove it to you.
*   Won't you allow me to come to Maine? I don't*
have to stay on Haven Point. I don't know what
would be best. Perhaps we could meet somewhere,
maybe away from everyone and the children.
*   Please, consider it. Allow me to see you?*
All my love,
Oliver

She felt confused, underwater again. She recognized
a bit of Oliver's old devotion, but something in the letter
muddied the waters. Unable to put her finger on it at first,
she read it over again.

It's the promise, she thought. What good was a vow
that "nothing like that will ever happen again"? Nothing she had ever known in Oliver explained what he
had done. On this count, he might as well be a perfect
stranger, and of what value was a vow from a stranger?
She put the letter back in its envelope and tucked it into
her bag.

A terrible inertia set in over the following days. She
continued to avoid Oliver on the phone. She made her way
around Haven Point, checking the boxes of her days with
a determinedly cheerful exterior, while inside she felt
numb and aimless.

They were meant to return to Washington in a few
weeks, and she had no idea what she would do. More than
once, she felt the urge to call her mother, but to what end?

Her parents would say she belonged with her husband, to forgive him, and she could not.

She did not reply to Oliver's letter. The more she thought about it, the cheaper it seemed. His promise had cost him nothing him more than the price of the stamp. She needed to know what was behind his betrayal, but to ask was to grovel, and that she could not bear.

A week later, Maren was on the porch when Maude came by, a black Lab on either side, like sentries. At Maren's invitation, she sat heavily on a chair. She pointed to the ground and the dogs lay obediently at her feet.

"How are you, Maude?" Maren asked languidly.

"Oh, fine." They chatted about nothing for a few minutes, though Maren could tell Maude had something particular to tell her.

"I'm afraid I've got more nonsense from Harriet to report," she said finally.

"Good Lord, what now?"

Maude leaned over to pet one of the dogs, avoiding eye contact. "She's telling people you're cozy with Finn Donnelly."

"Based on what?" Maren's mind reeled, wondering where Harriet had gotten the idea.

"She said you were at his house."

Maren exhaled, relieved. If Harriet knew she had hit on a kernel of truth, she would be dining out on it. She had scarcely looked at Maren since the horrible incident with Sassafras at the art show party. Harriet probably learned Maren had been to the Donnellys', and had just extrapolated from there.

"Well, I'm not 'cozy' with Finn Donnelly. I went by his house, but only to offer to take that horrible sculpture off his hands."

"I just wanted you to know."

"I know, Maude. I appreciate it."

Maude did not move to leave. She looked at Maren for a moment, almost curiously. "So, how are you?"

Maren paused and took a breath. "I'm not even sure."

"Have you decided what you will do about Oliver?"

"I can't seem to see past the nose on my face. I told him not to come up here, that it was too confusing right now."

Maude looked out at the water, her expression concerned.

"What? Do you think I've done something wrong?"

"Maybe." She looked at Maren again.

"Why?"

"I've seen this through the years, again and again. We think we have something special here on Haven Point. And it is special, don't get me wrong. But sometimes I think families sacrifice too much. Mothers here all summer, fathers away. It can wear on marriages. Little cracks can become canyons."

"Well, that may be, Maude, but keep in mind, Oliver is the one who insists I come up all summer, and it was Oliver who betrayed me."

Maren saw a flicker of surprise on Maude's face and realized she had spoken hastily. In saying Oliver "insisted" she come up, she had revealed her ambivalence about Haven Point. Maude let it go without comment.

"You don't have to convince me Oliver is wrong. He's wrong, from stem to stern. But family work is women's work, Maren. It always has been. Men are, well . . . men are what they are. If you think there's a prayer for you and Oliver, I think you have to get yourselves under one roof again."

"Thanks, Maude. I appreciate your concern. But I don't think I'm ready for that."

In some corner of her badly broken heart, Maren knew Maude had a point. But she could not imagine Oliver on Haven Point. In fact, she was considering asking him to move out of their house in D.C. before she and the kids returned.

A few days later, Maren returned to Fourwinds after a walk. Pauline had taken the kids to a junior tennis carnival at the country club and Irina had time off. From the moment she walked in the door, Maren sensed a shift in the atmosphere.

It was Oliver.

He stood by the window, looking out at a boat on the water. He spun around when he heard the door. His eyes were hollow. He had lost weight.

"Maren," he said, his expression beseeching.

She could not look him in the eye. A thousand emotions warred inside her: anger, anxiety, confusion (and, to her surprise, the tiniest hint of relief).

"I know you said not to come, but I'm sorry. I felt I had to."

"Did Maude call you?"

"It doesn't matter. I'm here. I've taken a leave from the practice."

"Oliver, I don't have anything to say. I don't want to talk. I can't talk to you about this." A part of her wanted to run to him, to believe he was in earnest, but her feet wouldn't go. She made to leave the room.

"Okay, but before the kids get home, please let me say one thing. I love you and I will do whatever I can to fix this. I can't do that when we're apart."

"I don't think I am ready for this, Oliver. I wish you

would leave before the children see you. It will be too late if they do."

"I'm not leaving," he said simply, almost apologetically.

"Fine." She walked out of the room, and a dreadful standoff ensued.

Oliver slept in the blue room. In a moment of uncharacteristic curiosity, Pauline asked about it, but she seemed satisfied by Maren's vague explanation about Oliver snoring. By tacit agreement, they behaved reasonably well when others were around. It wasn't so different from how they'd been for ages, orbiting around each other, passing through the busyness of their days with little affection or interaction.

The act might have passed muster to outside observers, but Maren was a mess. She was not sure what was worse, her listlessness and malaise before his arrival or the gnawing, unsettled feeling since. She could not get comfortable.

It went on for four horrible days—Maren feeling like she was jumping out of her skin; Oliver watching her closely, helping more than usual.

Adding to Maren's misery was Annie's fretfulness. She found Maren on the porch one day and squeezed next to her on the wicker love seat.

"Why did Daddy come back to Maine?"

"Why, to see you all, of course." Maren had been brooding, but she answered as normally as she could manage.

"Daddy doesn't ever come up in August, except on weekends, and you aren't being nice to him," Annie said, her tone accusatory.

Unsure how to respond, Maren gently pulled Annie down so her head was in her lap. Annie's legs were so long now, they hung off the edge of the love seat. Even curled up, she couldn't fit next to Maren. She had so rarely done that anyway; only when she was sick, which was almost never.

"Why do you say I'm not being nice to Daddy?" Maren stroked Annie's silky hair.

"You don't seem happy he's here."

"I don't? Oh dear. Sometimes grown-ups get so busy they don't make time to be kind. That's not right, is it?"

"No."

"Well, thank you for telling me. I will have to do better," Maren said, forcing a lightness she didn't feel. Annie seemed to relax a little on her lap, and a minute later she bounced up.

"I'm going to the beach."

Maren was relieved, but she knew the reprieve was temporary. Annie was too plugged in. They could not keep this up for long.

The house was empty for the first time in days, and Oliver seized the opportunity. Soon after the screen door banged, signaling Annie's departure, he found Maren and took the seat their daughter had vacated. Chastened by Annie's accusations, Maren didn't move. Something had to break the stalemate.

"What can I do or say, Maren?"

She looked back at him and remembered Maude's words. *Family work is women's work.* She took a deep breath and finally, after all the wretched days of resistance, let slip the question that had so oppressed her.

"Just tell me *why.*"

He was silent for a moment, and she braced herself. Would he try to call Khaki a temptress? Would he say Maren had done something wrong?

Oliver merely looked defeated. It was as if she'd asked the one question he couldn't answer, the only one she thought he should be able to. Surely, he had known this would come.

"I don't know. It was just some madness, some temporary madness."

"How do I know you won't have 'temporary madness' again?" she asked, the anger returning.

"I swear I won't. You're the most important thing to me in the world."

"What does that mean? You said the same thing in your letter. What is my guarantee, if I don't even know why you did this? And, God, Oliver . . . with *Khaki,* of all people." Her voice caught, but she took a breath. She would not cry. "I won't go through this again, and you are offering me no reason to trust you."

"I felt lonely, I guess. . . ."

"You were lonely? *You?* You wanted me up here all summer. You insisted we couldn't go to the Delaware shore, like I suggested, or somewhere else closer to home. And you were lonely? That's rich, Oliver, and what's more, I don't believe it. I just think it's all you can come up with."

He looked down at his hands, his long surgeon's fingers that did such precise, miraculous things. She knew in her bones his explanation had been a false gambit. She rose to go inside, too tired to be insulted, unable to be with him another moment.

Not fifteen minutes later he found her again in her bedroom, and her body tensed. Did he plan to chase her around until she submitted? In order to be reassured, she needed to understand. She had even summoned the humility to ask, but he had offered nothing.

"I don't know what to say, Maren. How can I make you believe this won't happen again?"

"How indeed?" Maren replied icily. "How do I know you won't see Khaki again, or find another woman—maybe someone else from Haven Point, someone who really *belongs* here?"

"What do you mean?" He looked genuinely confused.

"I need to understand why you did this, Oliver, and all you're doing is placating me. You'll say anything, and it means nothing."

"What if I don't know?" He looked ashamed and desperate.

"Then we're at square one. I think you should find an apartment, Oliver. I can't live with this. I can't live with you," Maren said. She stood and left the room.

She could not have imagined feeling any more miserable until she reached the landing and saw Annie sitting halfway down the staircase, back hunched, arms hugging her legs. She had heard.

"Annie . . . Oh Annie . . ."

Without a backward glance, Annie unfolded herself and darted down the stairs and out the front door.

Maren's knees were weak. She made her way to the door with the vague idea of going after Annie, but there was no catching her now. Ever, really. She turned to the living room, slumped in a chair, put her hands over her face, and cried silent tears. She felt as defeated as she ever had in her life.

"Was that Annie?" Oliver asked from the bottom of the stairs.

Maren nodded. She removed her hands from her face and looked at him, eyes wet. Oliver entered the room and sat in another chair.

"Do you know how much she heard?" he asked.

"I have no idea."

"I'm sorry, Maren. I don't know what to say. I wish to God I did." He looked wrecked.

"I just can't get over the hideous irony. You stick me up here with your mother, your angry father, friends who think I'm an interloper, and then this."

When he said nothing, Khaki's words again came into her head.

"Tell me the truth. Is it what Khaki said? That I don't belong here, or belong with you, that I'm not one of them?" She swept her arm toward the front door, toward the rest of Haven Point. A vision flashed in her mind of Finn Donnelly referring to "them" days before as he made a similar sweeping gesture, over the rocky barrier between his home and Haven Point.

"Oh my God, no, Maren." Oliver looked horrified. He paused, closed his eyes, and took a breath, searching for words.

"Maren," he said, finally and forcefully. "I married you because I loved you like I'd never loved anyone. I still do, though I know it is impossible for you to believe right now. I didn't marry for blood, but if I had chosen to, what better could I have done for my family than to marry a Larsen?"

Oliver shook his head, seemingly astonished at her confusion. "God, Maren, it shines from your every pore, and you don't even know it. That trueness, that fineness, it was everything I wasn't, everything *we* weren't." Oliver gestured around the room, leaving no doubt that the "we" to which he had referred was his family. "For as badly as I behaved, I never forgot that I am the luckiest man, our children the luckiest children. You make me better. You deigned to marry *me,* Maren, not the reverse."

Maren could not see in herself what Oliver saw, but

she recalled Oliver's proposal all those years before, how he laughed at Maren's idea that she might not be good enough for his mother. On this count, at least, she realized he was in earnest. His affair with Khaki was not about her being a Trumbull. Maren felt a glimmer of relief. If there had been even a grain of truth in what Khaki said that night, Oliver truly would have been a stranger to her.

"But if not that, then why?"

He looked at her despairingly, and her heart sank again.

She was so tired of going around and around with him. There seemed to be no way beyond the impasse. He couldn't answer, and she couldn't live without knowing. She felt sick, thinking of the children, especially Annie, but there was nothing she could do about that. She saw no other way out.

As she climbed the stairs, her mind coalesced around a plan. She would take the kids to Minnesota for a while. She had to pack, to make arrangements.

She was halfway up the stairs when she heard Oliver behind her.

"She needed me," he said, his voice low and shaking.

She spun around and looked down at him.

"What did you say?"

He seemed almost surprised at the words that had come out of his mouth, as if he'd not expected them to, but he could not have been as surprised as she.

"You want to know why." Now he looked a bit afraid, as if he knew she would not like what he was saying. "She needed me."

"You think your wife and children don't need you?" Maren asked, scornful.

"No, I don't think that." He looked down and spoke quietly. "I know my children need me."

She reeled, confused. "I don't understand. What are you saying?"

"She had nothing. She needed me. You don't. You never really have. Of course, it was wrong," he added, his words rushing. "I know it was wrong. There is no way I can make it right, but if you want to know why, that's why."

"That is just ridiculous, Oliver. I don't even know what to say." She was trying mightily to keep up her anger, but she saw shapes now through the fog. If nothing else, she could tell it had cost him something to say this. Once again, he was speaking the truth, or his truth at least.

She sat on the stairs, right where Annie had sat earlier. He climbed up and sat on a stair below her, back to the wall, long legs bent in front of him, feet against the banister, like a child.

"That's ridiculous. It doesn't make sense," she repeated, though with less conviction.

He sat, not touching her, waiting for her to lift her face. When she finally did, she saw his brow knit, the sorry look in his eyes.

"I needed you, Oliver." It was all she could manage. He reached out then, and took two of her fingers in his hand, gently.

"Needed?" he asked, sad, but resigned to the past tense.

It was a long time before she replied. He waited quietly.

"Give me time," she said finally. Oliver nodded and looked up at her, grateful.

She did need time. She needed time to forgive him,

and time to get to know him better. He was still a stranger to her in many ways, but of a different species than she had initially feared.

She needed time to consider whether all these years what she'd thought was her armor had actually been a weapon.

CHAPTER NINETEEN

August 2008
Haven Point

SKYE

Gran had arranged for Skye to be picked up by Hal Mahaney, a fiftysomething cousin of Georgie's who made a small fortune carting Haven Pointers to and from the Portland airport. He was a talker, and fortunately seemed content with what was largely a one-way conversation.

"Good thing you got up now, Ms. Demarest," he said. "Seems like we're gonna get some weather up here from that hurricane."

"Really? I didn't think they knew where it was going." The hurricane churning away off the coast of Florida was supposed to make landfall somewhere near the border of Virginia and North Carolina that night. Last Skye had heard, it was expected to move up the coast, but the exact path was uncertain.

"The old lobstermen don't like the look of it. Best case, it moves up offshore. But it's looking like it'll hit land again down near Long Island and come up inland."

"I didn't think you all even got hurricanes here in Maine."

"We don't get as breezed up, what with the cold air, but it's the flooding that's a worry to folks on the coast. If they come up inland and put us east of the eye, that's when we get the storm surges. And we've got a full moon coming. Of course, Georgie and your grandma got nothing to worry about, up there on the cliff."

When they finally reached the causeway, Skye asked if they could open the windows.

"Suit yourself." Hal shrugged.

The breeze was always a little wild here, more warning than welcome, but she felt a spark of life at the contrast to the stultifying D.C. August heat.

When they pulled into the driveway, Gran came out to the porch, a flash of coral against the gray. Gran was dressed as she might have been at any time in the past forty years—in a knee-length skirt, crisp button-down, and leather loafers—and Skye felt an unexpected rush of comfort at her tidy predictability.

Hal brought her suitcase up to the porch and left. Gran looked a little thinner than she had when Skye saw her in early June, but she gave Skye a sturdy hug then led her inside and upstairs.

Skye's room had not changed. The doorstop was the rock on which she had painted her name in bubble letters years before. Her favorite children's books still occupied the wicker shelf on the wall, and the picture of Skye standing between Gran and Pop on the beach was in its usual place on the dresser.

She knew she should see it as a testament to Gran's devotion that the bedroom always stood ready for her. Today for some reason, it vaguely irritated her, and the warm feeling she'd had moments earlier evaporated. So many things vaguely (or not so vaguely) irritated her lately. It was fortunate Adriene had skin as thick as a rhinoceros, Skye had snapped at her so often.

Skye unpacked, progress hampered by dresser drawers so swollen by salt air, she had to shimmy them back and forth to get them open. She took the back stairs to the kitchen, where Gran was getting dinner ready.

"Can I help?" she asked.

"I've got it. Go make yourself at home."

Skye wandered around the living room, examining the books, pictures, trophies, and art projects that filled the built-in shelves along the walls. For the most part, she felt as she usually did on Haven Point: like an anthropologist studying the artifacts of some ancient tribal culture. One photograph, however, stopped her in her tracks. It was of her mother and her uncle Billy.

Her mom looked about sixteen. She was laughing unselfconsciously, mouth open and face tilted up, as if she might drink from the sun. She radiated uncomplicated joy.

The image echoed Billy's words at her mom's memorial service. Skye had found it surreal, how everyone shook their heads in sadness at the great light that had been snuffed out so prematurely. Billy, Gran, Flora, even Adriene—all shed pure tears of sorrow.

"So tragic," they all said.

Who is this woman they are mourning? Skye had wondered. It wasn't like she had died in a car accident. From what Skye had seen in those final months, her death had been inevitable.

As Skye turned away from the image of young Annie, she spotted her own young face, framed alongside a poem she had written in third grade.

ICE CREAM
BY SKYE DEMAREST

Ice cream is so very nice
I'll eat it once, I'll eat it twice

It's tasty and sweet
Now take a seat
And feel the beat
Move through your feet
Ice cream all the time
In rain and shine
Put down that spoon.
The ice cream's mine!

"What have you found?"

Skye turned to see Gran standing in the dining area and wondered how long she had been watching.

"The ice-cream poem," Skye replied. "Pretty experimental stuff for an eight-year-old, wasn't it?"

"I love that poem. From the time you could talk you were so funny. And such an interesting turn of mind," Gran said. "Dinner's ready. Hope you don't mind eating in the kitchen."

When they sat down to roast chicken and cold blueberry soup, Skye could tell Gran had something on her mind. She finally came out with it.

"I assume you know Adriene sent me the toxicology report," Gran said.

The night Skye found her mother, Adriene had been her third call, after 911 and Gran. She had arrived in time to coax from the cops the probable cause of death: "polypharm overdose." Not a big surprise, given the pills Skye had seen on the floor next to the tub. She had offered to pull strings to expedite the tox report. (In D.C. government terms, "expedite" meant "get it in less than a year.")

As far as Skye was concerned, whether accidental or intentional, drugs, alcohol, or a combination, it amounted to the same thing: Her mother's demons got her in the end.

For some reason, Gran had seemed eager for the information.

Skye had no desire to know more about the toxicology report. When she asked no questions, Gran changed the subject, unfortunately to the one Skye had hoped to avoid.

"I'm sorry about your job, Skye," Gran said.

"Thanks."

"I wonder if it's an opportunity. You had so little time to look for work when you moved home."

"Well, I have plenty of time now, don't I?" Skye struggled to keep the tension from her voice. She'd had a break from Gran's questions over this past grim year, but she'd known they would start up before long. *Are you doing anything freelance? Keeping up with your friends in the sketch comedy troupe? Thought any more about screenwriting?*

It was all wrapped up in Gran's strange indulgence of her mother's so-called career. When Skye was little, Gran had stepped in to make up for her mother's shortcomings. When she was old enough, Gran taught her end runs around her mother's deficiencies.

No one ever said it outright, but she felt the message was clear. *Your mother is just too creative to be bothered. We must all work around her genius.* It was maddening. Skye had been raised to be the prudent and organized one, but now she had to face judgment for not being sufficiently creative?

"I'm sure it's not pleasant, but you're so careful with money. I don't think it hurts to take a step back from time to time," Gran said.

"You know what hurts, Gran? Chaos hurts. Uncertainty hurts," Skye snapped.

"You mean the kind of chaos and uncertainty you grew up with?" Gran replied evenly.

"Yes, Gran. That's exactly what I mean. And here's what I can't figure out: What happens when you're gone, if I take over as the family's artist-in-residence? Who's going to take care of, you know . . . life?"

Gran looked at her for a moment, more thoughtful than upset.

"Skye, I'm sorry if I seemed to trivialize what you're facing, or what you faced," she said finally. "There is no disputing the uncertainty you grew up with, and I can understand your fear now."

Skye took a deep breath, chastened by Gran's kindness.

"Thanks, Gran. I'm sorry I snapped. I'm just stressed. The thing is, Randall Vernon isn't just a politician. He's a powerful businessman."

"And what does that mean for you?"

"He's so vindictive. I promise he'll do everything he can to prevent me from getting another job."

"I know some men give an impression of being able to wield that kind of power. But it's my observation that many fewer actually can, and fewer still would bother to in the end." Gran looked at her with tender sympathy. "I think you'll come out of this okay, though I'm sure that's hard for you to believe right now."

Skye smiled, a little sheepish. "I'd like to, but the second I start believing it, my anxiety gets very suspicious."

"That anxiety. Such a troublemaker!"

"Adriene calls it my Neanderthal Greek chorus." Skye lowered her voice to caveman pitch. "Bad thing gonna happen. Must do something stupid."

Gran laughed as she took her dishes to the sink. "That reminds me. We should get ready for the sing-along."

"Oh . . ." Skye hesitated.

"You're coming, right? You can't miss the sing-along."

In fact, Skye would have liked very much to miss it. It was one thing to sit in Fourwinds with Gran, quite another to throw herself into Haven Point's social exigencies, the endless stream of events and traditions that filled the weeks there. But as she watched Gran at the sink, she felt her resistance crumble.

Gran still had the Nordic beauty of her youth. Her hair, though now white instead of blond, still gleamed. Neither age nor grief had dimmed her bright blue eyes. But Skye detected a strange hesitancy in Gran's movements, as if she'd been shattered and pieced back together, and was now worried the glue wouldn't hold. Gran's height, which had always signaled robust health, now made her appear more vulnerable.

Like she has farther to fall, Skye thought.

"Of course I'll come." She plastered on a smile. "Wouldn't miss it."

When they arrived at the yacht club, Georgie waved from across the room, As they picked their way through the crowd, Skye saw a few familiar faces. Most acknowledged them with small waves and smiles. New England minimalist greetings were appropriate in this community, where you were likely to see the same person the next day.

Georgie stood and gave Skye a perfunctory hug, a lavish display of affection for her.

"What's the news, Georgie?" Skye asked.

"Oh, Maren, you haven't heard this one yet. The Hellmonds are renovating Gull Cottage."

"Horrors." Maren laughed.

"I guess they're putting in some fancy Wi-Fi thing

so Jill can be 'virtual.'" Georgie lifted her fingers in air quotes.

"Georgie's suspicious of renovations," Gran explained with a smile. Skye was just pleased to discover that a woman on Haven Point actually had a job. From what she had observed over the years (and could see was still the case, looking around the room), the women of Haven Point all had some magical ability to find husbands and have kids, at which point they promptly quit their jobs.

They would encamp to Maine in June and decamp home when school started. When children were old and gone, they followed the sun to Boca Grande, the Hillsboro Club, or Jupiter Island. The way was paved so nicely for them.

A barely distinguishable stream of white teeth and Patagonia half-zips was filing into the yacht club. When the flow came to a sudden stop, Skye looked up to see Harriet Hyde Barrows in the doorway, gazing around imperiously, indifferent to the traffic jam she had caused. When she finally found an acceptable seat and moved aside, Ben's face appeared behind her.

Skye felt a jolt at the sight of Summer Ben: slightly tan, wavy hair just a touch longer than usual. She kept her eyes on the door, half expecting Charlotte Spencer to enter next, but the only person in his wake was a young man who, except for a sullen expression, looked like the seventeen-year-old Ben that Skye had known—probably his younger brother, Steven, who was in college.

Her first instinct was to pretend she had not seen him come in, to turn to Gran and Georgie and feign deep engagement in their conversation. She quickly realized that would be absurd. They would have to acknowledge each other at some point, plus the chair in front of hers was unoccupied, so she had an unobstructed view of where he was sitting. When he settled in and glanced around, she caught his eye and smiled.

A look of surprise crossed his face, and then he responded in kind.

At least he's being subtle, she thought. Gran knew she and Ben had seen each other a few times, but nothing beyond that.

Fortunately, just as Julian Stevens, who had been the song leader as long as Skye could remember, approached the piano, a man large enough to block her view slipped into the empty seat, sparing her the effort of not looking at Ben throughout the event.

"Page forty-eight, please. 'Polly Wolly Doodle,'" Julian said, after a few announcements.

As the pianist struck the first few notes and the well-trained crowd began to sing, Skye's old disconnectedness kicked in. She felt like she was at a living history museum where costumed actors brought quaint, old-world traditions to life. She could be charmed. She could marvel at small children knowing all the words to "Ezekiel Saw De Wheel." But, as ever, she was on the outside looking in.

After Julian led the crowd through "The Grandfather Clock" and "My Bonnie Lies Over the Ocean," he announced a song that broke through her detachment.

"All right, now. Time for 'Little Liza Jane.' Page twenty-three."

The room was suddenly alive with the sound of excited chatter and scraping chairs. Small children were passed around, until each was in front of, or in the arms of, an adult. As the pianist began to play and the crowd began to sing, Skye felt her throat tighten and tears prick at the back of her eyes.

*I've got a girl and you've got none, Little
Liza Jane
Come, my love, and be the one, Little Liza
Jane*

Skye had not heard the song in years, and, to her recollection, she'd never heard it here on Haven Point, but she
knew every word, just as she knew what would happen
when the crowd sang the next lines.

*O-o-o-o, Liza, Little Liza Jane
O-o-o-o, Liza, Little Liza Jane*

On the "O-o-o-o," every small child was tossed in the
air like a rag doll, just as Skye's mother had done when
she sang "Little Liza Jane." Like the children in the yacht
club, she had laughed, as wide-eyed and thrilled as she
would have been on an amusement park ride.

Skye had the same odd feeling she'd experienced
when she saw the photo of her mother in the living room
at Fourwinds. Skye had noticed her mother's name on
trophies. She'd seen photographs of her here on Haven
Point. For some reason, though, she'd never absorbed the
fact that her mother had an entire history here, one Skye
knew nothing about.

As the song ended and Julian moved on to "Casey
Jones," she took a deep breath and collected herself. By
the time he reached the traditional closing song, "America the Beautiful," she had regained her equilibrium, and
her mind turned to the more prosaic question of whether
she and Ben would speak after the event was over. He
was closer to the door, so she figured the ball was in his
court. He could leave with the exiting stream or wait for
her and Gran to pass.

He did neither. As soon as the crowd stood to gather children and belongings, Ben made a beeline in Skye's direction.

"Skye! It's good to see you." He kissed her cheek, and let his hand linger on her upper arm as he greeted Gran and Georgie.

Gran looked from Skye to Ben and back to Skye, a glimmer of curiosity in her eyes. Fortunately, she was distracted by a friend, and Ben and Skye detached themselves to join the other young and able-bodied in the effort to put the room back in order.

"How have you been?" he asked as they folded chairs. She saw genuine concern in his eyes.

"Okay, thanks." She gave him a rueful smile that she hoped conveyed the right message. *I know the last time I saw you was at my mother's memorial service, and obviously it's been hard, but perhaps we could leave it at that?*

"I heard you left Congressman Vernon's office. I'm glad you got out of there. It sounded like such a snake pit," Ben said. Skye wondered if he knew anything about the circumstances under which she left.

"Yeah. I was never going to last there. What about you? Is this your vacation?" she asked as they took the chairs to the storage closet.

"Not exactly. There's nothing on the dockets, though, and my parents are in Europe. They asked if I'd come up, just in case this hurricane causes problems."

"Hal was telling me about it on the way. What's the latest about the track?"

"I'm not sure," Ben said as they rejoined Georgie and Gran. "You all don't have to worry up where you are. You know how it is down on the beach, though."

"We do, indeed. We'll keep hoping it heads another way," Gran said.

Skye noticed Ben's brother eyeing them from the doorway, arms crossed.

"Ben, I think your brother is waiting for you. Don't let us hold you up."

Ben looked toward the door. Skye thought she saw a flicker of worry on his face, but when he turned back, his expression was clear.

"Yeah, I should probably catch up with him. Good to see you." He gave Skye's arm another gentle squeeze then maneuvered through the crowd to the door.

To her supreme annoyance, Skye found herself battling disappointment that Ben had not suggested they get together while they were both on Haven Point. As they joined the slower exodus from the yacht club, she did her best to put him back on the mental shelf, where she thought she had safely stowed him months before.

When they emerged, the stars were coming out. A faint purple line on the horizon marked the last vestiges of twilight, as the black silhouettes of sailboats bobbed at their anchors in the little harbor.

They had stopped on the lawn to enjoy the gentle breeze, when Skye spotted Harriet Hyde Barrows's tall, bony frame heading with great purpose in their direction.

Gran groaned quietly. She and Harriet still cordially despised each other.

Harriet always looked peeved, but as she drew near, Skye noticed even greater displeasure than usual.

"Maren, I noticed the bittersweet bushes are overgrown on your section of the cliff."

"Hello, Harriet," Gran replied coolly. "My landscapers are taking care of it this week."

"Homeowners on the cliff are responsible for their sections of the cliff path," Harriet continued, as if Gran had not spoken.

"Yes, I am aware of that. Which is why I have asked my landscapers to take care of it," Gran repeated.

"Bittersweet is extremely invasive, you know. It strangles everything in its way."

"Yes. I do know. Which, again, is why I have told the landscapers to clear it." Gran spoke slowly now, as if talking to someone very stupid, which elicited a snort of amusement from Georgie.

"Please see that they do."

Harriet's last comment, accompanied by a practiced sniff, sounded so much like a parting shot, Skye expected her to turn on her heels and march off. But with her diatribe behind her, she turned her steely gaze to Skye.

"You remember my granddaughter, Skye," Gran said.

"Yes, I do." Harriet tilted her head back and squinted down at Skye, like a doctor over a tongue depressor. Skye felt a flush of anger, and barely restrained herself from asking Harriet if she had identified another invasive species. "Hello, Skye."

"Hello, Mrs. Barrows."

"I was sorry to hear about your mother." She did not sound particularly sorry.

"Thank you," Skye said. There was an awkward pause.

"All right, then," Harriet said finally. To Skye's ears, it sounded like *All right, then. I did that condolence thing. Now I'm free to go.*

Harriet turned and headed up the lawn. When she was about ten steps away, they heard her voice again.

"The bittersweet, Maren. Don't forget!"

"Thank you for the reminder, Harriet," Gran replied in a weary tone. When Harriet was out of sight, they headed up the hill themselves.

"She's a piece of work, that woman," Georgie said.

"I thought she was going to ask me about my red hair again," Skye said. "Do you all remember that?"

"Oh, I remember it, all right," Gran said.

"When was that?" Georgie asked. "I just recall being so mad she put you on the spot."

"It was the summer before I was in ninth grade." Skye smiled, remembering how Georgie had put a stop to Harriet's interrogation. "And Georgie, you told her I got my red hair from Gran's brother, but later, I saw a picture of Gran and her brother at her apartment. He didn't have red hair!"

"Oh Lord, no. He was a blond Viking, just like your grandma."

They all laughed.

"I must say, though," Georgie added, as they reached her house, "if that storm comes, it's a good thing Ben's here. Fritz and Tenley are in Europe, and that Steven won't be much help."

"They've had some issues with Ben's younger brother," Gran explained. She didn't elaborate, but Skye almost laughed, thinking about what would qualify as an "issue" in Ben's family. Maybe he got a bad grade in economics. Or—horror of horrors—decided to play baseball instead of lacrosse.

After she and Gran got back from the sing-along, Ben texted.

Hey, Skye. So good to see you tonight. Glad we happened to be here at the same time. Any chance we could get together tomorrow?

Skye had been annoyed with herself for her disappointment earlier when Ben had not suggested they get together. Now she was annoyed with herself for how pleased his text made her.

Sounds great.

Can I come by after lunch?

Perfect.

A few minutes later, he texted again.

Alternatively, you could come to our garage and sit in an inner tube drinking beer while I play Wild Thing on the guitar.

What? You only know two chords?

THREE chords.

CHAPTER TWENTY

August 1966
Haven Point

MAREN

Maren clenched her fists and strained forward in her Adirondack chair, as if by some miracle of telekinesis she could push Charlie and Annie's stalled boat out of calm water.

She was comforted by the fact that the water around Fritz Barrows's boat was also smooth as glass. Fritz was arguably the best junior sailor on Haven Point. If he had found himself in the same predicament, it was hardly something for Charlie to be ashamed of. The rest of the fleet was catching up quickly, though, and would soon eclipse them both.

They were watching from the hill above the yacht club. As always, the race had attracted a large crowd, a smudge of salt-bleached reds and blues and greens, the standard Haven Point palette for sailing.

Before the start of the race, it had never occurred to Maren that Charlie and Annie might actually win. At eleven, Charlie was the youngest skipper to qualify for the Stinneford Cup for as long as anyone could remember. With Annie as mate, their crew weight was half that of the other boats in the race. A decent showing against much more experienced sailors would have been satisfying enough.

But Charlie's start had been masterful. Even Maren, who had never sufficiently overcome her landlocked youth to truly comprehend the sport, had been able to see it. It planted a tantalizing seed, and she had begun to imagine the multitude of sins that would be redeemed if he actually won the race.

Oliver sat back in his chair, threaded his fingers through hers, and looked at her with a rueful smile. It seemed he had also begun to hope.

"At least he'll increase his lead over Fritz here. Light wind helps lightweights," said Maude, who sat on Oliver's other side.

Georgie looked up from the dock, where she stood beside Leighton Ballantine, the yacht club commodore. She was this year's vice commodore, one of several jobs that rotated among women from old Haven Point families. With Maude too frail for such responsibilities, Georgie had taken up the mantle in a reluctant spirit of noblesse oblige.

She could not be too conspicuous in support of Charlie and Annie (among many reasons, Maren suspected Harriet had already mentally carved Fritz's name in the Stinneford Cup trophy), but Georgie patted her chest in a subtle mime of anxiety.

Charlie did manage to pull a little ahead of Fritz, but it seemed meaningless, since the other eight boats in the fleet were quickly making up time and appeared ready to pass them both at any moment. Maren leaned over to pet one of Maude's dogs, and tried to readjust her hopes back to their earlier, more modest level.

A few seconds later, Maude sat up a little straighter.

"Oliver, look," Maude said. Maren heard excitement in her voice.

Oliver looked through his binoculars then leaned forward, his posture rigid with anticipation.

"What is it?" Maren asked.

"Look at the water near Charlie, Maren."

Maren lifted her own binoculars and watched as the ripples in the water moved like a cloud from Gunnison Island toward Charlie and Fritz. Suddenly, the sails of their two boats filled and they picked up speed. The rest of the fleet slowed to a crawl in calm waters.

"Charlie read the wind shift," Oliver said, amazed.

"I've never seen one like him." Maude shook her head. "Not that young, at least."

Maren's heart warmed. Maude's Yankee thrift extended to compliments. They were all the more treasured for being so rare.

The race was down to Charlie and Annie versus Fritz and his crewman, Gibb Devereaux. Charlie had a small lead, but the heavier wind now gave the advantage to the heavier crew. Fritz pulled ahead just as the boats disappeared behind Gunnison Island.

"Oh no," Maren said.

"It's not over. The wind is lighter around the island," Oliver said.

It would be a couple of minutes before the boats would pass the mark behind the island and reappear. The crowd began to chatter as they waited, delighted with a Stinneford Cup more exciting than anticipated.

Maren, heart thumping, kept one eye on the water and the other on Oliver, who repeatedly checked his watch. When he squinted at the water and lifted his binoculars, she followed suit, just in time to see the top of a mast emerge, followed closely by another.

"Are the spinnakers up?" Maren asked. From this distance, the colors of the spinnaker sails were the only way to tell one boat from another.

"They should be. We'll see the stripes soon."

And then, there it was. The red stripe of Charlie's sail.

"He's in the lead!" Maren's cry was drowned by the roar of the crowd as everyone on the hill also caught sight of the sail. Seconds later, the British racing green stripe of Fritz's spinnaker came into view.

As they swiftly approached the finish line, Maren could finally make out the figures in the boats: Annie, deftly manipulating the ropes attached to the bottom corners of the triangular sail, and Charlie looking over his shoulder, shouting orders.

A shift in the wind acted like a crop to a horse's haunch, giving both boats a burst of speed. Fritz positioned himself right behind Charlie.

"What's he doing?" Maren asked.

"Trying to steal wind from Charlie's port side. If they block it, they can put Charlie in dead air."

By nudging his boat to the starboard side, Charlie kept his wind but lost some time. Fritz closed in, his spinnaker edging past the back corner of Charlie's boat.

It came down to the final fifty yards. The entire crowd on the cliff was on its feet, cheering on the eleven-year-old skipper. Maren dared not look at Harriet. Even if Fritz won, she would be livid at the bias shown toward Charlie.

Maren held her breath and said a silent prayer. *For Charlie, please, for Charlie . . .*

If the finish line had been ten yards farther, the race would have been Fritz's. But when the final shot of the cannon came, Charlie and Annie cleared the line ahead.

There was more hearty applause. Maren lifted her binoculars and saw Fritz lean over the side of his boat to shake hands with Charlie. She sighed deeply, a sense of satisfaction as pure as she ever remembered feeling.

"I wish Pauline had seen this," Maude said. Maren

smiled and resolved to call her that afternoon. Pauline's speech had degenerated, so it was hard for her to talk, but she could listen. This was indeed the sort of victory that would thrill her, even if she only dimly understood it. William's athletic triumphs had been too violent, too angry for Pauline to appreciate, but she always rooted for her grandchildren.

As the sailors made their way up the hill, Fritz grinned and chattered excitedly on the outskirts of the crowd surrounding Charlie. He seemed as dazzled as everyone by the race's results, by his little competitor's prowess. Maren noticed that he steered clear of his mother, who was unable to hide a cloudy expression.

When Annie wriggled out from the group of well-wishers, Fritz tapped her on the shoulder and extended his hand. She shook it and smiled, friendly enough but nothing special, then moved on to another friend. Fritz gazed after her with an expression Maren had seen on too many boys' faces.

Another conquest, Maren thought. She had suspected as much the past couple of weeks.

Charlie finally detached himself from the crowd and approached Maren and Oliver, who gave him great hugs and congratulations. Annie flitted over, picked him up, and twirled him in a circle.

"You are king of the WATER!"

"Put me down!" Charlie said, pretending to object.

"All right." Annie released him. "But only because I'm going to the beach."

"Annie, be home by six. Remember we're going to Phippsburg tonight." Whatever the outcome, they'd promised Charlie a special dinner. Annie waved in vague acquiescence and took off after her friends.

* * *

Later that afternoon, Maren joined Oliver on the porch. He had arrived the previous day and could only stay a week. She wanted to make the most of a rare moment alone.

Oliver smiled up at her, laid his medical journal aside, and made room for her on the love seat.

There had been a time when Oliver's smile had lost its power over Maren. Even when she knew their marriage was on the road to recovery, she had not expected to regain the intoxication of their early days. Didn't that always fade as years passed, and with children underfoot? But to her surprise, the old passion had returned, albeit in a more tempered form.

It had taken much effort on both their parts. Maren knew Oliver had been as surprised as she by his explanation for his affair with Khaki. Once conscious of it, though, he had put his great mind toward understanding it. In typical fashion, he did not share all his thoughts, but she could tell by the fruits it bore that he had undergone a rigorous self-examination.

She saw it in general ways—steadfastness, patience, presence—but also in specific gestures. Maren never told Oliver her fleeting notion that summer of taking the children to Minnesota for the pre-harvest, so she was surprised the following year when he proposed the idea himself. He had only occasionally joined Maren and the children on their post-Christmas visits, but now he insisted they all needed more time with her family.

Maren had been pleased, but it was not until they arrived for their first visit that she realized it was not simply kindness or respect that had prompted his suggestion. Oliver had always been cordial to her parents, but now she saw an aspirational quality to the way he interacted with them, as if merely being in their presence might allow him to absorb some of their goodness. Whatever indefinable quality he saw in Maren (something too deeply ingrained for her to fully comprehend herself) he seemed to want for himself, for his children. The visits had become an every-other-year tradition.

At first, Maren was too angry to examine Oliver's explanation. But while he never suggested she was responsible, and she refused to blame herself, over time she was able to see what Khaki had given him, what she had withheld. Maren had always disparaged women who complained about their neglectful husbands, but deep down, Maren *had* felt neglected. She had just been too proud to ask Oliver to spend more time with her, to sit and talk at the end of the day, or even just casually occupy the same space. She went off to her activities, made plans with her friends, and never let her loneliness show.

The effort to prove her independence to Oliver had been a catastrophic success. Khaki—diabolically smart Khaki—was cold to Maren, but she showed Oliver another side: vulnerable, defenseless. Khaki made Oliver believe she needed him, and he had responded.

In the end, they both learned that a marriage was more than just two people and all they brought with them. It was a creature of its own that needed care and feeding.

And that smile of his, which made him look astonished at his good fortune to have her as his wife, again ignited something deep inside her.

"That race was something," Oliver said, arms crossed behind his head, the picture of contentment.

"Wasn't it?"

"I wish we could find sailing's equal for Charlie at home," he said. Oliver was not involved in the minutiae of his children's lives, but Charlie's difficulties were pronounced enough to penetrate even his busy mind.

"You know it's not just sailing that makes it good for him here."

"It's not? You mean Haven Point offers something more?" Oliver teased. Maren cuffed him good-naturedly.

"He is a completely different boy here. He's good here."

The tetchiness and sensitivity that showed in small ways when Charlie was younger had burst into florid display in recent years. He went about satisfying his hunger for attention in the worst ways, acting out in school and picking fights, usually futile ones with older boys. At home they were forever waiting for another shoe to drop, for news of another incident arising from Charlie's false bravado.

In Maine, he was utterly transformed. Each of the children loved Haven Point, but Charlie needed it. Within hours of his arrival, his edges were smoothed like a piece of sea glass. There was something medicinal in the air and water, the people, the house. Everything was hard at home. Everything on Haven Point was easy.

The discovery of Charlie's prodigious sailing abilities had been the icing on the cake. For several years after Oliver's affair, they had agreed their marriage was in too tender a state for long separations. Maren had limited their time on Haven Point to a few weeks, at most, each summer. Even those short visits had provided sufficient time for Charlie to master the fourteen-foot boats the younger sailors used. The previous summer he had taken the helm of a 110, and it had been as easy for him as breathing.

He would leave for the yacht club early every morning and stay all day. Unlike at home, where he seemed to alienate everyone in a position of authority, the staff there loved him. Every evening he'd burst into the kitchen, erupting with excitement.

"The one-tens dig in the chine and carve to the weather, Mom! They just fly on the reach!"

He might as well have been speaking Greek, for all Maren understood, but she shared his joy. It was for Charlie's sake that Maren had suggested they come for a full season this summer. Their marriage was solid, but Charlie was not. That morning's victory felt to Maren like the ultimate affirmation of the decision.

As they sat watching the birds and water, she felt like a great knot had been untied.

Maren wasn't a full convert to the Haven Point religion, like Oliver and Georgie and the others who had such abiding faith in the place, its mission and meaning. She knew, of course, that Haven Point represented an extraordinary privilege, but she felt it needed the counterbalance of life at home. It was different now, though. It helped that she no longer felt exiled there, and that she was relieved of the burden of Pauline and all her attending chaos. She and the rest of Pauline's protectors had been able to lower their guards somewhat after William's death, but the Pauline-Irina-Sassy triumvirate had presented its own difficulties.

The previous October, in a fit of Russian passion, Irina had announced she could no longer handle the job of being Pauline's caretaker. Maren told Oliver she thought it was time to move Pauline into a home, and that it made the most sense for it to be in D.C. Oliver mounted weak resistance but ultimately relented.

Maren found the facility, saw to the move, and often brought the children to visit. Pauline listened sweetly to their stories and smiled at their rambunctious ways. An occasional comment or sharp observation, even with her imperfect speech, betrayed the intelligence Maren suspected she'd buried all those years with William.

Oliver visited less frequently, but often enough to gather what Maren had long known. Their children had no greater champion than his mother. He remained formal with Pauline, but his disdain was not quite so pronounced.

Maren sank further into the love seat and leaned on Oliver. He put his arm around her and kissed the top of her head. It was only when she heard Annie's footsteps bouncing down the porch that she realized she had dozed off.

Annie was wearing one of Billy's old T-shirts and wrinkled Bermuda shorts, evidently having changed into whatever clothes she found in the cabana. Annie never had an awkward phase in the usual sense of the expression, though she had been all long arms and legs until the past couple of years, when her limbs had arranged themselves more proportionally. She was an indisputable beauty, tall with thick blond hair and shining blue eyes, but hadn't an ounce of vanity. Shopping, clothing, and makeup bored her. She brushed her hair only when forced.

"Can I have some of this? I'm crazy thirsty!" She picked up Maren's iced tea and took a great swallow before Maren could answer.

"Help yourself," Maren said, after Annie set down the half-empty glass. Annie flopped on the wicker ottoman opposite her parents and stretched her legs.

"I'm proud of how you helped Charlie today," Oliver said.

"I just did whatever he told me." Annie shrugged. "He'd have won by more with Billy or someone heavier in the boat."

Maren felt a prickle of apprehension. The only wrinkle in an otherwise smooth summer was tension between Oliver and Annie. The two of them could argue about anything, even a compliment.

"Well, it was a great race," Oliver said, prepared to leave it at that for once. Maren knew Oliver actually felt as she did: Billy would not have been a better crewmate for Charlie. They had both been relieved when they realized Billy would be visiting friends in Camden during the Stinneford Cup. He was kind enough to his little brother, but they had a more typical sibling relationship. He would have struggled to do Charlie's bidding.

The same powerful intuition that had enabled Annie to tease out Oliver and Maren's troubles all those years before also gave her keen insight into her younger brother. She had nothing like Charlie's difficulties at home. In temperament and disposition, she was almost his perfect inverse. But while she would consider it traitorous to admit, she helped him on land just as she'd helped him on the water that morning. She remained Charlie's greatest ally, refusing to openly acknowledge his vulnerabilities even as she did all in her power to mitigate them.

Annie and Oliver, on the other hand, were often at loggerheads. For a time, Annie's performance in school was the main source of conflict. Billy, who would soon start his freshman year at Harvard, achieved academically as Oliver had, by reason and dogged effort. Annie, all impulse and instinct, had always been an indifferent student. When something captured her interest, they saw flashes of keen intelligence and ability, but Oliver found this more frustrating than encouraging. He wanted to mold a Demarest from the hybrid that was Annie.

Maren saw in Annie a fertile mind that didn't run in conventional directions. She finally persuaded Oliver to let Annie attend a school more focused on the arts, where she had shown the most interest. Annie had thrived, and Oliver seemed satisfied, but to Maren's dismay it had not diminished the conflict.

Maren had begun to think Annie's anger at her father went beyond normal teenage defiance. It was like a virus that lurked in her bloodstream, reactivating at random intervals. Every outbreak left their relationship weaker.

Maren wondered if a piece of it was rooted in what she had overhead between her parents all those years before. Despite their efforts, Annie had steadfastly refused to discuss it. Maren hoped Annie would eventually realize all was well with them, but the jury was still out.

"When do we leave for Phippsburg?" Annie asked.

"Soon. I'll get Charlie," Maren said.

She found Charlie in the attic, lying on a sagging twin bed in one of the ocean-facing rooms, his nose buried in one of Oliver's old books. The weak sun shone through the casements, creating a diamond-patterned light over his head.

"Charlie, time to leave for Phippsburg."

He looked up, confused briefly, as if he'd been transported and was surprised at the passage of time, but he quickly recovered and jumped up.

"Oh, good!"

"Before we go, I'd like to call Nonnie. I'm sure she'll want to hear about your big victory today."

Charlie smiled broadly, and they made their way to the phone in the downstairs hall. Dora, the most cheerful of the nurses at the home, picked up the phone.

"Miss Pauline is sound asleep, Mrs. Demarest, but I'll take a message."

"Hold on, Dora." Maren put her hand over the receiver. "Charlie, do you want Dora to give Nonnie a message?"

"Yeah!" He leaned forward and put his mouth near the phone. "Tell Nonnie I won the Stinneford Cup. Tell her the whole thing!" Maren laughed and stood a little taller to get the phone out of Charlie's reach.

"I'm sorry, Dora. Do you have a pen and paper?"

"I do. You just tell me everything, honey." With Charlie in the background, gesticulating and interjecting details, Maren relayed a message, punctuated with apologies for its length.

"Don't you leave anything out, Mrs. Demarest. This will cheer her up. You know she loves that Charlie. She usually has a good spell after dinner. I'll give her the good news then."

"She's gonna tell her?" Charlie asked when Maren hung up.

"The Stinneford Cup will be Nonnie's after-dinner entertainment."

Charlie beamed, and Maren felt a surge of the joy and relief she experienced whenever he was contented.

"We'd better run in before this gets going," Oliver said as they pulled into the Gale House parking lot. Dark clouds rolled in from the west, like a great charcoal blanket being pulled over the sky. A strong gust of wind ushered them inside.

The restaurant was open-air, with clear, vinyl roll-down curtains for the windows along three sides. Long strips of paper covered old picnic tables. It was a typical, busy Saturday evening. As the hostess led them toward a table, noise from one corner drew Maren's eye. She turned to see Finn and Mary Pat Donnelly, their kids, and a few other teenagers Maren did not recognize. As she passed, Finn smiled at her and raised his eyebrows.

Maren nodded and smiled primly. She avoided Finn when possible. On the rare occasions he caught her alone, he invariably paid her some extravagant compliment, but she was meticulously careful not to encourage him.

When they reached the table, Maren sat facing the

water, opposite Annie, whose eyes soon wandered eagerly in the direction of the Donnelly table.

"Look, Mom. The Donnellys are here." She craned her neck to get a better look. "There's Patrick!"

When Oliver looked up at this, Maren again braced for conflict. Oliver spent little time thinking about the Donnellys, but his old reflexes were in order. Just as a patient will kick when a doctor hits his knee with a percussion hammer, so Oliver sniffed when he heard the name "Donnelly."

"Yes, I saw them when we came in," Maren said, her tone carefully neutral.

"Why didn't you tell me?" She leaned over again, and lifted her hand to wave but then pulled it down almost as quickly, enthusiasm drained from her expression. She took a sudden interest in the menu, though she knew every item on it.

Oliver, having watched the exchange, opened his mouth to speak, but Maren shot him a look. Fortunately, he took the hint.

While Oliver surveyed the kids for their orders, Maren turned as if to get something from her purse and looked over to see what Annie had noticed. Patrick had his arm slung over the shoulder of a girl with a thick mane of black hair, heavily made-up dark eyes, and a snug floral blouse that could not contain her voluptuousness. She was laughing, eyes lit up, as if thrilled to be in such company.

So, Annie's jealous! Maren thought, turning back to the table. This was an interesting turn of affairs.

Annie and Patrick's friendship had faded in recent years when they spent so little time on Haven Point. During that time, the Donnellys had remained in their social limbo on the other side of the rocks, though it did not seem to bother them. Haven Pointers were minimalist entertainers who tended to limit houseguests (at least in part to keep the place a well-kept secret), but summer at the Donnellys was one long house party, with emphasis on "party." At any time, a dozen or more cars were parked outside their house. On sunny days, a great congregation of Donnellys and guests could be seen enjoying the water in front of their stretch of beach.

At night, more cars appeared, carrying more guests for their parties. Strains of music often wafted over the rocks and down the beach, the sound reverberating around the cove and into the open windows of every home on the point. While no Haven Point adult would be seen at a Donnelly party, they thought nothing of spending hours talking about them.

The Donnelly property offered so many enticements, neither parental disapproval nor the rocks at the end of the beach could keep the younger set away. The Donnelly kids rarely came to the Haven Point side, though Maren occasionally saw Patrick and his brothers at the end of the beach, playing in the pickup football and kickball games, which were more democratic affairs.

Though leaner and more striking than his father, in disposition Patrick struck Maren as more his mother's son. However vulgar and flashy Haven Point might deem him, Finn had an undeniable charm, a boundless self-assurance combined with cheeriness and optimism. Patrick had his father's confidence, but little of his charm.

By the time dinner was served, Annie had regained her equanimity. She wouldn't ruin Charlie's night with sullenness. The storm made for great theater as it passed overhead. Diners jumped at claps of thunder, while the waitresses remained oblivious. They lingered over coffee and dessert until the hardest of the rain stopped. The Donnellys were long gone by the time they left.

A breeze kicked up from the north, carrying with it some residual electricity, but it was only drizzling as they climbed in the car, full and laughing. Maren sighed, content, as she slipped into her seat. They drove home behind the western edge of the blanket of clouds and squished across the lawn to the kitchen door.

As they walked in, the phone rang. Oliver went to answer, while Maren urged Charlie and Annie upstairs and into their pajamas. She was getting ready for bed herself when Oliver entered the room. He walked slowly and looked perplexed.

"What is it?"

"That was the director of the home. Mother died tonight." Oliver sat in a chair near the window, an upholstered one Pauline had liked—too small for him, though he didn't notice. He looked out the window. The wind was still a little wild, and the screens glistened from the earlier drops.

Oliver seemed unsure what to do with the information he'd just received, and Maren felt something shift underneath her.

"Oh dear, Oliver. What did he say?"

"He put Dora on. She'd been with Mother earlier. Dora said she died peacefully in her sleep. She had been weak lately, as you know, though they had not necessarily expected this now."

Peacefully, in her sleep. Maren felt a twinge of relief, even pride. It had been the humble goal of the women all those years: Pauline might die from her drinking, but not in some horrible, public way.

Maren slipped on her robe, crouched beside Oliver, and placed her hand gently on his forearm. It was hard to know the precise words to say, given Oliver's complicated feelings, so she reverted to manners.

"I'm so sorry. This must be a shock."

"Dora said something I didn't understand, something about your story?" He looked as if he'd been told something in a language he struggled to translate. "The story made Mother happy, she said."

"Oh, the race. I forgot to tell you. Charlie and I called her. She was asleep, but Dora took a long message about Charlie and Annie winning the Stinneford Cup and promised to pass it along."

Oliver looked out the window, thoughtful and quiet. Though he had grown to appreciate his mother's kindness to the children, Maren did not think he had fully absorbed the beauty or purity of it. It was partly because he had fewer occasions to witness it, but she also suspected he was reluctant to acknowledge any goodness in his mother.

"She adored Charlie, and she understood him." Maren kept her tone matter-of-fact, to avoid the appearance of pressing a point. "She was sweet to him."

"She was that way with Daniel and me once," Oliver said, still looking out the window.

"Was she?" Maren knew this already, of course. She had heard it all from Maude and Georgie, about the poems she made up when the kids were little, the special brand of loving attention that had been lost to the bottle. In all the time Maren had known Oliver, however, these were the only tender words about Pauline she had ever heard from him.

She had long hoped Oliver would forgive his mother. Not for Pauline's sake, necessarily. Maren pitied Pauline's vulnerabilities and had been sincere in her desire to protect her from harm and humiliation, but she felt Pauline owned her troubles. With more strength of character and a better moral compass, she might have fought to be well.

Her choices damaged her children, and that had consequences.

She believed forgiveness would help Oliver. He was a better husband than the man she'd found in that room at the Waldorf Hotel, but some part of him was still closed off.

Though she knew it might not last, the innocent confusion she saw in his eyes gave her hope. He looked like a child with questions, open to answers.

CHAPTER TWENTY-ONE

August 2008
Haven Point

SKYE

Skye was simultaneously maneuvering a hinky-wheeled grocery cart and examining Gran's shopping list when she almost smacked into someone at the end of an aisle. When she looked up to apologize, she was surprised to see Ryan Donnelly.

Nearly as startling as running into him was his appearance. Ryan was usually smartly dressed and brimming with energy, but today he wore a tattered T-shirt that looked two sizes too small. His hair was stringy, and dark circles rimmed his eyes. Skye detected none of his usual animation. He certainly didn't seem happy to see her.

"Hi, Ryan. It's been ages. I didn't know you were going to be here this week."

"Yeah, Congress is out, as you know. I'm off for a bit." His eyes roved around the store as if he was in a terrible hurry to be anywhere other than where they stood.

"So, how are you?" Skye asked.

"Fine. I'm fine . . . uh . . ." He grasped for something to say. "Did you hear there'll be a clambake tonight?"

"Gran mentioned it. I'm going to try to come by. Seriously, are you okay?" She peered at him a little more closely. "You don't look quite yourself."

"Yeah, fine, totally. Just getting some stuff . . . Been

a little crazy . . ." Ryan's voice trailed off as he pointed imprecisely toward the deli counter.

"Okay, see you later, Ryan."

That was weird, Skye thought as she put the groceries in the car. It did seem fortuitous to have bumped into him, though. Skye was still bothered by her fangirl reaction to Ben the night before. Seeing Ryan, Haven Point outsider, was a reminder of what had bothered her about Ben in the wake of her mother's death: He was the consummate Haven Point insider.

Ben had said he would come by, but Skye wondered if he actually would, given the latest weather reports. The hurricane had moved north overnight, its eye hovering off the mid-Atlantic coast. D.C. had been pounded by rain, but winds were barely tropical storm levels, and it looked like it would pass east of New York City.

Unfortunately, it appeared it might then take an inland track, which had potential for catastrophe in New England. Skye was always skeptical of worst-case scenarios, but it appeared the storm would pack at least as much punch as a nor'easter, and everyone knew how much trouble those could cause.

When she got back to Fourwinds, the sun seemed to be winning its fight against an earlier mist. Skye decided to go for a run. After she put the groceries away, she slipped on her sneakers and headed onto Haven Point Road in the direction of the beach club.

The gravel crunched under her feet, and the damp pine air filled her lungs. She'd gotten out of the running habit over the previous year, and it took her a while to hit her stride, but by the time she reached the end of the beach and doubled back to run along the causeway, the endorphins kicked in.

For the first time in a while, she felt like she could put

her career anxiety into the background. She stopped at the top of the hill near the yacht club to stretch and take in the panoramic view. The fog had completely cleared by this point, and she could see all the way to the Portland Head Light.

As her eyes scanned the bay, she noticed one of the club's fleet of racing boats sailing away from the point with two people aboard, a man and a woman. Something about them drew her eye—the outline of the man, the breadth of his back and the way he moved. She picked her way through a clump of weeds to an old brass viewer that stood nearby. It was like the ones on the observation deck of the Empire State Building, except it didn't require coins.

The viewer was stiff and unwieldy, but she was able to train it in the direction of the boat and sharpen the focus. Even through the old, salt-covered lenses, she could see the sailors were Ben and Charlotte Spencer.

So, she is here.

Charlotte's eyes were shaded by Ray-Bans, her hair held back by a Jackie O–style headband, the kind that looks fabulous on women with silky hair, but which Skye could never figure out how to wear without looking like a Chia Pet. She and Ben worked together in perfect rhythm, the fruits of their labor evident in gloriously full sails.

Skye wasn't sure how long she had stood riveted to the spot watching them, but the sound of a car coming up Haven Point Road broke the spell, and it suddenly hit her that if she could see Ben, he could see her, as could anyone who happened by.

She let go of the viewer as if it were contaminated. As she ran back to the house, she was overwhelmed by a sense of narrow escape, like a sleepwalker who had awakened at the edge of a cliff.

To her relief, Gran was still out. Skye sank into a kitchen chair and called Adriene at work. She expected to get her voicemail, but Adriene answered.

"Hey! How are things at the Playground of the Waspocracy?"

Skye launched in immediately, describing the scene she'd just witnessed.

"So, she's there. He's there. You don't know what that means."

"You should have seen them. They're a total matched set. They looked like an ad for polo shirts or nautical rope bracelets."

"You can't draw any conclusions. Either way, why does it bother you? Just yesterday you were saying he wasn't your type."

"I don't know." Skye sighed, defeated.

"Ben is the only guy who has this effect on you, Skye. You were weird about him in high school. Then you date all those tortured artists and barely bat an eye . . ."

"Yeah, except . . ." Skye started, but Adriene was on a roll.

"Then Mr. Normal McNormalFace shows up again, and from day one you're standing over the relationship, ready to declare it dead and go rummaging through its pockets."

"First of all, you really must do something about your imagery. It's getting extremely gruesome," Skye snapped. "Second, you can hardly call it a relationship. We had a handful of dates."

"Because you pulled the plug!"

Because my mother died, Skye thought, though she

didn't say it out loud. It would have been a cheap shot. She knew Adriene was onto something.

When Adriene spoke again, her tone was gentler. "I think you need to figure out what you're afraid of, Skye."

After they hung up, Skye sat thinking. It dawned on her that the worst moment standing on the hill above the yacht club had not been when she saw Ben and Charlotte through the viewer. It was when she realized they could see her.

Being seen. That was always it, wasn't it? She wanted to control what people saw—to decide when the cameras rolled, when the laugh track came on.

She had tried to convince herself that her mother's death put the differences between her and Ben in relief, that he wasn't her "type," but the truth was rather rudely staring her in the face now. She was afraid because she had lost control of what he saw.

Adriene had been generalizing about her "tortured artists." Not all the guys she had dated had been tortured or artists. But they had been messed up in one way or another, and Skye had been able to hide in their darkness. In Ben's bright light, she felt exposed.

Skye had never felt the kind of connection she had with Ben, never enjoyed such easy laughter, such great chemistry. She hadn't wanted to admit it to herself, but she was wild about him. She had been for years.

A spark of hope had been ignited the night before. Seeing him sailing with Charlotte had almost extinguished it.

Almost.

While the twentysomethings would be at the clambake that night, Gran would attend a potluck for the older set at the Lawrences'. Skye had promised to bake a tomato pie she could take with her.

That afternoon, as she was arranging slices of cheese in the bottom of a pie crust, Ben knocked on the kitchen door and poked his head inside.

"Hey, Ben. Come on in." She fixed a pleasant look on her face. Ben seemed his usual cheerful self, his expression unblemished by guilt or worry. He came in and wrapped her in a hug.

"So good to see you," he said. He pulled back, looked at her closely, and brushed a stray hair from her face. It was a quick gesture, almost brotherly, but still intimate enough that she felt a grain of confidence.

"Good to see you, too," she said. She smiled and nodded at the piece of cheese in her hand. He took the hint, moved to the table, turned one of the chairs, and sat on it backward.

"So, what are you making?"

"Tomato pie."

He rose halfway to peer at her half-assembled creation.

"You're not supposed to see it." She shielded the glass baking dish with her hands. "It's my grandmother's recipe. Sacrosanct!"

"Is it made with ramen noodles?"

"No. No ramen noodles."

"Microwave popcorn?"

"No, not that either." She began to laugh.

"Bratwurst?"

"No. Tomato pie has no ramen noodles, microwave popcorn, or bratwurst in it," she said.

"Then don't worry. I couldn't make it if I wanted to."

"I don't know how you haven't shriveled up and died from starvation."

"People feed me. Or I scrounge," he joked. Ben was hopeless in the kitchen. Skye had once noticed a squash racquet on Ben's counter. He confessed he had used it to drain tortellini.

Skye knew she had no grounds to ask, but her desire to know where things stood with him and Charlotte weighed on her.

"Such a perfect Maine day, isn't it? You'd never know a storm was coming. What have you been up to?"

In the pause that followed, she could almost hear the engine of his mind at work.

"Nothing much," he said finally. "What about you?"

Like a ball on a roulette wheel, Skye's emotions cycled through confusion, disappointment, and humiliation, before finally landing on anger.

"Grocery shopping for this," she said, nodding toward the pie plate. "I went to the store in Phippsburg. Guess who I ran into?"

"Who?"

"Ryan Donnelly," she said brightly, as if she did not remember Ben's reaction when she'd brought his name up before.

"Really," Ben said, his tone flat.

"Yeah. He mentioned the clambake on the beach tonight." She continued to feign oblivion.

"Skye, how well do you know Ryan Donnelly?"

"I've known Ryan for a while. He works on Capitol Hill," she replied. She turned to get Parmesan cheese out of the refrigerator. "I know the Donnellys aren't up to snuff on Haven Point, but I don't get why you have such a hang-up about him."

Ben paused. His usually sunny countenance was overtaken by a stormy expression.

"So that's what you think? That I don't like Ryan Donnelly because he's not 'up to snuff'? Quite an indictment of me, Skye. Thanks for clarifying."

"Well, why don't you like him then?" she asked, finally daring to meet his gaze.

"Forget it. I'll catch you later, Skye." He sounded more sad than mad. He rose, flipped his chair back to the table, and left without another word.

Skye gripped the edge of the counter and closed her eyes.

Skye Demarest, you are an idiot, she thought. She sighed and pushed herself off the counter. After she put the pie in the oven, she went to her room and sat on the window seat.

Ryan had said Ben had been a jackass to him. Maybe he had, maybe he hadn't. Skye did not know Ryan that well, and while Ben was indisputably a Haven Point kid, she had to admit she had never seen him treat anyone poorly. Ryan might be a blind spot, but people are allowed the occasional blind spot.

Of course, the whole spat with Ben had been a proxy battle for her own fears and resentments. He had no way to know she had seen him sailing with Charlotte, or how vulnerable it made her feel. She had been on the fence about the clambake that evening, but she realized she needed to go and apologize. Perhaps she would even tell him the truth.

She wished she could get a handle on her mood. When she wasn't in a weird stupor, she was angry. Even this old room had annoyed her yesterday. Why on earth would she be irritated by Gran's desire to make her feel welcome?

She rose, pulled one of the old children's books from the shelf, and brought it back to the window seat—*A Time of Wonder* by Robert McCloskey. It was about two sisters on a family vacation on an island in Maine. The denouement is a surprise hurricane that rips through in the evening. No wonder it had caught her eye.

A Time of Wonder was her mother's favorite children's book. She had always admired its lyricism and simple illustrations. But as Skye reread it with fresh eyes, she also saw that it was a love poem to Maine.

Skye looked out at Gunnison Island, lying long and green in the sunshine, as if in defiance of the forecast. Her mother had loved storms. She'd even harbored a slight survivalist streak, though it ran crosswise of her disorganization. *So many flashlights, so few batteries,* Adriene used to joke.

One September day when Skye was twelve or thirteen, D.C. caught the tail end of an unusual tropical storm. Skye had gone to the teachers' parking lot after school and found her mother had beaten her to the car for once. It was raining pitchforks, and Skye ran to the door, closing her umbrella at the last second so she could stay as dry as possible. Her mom was dripping wet, of course. She had given up on umbrellas years before. On the rare occasion she remembered to bring one, she invariably left it behind.

"You won't believe what this car can do," her mom said. She had a big smile on her face, and her eyes were dancing.

"What?" Skye asked, surprised at her mother's enthusiasm. She had never taken an interest in cars, just drove whatever used model Pop found for her. (All heavy and slow, a hedge against her distracted driving.)

"Watch this." Her mom popped in a cassette. As Don McLean's voice filled the car, she turned on the windshield wipers then looked at Skye, eyebrows raised, waiting for her to catch on.

It took Skye a minute, but then she started to laugh. The wipers moved in perfect rhythm to "American Pie."

"This is my favorite car ever," her mom said as she pulled out of the lot.

The image brought a brief smile, but Skye pushed the memory from her mind. Certain recollections of her mother seemed to come with their own relentless gravitational force. If she did not resist, she felt certain they would pull her into some fathomless trench.

Skye had spent years lying to the world about her life. She was not about to start lying to herself. Gran, Billy, and the other mourners had tried to rewrite her mom's history with their varnished elegies. Skye knew the real story, though: a roller coaster of hope and despair that ended with flashing lights, neighbors' worried faces, and her mother in a bathtub.

Later that evening, Skye put on eye makeup, white jeans, and a green silk V-neck shirt she knew was becoming. The day had started blue and sparkling, but it was humid now, so she abandoned the idea of doing anything with her hair and settled for a loose bun. She tied a lightweight sweater around her shoulders and headed out the door.

The clambake was in front of the Van Sant compound, near the end of the beach. It was an old-school affair: clams, onions, corn, and potatoes wrapped in cheesecloth and cooked over firewood in a rock-filled pit.

By the time she arrived, Skip Van Sant was already plucking items from the pit and piling them on aluminum trays. A few people were filling plates from platters on long tables, but most were still milling about. Skye grabbed a beer from the cooler and looked around, trying to make out individual faces in the gathering darkness.

As she made her way around the periphery of the clam pit, she spotted Charlotte's familiar silhouette. Skye couldn't help but feel inordinately pleased that Ben was not by her side.

Something in the volume and quality of conversation suggested people had been drinking for a while. That, along with anticipation of the storm, gave the party an agitated, buzzy excitement. As she headed toward the bonfire, ten or fifteen feet beyond the clam pit, she picked up snatches of conversation.

During Hurricane Bob, the tide dragged the anchors, and sailboats crashed into each other. . . . Harbor staff said there wouldn't be any heroics. . . . We pulled our boats today and took them to Gull Harbor. . . . It's small, but deep, with good holding ground. . . .

She caught glimpses of faces, hands wrapped around bottles of beer, or red Solo cups filled with wine or gin and tonics. They were all as they had always seemed to her: preppy, confident, boozy. The girls wore white jeans and bright sweaters; the guys, expensive windbreakers and Nantucket reds or khaki Bermuda shorts. She spoke with a few people as she circulated. Everyone was pleasant enough, too certain of their place to snub her, but no one noticed if she left a conversation and melted into the darkness.

When she made a full tour of the party without seeing Ben, she felt deflated. From the chatter she picked up, most Haven Pointers down on the beach were clearing out. If Ben hadn't already left, he surely would the next day.

Just as she was debating whether to text him, she noticed that conversation around the bonfire had quieted. Something close to the water's edge had caught people's attention. She peered into the darkness.

It took a moment to hear the angry voices and make

out the shapes of two figures squared off, a foot or two apart. They leaned into each other, postures taut and menacing.

It didn't take long to discern the familiar shape of Ben's back. Even through the dark and distance she could see the tension in his shoulders. He raised his arm and pointed toward the other man's chest, an aggressive gesture unlike anything she had seen in all the time she had known him.

It wasn't until the other face was caught by the glow of the fire that she was able to make it out. It was Ryan, of course. Some part of her had already known. She strained to listen but could not make out individual words, just the sharp staccato beat of an angry confrontation.

She slipped into the crowd next to Tita Harwood, whom she knew slightly.

"Hey, Skye." Tita glanced at her quickly, then looked back toward the beach.

"Is that Ben Barrows and Ryan Donnelly?" Skye asked.

"Yeah," Tita replied, with a sigh that suggested that they were witnessing some variation of a commonplace scene.

"What is the deal with them?" Skye asked. Tita seemed as good a source as any. Though she came from an old Haven Point family, her aunt had married a Donnelly (an event still known as "the original sin" among some older Haven Pointers). While she was not necessarily a Donnelly partisan, she struck Skye as a semi-convert, less likely to rush to Ben's defense as a reflex.

"I'm not sure exactly. Ben's younger brother Steven was friendly with Ryan. I guess Ben didn't like it. He's been on Ryan's case this summer."

"Why didn't he like it?"

"I don't know. The Hydes and Donnellys have never gotten along." Tita shrugged.

Skye looked back toward the water in time to see Ben push Ryan away with one arm and stalk off in the direction of his grandmother's house. He was eventually swallowed up in the darkness. When Tita moved on to greet a friend, Skye slipped out of the light of the fire and walked in the same direction.

She found Ben slumped on an Adirondack chair in the grass atop the sea wall. There was just enough light from Harriet's house to reveal a grim look on his face. He took a swallow from a beer he'd evidently found somewhere and barely glanced at her before turning his eyes back toward the party in the distance. His jaw was set, and his body looked strained, such a contrast to his usual flopping casualness.

"Hey, Ben."

"Hi, Skye," he said woodenly.

"What's going on?" she asked, careful to sound gentle.

"I assume you saw that." His tone was challenging, as if he wanted her to go ahead and make her point.

"Your fight with Ryan, you mean?"

"It was hardly a 'fight.'" He said, scowling. "But yes."

"Argument, then. Whatever. Semantics. What is it with you two?" She was trying for curious and open-minded, but it was hard not to match his hostility and distance with some of her own. He looked at her, eyes shining.

"What's the deal with *you*, Skye? You're the one in my face about him."

"That's not fair," Skye replied, stung.

He hesitated before responding.

"The guy's a punk, okay?" His tone softened. "Skye, I honestly can't talk about this now. Sorry."

He rose from his chair, gave her half a wave, then turned and walked down the path toward the house. Skye leaned against the sea wall and stared into the inky darkness.

Well, that didn't go as planned, she thought. She had meant to apologize, perhaps tell him the real reason she had been annoyed earlier that day. She sighed and pushed herself off the wall. Just as she turned to head down the beach toward home, she noticed movement outside the circle of dim light. A second later, Charlotte appeared.

Oh, fantastic. Skye groaned inwardly.

Charlotte looked elegant and perfectly casual. Her glossy hair was tucked behind her ears, and she wore a silky floral shirt over white jeans, which looked like they'd been cut for her lean figure. But for all her polish, something was off. Her smile was tight, and she cocked her head in an unnatural fashion.

She's angry! Skye realized. She'd never seen Charlotte off-kilter, and it gave her a perverse boost.

"Hi, Charlotte," Skye said, summoning all the cool she could manage.

"Hi, Skye." Charlotte smirked, head still cocked, like she expected Skye to answer some unasked question.

Skye mirrored Charlotte's head tilt and raised her eyebrows, as if to say, *I'm waiting.* When Charlotte still didn't speak, Skye began to wonder if she might be drunk.

"Something on your mind, Charlotte?" Skye asked finally.

"What are you doing, Skye?" Charlotte asked, with an emphasis on the word *doing* that gave the question a hint of accusation.

"Just heading home," Skye replied, as if she thought

Charlotte meant the question literally. She turned and took a few steps in the other direction.

"Wait . . . Skye!"

She turned back slowly. "Yes?"

"Is there something going on with you and Ben Barrows?"

"What do you mean?"

"I mean, are you two seeing each other?"

Skye felt a swell of hope. Charlotte wouldn't ask this question if *she* and Ben were seeing each other (or seeing each other exclusively, at least). Skye had no intention of answering, though, and instead went with an old media relations trick: answer an unwelcome question with a question of your own.

"Why are you wondering? Are you still interested in him?"

"Me? What would give you that idea?" Charlotte responded innocently. She had evidently gotten some media training, too.

"I honestly don't know, Charlotte. I couldn't imagine why you'd care so much."

"I never said I cared 'so much,'" Charlotte said haughtily.

"Oh. Sorry. I guess I misread you. Good night!" Skye smiled, and turned toward the beach.

When she was far enough away that she knew she could no longer be seen, she looked back and saw Charlotte's silky blouse and white jeans bobbing along—not toward the party, but in the same direction Ben had gone.

There she goes, Skye thought with a sigh. She had probably walked that path a thousand times, always certain of her welcome. Charlotte, though, had the look of someone in pursuit, while Ben had not seemed in the mood to be prey. She might be making the wrong move for once.

And either way, even if Charlotte regained her status as princess with Ben once more her prince, there was something to be said for having knocked off her crown, if only for a moment.

CHAPTER TWENTY-TWO

MAREN

When Maren came downstairs, she was pleased to see Skye preparing to go for a run. She looked like she needed to let off some steam.

Too bad she can't play hockey here. Maren smiled to herself.

Hockey had been Oliver's idea. How he had worshiped that child. Skye could not possibly have known how much, since he was not jolly and effusive like some grandfathers. But Maren knew his "love language," as those new age books called it.

Skye had been nine or ten at the time, old enough to begin to understand her mother's behavior. She had spent a few weeks on Haven Point that summer. After they returned Skye to her mother, Maren and Oliver had been worried. Annie had seemed so shaky, and Skye was already beginning to behave like a little adult—anxious and vigilant, a tireless perfectionist.

A few weeks later, Oliver approached Maren.

"I have an idea for Skye," he said. "I think she should play ice hockey."

Maren tried not to let her surprise show. "Really? Why is that?"

Oliver paused. He looked so serious, so scholarly,

Maren was prepared for a scientific disquisition on the subject.

"Because," he said finally, "I think it would be good for her to whack at something with a stick."

Maren had burst out laughing.

"I'm sorry, I don't know what I was expecting, but that was not it," Maren said. "But now that you've said it, I'm interested. Why not golf?"

"Golf?" Oliver had sniffed. "She needs something far less civilized than golf, Maren."

Maren laughed again.

"She's fast, coordinated," Oliver continued. "I think it might be a good fit."

He had been right, of course.

Well, she'll have an outlet today, Maren thought. She would need Skye's help getting things ready. From what she'd heard at the Lawrences' potluck, this storm was shaping up to be a monster. Almost anything not tied down could become a missile in strong winds: the gas grill, porch furniture, potted plants.

Once she returned from her run, Skye helped lug and move and hammer, while Maren closed storm shutters in the attic and trimmed shrubs to make them more resistant to the wind.

She had asked Skye to leave two chairs on the porch, so after they showered and had dinner, they went outside to enjoy the last good weather they might see for some time. Maren brought her knitting, and Skye had her phone. They had only been outside a few minutes when Skye got a text. She looked at the screen and laughed.

"Oh my God," Skye said as she tapped out a reply.

"What is it?" Maren asked.

"My friend Colette from Vernon's office. She's going to call me in a few minutes," she said as she rose from her chair. "I'm going to take it in my room. I'll explain when I come back."

When Skye returned, it was with a look of amusement on her face.

"What was that all about?"

"Long story, and it relates to my getting fired," Skye said. Maren raised her eyebrows. She'd wondered what happened, exactly, but Skye had not wanted to talk about it. "I'll start with the latest, though. So, Shelley Vernon, the congressman's wife, suspected he was having an affair, which he was."

"How shocking," Maren said drily. Skye had told her a bit about Randall Vernon.

"It seems she hired a detective. He got the goods on the affair, and he found something else, too," Skye had a twinkle in her eye Maren had not seen in far too long.

"What's that?"

"Evidently, Congressman Vernon, in an effort to keep his wife from finding out, was underwriting the affair with campaign funds. He put all the hotel rooms, meals, and limo rides they shared on the campaign credit card. An hour ago, this came out. . . ." Skye smiled, clicked on a link, and handed her phone to Maren.

The headline from the *Richmond Times-Dispatch* story read:

SHELLEY VERNON FILES FOR DIVORCE FROM CONGRESSMAN RANDALL VERNON, SUBMITS EVIDENCE OF CAMPAIGN FINANCE VIOLATIONS TO FEDERAL ELECTION COMMISSION.

"What will this mean for the congressman?" Maren asked after she scanned the story.

"He'll say he planned to pay it back, but my bet is he's

toast either way. A billionaire using campaign donations to pay for his mistress? Not a good look."

"So, what did this all have to do with your getting fired?"

Skye relayed the story of her last day on the Vernon campaign, beginning with the campaign breakfast and culminating with her marching out of the office.

"Colette sent me a photo from a press event after the whole thing blew up, and Shelley looked so meek, I thought I had made things worse for her. Seems she was just getting her ducks in a row," Skye said.

Maren's heart swelled. Her granddaughter, who had an almost insatiable desire for order and stability, had put it all on the line for Shelley Vernon. Whatever Annie's failings as a mother, she had raised a daughter with a ferocious instinct to look out for other women when they were vulnerable.

"So, did you see Ben at the clambake last night?" Maren asked. She knew they'd had that one summer together when they were young, and had seen each other in Washington earlier in the year. Maren had spotted Ben's kind face at Annie's memorial service, though things had seemed to fizzle after that. Maren had put it out of her mind, until she saw the way Ben looked at Skye after the sing-along.

"Yeah, he was there," Skye replied.

"What ever happened with you two?"

"He's a good guy. We had fun. I don't know. . . ." Skye faltered. "I just don't think we have that much in common."

Maren had not planned to speak to Skye tonight about Annie, the ashes, any of it. She was still not sure what Skye knew, and she wanted to tread carefully. But she also sensed an opening.

"You don't strike me as lacking things in common, Skye. Similar age, both of you well educated, so good-looking. And you have Haven Point in common." She paused. "Or perhaps you see Haven Point as an area of difference?"

"Partly the latter, I guess. And when Mom died, I don't know . . . It didn't seem right."

"Why is that?"

"Because of how Mom felt about this place."

Maren stopped knitting and looked at Skye. "I've actually been wondering about this for some time, Skye. What did your mom say to you about Haven Point over the years?"

"Well, you know, she hated the 'elitism and hypocrisy,'" Skye said, making air quotes with her fingers. "Like, all that stuff with the Donnellys."

Maren paused. "What exactly did your mom tell you about the Donnellys?"

"Just little comments through the years, about how Ben's grandmother kept them out of Haven Point, how snobby and unfair it was."

And there it is.

For months—years, really—she had suspected that Annie had never told Skye the full story. Now it was up to her. With that realization came a terrible wave of grief.

"What is it, Gran?" Skye asked.

Maren looked at her granddaughter, that lovely face a reminder that she could not let it pull her under. She took a breath.

"You know, Skye," she said. "I think your mother gave you a rather simple rendition of her Haven Point story."

"Probably," Skye acknowledged.

"Her feelings for this place were far more complicated

than she led you to understand. I have something to show you."

Maren went to her room, opened the drawer of her desk, and pulled out a document. The toxicology report was also there, but it was not time for that yet.

Tread lightly, she reminded herself as she descended the stairs and returned to the porch.

"Your mother had an addendum to her will," she said, handing Skye the document. "She added this a year before she died."

Skye took the piece of paper and read it out loud.

I direct my body be cremated and ashes placed in a box. During the summer following my death, I request my mother, Maren Demarest, or my daughter, Skye Demarest, take my ashes to Haven Point, Maine. There, I request either my mother or daughter have a boat take her to open waters. The boat having reached a suitable distance from shore, I request all my ashes be scattered in the ocean.

Skye looked at Maren, dumbstruck.

"What is this? I don't understand."

"I know you don't, love," Maren said, her heart melting at Skye's confusion. "I have been wanting to share this with you for some time, but I haven't known where to begin."

"Where to begin what?" Skye practically yelled.

"It's about something that happened here," Maren said. "Your mother had her reasons for her opinions about this place. It's just, well . . . it was never the whole story."

CHAPTER TWENTY-THREE

SKYE

When Skye came downstairs the following morning, Gran was already up, sitting on a slipcovered chair, looking out at the water. She was almost perfectly still, ankles crossed on a small needlepoint footstool, hands clasped at her waist.

Skye felt as if she had intruded on a private moment. She went to the window and peered out. The tops of the pines lurched in the wind, and a layer of wispy dark clouds moved under a curtain of slate gray, like dancers in a dark ballet.

"Good morning," Gran said finally.

Skye turned to face her.

"Good morning, Gran," Skye said. "It's starting to look interesting out there."

"It's beautiful in its way, isn't it?" Gran's eyes were still on the weather, her mind seemingly elsewhere.

"It's not supposed to get bad until later this afternoon. How about a walk before breakfast?"

Gran looked at her skeptically.

"It's barely raining now. Please?" Skye's playful pleading seemed to snap Gran from her reverie.

"I suppose," she said. She pushed herself slowly from

her chair, but Skye detected the faintest hint of enthusiasm breaking through the opacity.

They put on hooded raincoats and made their way to
the muddy cliff path, carefully stepping around damp
stones. The sea was already more active than usual. When
they reached a spot where the cliff dropped off more grad-
ually than in front of Fourwinds, they stopped to watch
the great white explosions of spray as the waves collided
against the rocks.

Since it first made landfall in southeast Virginia,
the hurricane had mostly taunted the East Coast, like a
prizefighter sizing up his opponent, landing only the odd
glancing blow. On Tuesday night, it slammed into the
eastern tip of Long Island, powered up Narragansett Bay,
then raced north on I-95 like a summer traveler trying to
beat traffic.

Some forecasters predicted that hurricane-force winds
could sustain, even into Maine. Things would start getting rough that afternoon. Unfortunately for the houses
on the beach, the worst of it was expected right at high
tide.

As they walked, Gran kept up her end of the conversation, but Skye noted little twinkle or curiosity. Skye
had the sense she was rationing limited emotional re-
serves. The night before, Skye had been desperate to understand the strange provision in her mother's will. But
when Gran mentioned something that had happened here
on Haven Point, Skye had seen the veil slip. It was only
for an instant, but Skye was so chastened by the pain
etched in Gran's face, she managed to put aside her own
anxiety for once.

It was my mother in that tub, she reminded herself.
But it was Gran's daughter.

"It's late, Gran," Skye had said. "You can tell me about this another time."

Gran had nodded gratefully, and they'd gone to bed.

When they had neared the end of the walk, rather than doubling back, they took one of the overgrown paths that led back to Haven Point Road. As they made their way toward the house, Skye caught sight of one of the low wooden signs that marked an entrance to the Haven Point Sanctuary.

"Can we go back through this way?" Skye asked Gran. "I haven't been in the sanctuary this week."

"Sure," Gran said. "Keep yourself covered, hands in your pockets. It'll be buggy."

Skye had learned a lot about light at her mother's knee, how an overcast sky could be a photographer's friend, cutting glare and making colors more vibrant. The light, always spare and diffused here, was especially so today—greens and browns so saturated and vivid, they appeared unreal, like an animated movie.

The tree canopy provided shelter from the rain, and the wind was barely audible. Only the tops of the trees shivered. As they passed through, Skye noticed an odd quality to the sound, though it took her a moment to put a finger on what it was.

"Where are the birds, Gran?"

"In hiding, mostly. When a storm is coming, they pick up infrasonic signals and changes in air pressure. Strong flyers get in front of the storm and let the winds carry them. Woodpeckers go in their holes. Some shore birds fly inland."

"And the rest?"

"They hang on for dear life."

They emerged from the sanctuary into a stronger wind that buffeted them as they made their way back to the house. It was not unlike what they might experience on any stormy day on Haven Point, but there was something rousing in knowing it was a prelude.

"An awakening wind," Gran said as they hunched forward against it.

"Pardon?"

"Nothing, just a phrase I picked up somewhere," she said obscurely.

After breakfast, Gran got a book, and Skye fetched her laptop from upstairs. They turned their chairs to face the windows.

It was cooler now, and the light waxed and waned with the passing of darker clouds. Before long, the wind grew louder. Rain pounded the side of the house. Skye laid a lightweight blanket over her legs.

Finally, Gran put her book aside and sat up.

"I think I'm ready now, Skye, to tell you this story."

CHAPTER TWENTY-FOUR

August 1970
Haven Point

MAREN

Percy Stevens clapped his hands, and the din in the yacht club slowly ebbed.

"Hello? Time to get going?" Percy said, calling the room to order. In his Canadian accent, commands sounded like kind requests.

Maren glanced around the room one more time. Annie still hadn't arrived. At seventeen, she was not obliged to inform her mother of her every move, but Maren had not seen her since midday and was growing uneasy.

The room felt warm and close. They had opened the window flaps on the water side, but the breeze was too listless to help. Everything felt flat and insipid. Perhaps it was just the weather causing the malaise, but this summer, it was hard to tell. Oliver would arrive the following morning, and Maren hoped his presence would offer some improvement in what had been an odd, desultory season.

Percy read through the announcements then started the crowd on the first song, "Abdul Abulbul Amir," a nineteen-verse celebration of bloodthirst in the Crimean War.

> *Then this bold Marmeluke drew his trusty skibouk,*
> *Singing, "Allah! Il Allah! Al-lah!"*

Around the seventh verse, Maren sensed a change in the atmosphere in the room, a shifting in seats, eyes drawn to the yacht club entrance. She turned and saw the object of interest: Annie, picking through the crowd, Patrick Donnelly in tow.

They crept all the way around the room before finally taking seats well inside the building. Maren, whose ability to read Annie was both blessing and curse, knew Annie's little tour through the room had been gratuitous. She could have chosen seats near the door or walked around the outside to sit on the back porch with Charlie and his friends. But Annie was to rules as a kitten to a piece of string. While the sing-along was not technically closed, as a Haven Point family event, it might as well have been. To Maren's recollection, no Donnelly had ever attended. Annie wanted as many people as possible to see her with Patrick.

Once settled, Annie opened the songbook and began to sing. She held her chin up and tossed her mane of long blond hair over her shoulder, as if daring anyone to comment on her choice of guest. Harriet, who was seated opposite Maren, leaned over and whispered to her daughter, Polly, who nodded in her usual rote agreement.

Annie insisted the only reason Maren's generation disapproved of Patrick was because he was a Donnelly. While it was true that Finn and Mary Pat had never been accepted, despite the younger set intermingling, Patrick's reputation as a bad influence was not entirely due to his surname. Maren was still trying to tease fact from wild rumor, but she had heard enough that summer to be concerned.

Patrick, she noticed, did not join in the singing. She suspected he did not want to look foolish. He had settled on a posture of vague cultural interest, as if he was at a lecture or listening to a string quartet. *I am merely an observer,* his expression suggested, *not meant to sing.*

Annie and Patrick slipped out the porch door after the sing-along, before Maren could reach them. At home, she tried to read a book in bed while she waited for Annie to return, but she struggled to concentrate.

She had tried to convince herself Oliver's arrival would help things, but a niggling sense told her the opposite was likely true. Whatever was going on between Annie and Patrick seemed to be picking up steam, and Oliver would not like it.

At eleven o'clock, thirty minutes past Annie's curfew, Maren heard the door slam, then the sound of Annie trotting up the stairs and turning on the 8-track in her room. Even Annie's sullenness couldn't squelch her bouncing vigor. She was still a perpetual motion machine.

Maren climbed out of bed, crossed the hall, and knocked on Annie's door. It was best to pick one battle at a time with her daughter. Tonight, by necessity, it would be the music filling the hallway. The issue of the missed curfew would have to wait.

"What?" Annie sounded annoyed.

"Please open the door."

Annie opened it just wide enough for Maren to see her sneer. Maren consoled herself that at least Annie didn't appear impaired in any way. The whispering about Patrick had included mentions of excessive drinking, even drugs.

"You know the walls aren't thick enough for you to listen to music that loud, especially at this hour."

"Fine," Annie said with an exasperated sigh. She turned on her heels, lowered the volume, and looked at Maren, eyebrows raised, as if to say, *Satisfied?*

Before that summer, the only arguments they'd had

about music had been over volume. While "Bridge over Troubled Water" and "Raindrops Keep Fallin' on My Head" were not Maren's cup of tea, at least they weren't unpleasant.

Maren laid Annie's new taste in music, which she fervently hoped was temporary, at Patrick's feet. She recognized the ugly, discordant song Annie was listening to now. Patrick had been on the porch at Fourwinds a few days earlier, strumming this very tune on his guitar, while Annie gazed up at him as if he were some kind of oracle. Annie proudly informed her mother the song was called "War Pigs" by a new band named Black Sabbath.

When Maren returned to her room, she could still hear traces of the angry, bass-heavy strains. She wondered, not for the first time, what had happened that summer. Where had all the sweetness gone?

Late the following afternoon, Oliver and Maren were in the kitchen together, the rain having interrupted his tennis game and her walk.

"What's this about Annie bringing that Donnelly boy to the sing-along?" Oliver asked.

"Patrick, you mean?" Maren tried to sound nonchalant. She had hoped for a chance to talk to him before the reports about Annie and Patrick reached his ears, but she was not surprised he had already heard. Gossip was an Olympic-level sport on Haven Point.

"Yes. Frank Lawrence mentioned it at tennis. He seemed to think I should be concerned."

"She's been spending time with him lately."

"Frank says the kid is bad news, all kinds of wild parties and a lot of drinking."

"Patrick wouldn't be my first choice for Annie," Maren said with a sigh. "But we need to be careful, Oliver."

"Of course," Oliver said as he opened the newspaper.

Fifteen minutes later, Annie and Charlie came in the kitchen door, both also driven home by the rain. Annie looked irritated. A wise navigator of her humor would know to exchange pleasantries before discussing anything important. Her moods these days were like the great storm clouds that rolled over Haven Point. They caused their mayhem, but they always moved on.

Oliver, who was not a wise navigator when it came to Annie, launched in immediately.

"What is with you and that Patrick Donnelly, Annie?" he asked, putting down his newspaper.

"What do you mean?" Annie looked at her father, her eyes flashing. Maren suspected she relished this fight.

"I understand you brought him to the sing-along last night."

"There's no law against him coming to the sing-along."

"Maybe not, but you had to know it would get people talking."

"People bring houseguests," Charlie piped in. "What's different about Patrick? He was Annie's guest."

"Yeah!" Annie shot Charlie an approving look. "I don't care if people talk. What's your problem with Patrick anyway?"

"I've been hearing things," Oliver said knowingly.

"It's disgusting how uptight this place is about the Donnellys." Annie scowled. "Of course, everyone gossips about him."

"As I understand it, he's been having big parties with a lot of drinking and drugs. I don't want you to be a part of that."

"I know what this is about. He's a Donnelly, so you'll believe anything you hear about him."

"You might consider, Annie, that where there's smoke, there's often fire," Oliver said, his tone now weary, as if the conversation was beginning to bore him.

"You might consider, Dad, that you're just a big snob!" Annie shouted. She stormed from the room. Oliver shook his head and opened his newspaper.

Maren sighed. If Oliver would only show the smallest willingness to entertain Annie's perspective, perhaps concede that some of the treatment of the Donnellys was unfair, it would help. But she had little hope of that outcome.

She suspected Oliver didn't actually feel that strongly about Patrick or his family (not yet, at least). His patrician manners were deeply ingrained, and Maren was certain he considered them vulgar. As a rule, though, Oliver was rather oblivious to pedigree. At home, while they still socialized with the "cave dwellers," those members of Washington society who considered Oliver one of their own, they had many friends from disparate backgrounds outside that circle.

This was just another round of Oliver versus Annie, with both combatants staking out their usual corners. And as Oliver learned more, Maren knew it would only get worse.

That evening, Oliver and Maren were to attend a party at Woody Van Sant's house. When they came downstairs, they found Annie by the front door, shoving bottles of paint into a canvas bag. She had brushed her thick blond hair to silky perfection and was wearing her most flattering low-slung jeans.

"Where are you headed?" Maren asked.

"Jilly's. We're working on sets for the Sea Stars." As

the children's drama counselor that summer, Annie's duties included directing a production for the younger children.

"I don't want you over at that Donnelly house," Oliver said.

"I told you, I'm going to Jilly's!" Annie snapped, affronted, then marched out the door.

Annie was not accustomed to scrutiny of her comings and goings on Haven Point. Maren and Oliver had loosely adhered to the "Freedom with Safety" creed, by which kids were allowed a longer leash on Haven Point. The families all knew one another, and kids didn't drive anywhere, so it was hard to get in much trouble.

Maren had wondered through the years if parents might be too sanguine, but the question had been purely academic when it came to Billy, who was naturally cautious. Even without Patrick Donnelly in the picture, Maren expected they would have had reason to tighten the reins on Annie. Now, unfortunately, Annie would just see any restriction as proof of what she already suspected: that her father was unreasonably opposed to the Donnellys.

Woody Van Sant's house had become something of a bachelor pad since his divorce. Three years earlier, in one of Haven Point's epic scandals, Woody's wife Sarah had left him for Chip Thorndike, a fellow Haven Pointer. Once past his initial devastation, Woody forced himself into the dating world and found he'd done so at a fortuitous time. When his kids were with Sarah, he'd hosted one woman after another on Haven Point, many little older than his teenage daughter.

Woody extended the cliché by purchasing a speedboat—not a teak Chris-Craft (the only acceptable sort), but a huge cigarette boat that looked like something from a James

Bond film. The mustache he had grown also ran afoul of Haven Point taste. It was not of the timeless walrus-like variety, but an awful, skinny thing that made him look like a cartoon villain.

Worst of all, he had begun to dress fashionably. Tonight, he wore bell bottoms and a thick belt with a large brass buckle, shirt unbuttoned nearly to his navel. Woody's date was a blonde with bloodshot eyes, who had brought along a few friends, a messy lot who flopped vaguely around the party, talking only amongst themselves.

Haven Pointers had been wearing the same cotton ducks, floral skirts, espadrilles, and sailing shirts since the 1930s. Next to them, Woody and his girls looked like actors brought in to lend an authentic tone to a costume party.

Nevertheless, Woody was still one of their own, so a crowd had gathered to eat his horrible appetizers and drink his Sambuca. They could wait patiently until he got past this phase and returned to his former good sense and taste.

Maren spotted Georgie in the living room and left Oliver talking to Woody in the narrow entryway.

"Kitty looks good," Georgie said, when Maren approached. She nodded toward Chip's ex-wife, Kitty Thorndike. There had been tension between Kitty and Woody when they discovered what their spouses had been up to, but they'd ended up friends.

"She always did look good," Maren said.

"True. Kitty is certainly prettier," Georgie acknowledged. "That Sarah always was a sickly little chicken of a woman."

If attractiveness drove extramarital affairs, Chip's would have been inexplicable. He had left buxom Kitty for Sarah Van Sant, who had the body of a ten-year-old. Of course, as Maren knew, things were not always so straightforward.

"I don't know why they didn't just swap," Georgie said thoughtfully.

"Georgie, really . . . swap?" Maren laughed.

"I'm sure there's swapping going on," Georgie persisted.

"On Haven Point? I doubt it."

"Okay, maybe not here," Georgie said. She lowered her voice to a whisper, and leaned in to share what she obviously considered a fascinating tidbit. "But there's supposedly a key pitching society on Peaks Island."

"A *what*?"

"My friend's daughter works at the hotel. She said a group gathers on the beach at night. The men put their keys in a basket and the women pick a set as they leave. They go home with whoever's keys they grabbed."

"Oh, come on, Georgie. I've heard of that, but I don't believe it. People are willing to go home with *anyone*? No one is too repulsive?"

"That's what everyone in these groups have in common in the first place, that they're *swingers*." She uttered the word with relish.

"It sounds like a myth to me."

"That's not all. She closed the bar late one night and walked by the pool on her way out. A bunch of people were going off the diving board in their birthday suits, one after the other. They all did little dances as they jumped." Georgie bent her arms at the elbows, and shook her hips slightly to demonstrate. Maren nearly spit out her soda at the charade.

"Fortunately, we don't have to worry about that here," Georgie said, wrinkling her nose in distaste.

"Ugh. A bunch of naked Haven Pointers." Maren shuddered at the thought.

"No, I was talking about swimming pools," Georgie said. Pools were considered so gauche on Haven Point, not even the Donnellys had one.

While the more exotic trends might not have hit Haven Point, the Thorndike and Van Sant divorces were part of an epidemic. Whispers of indiscretions were loud and frequent enough that even Maren had heard them. A couple of summers earlier, Orwit Ballantine was in Phippsburg and saw Margeaux Peabody slipping out of the Red Lion in the middle of the day.

"Hey, Margeaux, you meetin' your lover?" he'd yelled. Poor Orry was only joking, but Margeaux burst into tears, and cried, "How did you know?'"

"Has Oliver heard about Annie and Patrick?" Georgie asked.

"Yes. They had a great row, of course."

"That Patrick's turned out to be a shady character, hasn't he?"

"I always thought he was a little oily, but it wasn't of much consequence until this summer. Annie seems completely in his thrall, and Oliver's reaction is sure to fuel the fire."

Patrick had been a great lothario in recent years. Every year he had a new girlfriend on his arm, sometimes more than one a summer, each submissive and devoted.

Through all that time, Annie had scarcely turned his head. If he had tried to fashion a way to fix Annie's interest, he couldn't have played it any better. Boys at home fell over themselves trying to get Annie's attention. Patrick's neglect was novel. When he arrived in July with no girl in tow, he barely had to snap his fingers to get Annie by his side.

Maren used to think Patrick's blithe attitude toward Annie might be good for her, that she could stand to be brought down a peg. This felt different, though, more perilous. She feared it would end in a hard lesson. It was not just that Patrick did not seem to care what Annie thought. He didn't seem to care what anyone thought.

"How does Oliver feel about his rabble-rousing on Vietnam? He can't like it with Billy in the navy."

"He doesn't know about that part yet." Maren grimaced.

"Oh dear." Georgie's eyes widened.

Earlier that year, at the end of a tortuous process, Billy had enlisted in naval Officer Candidate School in Rhode Island. Though Maren and Oliver had agreed to let Billy make his own decision regarding the war, Maren had not been able to hold her tongue when he was nearing college graduation. The draft boards were notoriously susceptible to manipulation, and she begged Billy to let her and Oliver help.

Billy, however, already felt guilty about the protection his college deferment had provided. He felt badly for his mother, agonized for her, but every conversation ended the same way.

No, I have no desire to fight, he would say calmly. *Yes, of course I'm ambivalent about the war.* But he would not let them intervene. In his usual, deliberative way, he'd considered his options and arrived at his decision.

In recent months, Maren had been gripped by a terrible foreboding. She had tried to reason with herself. Mothers whose sons were actually fighting had nothing like her levels of anxiety.

Oliver was calmer. Duty on a ship was safer and could actually be good for Billy, a top student with an interest in travel and diplomacy. But Oliver also had more sympathy than Maren for the war, or at least the original impulse behind it. He saw Korea and Vietnam as proxies to hasten the collapse of Communism.

Though he'd grown frustrated with how the war was being prosecuted, with Billy in the navy he had redirected his anger to the antiwar movement, especially those in its number who said men like Billy had sold out their generation. He grumbled as he read the paper every morning.

Maren, against the war from the start, had more sympathy for the protesters, but Patrick struck her as the sort of young man for whom the war was merely a convenient tool. If not for Vietnam, he would have found some other way to express his righteousness, some other outlet to exercise the terrible power of his magnetism.

"Oliver told me you all took Annie down to that big protest in D.C.," Georgie said.

"Well, we knew she would end up there no matter what. She's fascinated with all of this."

"That must have been a sight, all those hippies at the Lincoln Memorial!" Georgie actually brightened at this. She wouldn't like a hundred thousand antiwar protesters showing up in her own backyard, but it was the kind of spectacle she loved at a safe distance.

"Oliver was horrified. I thought it was interesting. Annie looked like she wanted to jump in the Reflecting Pool with all of them," Maren said. "I don't think she understands it all perfectly, but she loves the idea of being a part of a cause."

When Lillian Belmont approached, the conversation turned to golf, and Maren's attention wandered. Out of the corner of her eye, she watched one of Woody's young women. Maren had met her when they'd come in. She had some trendy name, like Tammy or Sherri, the kind they never heard on Haven Point, where everyone was named for some ancestor.

The woman stood by the record player, eyes closed, weaving in a sort of semi-dance. If she looked past the stringy hair and unfocused expression, Maren realized she actually resembled Annie, a similarity that added to her uneasy feeling.

Oliver joined them, looked around the room, and smiled.

"Interesting, what Woody's done with the place," he said. Woody seemed to have tried for the spare, modern look the Donnellys had affected so well, but the funky lamps and bright orange plastic chairs didn't work in an old Haven Point beach house with unfinished walls and creaky floorboards.

"Isn't it awful? Just as long as he doesn't tear it down, I suppose." Georgie wrinkled her nose.

"What is it with you and these houses, Georgie?" Maren asked. "I swear, one could be hanging together by embroidery thread, and you'd still think the owner should keep it standing."

"Well, first, there's no reason a house should get to that state. Haven Point homes have good bones and can be properly maintained." Easy for Georgie to say, since Graham men could fix anything. Georgie was forever needling Oliver about how helpless he was with household repairs.

"And second?"

"Second, once a house comes down, we don't know what will go up in its place," Georgie replied, unapologetic.

"I think it's more than that," Oliver said with a twinkle in his eye. Oliver loved Haven Point, but he had none of Georgie's sentimentality about the houses.

"Oh, I can't wait," Georgie said.

"You see, Maren, to Georgie, Haven Point houses are like churches. So long as they remain standing, they can welcome the prodigals when they finish wandering in the wicked world. If they're torn down, there is no body for the lost soul to return to."

"Oh, nonsense," Georgie replied with a little scowl, elbowing him in the ribs.

"Seriously, though," Maren said. "Do you all think things are changing on Haven Point? For the worse, I mean?"

"What do you mean, for the worse?" Oliver eyed her curiously. "I assume you're not talking about houses."

Maren had surprised herself, blurting this out, though it was something that had been tickling her consciousness for weeks.

"It's just . . . I don't know. All the divorces, the arguments about the war. There's a degenerative quality to it."

"Maren, I never thought I'd hear you fret about change on Haven Point," Oliver teased. "I wouldn't think you'd care if a band of gypsies set up camp by the yacht club."

"I am not fretting," she insisted. "Something just seems different this summer. I see it with Annie and all their friends. And Woody, and all this here." She looked around the room.

"This is just a thing Woody's going through because of Sarah," Georgie said with a dismissive wave at the gaudy furniture. "It'll pass. These are hard times with this awful war, and the kids behaving so badly. Haven Point will get back to normal. The country will get back to normal."

"As to Annie and her friends," Oliver added, "all I see is the Donnelly family having a predictably insidious effect."

Georgie nodded in agreement.

They had each responded in typical fashion. Oliver and Georgie saw nothing amiss in the fractured families, the disagreements, the misbehaving teenagers. To their thinking, nothing could crack the just and worthy foundation of the enterprise that was Haven Point.

As for Annie's rebelliousness, the equation was simple: She was off-kilter. She was consorting with a member of the Donnelly family (whom Haven Point had rejected, but who had taken up residence anyway). Ergo, Annie's behavior was the fault of the Donnelly family.

As the conversation wandered in another direction, Maren turned toward Woody's girl again. She finally remembered the name. *Denise.*

When the Beach Boys's "I Can Hear Music" began emanating thinly from the RCA Swingline record player, Denise lifted the needle and replaced it.

As Maren watched her sway drunkenly to "Black Magic Woman," another of Annie's new favorites, she felt certain Georgie and Oliver were wrong. Some larger, unseen force was at play, and it was tearing Annie away.

"Oliver, are you ready to go?" she asked abruptly. She wanted to get out, home to Annie and Charlie.

"Sure." He looked at her with some concern. He might not know what was on her mind but he could tell something wasn't right. She wanted to hug him for his willingness to leave on a dime.

"Want to walk up with us?" he asked Georgie.

"No, thanks." Georgie tilted her head toward the snacks, where Cappy hovered, trying to find something edible. "I think he's hoping to get a meal out of what's on that table."

"I wish him luck," Oliver said, casting a skeptical glance at the buffet.

As she and Oliver headed toward Haven Point Road, they saw three figures down the lane. Two walked away. When the third turned in their direction, Maren recognized Harriet's angular silhouette.

Even if she'd been invited to Woody's party, Harriet would not have attended. Having claimed her slice of the moral high ground for staying married, however superficially, she disapproved of all divorces, particularly the scandalous one involving these two couples.

"Hi, Oliver," Harriet said when they reached her. She smiled up at him warmly.

"Hello, Harriet," Oliver replied. He showed no sign of noticing Maren's exclusion from the greeting. Oliver remained oblivious to Harriet's ways, even after all these years, and Maren had never thought it worth enlightening him.

"Can you believe that racket?" Harriet looked at Maren and inclined her head in the direction of the Donnelly property, from which loud music was emanating. It was not band music, which would indicate Finn and Mary Pat were entertaining, but more modern strains.

"Awful," Oliver agreed.

"It must be hard, knowing Annie is over there, with Patrick and those other kids." Harriet attempted a look of sympathy, as if she felt for Maren and Oliver's plight with their wayward child.

"Annie's at the Donnellys?" Oliver turned to Maren. "She said she was going to Jilly's."

"Remember? This came up at the last minute," Maren said in a soothing tone, surreptitiously pressing her foot into Oliver's. Oliver got the message for once.

"Oh, of course. That's right."

"You know where they are, right? In that outbuilding they call The Stable. A bunch of bedrooms, basically." Harriet directed her comment to Oliver, whom she evidently felt was the only one who could possibly have any parenting standards. "I heard it's crowded with kids, beer bottles everywhere. Mary Whalen just told me they have these strange glowing light bulbs."

"Black lighting, most likely," Maren said nonchalantly. If Harriet wished to cast her as the atrocious modern parent, she figured she'd play along.

"So how is Polly doing?" Oliver asked, trying for a change in subject.

"She's fine. All the better for not taking an interest in the Donnellys!"

You mean they haven't taken an interest in her, Maren thought meanly. Harriet had an adaptable turn of mind when it came to her children. When charming, outgoing Fritz was around more often, Harriet was forever going on about how boring and introverted other children were by comparison. Harriet did an about-face, though, when Fritz staged his gradual escape from his mother, and began to spend more of his summers with his father on Watch Hill in Rhode Island. Polly's frailty and shyness were now the highest virtues, and livelier kids were out of control. She gossiped relentlessly about Annie.

Eventually, Oliver managed to get Harriet off the subject of the Donnellys and deftly wound down the conversation.

"Maren, what is going on?" Oliver asked as he and Maren walked up the hill. "This Patrick character sounds worse than I thought."

"I'm not sure." Maren sighed. "Honestly, I think Annie might be a little out of her depth. But again, Oliver, we really have to be careful. You know when we say up, she says down."

"I understand," Oliver said.

Maren was certain he did not.

CHAPTER TWENTY-FIVE

A s they sat in the semi-dark living room, waiting for Annie to get home, Maren felt a surge of the anxiety that had dogged her all these months. She thought it was about Billy, but now she realized it was free-floating, and had found a new place to land.

A half hour later, Annie walked in, shut the door quietly, and began to tiptoe up the stairs.

"Hello, Annie," Oliver said. "How was Jilly's?"

Annie spun around.

"Oh, fine," she said, trying to arrange her face in a casual expression. "I'm tired, though. G'night."

"Annie, come here." Annie approached, a little tentatively. Oliver stood.

"You were at Patrick Donnelly's house tonight. Why didn't you tell us?"

Maren could practically see Annie's mind working, trying to settle on a strategy. She evidently concluded the best defense was a good offense.

"Why? Because you're obviously prejudiced against Patrick!" Her face reddened, and she spoke through clenched teeth.

Another battle anticipated. Another battle relished, Maren thought.

"Do I smell beer on your breath, Annie?" Oliver said, leaning a little closer.

"So what if I had a beer?" Annie said, crossing her arms over her chest. "All the kids drink beer here."

"I told you I didn't want you at this boy's house, Annie, and this is why. Patrick Donnelly should not be giving beer to a girl who's underage."

"Patrick didn't give it to me, Dad. And you don't know him at all. Patrick is serious and committed. He's become really important in the college antiwar movement!"

Oliver paused, a dangerous beat. Maren felt a stab of regret that she'd not gotten ahead of Annie in letting Oliver know about Patrick's politics. She could not imagine a worse manner for the subject to come up.

"Oh, really? He's an antiwar activist?" Oliver spoke slowly, his voice laced with sarcasm. "Such a lovely lot! These are the people who object, for example, *to your own brother.*"

"He's finally opening some people's eyes around here! You know what your problem is? You and Mom aren't angry enough!" She leaned in toward Oliver, body strained. "And you're right. He would say Billy shouldn't have gone into the navy. It encourages Nixon when boys like Billy sign up."

"How edifying, Annie. Our family is now to take instruction from the son of Finn Donnelly?"

A look of gratification spread across Annie's face. "Of course, that's what it's all about. He's a Donnelly, not from a Haven Point family. You don't know him, Dad. Not one bit."

"I don't? Why don't you educate me, then?" Oliver's jaw tightened. He was barely containing his temper.

"Patrick is smart. He has written a *manifesto*!" She

crossed her hands over her chest as if this was the crowning glory of her argument.

"Oh, a manifesto!" Oliver said. Maren wouldn't have thought it possible to pack more contempt into his tone, but he managed. "Good God, Annie, who *hasn't* written a manifesto these days? They're as common as pig tracks."

"Oliver," Maren said, in a low, warning voice.

"You're wrong. Patrick is a real leader. He's even speaking at a meeting in Bath tomorrow!"

To Maren's surprise, Oliver's face relaxed.

"A meeting in Bath, you say? Tomorrow?" He turned to Maren. "You don't have any special plans for me tomorrow, do you?"

Maren shook her head slowly.

"I'll go to that meeting, then." As Oliver resumed his seat, Annie's mouth dropped open. She seemed to be grasping for the words to articulate why this was unfair.

"You are just going to make fun of him," she finally sputtered.

"I won't say a word, Annie. I'll just go and listen," Oliver said, the picture of complacence. Annie seemed to realize she'd fallen into a trap. Having implied they didn't know Patrick, what could she say to her father trying to do just that?

"Mom." Annie turned to Maren, eyes pleading.

"Annie, you said you wanted us to respect Patrick's activism. Your father said he would go and listen. We can take his word as a gentleman that he will say nothing during the meeting."

"But . . ." She looked from one parent to the other, her eyes wild, then turned and ran up the stairs.

"What do you hope to achieve by going to the meeting?" Maren asked Oliver, as they climbed into bed.

"I don't know, Maren," he replied. "Everywhere I go, people are warning me about this character. I just need to hear it from the horse's mouth."

Until now, Maren had sensed Oliver was clinging to what little authority he still had over Annie, but he no longer looked obstinate. Now in his eyes she saw vulnerability and helplessness.

Unfortunately, she'd seen the same in Annie's.

In the end, the meeting was anticlimactic. When Oliver returned from Bath and described what had transpired, Maren could not tell if he was relieved or disappointed.

Patrick and a local peace activist, a woman in her seventies, had delivered a presentation about the McGovern-Hatfield Amendment, which called for a total American troop withdrawal from South Vietnam by the end of the following year. A controversial measure, but tame by student radical standards, certainly on the less objectionable end of the activism spectrum.

"He was as pompous as they come," Oliver said. "But it was all rather bland. He yammered on about the amendment, which hasn't a prayer of passing Congress, and that was it."

"That's a relief," Maren said.

"I still don't like him."

"I don't either. But, again, we're in danger of making him more enticing."

"I suppose," Oliver said with a sigh. "I just can't shake the feeling that we are feeding Annie to the lions."

"We only have a few more weeks here, and then I think it'll be behind us. It's not practical for her to see him after that," Maren said. Oliver reluctantly agreed.

Annie had been grounded for lying, but a few days later she was emancipated. She worked in the morning, came home for lunch, then threw some things in a canvas bag and was off again.

It was a brilliant afternoon, so Oliver and Maren headed to the golf course. As they approached the pro shop, they saw Fritz Barrows by the door, pulling a golf glove from the side pocket of his bag. Fritz's visits to Haven Point were brief and rare these days, with most of his time spent on the golf course or a sailboat.

"Hi, Dr. Demarest, Mrs. Demarest."

"Hi, Fritz. Are you about to go out?" Oliver asked.

"Yes, I was going to play the front nine."

"We are, too. Why don't you join us?" Oliver asked. "We'll just call for our bags."

As they walked to the first tee, Maren wondered what Oliver was up to. Golf, like many things on Haven Point, was an intergenerational affair, and there was nothing odd in playing with someone much younger. However, Oliver was not in the habit of inviting a single golfer to join them.

Fritz seemed to sense nothing amiss and they chatted generally for the first couple of holes. It was not until they were about to play the third that Oliver revealed his purpose.

"So, Fritz, I saw Patrick Donnelly speak at a meeting in Bath the other day. He's at Harvard with you, isn't he?"

Maren saw something flash across Fritz's face, a trace of cynicism perhaps, but it quickly disappeared. He had to know Annie and Patrick were an item and that he should respond carefully.

"We're curious about him, of course," Oliver continued, as they approached the men's tee. Maren could not help but be impressed by Oliver's mild tone—how he accented "of course," giving his words a whiff of conspiracy, mutual understanding. He'd always had a superb bedside manner.

"I bet that was interesting," Fritz said, his tone neutral.

"Not particularly." Oliver laughed.

"What was the meeting about?" Fritz asked as he bent over and placed his tee in the ground.

"Oh, it was all very harmless. He and some local activist asked people to write their senators about the McGovern-Hatfield Amendment."

Fritz didn't reply immediately. He lined up his shot, hit the ball, and then looked back, first at Oliver, then Maren.

"I'm glad to hear he's doing something productive."

Oliver calmly placed his ball on the tee, and watched it arc gracefully onto the green. He was maddeningly good at golf, even when he'd not played in months.

They moved to the ladies' tee and were quiet as Maren teed up and hit her ball. "I take it Patrick was doing something less productive before?" Oliver asked, finally.

Fritz looked as if he was deciding how to respond, then finally let out a long breath.

"He was in a pretty radical organization, Dr. Demarest." His tone was apologetic.

"Was he? Which one?" Oliver asked calmly.

Maren's heart dropped. Oliver had been fishing for information about Patrick, but she knew this was bigger than anything he expected to catch.

"It was an offshoot of Tom Hayden's group, though it's hard to follow where one of these groups ends and the other begins. It wasn't just Harvard students. They were from all the Boston campuses. Patrick was pretty well known. He's a good speaker, as you probably saw yourself. He loves all that stuff, standing on the hood of a car, yelling into a megaphone with his fist up." He raised his own fist in a half-hearted imitation.

"Really?" Oliver asked, his tone friendly and interested, like this was a fascinating development.

"It got pretty intense this spring. I imagine you saw it on the news. They occupied administrative buildings, held huge protests. Someone spray-painted 'Baby Killer' on a veteran's car. Then a group went to the airport and jeered at soldiers returning home. Some of them got arrested, and the whole thing made the papers. Patrick managed to keep away from the cameras for once, but he was there. Everyone knew it."

"I see." Oliver's tone was even, though Maren saw a slight movement in his jaw.

"You know what's worse? I'm not even sure he was that committed to what they were doing."

"Curious. What makes you say that?"

"He just loves the attention. It got him a lot of great girls," Fritz added, then looked up at them sheepishly, as if he knew he'd tipped his hand. "You all probably think I'm bitter."

Maren smiled in return. His long-standing crush on Annie was an open secret.

"We don't think that, Fritz. But from what Oliver saw at the meeting, maybe his conscience got the better of him," Maren said. "He seems to be more in the mainstream now."

Fritz shook his head.

"You don't think he saw the error of his ways?" Oliver asked, genuine interest now audible in his tone.

"His conscience didn't get the better of him. His father did. When Mr. Donnelly heard about the scene at the airport, he hightailed it down to campus and told him to back off. Probably threatened to cut him off. Trust me. It wasn't his conscience that bothered him. I'm not sure he has one."

"Thanks for telling us, Fritz," Maren said, before Oliver could push Fritz any farther.

"I'm sorry," Fritz said. He looked as if he meant it.

"You have nothing to be sorry for," Oliver said, his voice reassuring. He turned the conversation as smoothly as he might turn a sailboat, around the shoals of this matter toward the safer waters of weather and sports.

After they finished the round of golf, Oliver and Maren got in the car and headed up the hill toward Fourwinds.

"Maren, do we need to filter what Fritz just told us?" Oliver asked as they approached the house. "I know he's always had a thing for Annie."

The question surprised Maren. She turned to him, ready to see traces of the stubborn, oppositional streak that Annie seemed to bring out in her husband, but he mostly looked sad. She realized Oliver had actually reconciled to a softer line on Patrick and sensed he was genuinely disappointed by what they'd just heard.

"No, I don't," she said with a sigh. "I think Fritz is right that Patrick doesn't care about anything. I don't sense he cares much about Annie, either. But I'm still not sure this should change our stance."

"Maren, I am ambivalent about this war. You know I am. But I can't stomach the people Patrick Donnelly was allied with. If the only reason he disengaged from that group was to save his own hide, I can't stomach him either." He pulled the car to the spot next to the garage, turned off the engine, and turned to look at her.

"I know . . ." Maren began, but Oliver wasn't finished.

"It's not just that. It's how slippery he is, how calculating. I see now, looking back, what he was doing at that meeting. He's rewriting his antiwar history, redacting his past. For all her bluster, you know Annie is innocent. She assumes everyone's motives are as genuine as her own.

I don't think we can trust her with him. You said yourself she was out of her depth."

"I don't disagree. But what do we do? She'll insist you're opposed to Patrick because he's not from a Haven Point family. And Oliver." Maren paused and softened her voice. "She'd have a point. You do have your prejudices."

She had never leveled this charge at him before, but he didn't blink.

"I would have the same reaction if he came from a Haven Point family."

"Except one thing: You don't think Haven Point could produce a son who behaved like Patrick."

"That's neither here nor there, is it?" His expression suggested that was exactly what he thought.

The truth was, Haven Point youth rarely strayed far beyond prescribed boundaries, which on the whole kept them from going very wrong. Maren wondered at times if it was less breeding than lack of courage or imagination that kept them on the straight and narrow. Regardless, Patrick had taken part in something base and ugly, then made it worse with dishonesty.

The fact that Oliver's issues with Patrick aligned with his predispositions did not make him wrong. Unfortunately, Annie was too invested, and her thinking too black-and-white, for her to see that.

"What do you plan to say to her?" Maren asked, finally.

"I'm not sure."

"Be gentle, Oliver. It's the best way. She needs to know you are on her team."

When they entered the house, they heard music from Annie's room. Maren went upstairs and asked her to come down to talk to them.

"In a minute," Annie said. When she finally descended,

she had her canvas bag over her shoulder, ready to go out somewhere.

"What?" She entered the living room and sat on the edge of an armless needlepoint chair, poised to spring at the first possible moment. Oliver and Maren sat on the sofa.

"Annie, we had occasion to talk to someone this afternoon who knows Patrick Donnelly from school. We heard a little more about what he's been up to on campus," Oliver said.

"And?"

"It appears Patrick was involved in some things your father and I find disturbing," Maren cut in.

"What things?"

"A number of them," Maren continued, "all of which have one thing in common: Patrick associating with people who treat American soldiers with contempt."

"Who told you that?" She looked dubious.

"Well, you did, first," Oliver said, hints of annoyance emerging in his voice. "You said Patrick thinks soldiers like Billy 'encourage Nixon' by enlisting."

Annie looked confused now, as if she wasn't sure of the best, most tactical way to respond.

"And we had confirmation from one of his classmates," Oliver added.

Annie's eyes flew open.

"Wait . . . was it Fritz Barrows? It was Fritz, wasn't it? He hates Patrick. His mom hates the Donnellys! You can't listen to him!" She was speaking quickly, eagerly now. She seemed to think she had a trump card.

"Oh, I think we can, Annie." To Maren's dismay, Oliver had reverted to his slow, patronizing tone. "We do not want you seeing Patrick Donnelly anymore."

Maren flinched. Oliver might have assumed she was

on board with this consequence, but he'd been peremptory. While Maren was no longer certain they should just let things with Patrick run their course, she had not signed on to this. But they needed to present a united front, so she kept quiet. She wasn't sure she had a better idea anyway.

Annie's mouth opened and her eyebrows flew together. She did not look disappointed. She looked terrified.

"You can't just order me not to see him. I'm old enough to decide who my friends are!"

Oliver remained seated, but he was stretched tight, his demeanor rigidly controlled.

"You may be old enough to pick your friends, but we have a right to step in when you consort with someone whose values we find reprehensible. You aren't helping matters with your attitude, Annie. You don't even seem to see the problem with Patrick's choices."

"But you don't even know if what Fritz said is true!" Her pitch rose as her voice lost strength. She sounded childish and desperate.

"Annie, I think we do, and I think you do, too," Maren said, more gently. Annie looked at her, unable to argue.

"But you didn't have a problem with him after you went to see him at the meeting. So, what he's doing now is fine, right?"

"Annie, not six months ago, he was involved with a group of people who mocked soldiers when they returned home from the war. What if Billy had been one of them?" Oliver asked.

Annie, stubborn as Oliver, kept her expression implacable. Maren knew Annie's mind was too muddled to even entertain Oliver's hypothetical question. She probably barely heard it. Oliver, however, would interpret her lack of response as Annie choosing Patrick over her own brother.

"How about this, then," Oliver said. "Why don't you take a little break from Patrick?"

"A break? How long a break?" She looked fearful again.

"I don't know. Until Labor Day?"

Annie had to know they would not permit her to see Patrick when summer was over, that Oliver intended this as the death knell of the relationship. She burst into tears and ran upstairs, more distraught than Maren ever remembered seeing her.

CHAPTER TWENTY-SIX

August 2008
Haven Point

SKYE

The kitchen door slammed, and Georgie appeared in the living room. She carried a tattered canvas bag and wore a yellow slicker with a yellow rain hat that was larger in the back, like the Gorton's Fisherman.

Gran did not appear surprised to see her.

"Ugh, that infernal dog!" Georgie shook herself off. "I'm staying here tonight."

"What's wrong?" Skye asked.

"Skipper. My black Lab. He's afraid of storms." Georgie pointed out the window, where the wind whipped through the trees and the rising tide was sending up a spray so high, they could see it even up on the cliff.

"Cappy insisted we keep him on Haven Point with us, but he's cowering under the table, moaning and barking. I told Cappy I'd ride it out over here. My mother's dogs would never have dared be afraid of anything. It wasn't allowed."

"We all behaved for your mother, Georgie, man and beast," Gran said. "Come on in."

The dog's a cover, Skye realized. *She's here for Gran.*

"I've got a piece of news that probably won't surprise you," Georgie said, after removing her wet things. "Harriet Hyde refused to evacuate."

"She's still down on the beach?" Skye asked. She wondered if Ben had stayed behind with her. She couldn't decide which was worse—the idea of his leaving without getting in touch, or that he had stayed without getting in touch.

"I bet she thinks she can put up her hand and stop a storm surge," Gran said. "She shouldn't stay down there, though. Can we get her to come up here with us?"

"She won't. Cappy already asked her."

"Well, there's nothing for it but to pray, then," Gran said. "Have you eaten, Georgie? We were just talking about lunch."

Skye pushed Ben from her mind as they assembled turkey sandwiches, gazpacho, and Gran's oatmeal cookies. All the while, the wind grew angrier. The walls of the house were thick, but trim and junctures were worn with age. Skye was so agitated by the sound of the kitchen door rattling in its loose frame, she finally braced it closed with a chair.

Just as they had almost finished clearing the table, the lights flickered twice then went out. It was only mid-afternoon, but it felt dark as midnight with the black and gray cloud cover.

"I knew we couldn't stay so lucky," Gran said. "It's probably a transformer on the mainland. But have no fear. Ever the Boy Scout, Billy brings me a newfangled light every time he visits."

She headed for the pantry and returned with an armful of candles, flashlights, and LED lamps. Skye washed the dishes then rejoined Gran and Georgie in the living room, now illuminated by a battery-operated lantern and large candles. They could no longer see the great clouds rushing by, or the trees doing their frenzied dance in the wind out the windows, just the reflection

of their distorted figures and the flickering light. It felt
odd, closed in.

As they listened to the wild noises outside, Georgie
pulled knitting out of her bag, and Gran even read for
a bit. Skye wondered if Gran's story was on hold until
the storm had passed, but then Gran put her book down,
placed her hands on her knees, and leaned forward, as if
calling a meeting to order.

"Georgie, before you arrived, I was telling Skye about
the summer of 1970, when Annie was seeing Patrick Donnelly."

"Ah, yes," Georgie said casually. She looked over her
reading glasses, knitting needles clicking. "Carry on."

She's definitely *here for Gran*.

CHAPTER TWENTY-SEVEN

August 1970
Haven Point, Maine

MAREN

Maren slipped off her shoes at the top of the beach club stairs. She had been eager to escape the house, thick with tension since Oliver had laid down his decree earlier that afternoon. She inhaled deeply, hoping salt air and exercise might help.

By midday, the morning's bright sunshine had turned milky, and was eventually overtaken by thick gray clouds. The beach was empty except for a few stalwart families in scattered encampments. She walked briskly along the edge of the water where the sand was firmest, watching seabirds dive and nervous plovers skitter before her.

She was troubled by how Annie had reacted to Oliver's ultimatum. Maren had expected anger, but also some hint of poignancy, a sense that Annie had become the heroine in a coming-of-age novel about a sweet but doomed first love. Instead, Annie was twitchy and anxious, completely unlike herself. It was as if Patrick had changed her very constitution.

It's time to go, she thought. *This summer just needs to end.*

As she neared the rocks at the end of Haven Point Beach, she saw a man standing on the sandy strip between the Donnelly property and Haven Point's. It took only a moment to recognize Finn's broad, sturdy frame. Still as a statue, he gazed at a point in the distance. Maren cast her eyes in the same direction, but saw only open sea—no boat, no creature of interest. Finn was ordinarily so purposeful, it felt intimate somehow to witness him in such a meditative posture.

He turned when she approached. "Maren Demarest." Though he didn't smile, she still had the feeling he was mentally undressing her.

"Hello, Finn." Maren stopped a few safe feet away.

"Nice day, wasn't it?"

"It was. I think it's going to rain tonight, though." They both looked out at the water again, silence hanging between them. Finn finally spoke.

"So, I gather your husband was angry at Annie for being at our house the other night." He spoke lightly but did not make eye contact.

"He was. Annie had lied to us about her plans."

"It was her lying, then, that upset him? Not something about Patrick?"

Maren paused. She felt she owed him an explanation. Finn was likely to hear about Oliver's injunction anyway.

"Can I be candid?"

"Please do." Finn turned to face her. His expression was neutral, but she saw a glint in his eyes, a keen interest in her answer.

"With our eldest son in navy OCS right now, Oliver and I are sensitive about certain elements of the antiwar movement, and Patrick's activities on campus trouble us."

"You're not the only one." The mask dropped, and he grimaced. "I've been after him about it. What the hell do they mean, 'make love, not war'? Christ, in my day, we did both."

Maren studied him for a second. Though Fritz had

made it clear Finn disapproved of Patrick's controversial activities, she had still expected him to circle the wagons. His discomfort aroused her pity.

"Thank you for understanding," she said. She heard the hint of regret in her own voice, and it sparked a memory of a day long before, when she had stood at his front door and rebuffed his advances. She had been certain about her decision at the time, but sorry, in a way. And she was sorry to cause him pain now. It was strange, this link between them.

"So, what is the bottom line? Have you told her to steer clear of Patrick?"

She hesitated before replying. "Yes, that's about the sum of it."

He nodded and looked back toward the water.

"Well, I'd better be heading back. I need to get dinner on the table. Bye, Finn," she said, turning to head home.

"Maren," he called. She looked back.

"That's it?" He tried to look nonchalant. "The antiwar stuff? That's the only reason?"

"That's it, Finn," she lied, and headed toward Four-winds.

Annie spent that evening and the following day in a state of high dudgeon, moving about with the look of a caged animal. She paced and fretted, unable to concentrate on any activity. She barely spoke to Oliver. His stubbornness was equal to Annie's, though it presented as unshakable certitude. This was a good quality in a doctor trying to reassure a patient, but had the effect of further irritating Annie.

Annie finally went sailing with Charlie at midday, and out with her camera in the afternoon. Maren hoped fresh air would help. But when the sky took on a sickly hue and began to spit rain, she was forced back indoors. From the moment she walked into the kitchen, it was clear the time outside had not worked its usual magic. She was surly and tense, snapping at everyone.

Maren was pleased when Annie announced at dinner that her friend Sarah was having some kids over. She would get out of the house and among friends, but as Sarah didn't consort with the Donnellys, there was no danger of Annie seeing Patrick. Annie helped Charlie with the dishes, grabbed a slicker, and marched out the kitchen door with a mumbled good-bye.

Maren sighed. With a pang of guilt, she realized she was looking forward to Oliver's departure on Sunday. She would have sole responsibility for keeping Annie and Patrick separated, but it would surely be less tense.

"Georgie, you are making up the rules as you go along!" Cappy said, looking at the card she had laid down.

They sat at the folding card table in four mismatched chairs, playing an obscure and incomprehensible version of poker Georgie claimed to have learned from her brothers.

"I am not! This is exactly how I explained it."

"Stop arguing or we'll have to go back to playing bridge at the country club," Maren said.

Maren had hated bridge night. With Oliver often absent, she was forever rotating partners, invariably feeling she let them down, since she cared little about the game. Bridge night had been even worse for Georgie and Cappy, who bickered like the eighth graders they had been when they first met.

"It's not worth the end of your marriage," Maren had finally said a couple of years before, when she proposed card night as an alternative. They played poker, gin, hearts—anything but bridge.

After a few hands, Maren glanced out the window. The wind was picking up and rain clicked at the window like fingernails. She felt uneasy and struggled to keep her mind on the game.

"What's Annie up to tonight?" Georgie asked, after a while.

"She's at Sarah Echelson's house. I actually thought she'd be back by now," Maren said.

"I'm going to give her another half hour or so, then go fetch her," Oliver said, looking at his watch before throwing out his card.

Maren went to the kitchen, ostensibly to get more snacks, but really to shake off her strange mood. She wanted to kick herself for saying she expected Annie home by this time. It had only aroused Oliver's suspicions. She refilled the bowls of nuts before returning to the table.

As she took her seat, she heard the kitchen door. She felt a surge of relief, thinking Annie had come home, but the sound was followed by neither greeting nor footstep.

The wind, she thought. That, or her imagination, which was on high alert. About a half hour later, Oliver checked his watch again, then looked back at his cards. Once they were through with this hand, Maren suspected he would make good on his promise to find Annie.

He did not have the opportunity. They had not quite finished their game when they heard banging on the front door. Maren went to answer it, mystified as to who it could be. Few people used that door, and almost no one on Haven Point knocked. She opened it to find Finn Donnelly, dripping wet on their front porch.

"Finn. What is it?" Maren asked, as Oliver, Georgie, and Cappy materialized behind her.

"Maren, I've got some bad news. You and Oliver need to come with me."

"What's going on?" Oliver asked.

"Charlie is on his way to the hospital in Bath. He had a fall on the rocks."

"Charlie? But he's . . ." Maren started, mystified. She gestured vaguely up the stairs, which Oliver was climbing, three at a time. She stopped and listened as Oliver opened Charlie's door. In seconds he was back on the landing.

"He's not there." He descended the stairs, brow furrowed.

"I don't understand." Maren felt stuck, as if in quicksand. She turned toward Cappy and Georgie.

"We'll stay until Annie comes home," Georgie said quickly.

"Maren," Finn said, a look of surprise and consternation on his face, "Annie's with Charlie."

"Good God, what on earth is happening?" Oliver said under his breath. They grabbed raincoats from pegs by the front door and followed Finn to his car, which was parked at a careless angle, engine running and driver's side door open. Maren had a flash of memory to the first time she met Finn, how he'd picked her up in a downpour, how she'd worried about soaking the seat.

"We can take our own car," Oliver said.

"Just get in, Oliver, please," Finn said. "I have my houseman there with another car. We'll get you back." This was as many words as the two men had exchanged in all these years.

"I think we should have a car there, too. Maren, go

with Finn and find out what happened. I'll see you at the hospital."

Maren climbed into the passenger seat of Finn's car, and they sped off as soon as she shut the door. A million questions churned in her mind. She wished Oliver were there. He would know what to ask. Finn was his usual enormous presence, staring intently into the rain, now pouring down in great sheets. His massive hands gripped the steering wheel in a way that unnerved Maren. She finally managed to pluck a question, the most obvious, from the jumble.

"What happened?"

"I don't know exactly." Finn's voice was thin, devoid of its usual cocksure manner.

He is frightened, Maren realized, and her stomach began to roil.

"Patrick came running up to the sliding glass door and said Charlie had fallen on the rocks. He said it was pretty bad. I ran out to see. He was bleeding a lot."

"Was he conscious?"

Finn didn't answer at first. Maren looked at his profile. He finally shook his head. She gasped.

Just stay in control. Just stay in control and it will be in control. Maren repeated the mantra to herself, despite creeping dread.

"He came to for a moment, and I asked him his name. He said 'Charlie,' but then he was out again. We put blankets around him, wrapped clean towels around his head, and put him in the back of one of our cars. Annie got in the back with him to keep him stable. My houseman drove them, and I came for you. He's not far in front of us. It takes so long to get an ambulance. I didn't think that was the thing to do."

"I'm sure you're right," she said. "I still don't understand what Charlie was doing there, or Annie, for that matter."

Finn was silent for a moment. "I gather Patrick was with Annie when Charlie showed up," he finally replied.

A picture began to form in Maren's mind, a notion of how it had all come to be. They rode in silence. Finn drove swiftly but with expert care on the wet roads. The lights from Oliver's car were in the rearview mirror. He was close behind, and Maren could practically feel his anxiety.

An ambulance would indeed have taken longer. The volunteer service would have to come from Phippsburg before turning around to go into Bath. She cursed the remoteness of Haven Point.

The eighteen-mile journey seemed to take forever, but they finally pulled up to Bath Memorial Hospital, the best facility outside of Portland. Oliver caught up with them as they walked briskly to the entrance.

"Where did he hit his head . . . I mean, what part of his head?" he asked Finn unceremoniously. This was obviously the question that had most pressed on him during the drive.

"On the side," Finn replied. He reached up and touched the right side of his head. Oliver grimaced. They ran in and looked around the small waiting room.

Annie was curled in one chair. A burly man with dark, greased hair was in the chair next to her; his sad, helpless expression was incongruous with his rough exterior. Finn's houseman, Maren assumed. Despite her great height, Annie looked so small, and so terrified. She sprang up, burst into tears, and ran to Maren.

"Mom, he came looking for me. He was looking for me," she gasped through her sobs.

Maren opened her arms for Annie, who melted into her, shoulders shaking. Finn sat next to his houseman and began asking questions in hushed tones, as Oliver approached the tired candy striper behind the registration desk.

"Annie, love. Come sit with me." Maren led her to a bank of chairs. Annie leaned her head on Maren's shoulder and continued to cry. As Maren sat quietly and waited for the sobs to ebb, Oliver rejoined them.

"The doctor will be out soon to talk to us," he said. "Annie, what happened?"

Oliver's gentle tone somehow triggered more tears, but after a moment she composed herself and lifted her head from Maren's shoulder.

"I went to meet Patrick." Annie hesitated and looked at her father.

"It's all right, Annie," he said. "I just want to know what happened."

"No, you don't understand." Her voice rose again, and she struggled to get the words out. "I told Patrick I had to meet him. I just had to see him, to explain, so he didn't think I just disappeared. I asked Charlie to get me if he thought . . . He heard you say something . . ."

Oliver looked confused, but the puzzle pieces snapped together in Maren's mind. It was as she had suspected.

"You mean Charlie heard us say we would come get you at the Echelsons' if you didn't come home soon," Maren said.

"Yes!" she wailed, her voice thick with regret and dismay. "He came to tell me. He was calling to me, saying, 'Dad is coming to find you,' when he fell."

It had not been the wind Maren heard during the card game, but Charlie slipping out the door to summon his sister home. Loyal Charlie, always seeking a way to repay Annie's kindnesses.

"I was supposed to meet Patrick on the beach, but he was on the rocks because the tide was up. We heard Charlie calling and saw him climbing up, but it was so wet. He was almost to us when he fell. . . ." She trailed off then, struggling to get the words out amid sobs and uneven breaths.

"He fell hard, Dad. He fell really hard," she managed. She looked terrified.

Maren looked around for a second. "Where is Patrick?" she asked.

"He didn't come," she said. "His dad left him there. Mr. Donnelly . . ." She trailed off again. *Finn thought we wouldn't like it,* Maren thought.

A set of double doors to the waiting room opened, and a doctor emerged, bespectacled and somber. He looked around, spotted Maren and Oliver, and approached.

"Dr. and Mrs. Demarest? I'm Frank Griffin," he said. They nodded. "Won't you come with me?"

"Annie, you stay here, love. We'll be back soon," Maren said.

Annie nodded, eyes wide with anxiety. She pulled her knees back to her chest and curled her hair around her finger, as she had done as a little girl when she was tired or fretful. Maren hated to leave her, but Finn would come to her aid if need be. She followed Oliver and Dr. Griffin through the double doors into the hallway beyond.

The harsh lights and smell of antiseptic resurrected a mélange of memories from Walter Reed, of doctors and nurses trying to heal, trying to repair, and sometimes failing. She felt the return of the monstrous anxiety that had plagued her for so many months. First Billy, then Annie, and now Charlie.

"I am going to take you to your son's room. He woke up and was speaking, though he's asleep now. His vital signs are stable. His wound is clean and bandaged."

"He was speaking cogently?" Oliver asked.

"He was," Dr. Griffin said as he pushed the door open to a room off the hall. Oliver looked relieved and Maren allowed herself a glimmer of hope.

Charlie's eyes were closed, and a large bandage covered the wound. A nurse was at his bedside, her appearance and movements crisp and efficient.

"I understand he was hit on the side of his head," Oliver said.

"Unfortunately, yes," Dr. Griffin replied. "In front of the temple."

"Is it bad? The injury?" Maren asked.

"I have seen worse. Our concern is intracranial pressure. The fact that he was reasonably alert is encouraging, but I am concerned about the location of the injury. They can better monitor that at Maine Medical in Portland. I think he should be moved as soon as we can arrange it."

Maren felt bile at the back of her throat and wondered how much more she could hear without vomiting. She knew about intracranial pressure. It was common on the battlefield, but she never saw it at Walter Reed, because it killed a soldier long before he made it stateside. There were ways to relieve it, crude and imprecise back then and better now, but it was still a terrible danger.

"If there is bleeding, they are better equipped to pinpoint the source. There is always some risk in moving a patient in his condition, but I cannot in good conscience suggest we keep him."

Oliver nodded in agreement. While he and Dr. Griffin talked through arrangements—*An ambulance is waiting, you'll follow behind, Maine Medical has everything you need*—Maren went to Charlie's bedside. He was still, except the subtle rise and fall of his chest. He looked calm and peaceful, with no trace of his usual agitation. She touched his hand. It was warm, but he showed no sign of recognition or response. She gently squeezed it.

"Charlie?" she said quietly. "Charlie. It's Mom."

She looked up from his hand and saw his eyes move behind closed lids. A gentle moan came, and his lids fluttered. His eyes opened and roamed a little before settling on his mother's face.

Please know me, she thought. *Please know who I am.*

He moaned again and his lids dropped, as if the effort of keeping his eyes open was beyond his poor powers. She waited and prayed silently. Then she heard him mumble:

"Mom . . ."

"Charlie, love, we are here. Your father and I are here."

"I fell," he said. "I'm sorry. . . ."

"Shh, it's okay, Charlie. It was an accident. We love you."

"Love you," he mumbled, his voice thick and lazy.

"You just sleep, Charlie," Maren said.

Maren felt some relief from her crushing anxiety. How bad could the damage be if he communicated sensibly, if he recognized her? Maren left Oliver and Dr. Griffin to the frenzy of activity that would precede the move and returned to the waiting room, where Annie again rushed into her arms.

"He woke up and spoke to me a little," she told her daughter.

"So, is he going to be okay?" Her expression was cautiously hopeful.

"We are going to move him to Maine Medical to be

with Mr. Donnelly now. Your
ambulance."

ed and she gripped her mother's

tically shouted. "I'm coming with you.
home. I can't go home!"

thought for a moment. She didn't think she
ght Annie even if she wanted to, and perhaps it
cruel to keep her away.

"All right then. I expect we'll be leaving soon."

She approached Finn and told him the plans. He looked alarmed, but she explained it was just a precaution. She called back to Fourwinds and updated Georgie, and then they were again on the road, traveling the forty miles south to Maine Medical, rain still lashing against the windshield.

When they arrived, they raced to the front desk, a more complex affair than the one in Bath, and learned Charlie was with the doctors. Someone would find them when there was news.

The waiting room was a ghoulish place, even by hospital standards, with shabby orange love seats in an easy-to-clean faux leather. The fluorescent overhead lighting hummed and cast a greenish hue. Magazines cluttered the surfaces of mismatched end tables. A middle-aged woman in a wrinkled housedress snored in a corner, a newspaper spread across her chest. They moved to the opposite corner and began the vigil.

They waited calmly for a while, but as time ticked by, Maren grew restless.

"I don't understand why they won't tell us anything," Maren finally whispered to Oliver. "I thought they were just checking on him?"

Oliver looked concerned, too. He approached the

nurses' station. The nurse on duty disappeared [
minutes. When she returned, she and Oliver en[
an earnest conversation.

Something is happening. Maren watched Olive[
the side of the counter, his face grim. He appeared [
asking urgent questions, ones the nurse was ill-equip[
to answer. He finally returned to Maren.

Her heart resumed its unpleasant racing. She knew
whatever Oliver was about to repeat would threaten the
sense of well-being she had so carefully constructed when
she saw Charlie's eyes open, when she heard him speak.
Oliver led her to another corner of the waiting room, away
from Annie, who had her nose in a magazine and was not
watching.

"They are prepping Charlie for surgery," he said.

"Surgery?" Maren went slack.

"The nurse didn't tell me much, but she's taking me
back to talk to the doctor. I'll let you know what I find
out."

Annie had finally taken notice of her and Oliver, so
Maren managed a small smile, patted Oliver's arm, and
returned to their corner.

"What's going on?" Annie asked.

"They're having a look, I guess. Dad's going back
to see. We'll hear something soon, I'm sure." Annie
looked at Maren searchingly—on the hunt for clues, as
always. Maren did her best to keep her expression neutral. Annie did not seem convinced, but, too tired to
probe, she leaned her head against the wall and closed
her eyes.

Maren's effort to keep a calm exterior left her no outlet, and her anxiety intensified. Other than bleeding in his
brain, she could conceive of no reason for Charlie to be
in surgery.

When Oliver finally emerged, he looked defeated and aged, as if the doors to the waiting room had been a time portal. Annie noticed, too. She sat up straight as he approached.

"I am afraid I have some bad news."

"Oh God. What is it, Dad?"

"Charlie was able to answer some questions when he arrived here, but after they moved him to a room, his speech was garbled, and he became unresponsive. As Dr. Griffin feared, it appears blood is putting pressure on critical areas of his brain."

Annie's eyes filled with tears and her lip trembled. "What does that mean? What are they doing?" She made fists with her hands and held them together.

"The neurosurgical resident has him in surgery. Fortunately, they caught it quickly. If they can stop the bleeding, it's not likely to damage the brain tissue. There shouldn't be lasting effects."

Annie's eyes darted between them, her expression imploring. She wanted someone to promise things would be okay. Maren wished she could provide such reassurance, but that was not possible unless her own confidence in a good outcome was replenished. The most likely source would have been Oliver, but he looked just as uncertain. He sat on his little chair across from them, holding their hands. His posture was rigid, and Maren knew he was doing all in his power to mask his worry.

"How long will it take?" Maren asked.

"It could be a while. They have to find the source of the bleeding."

Maren thought nothing could be worse than the gnawing anxiety as they waited. But it was not long before she discovered she had lacked imagination. There was indeed something worse: the sight, far too soon, of a young surgeon's grim face through the window of the swinging door that led from the waiting room.

Only Oliver had met the surgeon, so Maren's last faint hope was that the face she saw belonged to some other tired resident.

She squeezed Oliver's hand, and his eyes followed hers to the doorway. His brow creased and she saw a flash of something in his eyes. *Fear.* He released Maren's hand and walked to the door. Annie noticed the doctor and saw her father rise to meet him, but she had not done the terrible math. She did not understand it should have been hours before they saw the surgeon. Any anxiety in her expression was still mingled with exhaustion and that little bit of hope.

Maren wished she could freeze this moment, before she herself knew utterly what was all but certain, before the words were said—before Annie had to know, everyone had to know.

But she could not.

The next hour of her life she would only ever remember as a series of hideous flashes. That first moment, looking through the window in the swinging door, as if she were watching a scene on a muted television set. The young doctor in his scrubs, touching Oliver's upper arm, Oliver slumped against the wall. She remembered feeling she should rise. *Go to him, hear what he is hearing,* but she could not get up. Oliver would have to come to her, come to them.

A terrible darkness took hold of her, a sensation unlike anything she had ever experienced. She felt it acutely in her chest, her heart, in the deepest place.

An odd thought struck her. Until this moment, she considered tragedies like this, especially the death of a child, something that happened to other people. It was not conscious, but it had been there, underscoring every-thing, making her feel safe. And she knew why she had unconsciously clung to that myth of exemption—why everyone does, to some extent. The alternative was this, a feeling of such irredeemable misery, the knowledge that life was forever changed. Only the presence of An-nie kept her from screaming or vomiting.

Annie gripped Maren's hand tightly as Oliver moved somewhat unsteadily in their direction.

He delivered the news as gently as he could. *They had done all they could. . . . The bleeding had damaged the brain stem. . . . Even if they had taken him straight here, nothing could have been done. . . . He knew no fear.*

Annie made a terrible, primal keening sound. "Oh God, oh God, oh God," she cried as she collapsed onto Maren, her eyes filled with sick confusion and lost inno-cence, robbed at seventeen of her sense of well-being, far too young to know she was not exempt. With one child gone and another rent by the news, Maren was swept deeper into the darkness.

They formed a triangle, Oliver to her left, but close enough to touch Annie, his face a picture of hopelessness and anguish, Annie on the other side, clinging as if her own life depended on it. Maren seized on Oliver's words, *he knew no fear,* and tucked them away for later, looking for some glimmer, some infinitesimal source of future relief.

How can we move? How can we do anything? She tried to pull her mind from the black fog. Mustn't they rise to do what must be done, and then leave this horri-ble place? But she could neither move nor talk. Oliver seemed as powerless. She began to weep, her shoulders shaking like a child's.

We cannot move. How can we even move?

And then an angel arrived. It was Cappy, standing at the entrance of the emergency room, water dripping from his yellow sailing slicker. Georgie had sent him when Maren had called from the hospital in Bath. He took in the sight of the three of them, and his mouth fell open.

Oliver somehow rose and approached him. Cappy put his strong arm on Oliver's shoulder, and Maren watched as Oliver, silent tears streaming down his face, somehow managed to get the story out. Cappy's eyes widened and his face contorted in that expression that is uniquely grief, but looks so much like fear. He pulled his lips thin and covered his mouth, as if to prevent something from escaping.

After a moment he lowered his hand and took a breath. He looked toward Maren and Annie, eyes damp and filled with compassion, and moved toward the desk. Maren could practically see his effort as he sought and found some power the rest of them had lost.

He would do what needed to be done right then. He would get them through those next moments, and he would deliver them home.

CHAPTER TWENTY-EIGHT

The minutes, the hours, the days that followed were a blur, defined mostly by the most inexpressible horror Maren had ever known, would ever know. It was hard to imagine being more miserable than she had been, sitting in that dreary waiting room with its sickly, humming light, but darker times were to come.

Oliver said almost nothing on the desolate ride home. Annie continued to cling to her in the car, occasionally looking at her parents with an expression of supplication, as if begging them to tell her this had not happened. Maren could do nothing but hold her.

When they returned to Fourwinds, they said good-bye to Cappy, who promised to return first thing in the morning. They got Annie to her room. She fell onto her bed, fully dressed. Maren and Oliver stayed beside her, Maren silently rubbing her back until somehow, finally, she slept, and they returned to their own room.

Oliver slumped onto the chaise, covered his face with his hands, and wept. Maren could tell he wanted to speak, so she sat beside him and waited.

"I did this," he said finally, voice muffled.

"What?"

"I did this." He looked up. "It's my fault. If I hadn't

told her to stay away from him, this wouldn't have happened."

Maren was swimming, nearly drowning, in her own terrible sea, but she had just enough wherewithal remaining to know how vital her response was. She was reminded of the moment on the stairs all those years ago, though that episode seemed quaint and trivial in comparison. But now, as then, she knew if she got this wrong, everything would be wrong.

She took his face in her hands, and looked at him.

"You cannot do this, Oliver. Down that road lies hell," she said ferociously, tears streaming down her own face. "It will be our ruin. We can make it through, somehow. We can survive, but you must acknowledge he died because he fell, that he died in an accident. Please, Oliver, I beg you not to blame yourself. If you do, I think it might kill me."

"But . . ."

"No, Oliver. I mean it, like I've never meant anything," she said, her tone more forceful. "Charlie died in an *accident*. No one is to blame. It happened because terrible things happen. You must put that out of your mind. For me, Oliver. You have to do this for me."

He looked at her, concentrating, as if trying to do this thing she asked. If it was for her, perhaps he could find a way to choose what to believe, what not to believe. He put his arm around her and squeezed. She leaned into him, as close as she could get.

If we can do this together, she thought. *If we can just do this together . . .*

They finally made their way to the bed and clung to each other through the sleepless night. Oliver did not mention his feelings of culpability again that night, or ever. Years later, Maren marveled at the vehemence she had called forth, the energy and purpose she found to convince Oliver that Charlie's death was a terrible, unfortunate accident, and must forever be considered such. She had made him believe, and it had been their salvation.

If only she had been able to do the same for Annie.

The following morning, she stared out the window as the first hint of orange appeared on the horizon, and her mind turned to the task ahead. They would have to tell people. Billy first. Cappy would have told Georgie and Maude, but there were Maren's parents and brother; Gideon and Clara. So many people at home.

At least she would be spared telling everyone on Haven Point. The thought of how quickly the news would spread brought something else to mind. She turned to Oliver. He was staring blankly at the ceiling, arm folded behind his head, his brow knit in sorrow and confusion. She moved into the crook of his arm. Tears stung again. She hated to make him feel worse, but there was something she felt he needed to understand.

"I think this is going to be too much for people here, Oliver," she said into his chest. "I think they will turn away. It is too horrible."

His only response was to pull her closer to him, and she worried he had not heard. It felt vital to prepare him for the fact that this little community could not possibly reconcile Charlie's death with its sense of itself as a haven, where children had freedom with safety. There was no place for this in their naïve worldview. They would have to tuck it away on some other shelf, make it something or someone's fault. *Probably mine,* she thought, though she didn't care. *Make it my fault.*

Regardless of how, she was certain Haven Point would find a way to protect itself from this tragedy. Not Georgie or Maude, but the rest. Whether they placed blame or merely averted their eyes, she feared the reaction would be too much for Oliver to bear.

We have to go home soon, she thought. *We will have to face this in Washington.*

"I'm not sure about that," Oliver replied vaguely. She looked up at him sadly, certain he would face another reckoning.

Within hours, however, she discovered Oliver was right. And that she had been almost perfectly wrong.

Haven Point did not turn away. Without faltering, without wincing, Haven Point looked them straight in the eye. There was no gossip. There was no blame. In those weeks and in all the years that followed, Maren never detected a single untoward reaction to Charlie's death.

The people of Haven Point came to them. Quietly, steadfastly, they did for them every single thing that had to be done. With their old reserve, once deplorable but now so welcome, they kept their upper lips stiff and did it all without drama or discussion.

Maren and Oliver's job was to survive and to help their children survive, while their neighbors carried them through, seeking nothing but the privilege to serve.

To ask what they needed was to burden, so no one asked. They divined. Maren's parents appeared from Minnesota, picked up at the airport by someone, she was never clear who. When James Barrows heard the news from Harriet and Fritz, he walked out of his house on Watch Hill in Rhode Island, went directly to Newport to pick up Billy, and drove him to Maine. As plans came together, friends from Washington were housed all over the point, cared for and made comfortable. Someone tracked down Dorothy in Europe and gave her the news. People were in and out of Fourwinds in a stream that seemed guided by some unseen hand. There was food, so much food, and women in the kitchen preparing it, putting it out, or putting it away, making it all make sense. Maren noticed Harriet helping with flowers, conjuring vases and putting arrangements throughout the house—able, for once, to stay in the background, to be just another part of the whole.

At first, Maren's parents were lost amid the strangers, but just when Maren wondered how she could give them comfort when she had so little in reserve, Maude appeared. She was frail, but Georgie got her there, and she spent many hours with Maren's family. They spoke of Charlie, but also of farming and other familiar things.

Georgie was perfection. Maren would have expected her dear old friend to be solid, but something deep within Georgie's grain emerged. She hurt so much, Maren knew, but never showed it. Georgie knew when to sit and be quiet and when to make Maren laugh. One afternoon, Maren sat dazed in the kitchen with Billy, Maude, and Georgie. Georgie removed the foil from a plate to reveal some concoction from the Palmers, who latched onto every health food trend. She plunked the plate of gritty, unappetizing cookies on the kitchen table.

"Wheat germ molasses cookies, anyone?" she asked. "Or I could go peel some bark off a tree if you'd rather."

After that first night, Maren never considered going home to Washington. Charlie would be memorialized on Haven Point and buried in the little cemetery there. Why would they take him home to D.C. where he had merely endured, instead of laying him to rest on Haven Point where he had truly lived?

The flip side of the relief from day-to-day burdens was the time it left for grief. Attacks, awesome in their power, came at random. Maren would be feeling something close to normal when she would be struck by what she came to call "the nevers"—thoughts of what Charlie would never again do, what he would never become, that she could never hug him again. She would double over, unable to move. Her tears were unpredictable. Sometimes she hid in her room and directed wrenching sobs into her pillow, so her children would not have to hear.

Billy and Oliver seemed to be walking across hot coals, too, their pain close to the surface, but Maren knew something was terribly off about Annie. She was resistant to attention of any kind and seemed more angry than grief-stricken. She rarely left her room. Maren and Oliver gave up trying to coax her out, but they spent many hours with her. They hoped their presence would bring comfort, but she was so terribly remote. Something inside Annie seemed tied in a knot that they had no idea how to unravel.

As the memorial service grew closer, it became a source of anxiety for Maren. The plans had come together well enough: Above all else, it would be a celebration of Charlie's life. Billy would deliver the eulogy and had been soliciting stories and impressions from Charlie's friends. She knew he would do a fine job. The kind local minister who held services at St. Dunstan's, the little Episcopalian church on Haven Point, would preside. Annie wanted no official role, and they had not pressed. Maren had one special request, an unconventional idea for the music, and there had been no objection.

The memorial service makes it final, she eventually realized.

That morning, Maren rose after a sleepless night and put on the black dress someone had found for her that week, since she kept nothing like it on Haven Point. She managed to go through the motions of brushing her hair, putting it in a knot, and seeing to Billy and Annie, but through it all she was racked by anxiety. When the time came to go downstairs, she sat on the edge of her bed, feeling as if she might be sick.

"I'm not sure I can do this, Oliver."

"I'll help you," he said. She looked up at him skeptically, doubting he had strength to spare. He seemed diminished, his eyes darker and shadowed. But when he extended his hand, she took it and, somehow, they made their way downstairs together.

Georgie, Cappy, Maren's parents, and the children stood waiting in the living room, a gloomy lot, dressed in their black clothing and pained expressions.

I can't do this.

Even as they moved across the lawn toward the road, she had the sense of something tugging her back toward the house. Lacking any alternative, she put one foot in front of the other and willed herself to make this short walk to St. Dunstan's, the longest walk of her life.

Then came another miracle. As they passed the hedge, she looked up to see that they would not make this walk alone. At least a hundred people lined the road, almost all of Haven Point, waiting to escort them to the service. As they started toward the church, their friends and neighbors quietly fell in around them. No tears, just the stolid, dependable, chin-up Haven Point expressions that in their minimal sentiment had brought such comfort those days. Her anxiety dissolved, almost in the moment.

They reached the door just ahead of the great procession. She had no idea where it had come from, whose idea it had been that the Demarests should be escorted to the service. But she had needed to be carried, and she felt as if she had been.

How did they know? she wondered for the thousandth time. *How do they know what we need?*

The service had poignant moments and even laughter, and the room fairly teemed with love for Charlie. Maren had asked that the standard final hymn be replaced with Charlie's favorite from the weekly sing-along. So, when the time came, the voices of Haven Point rose up full and hearty to sing "The Skye Boat Song," an old Scottish folk number about Bonnie Prince Charlie. She could practically see the notes sail out the open windows, through the trees, carried by the salt air to the sea Charlie had so loved.

> *Speed, bonnie boat, like a bird on the wing*
> *Onward! The sailors cry*
> *Carry the lad that's born to be king*
> *Over the sea to Skye.*
> *Loud the winds howl, loud the waves roar*
> *Thunderclaps rend the air*
> *Baffled, our foes stand by the shore*
> *Follow they will not dare.*
> *Though the waves leap, soft shall ye sleep*
> *Ocean's a royal bed*
> *Rocked in the deep, Flora will keep*
> *Watch by your weary head.*
> *Speed, bonnie boat, like a bird on the wing*
> *Onward! The sailors cry*
> *Carry the lad that's born to be king*
> *Over the sea to Skye.*

"Come on over. A change of scenery will do you good." Georgie had been after her for days.

"Oh, all right," Maren said. To resist Georgie took as

much energy, if not more, than to relent, so she slipped on a cotton dress and sneakers and headed out the door.

Maren had not been sleeping. She wavered between disoriented stupor and terrible, desperate darkness. She felt drained of all competence. Oliver was nearly as paralyzed, though he had managed to go sailing that morning. While it was an activity he could perform almost entirely by instinct, she envied his ability to do anything at all.

Georgie's porch was its usual late-August riot of plants potted in every kind of container. Flowers and greens and herbs spilled over each other, as if, given another month of summer, they might grow together and completely take over.

A morning fog had lifted, leaving behind a damp smell of salt and fish. Maude sat darning an old sock. At her feet were two dogs, lying as close as they could without being rolled under the old cane chair's rockers.

Maren slumped in a chair and felt vaguely sick, though she did sense the tiniest glimmer of novelty in being outdoors.

"How's Annie?" Georgie asked.

"I don't know. She has hardly left her room." Maren sighed. Oliver had taken Billy to the train that morning. She'd been perversely relieved by his tears when he said good-bye. He was so broken, but she knew somehow that buried deep in the suffering were seeds of vitality—that someday those cracks and fissures would make room for grace and mercy, for transcendence and healing. Annie was broken, too, but along the wrong fault lines.

"Last night she came into the kitchen with red eyes, and I thought something was finally breaking through. But all she said was, 'Has he called?'"

"Has who called?" Georgie asked.

"Patrick. She had that stubborn look, as if it taxed her dignity to ask, but she wanted to know. Her tears were for him. I didn't have a good answer, of course. We haven't heard from him since the night Charlie died."

"He was at the service, though," Georgie said.

"He came to the church with Finn and Mary Pat, but not the reception. It was so obvious Annie was looking for him that Finn finally gave her some flimsy excuse."

"I didn't realize she was still so fixated on him."

"I'm not sure we realized how much of a hold he had on her until Oliver told her to stop seeing him."

"What a disgrace, his avoiding her like that," Georgie said.

"Patrick's chief concern is Patrick. This is too messy. He can't be bothered."

"So strange. Annie's always had the world by the tail," Georgie said. "Sounds like she's more upset about him than Charlie."

Maude looked up from her needlework, her expression a cross between admonition and sorrow.

"It's easier to be upset about Patrick Donnelly," she said.

When Maren got home that afternoon, she knocked on Annie's door.

"What?" Annie's voice was dull. Maren opened the door to find Annie on her unmade bed, looking out the window. A Three Dog Night song played on the 8-track. She turned and looked at Maren blankly.

"I wanted to check on you. I've been at Georgie's."

"Oh."

When Pauline died, Annie had been an open book, her grief acute and intense, so different from what Maren saw now. Annie seemed underwater, weighed down by something bigger than grief.

"Would you like to get outside for a little bit? I'm going to walk to the beach."

"I don't know," Annie replied, her voice still listless, eyes unfocused.

"You could bring your camera," Maren added. "We can just wander."

The tiny spark of life Maren detected in Annie's eyes confirmed her suspicion. Annie's abundant energy could not simply dissipate. At some point she had to let it out.

Sure enough, Annie got up slowly, took her camera off her dresser, and put the strap around her neck. Annie looked at Maren again, her expression still vacant. She would come, but Maren had to lead. Maren suppressed the urge to show how happy it made her.

They made their way down the hill to the beach club, Maren venturing an occasional innocuous remark, Annie silent.

"Are you hungry?" Maren asked when they arrived. Annie had barely eaten for days.

Annie shrugged, moved to one of the tables that overlooked the beach, and slumped in a chair. Reading this as acquiescence, Maren ordered sandwiches and brought them to the table. The beach club was crowded, but other than some pats on the arm and gentle smiles, people left them alone.

Annie took the seat that faced north, which gave her a direct view of the rocks where Charlie had fallen. After a few minutes, something up the beach seemed to catch her eye. Maren turned to see two men working at the part of the sea wall where it met the rocks.

"What is going on up there?" Annie asked.

"I'm not sure."

Lillian Belmont sat at the next table. Maren saw her shift in her seat, a speaking look in her eyes. Annie picked up her camera and trained her telephoto lens in that direction.

"Mom, they are doing something above the rocks."

"Lillian, do you know what they're working on?" Maren asked. Lillian hesitated.

"They are cutting a path," she said finally.

For years, Annie and her friends had pressed for a path to allow easier access to the Donnelly property, a way through the snarl of trees and vegetation above the rocks that separated the beach and the compound beyond.

Annie, eyes wide, turned to face Lillian. "A path?"

"It is too late for Charlie." Lillian spoke plainly, as everyone had that week. "But they are doing it now."

Annie pushed her chair back from the table with a great scrape, her eyes wild.

"Annie, please sit down," Maren said quietly.

"NO! I'm not staying here. I won't stay here," she shouted. When everyone at the beach club fell silent, Annie seemed grateful for the opening. She flung an arm in the direction of the Donnelly property.

"*Now* you let them cut a path? We asked for that path, but you all were so stuck-up. You just hated them too much, you wouldn't do it. But now you see what could happen to your precious kids, so it's finally more dangerous than letting them hang out with the Donnellys. This place makes me sick."

She burst into tears and ran out of the beach club.

Maren sat paralyzed. Lillian rose from her table, sat in what had been Annie's seat, and took her hand. "I am so sorry. I didn't know what to say other than the truth."

"It's all right, Lillian. It's not your fault."

She stayed for a few more minutes. Someone wrapped

her sandwiches for her. There had been a day when Maren would have resented these people witnessing Annie's scene, or mistrusted their response, but at that moment she was more comfortable sitting among them than going home to face Annie.

But face her she must. She declined Lillian's offer to walk her home and trudged up the hill alone. When she reached Annie's room, it was to find her packing.

"I have to get out of here. I can't stay." Annie seemed less angry, but her breath was short, as if she were having an allergic reaction and had to escape something unhealthy in the air. "I want to go home. I can stay with Laura or Gwen."

"Annie, I need to say something. Please sit down."

Annie stopped for a moment, resistant.

"Mom, please?" Her expression was pleading. Maren looked at her gently and patted the bed. Annie finally sat.

"Annie, I beg you to listen. I had to say something similar to your father earlier this week. It is so very important you understand. Charlie's death was an accident."

"But it didn't have to happen," she insisted, her eyes flashing. "If we had a path, if everyone hadn't hated the Donnellys so much, it wouldn't have happened. Don't you see? They wouldn't let them past the rocks. I can't stand it here. I can't stand it."

She clenched her hands into tight balls and covered her eyes as she began to cry. Maren had a memory of Annie's tantrums as a little girl, the tears that would come so fast, as if pressed out by the wellspring of her great energy. Maren put an arm around her back. This would not pass so easily. Annie was as tangled as the mess above the rocks. Maren wondered if there was any way clear.

"Annie, I know how you feel about people here, but it's a dangerous thing to assign blame. If we could go back in time, we could take a thousand things from the equation and Charlie would be here. You can blame the rain. You can blame me, or Dad."

Annie looked up quickly. "No. It's not your fault, or Dad's." She pulled herself together to get the words out through her tears. "Dad had reasons for me not to see Patrick. I didn't agree, but it wasn't the same as everyone else. They just wanted to keep them out. They always did."

Maren could tell Annie had gone to great pains to reconcile herself to what she was saying. She felt a surge of tenderness at Annie's desire to absolve her father from blame, and of deep relief that Annie did not seem to blame herself.

At the same time, she was troubled by Annie's persistence in defending the Donnellys, even after Patrick had so clearly abandoned her.

"Annie, do you think that is why Patrick hasn't come around?"

"Obviously!" she practically screamed. "They finally drove him away. He got the message. A person can only take so much!"

It was the most peculiar logic, the idea that Patrick had thrown up his hands after some final affront from Haven Point. But Annie had seized on it as the explanation for his disappearance. In her perversion of history, she was the baby Patrick had to throw out with the bathwater. Maren suspected Annie had spent many hours fixating until she fashioned an explanation for his betrayal that implicated Haven Point without insulting her.

Maren looked at Annie, deciding whether to dispute her twisted analysis. She knew Patrick had not rejected Annie because he felt slighted by the people of Haven Point. He had abandoned her because Annie's grief was troublesome and inconvenient. Even if it stung, would the truth free her?

Only if she could believe it, Maren thought. Annie did not seem remotely open to the truth.

Maybe, like the ancient Hebrews who cast out one goat to assume their collective sins, Annie needed something to cast out. Maybe it would be best to allow her to respond to that old primal desire for some creature to take on all iniquity. It was wrong in many ways. It wasn't truth. But perhaps a scapegoat would help her get beyond this. While it was sad that Annie would make Haven Point the guilty party, at least she didn't blame herself, or Oliver. If Maren agreed, it might bring Annie back.

"We're leaving in a few days anyway, Annie. Please stay."

As always, it calmed Annie to feel understood. She sniffled again but seemed to relax.

"Fine," she said. "But I'm not leaving this house. And I'm never coming back here."

Annie did not leave the house for the rest of their stay, and she never went back to Haven Point. It was many years before Maren realized the error. Annie Demarest could not cast Haven Point out like an old Hebrew goat.

She had exiled herself instead.

CHAPTER TWENTY-NINE

August 2008
Haven Point

SKYE

I know this was rather a lot for you to take in," Gran said. She looked at Skye with gentle sympathy, as if it wasn't Gran's terrible loss she had described, but Skye's.

Georgie had remained next to Gran all afternoon—listening, knitting, occasionally interjecting a piece of information. Mostly she was just there, as she had always been.

"I don't understand why no one told me this before," Skye said. She took a tissue from the box Gran handed her and dabbed her eyes. "I thought Charlie died in a car accident."

Skye wasn't sure if she had assumed this or her mother had misled her. It was something she had believed as long as she could remember.

"I knew you thought that at one point," Gran said. "You were at my house once, maybe seven or eight years old. You saw a picture of Charlie and asked who he was. When I told you, you said, 'He died in a car crash.' Pop and I felt it was your mother's story to tell, or not. I suspected she called it an accident, and you assumed the rest. I was never sure if your mother ever told you the truth."

"I'm so ashamed I wasn't more curious," Skye said.

"Don't be. Your mother led you to believe his death was not significant to her," Gran replied.

Skye had a hazy recollection of her mother brushing aside questions, her sense that this was a subject to avoid. No one profited from pursuing something Anne Demarest didn't care to discuss. And while extraordinary in light of what she had heard, Skye could see how as a child she might readily have accepted that her mother had simply gotten over Charlie's death. In her own way, she'd powered through difficulties like a bull through a red cape. Why not power through grief in the same manner?

"And if everyone acted like it wasn't a big deal, why would you think otherwise?" Georgie interjected.

"Because it was her brother . . . And your son!" Skye's tears came again in earnest.

"It's been many years, Skye," Gran said with a sad, resigned smile. "I didn't get over it. You just don't. There is no true reconciliation for losing a child. But a time comes when it's not what you wake up to every day."

"I'm still not sure I understand why she wanted her ashes spread here, though," Skye said.

"Well, for a long time . . . ," Gran began, then paused. She closed her eyes, took a breath, then started again. "For a long time, I sensed she still had some love for Haven Point, buried deep."

"Maybe," Skye replied. "But if she did, it was buried awfully deep."

Georgie stopped knitting, glanced at Gran, then looked at Skye over her reading glasses. "Well, think about your name."

"What about it?"

"The song we sang at Charlie's memorial service?" Georgie said. "It was called 'The Skye Boat Song.'"

"You think she named me after that?" Skye was skeptical.

"We wondered," Georgie said.

Skye had asked about her name. Her mom had just said she liked it. Had it been a tribute to Charlie, perhaps even to Haven Point? The idea gave her a little rush of warmth.

"But Gran, had she said something about Haven Point recently? You said she put the instructions in her will a year before she died." The timing implied a sentiment right at the surface, not "buried deep."

Gran opened her mouth as if to speak, but before she could get a word out, her face crumpled in anguish.

"Oh Gran, I'm so sorry."

She nodded and waved a little, as if to say, *I just need a moment.*

"So, what happened to Patrick?" Skye asked Georgie. She hoped she had chosen a safe change of subject.

"He married a wealthy heiress," she replied. "Ran for a seat in the New York legislature, but he caused a huge scandal when he got some young staffer pregnant. His wife divorced him, and he's had two more wives since. He never changed."

"Does he still come to Haven Point?"

"He used to occasionally, but he doesn't get on with his family very well," Georgie said. "Even the Donnellys know he's bad news. He went to law school at some point. He's an ambulance chaser in California now. You know the guys in the ads? 'Have you been harmed by asbestos?' That sort of thing. He's made a lot of money," Georgie grudgingly acknowledged.

"His son comes up here, though," Gran said. She'd wiped her eyes and nose, and though Skye heard fatigue in her voice, she seemed to have mastered herself.

"Oh, that reminds me." Georgie, her eyes suddenly alive with news, turned to Gran. "I heard they finally arrested him. I doubt we'll be seeing him again this summer."

"Wait . . . which son of Patrick's?" Skye said, feeling a sudden dread.

"His younger son, Ryan," Gran said. "Oh, that's right. You probably know him from D.C."

"Yes, I know him! What on earth are you talking about?"

"Oh, steer clear of that guy," Georgie said, shaking her head, clearly not aware that Skye was about to jump out of her skin. "He's even worse than his dad."

"What did he do?"

"He's the one responsible for Steven Barrows ending up in rehab. The Barrows Family has had a bad summer, I tell you. Not just Steven . . ." Georgie turned toward Gran again, about to go off on another tangent.

"Please, Georgie. I really need to know what happened." Skye gripped the tops of her thighs with her hands.

"Ryan Donnelly was dealing Ecstasy. He came up here a lot last summer, hosting big parties in The Stable," Georgie said. "At first no one thought twice about younger kids being over there. Ryan has a lot of younger cousins, so of course they'd invite their friends. Some rumors went around about drugs, but it was hard to separate the wheat from the chaff. People weren't sure what was up."

Skye's heart sank.

Ben knew what was up last summer, she thought. She felt a rush of shame as she remembered how Ben stiffened when she first mentioned Ryan's name to Ben in February, and how she'd assumed it was due to snobbery.

"What happened this summer?" Skye asked, her dread giving way to humiliation.

"He was back and forth again this July. He just gave the drugs away at first, then he started selling them. That's what they do, get kids hooked, turn them into customers," Georgie said knowingly, even in this story able to find fodder for her fascination with the world's underbelly. "One night, Steven wound up in the ER, paranoid and hallucinating. He told the police what happened, that he'd gotten Ecstasy from Ryan. Ryan had hightailed it back to D.C. by then. The detective in Phippsburg figured he'd be back later in the summer, so he bided his time. They caught him in town the other night and arrested him for possession."

Sunday night, Skye realized with a groan. That was why Ryan acted so strange when she ran into him at the grocery store the next day. She cringed, remembering the fight she'd picked with Ben that afternoon. She had been upset about seeing him sailing with Charlotte, but she let him believe it was about Ryan. No wonder he hadn't explained. He was probably just keeping his brother's confidence.

"His grandfather bailed him out and his dad got him a fancy lawyer," Georgie continued. "They might not like him much, but the Donnellys take care of their own."

"I'm surprised I didn't hear about this," Skye said, her voice a little thin.

"They kept it quiet," Gran said. "They wanted to protect Steven and make sure Ryan didn't realize they were onto him. Tenley Barrows told Georgie and me, though, so I think they're speaking about it more openly. Don't mention it to anyone, though."

"I won't," Skye replied glumly as the self-recrimination came, fast and furious. She had been as blind in her positive opinion of Ryan as she had been in assuming Ben's prejudice against him.

After the sing-along, when Gran mentioned that Ben's family was having some issues with Steven, Skye had fully assumed it was something frivolous. No "real" problem could touch a Haven Point family. Had she been willing to give it a nanosecond of thought, she would have recognized what a ludicrous notion this was, and how deeply unfair.

Given the radio silence, she was pretty sure she had blown any chance of rekindling the spark between her and Ben, if such a chance even existed, but she still owed him an apology. And an explanation.

Outside, the sky had taken on a sickly greenish tint.

"I think it's getting bad out there," Skye said. Gran and Georgie looked out the window.

"You're right," Gran said. "We should probably have dinner now."

They made sandwiches and heated soup on the gas stovetop. By the time they returned to the living room, it had grown even darker. Skye tried to read a magazine, but she couldn't focus. Gran seemed equally distracted, frequently looking out the window. Only Georgie was blasé, blithely continuing her knitting.

Until that point, little except duration had distinguished this storm from any other. But as the wind grew stronger, it began to find its way through the cracks in the house. The rain slashed against the windows, almost horizontal.

"I lost my cell connection," Skye said. "Last time I saw a forecast, though, it predicted the storm would pass to the west of us pretty soon."

A few minutes later, they heard an odd sound. Georgie laid down her knitting, and they sat still and listened. At first a loud whisper, it grew until it sounded more like race car engines. Before long, it was louder still, as if a train were rumbling by. The wind blowing through the attic created another sound: a low, eerie moan, almost human.

Skye knew the eye was near. Soon it was so loud, had they tried to speak they would not have heard each other. Papers flew off a table near the door, though it was hard to know where the wind had come from to carry them. A bang from upstairs announced some unsecured object had blown from a perch in the attic. They sat paralyzed, fascinated, looking at each other and around the room, listening.

A half hour later, it grew quiet again. Skye went to the window. The clouds still covered the moon, though not as thickly. She could even make out the outline of the cliff, and the line between the dark gray sky and darker ocean below.

"That's not the end of it. This is just the eye passing over," Georgie said.

Sure enough, a few minutes later, the wind kicked up again. Skye returned to the sofa and pulled a blanket over her legs as if it were armor. Their words were again drowned out by the sound, even louder this time, like a scream. They heard more thuds and bumps from the attic, and a huge cracking sound from outside. The rain was so heavy, it sounded like a stream coming off the roofs, overtopping the gutters and pouring down the windows.

Suddenly, from the front hall came an enormous crash as the wind blew the front door open and burst in like an angry intruder. Rain poured into the house. A lamp from the hall table fell and shattered.

Skye fought the wind and made her way to the door. Using her shoulder, she somehow managed to close it and turn the rarely used dead bolt. The wind howled and moaned, as if furious to have been cast out.

Her heart raced. She felt a rush of adrenaline, a primal energy. She began to laugh, a wild sort of laughter that nearly circled back to tears. Gran and Georgie, eyes wide, joined her near the door, seemingly propelled by the same strange energy. Gran also began to laugh.

Unable to hear one another over the wind, they proceeded to do what women do when confronted with anxiety and a great mess: they cleaned. They moved about as if it were a matter of great urgency, stacking papers and sweeping particles of lamps and vases that had crashed to the floor, mopping the water in the hall, working in silent cooperation while the storm continued to rage.

And then, as if some heavenly being flipped a switch, it was over. The rain stopped. Soon, the only sound from outside was the odd gust of wind, racing to catch up with the storm. Cleaning finished, noise abated, they returned to the sofas.

"I can't imagine what sort of mess this left behind outside," Gran said. She picked up a tidal chart from a side table and studied it. "Timing-wise, it could have been worse, but not a lot worse."

"That was a gully-washer." Georgie shook her head.

As Georgie and Gran began to speculate about the condition of their gardens and gravel drives, Skye felt a strange, unpleasant sensation take hold. She looked down at her hands and saw they were trembling. Tears stung her eyes.

"I think I'll head upstairs," Skye said. "I'm really tired."

Was tired the word? *Spent.*

Gran looked at her with a slight, worried frown.

"I'll come with you."

CHAPTER THIRTY

MAREN

Maren followed her granddaughter up the stairs to her room. Her heart ached as she watched Skye stumble onto her bed.

"You don't seem quite yourself," Maren said.

"I'm not." Skye covered her face with her forearm.

Maren sat on the edge of the bed and gently stroked Skye's arm. Eventually, Skye began to cry.

"Maybe I should have waited until after the storm to finish this saga. That was a little melodramatic, wasn't it?" Maren smiled.

Skye managed a laugh through her snuffling. Maren got a tissue from the dresser, while Skye climbed under the covers.

Maren returned to her spot at the edge of the bed and considered how best to help her granddaughter. She had not yet told Skye what had been going on with Annie during that last year, and she did not want to overwhelm her. But she wondered if she might be ready—if not for revelations, then for recollections.

From somewhere in the recesses of her mind came a poem her mother had loved. She could not recall the title or the author. Only the last two lines had lived on in her memory.

And with the morn those angel faces smile
Which I have loved long since and lost
awhile

Would it help Skye to remember what she had "loved long since and lost awhile"?

"Skye, I think your mother struggled at times with recognizing how many things can be true at once," Maren said finally. "She could be a little black-and-white."

"You think?" Skye replied, with a faint smile.

"We all struggle with that, though. Human beings are pattern seekers. We use our stories to try to make sense of the world. You know your mother suffered, and that you suffered as a result. And now you finally know a bit more about why. But I think it's important to remember that's not her whole story."

Skye did not say anything, but when she turned to face Maren and pulled the covers up to her chin, Maren saw acquiescence in her eyes.

"We worried, Pop and I, about your mother with a newborn baby," she began. "But we were so wrong. She was made for it."

Annie had adored the infant stage; she reveled in little things like Skye's lips, which she said looked like tiny cowboy hats. When Skye colored on the dining room wall, her mother mounted a frame around the scribble, two feet above the baseboard, and placed a gallery label next to it. "*Orange Study* by Skye Demarest." When Skye grew attached to a worm she had found and wanted to bring it to school, Annie had simply shrugged. "That's fine." She sent Skye off with the worm in one pocket and a note to the teacher in the other. "Skye has befriended a worm. His name is Bernie. He's in her pocket. Just wanted to give you a heads-up."

As Maren relayed these tales, she watched Skye's face soften and realized her instinct had been correct. Her granddaughter had probably never heard this version of her childhood. The narrative constructed from her memories was of an enduringly skewed dynamic, with Skye forced into the role of caretaker. It wasn't wrong—just incomplete.

Skye's eyes grew wet, but she was smiling gently. So, Maren pressed on, determined to remind Skye that, despite her demons and many imperfections, her mother had loved her fiercely.

CHAPTER THIRTY-ONE

SKYE

In her dream, Skye and her mom were at home, sitting next to each other on the living room sofa, laughing at something. Skye tried to turn to look at her, but she felt like her head was stuck to the back of the sofa, as if by centrifugal force, like on an amusement park ride.

Though frustrated by her inability to see her mother's face, Skye reveled in the sound of her laugh. When some distant noise tried to drag her from her slumber, she was reluctant to awaken. She finally swam from her dream, and realized she was not with her mother, but on Haven Point, and that someone was banging on the front door.

The lights were still out, so she grabbed the lantern and headed to the landing, just as Gran and Georgie emerged from their rooms.

"Who on earth is it?" Georgie said. "It can't be Cappy."

They went downstairs, and Skye opened the door to find Ben with a great bundle in his arms and an anxious look on his face. It took her a moment to realize the bundle was his grandmother, long legs hanging over his left arm, head dangling from his right. She held the lantern closer and saw Harriet was unconscious, blood pouring prodigiously from a wound on her head. Ben was muddy and soaked, hair going in every direction. He struggled under the burden.

"Oh God, Ben! What happened? Come in!" She opened the door wide.

"I didn't know where else to go. The causeway is flooded," he said between labored breaths.

"Take her upstairs," Gran said. "The green room, next to the master. I'll get my first-aid kit." Gran was still a nurse, if not certified, and everyone on Haven Point knew it. She was able to treat a wound as well as any doctor might.

Skye led Ben to the green bedroom and fetched clean towels from the linen closet. Ben laid his grandmother on her side and put a towel under her head. Her pajama pants were soaked and clung to her thin legs.

It was hard to see exactly where the blood was coming from, but from what Skye could tell, the wound was near the crown of her head. Her stiff brown hair, usually so well styled, was snarled and rust-colored from blood, her quilted robe bloodstained.

Gran returned with reading glasses, the first-aid kit, and matches. Georgie followed close behind with more clean towels and bottles of water.

"The house flooded," Ben said. "It's a mess down on the beach. She went downstairs to get something and fell."

He looked down at his grandmother, his face a little gray.

"She's bleeding everywhere," he added unnecessarily.

"It's all right, Ben. Head cuts bleed a lot," Gran said. She moved the lantern to the bedside table, found the source of blood, and gently began to clean the area with an antiseptic wipe. Skye was relieved when Harriet groaned, her first real sign of life.

"She'll be all right," Gran said after a moment. "It's

too deep for a butterfly bandage, though, so I'll have to stitch it. Who knows when we'll be able to get her across the causeway?"

Skye and Ben watched as Gran sterilized the needle.

"Where did this happen?" Georgie asked.

"In the living room," Ben replied. "It was crazy. The storm passed, and I thought we had gotten through it, but then we heard this terrible sound. Like a wave, as if we were right on top of the surf. We looked downstairs, and all we could see was water, a foot at least. A storm surge, I guess. We had moved most of the rugs and furniture to the second floor, but she was worried about some table. She slogged through the water and fell. I don't know what she hit her head on." He winced at the memory.

"Okay. You and Skye go downstairs and you can dry off. Georgie will stay with me. Do you need clothes? I'm sure we can find something."

"It's okay. I have stuff in my car. I parked it on the hill before the storm hit."

Skye had to smile at this. Ben always used his car for auxiliary storage. He probably had everything from bathing suits to formal wear stashed in the trunk.

After he got his things, Skye showed him to the downstairs bathroom, where he could clean up and change. By the time they went back upstairs, Harriet had come to, and Gran was stitching her wound. Harriet's eyes were shut, her jaw clenched against the pain.

Skye felt a little weak just watching. Ben looked no better. Gran looked up at them briefly and smiled.

"Go on, you two. Georgie and I have this well in hand. Your grandmother was able to answer a few questions. She'll be fine."

"Okay," Ben said, obviously relieved. "Let us know if you need anything."

"Good thing neither of those two tried to make a living in medicine," Georgie muttered as they left the room. Ben and Skye exchanged a brief smile.

Skye led him to the living room, turned on battery-operated lanterns, and lit a large candle in a hurricane vase.

"Can I get you a beer? The refrigerator's probably still cold."

"Sure, thanks," Ben said.

When Skye returned, she handed Ben his beer, then sat down on the sofa and gestured to him to join her. He sat at the other end, an empty cushion between them. He took a swig of his beer, closed his eyes, and leaned his head back.

"I'm glad you came here," Skye said. "Gran will take care of her."

"I know. Thank you. I had no idea what to do. What a disaster." He shook his head, eyes still closed.

"Why didn't you all leave?"

"She wouldn't. I had to pretend I wanted to stay, too. She would have sent me packing if she knew I was here to keep an eye on her."

"She's stubborn, I guess."

"That's an understatement." He managed a little smile at this, but it faded quickly. "It was horrible. She was totally out. At first, I wasn't sure she was alive. I dried her off as best I could and carried her down the lane. The water was above my knees. Thank God my car was on the hill."

"It sounds horrifying."

"There are so many trees down and branches in the road, I had to drive over some people's yards to get here. If you hadn't been around, I was going to try the Grahams'."

At least he came here before Georgie's, Skye thought. She would hate to think she'd become such a pariah that he would only come to Fourwinds as a last resort.

As they sat quietly, Skye's mind kept returning to what she had learned earlier about Ryan Donnelly, how badly she had misread Ben's motives. He looked so tired, and she knew it was selfish under the circumstances, but the need to relieve her guilt pressed on her.

"Ben, I owe you a huge apology. I know it's not the right time, but I learned about Ryan tonight, about the drugs and everything. I'm ashamed of myself, of the assumptions I made. I just want to tell you how sorry I am."

He hesitated a moment, eyes still closed.

"It's okay," he said finally. He turned to look at her, his head still resting on the back of the sofa. "I couldn't tell you, so what else were you supposed to think?"

"Don't be magnanimous. It'll just make me feel worse," Skye said, shaking her head. "I've just always had this idea that everyone here lived such easy, perfect lives. It's so absurd."

"I can understand that. People here are pretty buttoned up."

"You're still being magnanimous," Skye scolded.

"Sorry," Ben said, feigning contrition. "Nasty habit."

"Another thing I should tell you, Ben. The other day in the kitchen when we had that argument about Ryan? I was actually upset about something else."

Skye saw the question in his eyes. It felt like climbing out on a thin limb, but she knew she had to stop being so fearful. Even if his response stung, he had more than earned the whole truth.

"I saw you and Charlotte sailing that morning, and I got angry when you didn't mention it." She spoke quickly, as if to force the words out before she could stop them.

Ben's brow furrowed, as if he was mentally assembling a puzzle.

"Okay. Wow. I can imagine how that must have seemed." He shook his head a little, as if to clear it of surprise. "Okay, so first, about Charlotte. Here's the thing. . . ."

He stopped. Now he was uncomfortable. Skye nodded, encouraging him to continue.

"You might know we dated for a long time," he said finally.

"Of course I know." Skye laughed, wondering how he thought that fact could have escaped her.

"I'm not sure what's going on with her," he continued, searching for the right words. "I think Charlotte was trying to figure out where things stood. Like she . . ."

When he could not complete the thought, Skye realized what held him back. He was too much the gentleman to betray Charlotte's confidences. Skye, on the other hand, felt no such compunction.

"She wanted to get back together?" she prompted.

"Yes," he said finally, with reluctance. "She wanted to give it another try."

"I see. And you don't?"

"No. I don't. Charlotte and I aren't going anywhere," he said, his tone certain. He picked at the label on his beer bottle and laughed—just a little laugh, but to Skye's ears it sounded like church bells, angels singing.

"I see," Skye replied.

He sighed, as if relieved to have that business dispensed with, then sat up straighter and regarded her, a gleam in his eye.

"So, Ms. Demarest, I have a question for you now," he said in a lawyerly tone.

"Okay," she replied warily.

"You were angry I didn't mention sailing with Charlotte. Why was that?" He crossed his arms and tilted his head in a spirit of playful inquisition.

Skye looked down. Now it was her turn to struggle for words.

"I don't know. I knew it was none of my business. I just . . ." She trailed off.

He waited a beat before he spoke again. "You didn't think it was your business?" he asked, his expression inscrutable.

Put up or shut up, Skye.

"I guess I should say I wasn't sure it was my business, but . . ." Her cheeks felt hot. "But I wanted it to be."

She glanced at him and discovered he was not just smiling, he looked downright amused. With his eyes glued to her face, he reached down and plucked her hand from the back of the sofa and pulled her toward him—not forceful, but commanding.

"Now, this is a very interesting development." His lawyerly tone was back as he grinned down at her. He lifted her chin, and she looked up at him, her heart thudding in her chest. His eyes explored her face, then his hand slid behind her head and he leaned toward her.

Just as his lips met hers, a heavy clomping on the stairs signaled Georgie's arrival. He groaned quietly and they separated.

"How is she?" Ben asked, when Georgie stepped into the light of the lanterns. Skye hoped she didn't look as flustered as she felt.

"Your grandmother cleaned and stitched the wound. Her head hurts like Billy Hell and she probably has a concussion, but she's awake. Making as much sense as she ever did." Georgie sounded weary. "You can see her. I just wanted to let you know. I'm going to bed myself."

They said good night, and Georgie disappeared back

into the darkness. When they heard her on the landing upstairs, Ben pulled her toward him again. He kissed her,
deeply now.

After a moment he pulled back, looked at her, and
shook his head. Skye felt like she was seeing her own
feelings mirrored in his eyes, that sense of wonder that
someone with whom you could share so much laughter,
whom you had known, really, for so little time but who
felt like the dearest of old friends, could also ignite such
powerful desire. He pulled her down so they were lying
on the sofa. Her hands wandered over his broad shoulders
and brushed the sides of his waist.

Under any other circumstances, Skye was certain
nothing would have stopped them, but simultaneously
they both seemed to recall the situation, the presence of
their grandmothers upstairs. He groaned again, theatri-
cally this time, and they both began to laugh.

"We should probably go upstairs," he said, eyes to the
ceiling. Before he got up, he looked down at her again and
smiled. "But this is a nice way to end a bad night."

When they poked their heads into the green bedroom, the
light was dim. Harriet, clean and dry, was wearing one
of Gran's nightgowns. She was covered to her waist with
a quilt. Her head, wrapped in gauze to keep the wound's
dressing in place, rested on two pillows.

Harriet's expression was mild. Skye hadn't realized
what a constant feature Harriet's look of disapproval had
been until now, when it was absent.

By far the strangest aspect of the scene was Gran,
seated on the chair beside the bed, Harriet's hand in her
own. Skye's eyes widened. Gran responded with a be-
mused look that promised a story to come.

"Hi, Grandma," Ben said.

"Hello, Ben." Harriet kept her eyes closed. "I'm sorry about all this."

The apology was another stunner.

"She'll need to get to Bath when you are able, but she'll be fine," Gran announced.

"Thanks, Mrs. Demarest. Grandma, I'll stay here tonight and get you out in the morning if the causeway is clear. Do you need anything?"

"I'm well, thanks to you and Maren." Harriet began to open her eyes and turn her head toward him, but she seemed to think better of it and sank deeper into the pillow instead. "Just go on to bed. It's late."

Skye grabbed sheets, towels, and a flashlight from the linen closet and brought them to the room next to hers. Once she and Ben finished making up the bed, he pulled her to him and kissed her again.

"So, we might have to wait a bit to tell people about us," Ben said with a smile when they separated. The quiver of pleasure Skye felt at the idea of an "us" was promptly dampened by the words that came out of his mouth next: "I have to give my parents time to get used to the idea."

Skye froze, bewildered. He had spoken lightheartedly, but his meaning seemed inescapable.

"Okay, Ben. No problem," she said coolly. He stood motionless as she moved toward the door. When she reached for the knob, she felt his hand on her shoulder.

"Wait, Skye." He turned her toward him, his eyes searching her face. "I'm sorry. I think you misunderstood me just now."

"You're worried what your parents would think about us. What's to misunderstand?" she said stiffly. He looked at her for a second, then put both hands on her shoulders, guided her to the bed, and gently compelled her to sit.

"I was making a dumb joke, Skye, because of how I was last time," he said as he sat next to her.

"What do you mean how you were last time?"

He paused. "Oh my God, Skye, I thought you knew this. It was kind of an open secret around here."

"What was?"

"So, um, when you blew me off after that summer in high school, I didn't take it very well." He seemed a little embarrassed.

"I didn't blow you off." She looked at him, still baffled.

He smiled a little and raised an eyebrow. "What else would you call it?"

Skye tried to recall what happened after she left Haven Point that summer. Ben had called a few times. Skye remembered that he suggested they get together, and she had resisted. It never occurred to her she had hurt him, though. Or that she could.

"I had no idea."

"It's okay, but please understand, I was totally kidding about my family. You and I had a couple of weeks together when we were seventeen. I was kind of a mess after, but it ended up being sort of a family joke. 'Ben's Blue Period,' they called it."

"Still. I'm sorry." She frowned and squeezed his hand, still struggling to take it in.

"I should clarify." Ben lifted an index finger. "I was a very manly kind of mess."

"Oh, goes without saying." She nodded. "Five o'clock shadow, empty liquor bottles."

"Exactly. Hole-punched-in-wall type stuff. Angst, but manly."

"Of course," Skye said solemnly. "Mangst."

They both laughed. Though it was ancient history and

they had joked their way through the awkwardness, Skye still felt he deserved some honesty from her in exchange for his own.

"For what it's worth, Ben, that was a confusing time for me. I felt a bit like I was playacting that summer, like it wasn't really me here."

He looked down thoughtfully, his thumb rubbing her knuckle. After a moment, he smiled gently and peered up at her from under his lashes.

"And I'll just say for what it's worth, in every way that matters, you are just as I remembered."

He stood, pulled her from her perch, and wrapped her in a hug. He smelled like salt water, wind, and sand. Like Haven Point. She wished more than anything she could join him in the little twin bed with its American flag comforter, but she released him, rested her hand on his cheek for a moment, then picked up her lantern and went to her room.

As she climbed into her own bed, she considered Ben's very different construction of that long-ago summer. She thought she had presented a false front, a carefully edited story about her mother, her life.

Perhaps there was another way of looking at it. Maybe what she had presented was just a more forgiving perspective. That wasn't lying. In its own way, it was growing up.

For the first time, she saw herself as Ben saw her that summer: not as a girl, broken and dissembling, but as a young woman, telling her truth and learning to love.

CHAPTER THIRTY-TWO

SKYE

When Skye struggled awake from her deep sleep, she was assaulted by flashes of memory. *My mother . . . Uncle Charlie . . . the door flying open, wind raging through the house . . . Harriet . . . a wound.* She pushed herself up on one elbow and rubbed her eyes. She opened them to see Ben at the end of her bed, a mug of steaming coffee in his hand. She smiled, remembering the night's happier ending. *Ben.*

"That was like watching my three-year-old nephew wake up," he said with a grin. He handed her the mug.

"Is that for me?" She sat up and took it gratefully.

"Your grandmother sent me up with it."

His hair was tousled. He needed a shave. He still smelled faintly of sweat and rain. She thought he looked beautiful.

Did all that really happen?

As if in answer, he grabbed ahold of her blanket-covered foot and jiggled it playfully. They exchanged a smile. As she took another sip of coffee, something in her peripheral vision caught her eye. She looked at the nightstand and saw the clock blinking.

"The power's on? Hallelujah!"

"It is. I'm heading out now to check the road. Your grandmother says to come down when you're ready."

He returned a half hour later, as Skye and Gran were making breakfast. The causeway was clear, so he could take his grandmother to the hospital in Bath. His aunt Polly would meet them there and take Harriet to Hartford when she was discharged, while Ben would return to Haven Point.

After Skye ate and saw Ben off, she went to have a look outside. The yard was littered with debris—branches, shingles, and roof tiles everywhere. A random wooden door was in the driveway, evidently blown off someone's shed or garage. A giant limb of the ancient oak in the center of the yard hung limply, twisted and shorn almost clean off. Other trees were stripped nearly bare of their leaves. Even the pines looked scraggly and thinner for their ordeal.

Skye did what she could. She cleared branches from the driveway and flower beds and returned items they'd stowed in the garage to their rightful places.

When she came in, Gran beckoned her to the porch, where she had iced tea waiting.

"You and Harriet looked chummy last night," Skye said.

"You won't believe the half of it."

"I'd believe about anything after yesterday. What happened?"

"Well, when she finally came to, she was crabby as ever and a little confused. When she put the pieces together, I think she was humbled. She looked at me at one point and said, 'We never have been friends, have we, Maren?' And I said, 'No, we haven't. You've never liked me, and I always wondered why.'"

"Wow, Gran. Bold!"

"Wasn't I?" Gran said, pleased with herself. "She tried to deny it at first, but I'd have none of that. She got really quiet for a minute, then she said, 'You don't know why?' I told her I truly did not."

"What, that she loved Pop?"

Gran's eyes widened. "How do you know that?"

"What else would it be? You told me she got married soon after you did. She had known Pop her whole life. She was probably waiting for him all those years, then the pretty nurse from Nowheresville snatched her fellow out from under her."

She smiled. "Harriet didn't put it that way, but that's the gist." Gran shook her head and leaned over to pick up some papers from the coffee table. "On another subject. I understand why you weren't interested in seeing this, Skye, but after our conversation yesterday I think you should know what it says."

Skye looked at the cover. *Government of the District of Columbia. Office of the Chief Medical Examiner.* The toxicology report.

She opened it and looked at the first page. It contained a list of substances for which her mother had tested positive. She didn't recognize the names. Below the list, under "Cause of Death," it said, "accidental multidrug intoxication."

"Don't they call it an accident unless they're one hundred percent certain?" Skye asked.

"Probably, but in this case, I think it's accurate. I am almost positive your mother died from serotonin syndrome."

"What's that?"

"She tested positive for three prescription drugs: an antidepressant, a migraine medication, and Xanax. You aren't supposed to mix medications that raise serotonin levels. My guess is the first two got her heart racing. She then self-diagnosed anxiety and took the Xanax. In this combination, it was toxic."

"Wouldn't she know not to mix them? Didn't the doctor or pharmacist tell her?"

"I suspect she didn't mention the migraine prescription to the pharmacist. As you know, her migraines were bad but infrequent. The prescription was old." Gran grimaced. "Expired, actually."

"Oh my God." Skye put her head in her hands and groaned. *Classic.* Her mother always said expiration dates were a conspiracy.

"Absurd, but it makes a certain kind of sense," Gran said. "If she intended to die, she could have taken a fistful of those, or any of a half-dozen other medications. There was no reason to take all three, unless it was a mistake. She was definitely careless, heedless of her life on some level, but in the end mostly unlucky."

Skye felt unsteady, as if sands were shifting beneath her. She had claimed to be indifferent about the cause of her mother's death, but it was only because she had assumed it was suicide one way or another. Why was she so unnerved to find out it was more likely an accident?

"You knew, didn't you?" she asked, recalling Gran's curiosity when Adriene had offered to expedite the toxicology report.

"I had a hunch," Gran said. She paused, and Skye saw her lips quiver. She took a few breaths before continuing.

"The last time your mother got out of rehab, she called, wanting to talk about Charlie. You have to understand how unexpected this was. She'd scarcely spoken his name to me since he died. We reminisced for a while that day, and we continued to do so over a number of similar conversations. One day she broke down. 'Why did he die, Mom?' she asked."

"Oh no." Skye began to cry.

"I know. It is horribly sad to think of her in such pain," Gran said, her eyes damp. "It was a good thing, though. She was finally grieving."

Her grandmother paused, and reached for her hand. "This is what I wanted to tell you most of all. She wanted to be well, Skye."

"Isn't this worse, though?" Skye asked, tears streaming down her face. "Is it better to lose her in an accident? To have her trying to heal and then make a stupid mistake?"

Gran looked at Skye sadly. "We lost her either way, Skye." Gran paused then added, "It's not worse. It just might be harder."

Not worse. Harder.

The words hit Skye like a blow to the solar plexus. She bent forward, as if trying to keep something within, but it would not be contained. She heard a sound emerge from her throat, and began to weep—not the sweet tears of the previous night, when Gran opened the door to childhood memories, but wrenching sobs. She understood with a terrible clarity why it was not a relief to discover her mother's death was an accident.

When Skye moved home, she had seen a woman who couldn't cope, a woman in a steady and inexorable decline, a woman whose death was inevitable. She had held on to that view for the same reason people so often cling to a story: because she thought it made it easier.

But her mother did not have to die. It had not been inevitable. Suddenly, stripped of her illusion, she saw her mother as she had been, not in black and white, but in all her color—the messy, beautiful, addicted, creative, funny, maddening, original whole of her—and she was consumed by a feeling of loss so acute, she wondered if she could bear it. She could not imagine anything ever filling the huge, gaping hole.

Gran moved to the ottoman next to her chair, took her hand, and sat patiently, while Skye did what she had long needed to do, what her mother had so belatedly done: looked grief in the face.

After a time, Skye took a shaky breath, looked up at Gran, and shook her head.

"The clarity of tear-washed eyes," Gran said tenderly.

"What about her ashes, Gran? Do you think she wanted to be close to Charlie?"

"Yes, and I think she had begun to reconcile her feelings about Haven Point. It was mostly an existential question, when she asked why Charlie died, but she seemed to have relinquished the idea that this place was to blame. She loved it here, Skye. Until the day we lost Charlie, she truly loved Haven Point."

"I believed her, though," Skye said. "About Haven Point, I mean."

"She was persuasive. She had to be, to convince herself. And make no mistake. Haven Point has its flaws, of course it does. But while it might not be the magic that some pretend, there was never really the rot she claimed either. You can make a case against anyone, against anything, if you choose to."

Skye nodded.

"For years, it saddened me that we took such opposite lessons from Charlie's death. Annie blamed Haven Point, while Charlie's death helped me see this place for what it is—just a bunch of human beings with all their sins and flaws, trying to create some community. It taught me, as Auden said in that poem, 'to love my crooked neighbors with all my crooked heart.'"

"Do you think Mom would have eventually told me all this herself?"

"I do. She was still trying to work through her feelings, but I feel certain she would have. The provision in her will said either of us could scatter the ashes. So, at the very least, we know she was prepared to outlive me. . . ." Gran stopped and closed her eyes. When she opened them, she continued, her voice shaky. "Had I died first it would have fallen to you. She was hard to understand at times, but it would not have been like her to leave some puzzle for you to decode."

"No, she wasn't exactly an international woman of mystery," Skye said with a smile. "In the end, it *was* left to you to tell me, though. I'm sorry. And thank you."

"Well, save your thanks, because there's one more thing I'd like to say," Gran said, a warning look in her eye.

"What's that?" Skye braced herself.

"The other day, when we were discussing your job, you referred to the chaos you grew up with. I agreed with what you said, and I still do, but I do think you have conflated some things in your mind."

"Like what?"

"I think, Skye, you experienced your mother's creativity and passion, her disorganization and chaos, and her drinking as one big mess."

"Wasn't it?"

"I don't think so. The chaos? That was garden variety Anne Demarest. Your mother always ignored what bored her. But she went after what interested her, hammer and tong. Her art was not a symptom of some pathology. It was the truest thing about her. Until that last year when she struggled so much, she never stopped learning and creating."

"That's true," Skye conceded.

"Here's why it's important for you to know this." Gran took her hand. "You got all the good, Skye. You have her humor and her intelligence. And you have her creativity, even if yours runs in another direction. But you got none of the bad. Your life will never be like hers, like what you experienced growing up." Gran paused and looked at her closely. "That was never the danger."

"The danger is my overcompensating?" She stiffened a bit, but mostly as a reflex. For once she felt like she might be able to hear what Gran was saying without defensiveness.

"Well, I don't know if there is any danger, per se. Remember your mom's expression? 'Everything depends on the quality and direction of light.'"

Skye nodded.

"I think if you tilt the prism a little, you might find it freeing."

The sound of the kitchen door announced Georgie had arrived for lunch. Gran patted her hand and went inside.

Skye stayed on the porch and considered what Gran had said. It was true that when Skye thought about her mom, especially in recent years, she had placed "Anne Demarest, the artist" in the darkest part of the picture, the occlusion shadow. If she walked around to another side and cast a warmer light on the subject, she might see the beauty again, and perhaps consider what was possible in her own life.

Possible. Skye had always struggled to understand why people attached such positive meaning to that word. When Skye considered what was possible, it was to war-game every conceivable outcome, to get in front of the worst-case scenario.

Could she completely exorcise her anxiety about work? Probably not, but for the first time in as long as she could remember, she felt a sense of possibility that was infused with at least as much hope as fear.

Haven Pointers who lived within an easy drive were pouring in to help overwhelmed caretakers. When Ben returned from Bath, he and Skye headed to the country club to lend a hand.

It was jarring to see what the storm had wrought beyond Fourwinds's yard. So much gravel had washed off of Haven Point Road, it looked more like a donkey path. As they passed one of the entrances to the sanctuary, Skye peered in and saw that a huge swath down the middle was a skeleton of its former self, treetops cut clean off as if scalped, branches jagged and leafless. It looked like something from a picture in a fairy tale after a witch casts a terrible spell. When they reached the Ballantines' house, Skye stopped and gasped.

"Oh no." A massive tree had crushed Mrs. Ballantine's lovely garden gate. Almost nothing was left of the roses she had painstakingly trained over its top. The few remaining blossoms peeked pathetically from under a huge branch.

As they walked onto the country club property, a truck full of lumber turned onto the grounds. A sign on its side read DONNELLY CONSTRUCTION.

They got marching orders from Georgie, who was manning phones and sending people out to various houses. They spent the next few hours at Ben's grandmother's house and in several others, taking photographs and doing what they could to prevent further damage in advance of insurance adjusters and repairmen: mopping and sweeping, covering broken windows, and moving valuables from exposed places.

When they were done, they walked back on the beach in the direction of Fourwinds. It was calm this evening, as if the sea were tired from the previous night's ordeal. Before they reached the beach club, they stopped and hoisted themselves onto the sea wall to watch as the setting sun painted gold onto the water and rocks.

"You love it here, don't you?" Skye asked, watching Ben's face as he took in the scene. "All the traditions, the families coming back year after year?"

"I do. I mean, Haven Point's ridiculously homogenous, but it's beautiful, and I have my family and a lot of friends here."

"Wait, what did you just say?"

"What? About family and friends?"

"No, before that."

"Oh, that it's homogenous?"

"Yes." Skye began to laugh. "So . . . you *know* that?"

"Kind of hard not to," Ben said, looking at her a little quizzically. "These summer communities are all still pretty Waspy. It won't happen overnight, but I know a lot of people our age would like that to change."

"They would?"

"Of course," Ben said, as if this were obvious. "I understand, though. Haven Point isn't for everyone. I gather your mother didn't like it here."

Skye waited a moment before responding. "That's not completely true, actually."

"What do you mean?"

"Gran started telling me some things this week, about my mother and this place, and I've learned it wasn't quite so simple."

He was quiet, offering an opening, but he wouldn't probe. Skye finally felt safe, though, loosening the reins of her story.

She began at the beginning and told him everything—about Gran and her uncle Charlie, about her mother's refusal to return to Fourwinds, about the request in her will about her ashes. Ben was kind, curious.

"I'm surprised I hadn't heard this either, with all the gossip around here," he said, when she had finished.

"I guess it was an unwritten rule." Skye was amazed herself by that detail, that everyone, even Harriet, had kept to an unspoken agreement. "People talk to Gran about Charlie all the time. They keep the memory of his life alive, but they rarely talk about how he died."

"You know, my dad didn't come here for a long time either," Ben said.

"Really?"

"Yeah. My grandparents' marriage was awful. And, well, you know my grandmother. My father hated her judgment, how she kept his sister, my aunt Polly, under her thumb. Everyone thought he was a cheerful kid, but I think he was in a lot of pain."

As Skye listened, she was struck by how much her own perspective had been warped by shame. She had been shocked to hear that Steven Barrows had a drug problem, astonished to discover she had hurt Ben when they were teenagers, and was again surprised to learn about his father's painful childhood. She had been so busy feeling ashamed, trying to get out in front of other people's assumptions about her, she never stopped to think she might be making assumptions about them.

"When did he start coming back here?"

"When he and my mom started dating. He said it took him by surprise, but he suddenly realized how much he wanted to show her Haven Point. It held so much of his history; not just his or his parents', but his grandparents' and great-grandparents'. I guess I feel the same way, even after all this stuff with Steven. Good and bad, it's part of my history, too," Ben said.

History. His story.

Skye had never felt she had any claim to Haven Point. With her genetic mystery dad, alcoholic mom, and off-beat childhood, she thought she didn't belong among these shiny, perfect people.

But they weren't shiny and perfect. She didn't know exactly what it meant to her, but for the first time, she saw that Haven Point was part of her history, her story, too.

"What's the plan for your mother's ashes?" Ben asked.

"I'm not sure," Skye said. "Gran said we could figure something out tomorrow."

"I've got our little outboard on a trailer. I can put it back in the water," Ben said. "You all might want this to be private, but if it would help, I could take you all out."

"Actually, that would be nice, thank you."

They didn't speak for a while. The only sound was Ben's foot gently kicking the sea wall. A pleasant tension hung between them.

"I don't mean to jump the gun here, Skye," he said finally. "But I hope this works, you and me."

"Me, too," Skye said. She suddenly felt a little shy.

Ben hopped off the wall, lifted her down, and kissed her, a kiss unlike any before, one that felt like a promise. Then they continued down the beach as the sun began to set and the sea grew copper.

CHAPTER THIRTY-THREE

MAREN

As Ben navigated around the point, Maren looked up and remembered her first impression of Haven Point, how the houses appeared to be standing guard. And there was Fourwinds, a grizzled old soldier: its foundation uneven and shingles faded, but still standing strong.

Maren had not told Skye that Fourwinds would be hers someday. She had decided it was not necessary. It was lovely, of course, imagining Skye holding on to the house, carrying on the Demarest tradition. For now, though, it was enough that Skye knew the truth about her mother and Haven Point. Once she had more time to reconcile her past, she could decide whether Fourwinds had a place in her future.

Ben continued around the point until the beach club was in view. Though they were well offshore, they could see figures moving in and out of the houses—cleaning, clearing, making things right again.

Maren widened her focus and took in the broader view, the older homes to the south of the rocks, the Donnelly complex to the north. The contrast was stark, like a "before and after" picture. Haven Pointers saw it as a cautionary tale. *If we are not vigilant, see what we will become?* But in the big world, where people weren't so hidebound, the juxtaposition of old to new might tell a story of progress, success.

Maren considered how Annie would have seen things from this vantage point. Her eyes would not have lingered on the contrast between the homes. They would have gone straight to the rocks themselves, symbols of separation and injustice. And, ultimately, of terrible loss.

She and Skye exchanged a glance. When Skye shook her head, Maren knew she had come to the same conclusion: Annie's ashes did not belong here.

"Can we go around Gunnison Island?" Maren asked.

Ben nodded, calm and unhurried. When they got behind the island and the coastline was no longer in view, Maren asked him to cut the engine.

She looked up at the island's rocky shore. She had hoped she would somehow just know when they had found the right spot, but she supposed that was just silly superstition. And this was as auspicious a location as any. It was back here, out of view of the spectators on the shore, that Annie and Charlie overtook Fritz's boat, leading to their victory in the Stinneford Cup. She recalled what a good sport Fritz had been on the occasion of his defeat. There was some poetry in Fritz's son being the one to bring them here today.

A flash of motion caught her eye, and Maren looked up to see that a bird had landed on a little ledge.

"Ben, do you think you could get a little closer to the island?"

Ben restarted the engine and moved the boat closer. The bird seemed to be watching them, but it stayed put. When they were near enough, she could see its yellow feet, and the back of its head, with the curly tufts that looked more like hair than feathers. It was a snowy egret, the bird her mother-in-law had so loved.

Thank you, Pauline, Maren thought.

"Skye, what do you think? Can we do this here?"

Ben cut the engine, and Skye pulled the box from the canvas bag.

"Go ahead, love. I don't have anything particular I want to say," Maren said.

Skye looked thoughtful for a moment. In the end, she seemed to decide that the truest thing was enough.

"I love you, Mom," Skye said as she tipped the ashes into the water.

Maren saw another flash of motion and looked up as the egret took flight, wings beating against the backdrop of the sky—no longer a delicate ornament adorning the shore, but a creature of strength and power, certain of its destination.

ACKNOWLEDGMENTS

The writer Anne Lamott says "help" is a prayer that is always answered. That was certainly true with this novel. I was astonished at how the right person materialized, at the right time, with just the right kind of support. It took a battalion of helpers to get this to the finish line, and I'm indebted to all of them.

First, my everlasting thanks to my editor at St. Martin's Press, Sarah Cantin, who is simply *magic*. Sarah loved and understood this story from the first, and she saw what it could be. This novel is much better for her extraordinary vision and gentle editorial guidance.

Thanks, too, to my agent, the unflappable Susanna Einstein—an excellent editor in her own right, and every bit as smart as her name would suggest.

I worked with a world-class team at St. Martin's Press, led by Jennifer Enderlin, Sally Richardson, Lisa Senz, and Anne Marie Tallberg. Many thanks to Tracey Guest and Jessica Zimmerman in publicity; Brant Janeway and Erica Martirano in marketing; Olga Grlic, who created *Haven Point*'s gorgeous cover; audio producer Katy Robitzsky; Tom Thompson, Kim Ludlam, Dylan Helstein, Michelle McMillian, and Anne Marie Tallberg in creative services; and the always kind (and patient) Sallie Lotz.

I'm grateful to early readers, who had the dubious distinction of reviewing the original "extended disco version" of the manuscript. Christine Pride's incisive suggestions made the story much better (and shorter!); Jennifer Entwistle and Ginny Wydler offered valuable feedback and encouragement. Caroline Teasdale Walker was not only a helpful reader, but also a chief recruiter for my army of angels. She introduced me to the brilliant poet Kristina Bicher, who gave so generously of her time and talent; and Emi Battaglia, without whom I would probably still be looking for an agent. Many thanks, too, to Page Robinson, who made sure I didn't accidentally profile anyone.

I'm obliged to writer friends, new and old, who graciously shared their wisdom: Beth Brophy, Eric Dezenhall, Sarah Pekkanen, Jim Wareck, Beatriz Williams, and especially Kathy Murray Lynch, who cheered me on (and up) over countless coffees and croissants.

I made at least one good decision during my freshman year of college: I found a friend who was fearless enough for both of us. In one way or another, Beth Rives Chesterton is on every page of this novel. How wonderful to discover that Beth's uncanny insights about people could be applied to fictional characters. (And since I basically flunked sailing at camp, I'm grateful, too, to her husband, Paul Chesterton, who helped me with the Stinneford Cup.)

Many thanks to Jo-Anne Goldman Chase, with whom I have clocked so much phone time over the years; she can still imitate the receptionist from the office where I worked in my early twenties. ("Hud-on.") Jo-Anne has listened to all my trials and tribulations over the years, and she also listened over several evenings at her house, as I read the entire manuscript out loud, start to finish.

I'm grateful to Caroline, Lisa, Ann, and other friends

and relatives who spent childhood summers in places like Haven Point. Their anecdotes, impressions, and memories were a wonderful help. Thanks to my friends in Maine, who will recognize traditions, some descriptions, and the universal summer community challenges. Any similarity to real people is entirely coincidental, however. Their kind welcome has made for lovely summers, but would not make a very interesting novel. Thanks, too, to the two Harriets in my life, who are so lovely I could use their name for a character without anyone thinking they had inspired it.

My family and home would have descended into chaos without the many wonderful women who have helped me over the years: Gladys Rubio, Rosa Aquino, Antonia Surco, Meghan Montecinos, and Meghan's late mother, Luly Salinas. I appreciate their help and advice, and for not laughing at the made-up language I pretend is Spanish.

My parents, among many gifts, instilled in me a love of books and stories, and ensured I got an excellent education despite my (not inconsiderable) resistance. Eternal thanks to my mother, Clare Hume, who is loving, generous, an astute reader, and a font of anecdotes from her summers on Old Black Point. I am so grateful for all she does for me and my family, and for always supporting my creative endeavors. (Well, except singing. Because, let's face it, everyone has their limits). My father, Brit Hume, from whom I inherited a practical streak, was on board from the first with this most impractical venture. (He seemed more certain than me, in fact, that this was what I was meant to do next). I'm grateful for his love, wisdom, and support, and for teaching me that the right word matters. Thanks, too, to Kim Hume, for her contagious enthusiasm for this novel.

Finally, I am most indebted to the three people who had to live with me throughout this process. My daughters, Mary Clare and Helen, inspire me every day with their humor and spirit and intelligence. I'm grateful to them for many things, not least for acting pleasantly surprised when I actually made dinner, rather than disappointed when I didn't. Last but certainly not least, I'm grateful to my husband, Drew Onufer, to whom this book is dedicated. Drew does it all—slays the bugs, laughs at my jokes, and plans, well . . . *everything*. He is our family plumb line, always bringing us back to center when we veer off. I'm blessed every day by his decency, good nature, and unswerving support.

AUTHOR'S NOTE

In attempting to bring to life World War II–era Washington, D.C., I relied on a number of resources, including David Brinkley's *Washington Goes to War*, Paul K. Williams's *Washington, D.C., the World War II Years*, John Morton Blum's *V Was for Victory*, Scott Hart's *Washington at War: 1941-1945,* and Mary W. Standlee's history memoir, *Borden's Dream,* about Walter Reed Army Medical Center.

Other than liberties I took with timing, I did my best to faithfully portray the Cadet Nurse Corps. It was, at the time, the most significant experiment in federally subsidized education in the nation's history, and the first integrated uniformed service corps. The 120,000 cadets who fast-tracked through nursing schools included 3,000 African Americans, 350 Japanese Americans, and 40 Native Americans. The program prevented the collapse of civilian nursing care during the war.

I was delighted to discover that the Cadet Nurse Corps was the brainchild of Ohio congresswoman Frances Payne Bolton, a great champion of nursing and nursing education. Though I didn't have the pleasure of knowing her, if her children and grandchildren are any indication, she was a wonderful woman.